THE EXCALIBUR CODE

BOOK FOUR OF THE HUNTER FILES

ROB JONES

Boldwood

First published in 2022. This edition published in Great Britain in 2025 by Boldwood Books Ltd.

Copyright © Rob Jones, 2022

Cover Design by Tom Sanderson

Cover Images: Adobe Stock and Shutterstock

Every effort has been made to obtain the necessary permissions with reference to copyright material, both illustrative and quoted. We apologise for any omissions in this respect and will be pleased to make the appropriate acknowledgements in any future edition.

A CIP catalogue record for this book is available from the British Library.

Paperback ISBN 978-1-80600-027-2

Large Print ISBN 978-1-80600-026-5

Hardback ISBN 978-1-80600-025-8

Trade Paperback ISBN 978-1-80635-344-6

Ebook ISBN 978-1-80600-028-9

Kindle ISBN 978-1-80600-029-6

Audio CD ISBN 978-1-80600-020-3

MP3 CD ISBN 978-1-80600-021-0

Digital audio download ISBN 978-1-80600-024-1

This book is printed on certified sustainable paper. Boldwood Books is dedicated to putting sustainability at the heart of our business. For more information please visit https://www.boldwoodbooks.com/about-us/sustainability/

Boldwood Books Ltd, 23 Bowerdean Street, London, SW6 3TN

www.boldwoodbooks.com

For my children

1

'"An inheritance may be gotten hastily at the beginning; but the end thereof shall not be blessed."'

Max Hunter turned to the bright young woman standing beside him and smiled at her. The approaching sunset was shining through the French abbey's impressive stained-glass windows, illuminating her blonde hair almost like a halo. Suddenly, he was very happy she had joined the project. He broke eye contact and found something to look at near his boots. A few inches away was a hole they had recently made by breaking through the ancient flagstone floor. 'Is that another quote from the Bible?'

'Proverbs 20:21, King James Version,' Lauren Lane said with a wink.

'And what does it mean? You'll have to forgive me, but I'm not much of a religious scholar.'

'It means that something gained by fraud, cheating or stealing seems like easy money at first, but sooner or later ends up biting you in the rear.'

'We're here at Mont Saint-Michel on official UN-ESCO business and whatever we find is part of a lawful archaeological exploration. There's nothing ill-gotten about any of this.'

'Not us, silly. I was thinking about what you told me about all the thieves and smugglers you've come across in your career. And it's a quotation, not a quote. A quote is what your builder gives you.'

Hunter's laugh bounced off the thousand-year-old walls surrounding them. He returned his eyes to her and leaned in closer, speaking through his grin. 'And you're no builder. I can tell by your physique.'

She narrowed her eyes and sighed. 'Dr Hunter! Professor Bonnaire told me you were in a relationship with an American CIA agent.'

'How discreet of her.'

'She meant well. I think she was warning me to resist your charms. Is it true?'

Hunter weighed that up. 'Agent Amy Fox and I spent some good times together but we ran a little hot and cold and so we decided to give ourselves some space. Then Juliette called from UNESCO and hooked me up with this job, so I flew back to Europe to help her out. I haven't seen Amy for several weeks.'

'I see,' Lauren said, her smile fading as the awkward moment passed. 'Anyway... as you say, I am certainly no builder, but it sure looks like this place is going to need one after all the mess we made here today.'

Hunter swept his hair out of his eyes and smiled at her little joke. He had also felt a slight frisson between them, but having just reminded himself of Amy over in Washington, he decided to stow it away and take up the opportunity given by Lauren to move things along. 'This mess is nothing to worry about. As you're aware, the island of Mont Saint-Michel, including the abbey and the entire bay surrounding us, has been a UNESCO world heritage site since 1979. We have every right to be here and make as much mess as we need to get to our little treasure.'

'Since 1979, eh?' said the perky young woman from Oxford with a sly grin. 'I wouldn't know about that. That was twenty years before I was even born.'

Hunter suddenly felt older than the abbey. Time to turn it back around on her. 'Don't worry about a thing like that. You might be inexperienced now, but after a few years of working and studying hard, completing some more research and getting muddy out in some serious fieldwork, you'll begin to know almost as much as I do.'

'Twenty-three years old and I have a First-Class degree in Archaeology from Magdalen College, Oxford, a Master's in Anthropology from Harvard and I'm in the final year of my Cambridge PhD in Medieval History, specialising in the theological scholarship of Xavier of Normandy. I heard when you were twenty-three years old you were doing press-ups in a muddy trench and getting shouted at by a drill sergeant. Have I got that right?'

Hunter's smile faded. 'Let's move things along, shall we? I believe the authorities have only permitted us to excavate this location until sunset, and as we can see, the golden hour is almost upon us.'

She looked across the abbey and through a large open arch at the sky. 'That's the most beautiful sunset I've ever seen.' She took her phone out of her pocket and started taking some snaps for posterity, or maybe bragging rights. Hunter didn't care; he'd done the same thing many times. 'I just want to get a picture of that before the sun goes down.'

'I'll join you,' he said. 'I'm a real sucker for beautiful things. Cannot resist them.'

She gave him a sideways glance and hid her smile

as they walked away from the excavation site and across the abbey's expansive nave. They arrived at three broad, open arches offering a breathtaking view over the wide, flat bay below. In a display of unparalleled beauty, the low sun reflected off a shallow pool of seawater trapped in a dip out in the estuary, making it shimmer and sparkle. As Lauren snapped some pictures, Hunter simply stared and drank in the view until yet more memories of his time in Washington interrupted the moment.

In the short time he'd known the HARPA team, he'd made some great new friends in Sal Blanco, Jodie Priest, Ben Lewis and even to a certain extent, young Quinn 'Ghost' Mosley. With Amy, it had been more than friends almost right from the start, but since going on a break and then his flying back to UNESCO in Europe, it was all starting to seem like a dream. He turned and fixed his eyes on Lauren. Yeah, there was the age difference, but she was early-twenties, smart and beautiful and shared his interests. She looked back up at him and they slowly moved closer until their lips were inches apart.

'Hey, is there anyone still up there?'

Hunter and Lauren were still staring into each other's eyes when they heard Scott's voice. Eyes widening, they spoke at the same time: 'Shit!'

Running back over to the hole in the nave floor, Hunter dropped to his knees and stared down inside it, peering into the dusty gloom until the figure of his second doctoral assistant slowly merged into view. 'Sorry, Scott. I was just enjoying the view.'

Lauren raised her eyebrow at the comment as Scott called back.

'Yeah, that's great, Dr Hunter. Meanwhile, I think I might have found something important.'

Hunter and Lauren shared a glance, both fighting to hide their excitement in case Scott had made a mistake.

'You found the jewels?' Lauren asked.

Scott laughed. 'Good news or bad news?'

'You choose, Scotty,' Lauren said.

'Bad news is that I cannot see any sign of the jewels.'

Hunter cursed, inclining his head further to get a clearer view of Scott. 'In that case, I'm more than ready for the good news.'

'The good news?' Scott called back. 'Oh, that's nothing. Just that I found a very old treasure chest with the words "Res Principis Arturus" on top of it. I don't speak Latin, but does that mean anything to either of you?'

Hunter and Lauren locked eyes. Hunter said, 'Say that again.'

Scott repeated his sentence word for word. 'What does it mean?'

'The Property of Prince Arthur.' Hunter scratched his head. 'Which is a little odd. I'm not sure why the crown jewels would have the title Prince Arthur inscribed anywhere on them. Are you sure about what's written on the treasure chest?'

Scott gave a petulant sigh. 'I can read three words, Dr Hunter. So, yeah.'

'Fair point,' Hunter said. 'Any chance we can get a look at it before they throw us out of here?'

'Sure thing, Max. I'm on my way up now.'

Hunter was playing it cool, but the truth was he hadn't been this excited since HARPA had uncovered a site in South America, now locked down, containing a mysterious source of water which some were already describing as the elixir of eternal youth. That remained to be seen, but somehow, he and Amy and the rest of the team had also managed to fit raising the *Titanic* into the field trip. The famous wreck was now undergoing massive restoration in a private Norwegian drydock under the direction of Olav Skulberg with a view to one day being opened to the public. It was one of the highlights of

Hunter's brief but illustrious career, and its salvaging rep-
resented a few days he could never forget, but it was already receding into the past, and these recent few weeks
he'd spent at UNESCO had been boring in comparison.
As he watched Scott Wright climbing up the telescopic
ladder with the small treasure chest, he realised just how
bored he'd been and grateful for the opportunity given to
him by Juliette Bonnaire to lead the field trip.

Scott had reached the top of the ladder and was
struggling to get out of the hole with the box under his
arm. 'Don't anyone help or anything.'

'Sorry,' Hunter said. 'Allow me.'

'Thanks.'

Hunter took the box and left Scott to clamber out
of the hole on his own. Turning to face the last of the
golden light streaming in through the windows, he
held the box at arm's length and admired its intri-
cately carved hardwood sides and burnished brass
edging. After he'd examined the box for a while, he
concluded that the age was certainly much older than
the thirteenth century, when the crown jewels disappeared. Lauren was beside him, taking pictures of the
box with her phone. Hunter turned and smiled into
the camera.

'Would you like one with me in it?' he said.

'Not much,' she said, sliding the phone back into her pocket.

'Thanks for all the help, guys,' Scott said, finally out of the hole and brushing dust off his shirt.

'Always welcome,' Hunter said. 'You know that.'

Behind them, they heard a metallic clang. Turning, they saw one of the abbey's security guards moving a stainless steel, crowd control barrier post out of his way before walking in their direction.

Hunter looked one more time at the box in his arms. Blowing some dust away from the inscription on its wooden lid, he read aloud what it said. '"Res Principis Arturus. Property of Prince Arthur."'

'Wow,' Lauren said. 'And I mean, wow. That's amazing.'

Hunter looked at her. 'You think my Latin is amazing? Thanks.'

'Agreed,' said Scott. 'And not with what you just said, Dr Hunter. I agree with Lauren. It's not every day you find the personal possessions of a monk from eight hundred years ago.'

'It most certainly is not,' Hunter said. 'We're supposed to be on the trail of the missing crown jewels, but instead we find this little box with the name Arthur on it. Maybe we got our hypothesis wrong, but it still has the potential to be a very valuable find. Let's see what's inside Arthur's little chest.'

The guard had reached them now. He stood twirling a key on his retractable keychain. He knew who they were, so he spoke in broken English, but his eyes were crawling all over the newly discovered treasure chest in Hunter's hands. 'It's time for me to lock up, Dr Hunter. You and your assistants will have to leave now and come back in the morning. Unless, of course, you already have what you need and will not be coming back.'

'We're not sure yet,' said Lauren. 'We haven't looked inside this chest.'

'I see,' the guard said. 'Well, either way. You have five minutes and then I'm sorry, but I have to ask you to—'

The first bullet blasted through Scott Wright's shoulder and knocked him to the floor. The young scholar never knew what hit him, but Lauren was screaming hysterically even before his wounded body collapsed in a heap. The security guard spun around and reached for his radio. Dimly aware of several figures moving in the shadows at the far end of the darkening abbey, Hunter grabbed Lauren and pulled her away from the guard just as someone opened fire with an automatic weapon. Lauren screamed again as the rounds ripped through him and burst out of his back, leaving fist-size exit holes. When the guard hit the floor just yards from Scott, his radio was still crackling in his dead hand. Another guard called out and also reached for his radio, but a bullet instantly hit him in the head and tore off a quarter of his skull, killing him on the spot.

Hunter had already pulled Lauren over to the hole. 'Get down that ladder, now!'

Lauren didn't need to be asked twice. Fit and strong, the young woman slid down the sides of the ladder in a heartbeat. She looked up in the gloom with desperate eyes. 'Dr Hunter!'

'Catch!' He threw the box and was already making his way down the ladder's rungs by the time she caught it. Another roar of gunfire boomed inside the abbey, and he heard men shouting and boots smacking down on the flagstones. Guards yelled at the intruders as they streamed into the abbey, only to be met with wild fusillades of automatic gunfire.

Hunter reached the bottom of the ladder, breathless and his heart pounding in his chest, and turned to Lauren. In her early twenties and on her first real field exploration, she had visibly paled and was shaking in the dark of the tomb.

'What's happening, Dr Hunter?' she asked.

'Nothing good. I need to make a call, right now.'

She was still trembling and had begun to hyper-
ventilate. 'I asked what just happened, Dr Hunter?
What happened to Scott? Is he dead? And what about
the guard? Who are those men? Are they going to kill
us? What if...'

Hunter was holding his phone to his ear, praying
for reception and waiting for the emergency services
to pick up the call. 'Lauren, stop talking and take a
deep breath.'

'I'm sorry. I'm sorry.'

'Don't apologise,' he said, pushing her into the
shadows, out of sight from anyone above. 'And no,
Scott's not dead. He took a bullet in the shoulder and
fell. He's playing dead. He'll be okay as long as he
keeps it up.'

'You're sure?'

'I'm sure. He looked at me just before I came down
here. And no, we can't go and get him because the
place is crawling with gunmen.'

She blew out a deep breath and tried to get a grip
on herself. 'Who are you calling?'

'An ambulance for Scott and any of the guards
who just got shot, if they're still alive.'

After Hunter placed a call with the emergency services, he started to make another call.

'Who are you calling now?' She was still breathing hard and fast.

He peered up into the hole. He could hear the men but there was still no sign of them. 'The director of UNESCO World Heritage. She can get us some help if she answers. Let's hope she's not in the middle of one of her legendary three-hour meals.'

Lauren frowned. 'Why not call the police?'

'Experience. Damn it, it's gone to voicemail. No... she's picking up the call. Is that you, Juliette?'

'Yes, *c'est moi*, Maxy. How is my *petit chiot*?'

Hunter blushed, instantly flicking the speaker function off again. 'I do wish you wouldn't call me that.'

'It's a term of endearment.'

'It means puppy.'

'*Oui, c'est ça.* But where are you? You should be wearing the little GPS tracker I got you. The one on your army dog tags.'

'First you call me a puppy, then you make me wear a GPS tracker around my neck. I'm starting to wonder if you might be the possessive sort.'

'Nonsense. Tell me, how many times have those GPS tags saved your life?'

'I forget.'

'Six.'

'But you remember.'

'Of course. If you had them on now, I would know where you were.'

'Or I could just tell you. Then again, you probably wouldn't believe me.'

'Try me.'

'Fine. We're at the site inside Xavier's tomb and someone just started shooting at us. They injured Scott and killed at least one of the guards, probably more. You need to alert the local authorities and HARPA. I just called for an ambulance.'

'Okay, I will do so immediately. You must get yourselves to safety at once!'

'I'm on it, Juliette. Speak later.'

Hunter cut the call.

'You think she'll get help?'

He shrugged. 'Impossible to be sure, but she's a pretty switched-on lady. Listen, Lauren. We have to find a way out of here and we have seconds to do it and nothing to light our way. First, this ladder is coming down. They want something to do with either us or what we found in this tomb. It's our job to make their job as difficult as possible.'

He pulled the telescopic ladder away from the edge of the hole and collapsed it. Above, some men wearing balaclavas appeared at the top of the hole. They shone torches down inside and began searching, the beams sliding across the walls and floor of the tomb like searchlights, but Hunter pushed Lauren up against one of the walls, just inches out of their reach. The men above him in the abbey argued for a few seconds. Hunter listened carefully, picking up a mix of English and Swedish.

Lauren stared at the collapsed ladder and lowered her voice to a whisper. 'Will that stop them? I mean, removing the ladder?'

Hunter wiped the sweat from his brow, his mind racing with ideas. 'I want to say yes, but I'm guessing anyone who decided to storm the abbey at Mont Saint-Michel probably came equipped to play in any conditions.'

'Meaning?'

A thick, black nylon rappelling rope tumbled down into the hole like a giant black python, its tip winding up just a few inches above the floor.

Hunter sighed. 'Meaning, they probably brought one of those.'

She moved closer to him until their arms brushed together. 'Okay, now I'm scared. This is just shooting fish in a barrel.'

The imagery galvanised Hunter. 'No time for fear, Lauren. Start looking for a way out of here. Right now, or we're both dead.'

2

Amy Fox was alone in her office when she got the call. The man was speaking on behalf of the deputy director of the CIA. He introduced himself as Brent Reed. After less than a minute of small talk about the weather, he got to the point and the point was not good.

'What do you mean Director Gates is on leave?' she asked, astonished by what Brent had just told her. 'He never told me he had any plans to go on leave and he always keeps me very well informed.'

'He's off the job, is what I meant, Agent Fox. I was putting it delicately.'

'You don't need to be delicate with me, Mr Reed.

I'm no shrinking violet. I just got back from a mission involving the discovery of the Water of Life and the raising of the *Titanic*, all of which was led by James Gates without fault, I might add.'

'No one is questioning Mr Gates's competence. Everyone in the Agency is more than aware of his record both in the US Navy and in HARPA. He is a highly decorated senior officer, a much-respected man and a valued member of the Agency.'

'Then why are you telling me that you've taken him off the team?'

With surprising speed, Reed replied, 'Because those are my orders.'

Amy thought about that before replying. Her experience working inside the agency told her those five simple words were concealing a whole world of trouble. 'If this isn't your decision, Mr Reed, then whose is it?'

'I'm not at liberty to say, but then I guess you knew I was going to say that before you even asked the question.'

She sighed. 'All right, fine. At least tell me why.'

'I'm not at liberty to say that either.'

'Is it that you won't tell me or you can't tell me?'

Reed paused a beat, considering her question. 'I

shouldn't be saying this to you and if they find out that I did, my ass is fired. You understand what I'm saying right now?'

Amy felt a surge of hope. Maybe she was getting somewhere after all. 'I assure you whatever you tell me will be treated in the strictest confidence.'

'It had better be. Now, listen carefully. My boss works closely with the deputy director of the CIA and he told me that the deputy director was ordered personally by the director to freeze Gates out. Whether or not the order originated with the director, I don't know. But I think this goes way higher, right to the very top. And I'll say one more thing. This has something to do with the mission you just referenced. You and your little team upset some big movers and shakers while you were galivanting around looking for your elixir and raising old shipwrecks.'

'It wasn't just any old wreck, Mr Reed. It was the *Titanic*. And HARPA didn't raise it. That was done by a third party, Olav Skulberg, as I believe you must surely know. When you say we upset some people, can you tell me more?'

'No, other than these are powerful people who have some clout when it comes to helping the CIA director make her decisions these days. Along the way, I heard the word Illuminati, but I think I must have imagined it because I'm not the sort who inclines towards the fanciful or fantastic and neither do I entertain conspiracy theories. However, one way or the other, Gates is on leave until further notice and Team HARPA is out of business. You've got an hour to hand in your security passes and leave the building. All six of you.'

Amy was shocked by what she was hearing. 'Wait a minute, putting Jim Gates out in the cold is one thing but you're also suspending me and my entire team?'

'Yes, but it's not my decision. I think I already made that clear. This comes from a thousand miles above my paygrade. Whoever's pulling these strings is so high in the stratosphere, you'd need bottled oxygen to go argue with them about it. And I'll make the following point again. If you tell anyone I told you this, then I won't even have a paygrade. We still have a solid understanding on that point, right?'

'We do.'

She said this, but she wasn't happy about it. She understood why he didn't want anyone in the wider agency knowing what he'd told her, but there was no way she was going to keep it from the rest of the HARPA team. They had a right to know, and besides, she would have to tell them something. They were about to get suspended from their jobs.

'What'll I tell my team, Agent Reed?' she asked.

'How the hell should I know? Make up some shit about the funding getting drained. You know them all better than anyone. You know what they'll swallow. Be smart and tell them not to rock the boat, to go quietly into the night. That includes you contacting Gates. Let him be. It's better for everyone this way. And that's the end of our conversation. I'll be in touch, and stay out of trouble, Agent Fox. Don't do anything stupid.'

Reed cut the call and left Amy sitting in the gloom. What he had said about the HARPA team was true enough; she did know them better than anyone else, but that didn't make it any easier to tell them they no longer had jobs, to cut them loose.

She looked at her watch, saw it was nearly midday and wondered what they would all be doing. Weeks had passed since they'd stood on the deck of Olav Skulberg's ship the Ostøya in the North Atlantic and watched the raising of the *Titanic*. Those were happy days, but after the mission, the team members split and went their own way. She knew Jodie was back in California wrestling with unexplained family issues. Sal was in New York helping his brother out at his pizza restaurant. Ben was right here in DC with his wife and new baby. That left Quinn and Hunter. No one ever knew where Quinn went, and that included Amy right now, and while she didn't know where Hunter was, she could make a guess or two.

She had been twiddling a pen while talking to Reed. Now she tossed the pen on her desk and leaned back in her chair. She was confused and concerned by what he had just told her, but she was sure about one thing. If he told her not to make contact with Jim Gates, that was the first thing she was going to do. She fired Zoom up and navigated to Gates's account, calling him up without delay.

The call rang and rang and her mind filled with worries. Maybe Reed had been a little elastic with the truth. Maybe Gates had been more than suspended. What if their crossing swords with the Illuminati during the *Titanic* mission had ruffled some important feathers? Maybe a more permanent solution had been applied to her old friend. Her fears were soothed when Gates answered the call and his familiar face suddenly appeared on her computer screen. His hair was a mess, he was unshaven and he looked tired, but he was alive and giving her his famous crooked smile. But he wasn't in his DC home. Behind him, she saw a lot of dark wood and the flickering light of what could only be a real fire.

'Amy, I was kind of expecting you to call. You never let me down.'

'That's me. Reliable to the point of boredom.'

His grey eyes narrowed and his smile began to fade. 'As a matter of fact, I was going to call you later today. I guess you already know they suspended the whole HARPA operation.'

'I just spoke to a man named Brent Reed. He was kind of an asshole, by the way. Didn't give a damn about anything, just told me HARPA was suspended and I should keep my nose out of it until I heard further information from his office. He also told me not to speak to you.'

Gates nodded sagely. 'That's Brent, all right. I'm pleased to see you regarded his advice with a healthy dose of your usual scepticism.'

'I see you're not in DC.'

'That's right. I'm in Colorado, at my ski lodge. It's no secret. Telluride is so beautiful right now, and when they suspended me it seemed like the right place to be.'

She'd heard him talk about the lodge before, but had never seen it. 'You're safe, then.'

'We're fine.'

'Your wife is with you?'

'Susanna is here, of course. And our dogs Zack and Lucy. We're having a great time.'

Amy realised he was playing down the threat of whatever was happening. His wife had an important career in DC and it was unlikely she would drop everything for an indeterminate vacation in the Rockies unless things were more serious than her boss was letting on. She considered challenging him, but knowing he would never admit it, she let it go. Instead, she decided on a more neutral and generic line of questioning.

'What's this all about, Jim?'

'I know probably about as much as you. Brent delivered the news to me late last night. Luckily a good friend of mine with a plane agreed to fly us out here in return for a few days at the lodge over Christmas. It was a good deal. As you know, we usually go to Florida at that time of year anyway. So we took the opportunity to get the hell out of DC and as far away from Brent Reed and his office as humanly possible. Some say Reed sleeps in a coffin, but that's just hearsay.'

She laughed politely at his attempt at using humour to lighten the mood, but inside she felt anything but calm. 'But this goes higher than Reed, right?'

'You bet it does. Brent is just a minion working for

his masters. How high it goes, I have no idea as of this moment. I've got Zack and Lucy working on it.'

She smiled again at his second joke but pressed on in her search for answers. 'Reed told me his boss works closely with the deputy director of the CIA, but does that office have the remit to suspend HARPA or is that coming from the director himself?'

'Working on that too, but from what I've gathered so far, this goes higher than the director.'

'But the director of the CIA reports directly to the director of National Intelligence, Karin Svoboda. That's a Cabinet-level position, Jim. Director Svoboda reports directly to the President of the United States.'

'Let's not get ahead of ourselves, Amy. The order to suspend HARPA may not have been official; it might have originated horizontally and not vertically if you catch my drift.'

'You mean someone outside of government has the influence to push the DNI around?'

Gates broke into a laugh. 'Amy, take it easy. We'll work it out.'

'I'm sorry, I'll dial the paranoia down a notch. But I'm not letting this go. HARPA has proved its value to the government many times in a relatively short period. It doesn't get shut down on a whim unless there's some kind of hidden agenda. All of this happened very fast right after we ran into the Illuminati, Jim. I can put two and two together.'

'And make four?'

'Let's just say we proved how adept we are at getting to the bottom of mysteries from the deep past and uncovering secret societies who would rather remain in the shadows. Then next thing we know, we get shut down.'

'Maybe, maybe not. Enquiring minds and steady nerves, Amy. That's what's going to get us through this and out the other side.'

Amy watched Gates take a second out to shoo his two dogs away from the laptop. Lucy, the golden retriever, wandered out of view while Zack, the young black Labrador, slumped down by the fire, sighed gratefully and curled into a ball to sleep in front of the crackling flames.

'Reed talked about how he didn't believe in conspiracy theories, but saying HARPA's suspension isn't connected in some way to what we've discovered on our missions seems like a closed-minded coincidence theory to me.'

Gates's jovial expression faded. 'I never said there's no connection. I said we need to keep an open mind to make sure we get to the truth. And yes, they may be targeting us to put us out of business.'

'That's certainly what I think. I don't believe in co-incidences. Someone wants us out of the way before we reveal any more ancient truths.'

'You might be right, but for now we follow the pro-cedure. It's a bureaucratic thing. You know that. You're an even bigger bureaucracy nerd than I am.'

She smiled, his calm manner finally making her relax. 'You want me to go ahead and tell the others they're all unemployed until further notice?'

'Looks like you have little choice, but I'm sure it's only temporary. Wait a minute.'

Amy saw him look off-screen. 'What's up?'

'Susanna just brought me my phone. There's a missed call from Professor Bonnaire. Just a few moments ago. She doesn't normally call me,' Gates said with a frown. 'Unusual.'

Then, Amy's phone rang. She looked down and saw it was also from Juliette Bonnaire. 'Now she's calling me, and that's just as unusual. She normally makes contact with the team through Max. I think I'd better take this, Jim.'

'Sure thing, Amy. We'll stay in touch. And let me know if you need anything. Officially, I'm out of the loop, but that's just officially. I also do a good line in unofficial stuff.'

'Thanks, Jim. It helped to talk to you.'

They ended the Zoom call and Amy picked up her phone. 'This is Amy Fox.'

'Amy, thank God,' Juliette said. 'I just tried to call Director Gates but there was no reply.'

That makes sense, Amy thought. 'What's the matter, Professor? You sound concerned.'

'I am concerned, very concerned. I need to speak to you on Zoom right away. I think Max might be in grave danger.'

3

Hunter was deep inside Mont Saint-Michel abbey, and his eyes were still adjusting to the tomb's darkness by the time the men appeared at the top of the hole in the floor above him. They were all wearing plain, black cloth masks. The English archaeologist and former Grenadier Guards officer was certainly no stranger to potentially lethal situations, but this one was shaping up to be one of the most dangerous he'd ever faced.

Then, a man spoke. His voice was cool and calm. 'You can run but you cannot hide, Dr Hunter.'

That took Hunter by surprise. How did these people know his name?

'But I can fight,' Hunter called up. 'Why not throw some shooters down and make it a fair fight?'

The man laughed. 'I think not.'

Lauren turned to Hunter, her eyes wide with fear. 'You know these guys?'

'Is that what you think of me? That I'm the kind of man who consorts with violent, gun-toting thugs and murderers?'

'Oh no, Dr Hunter. I think much worse of you than that.'

They shared a look. 'Thanks, but this situation is a little too serious for even your legendary wit to lighten the moment.'

'He's right, it is serious,' the man called down. 'Very serious. You might even say Dr Hunter has dragged you into a life-and-death situation. An expert in archaeological endeavours he may well be, but when it comes to downright dirty thieving and smuggling, he is, in the present company, a mere parvenu.'

'I'm no thief or smuggler,' Hunter called back. 'But thanks to that delightful introduction, at least I now know who I'm dealing with, although a name would be nice. You have me at a distinct disadvantage.'

'And I think we can keep it this way because I always like to have the advantage, as you put it.'

Another man appeared. When he pulled his mask

down to scratch his face, Hunter pulled his phone out and snapped some pictures of him. Seconds later, the mask went back up and Hunter began desperately scanning the tomb for a way out. 'That's not polite. If I don't know your name, then what should I call you? You're clearly military. Maybe I should call you Major Arsehole?'

The man's laugh turned sour. 'That would be Mr Arsehole to you, but do you think it's wise, provoking a man with a gun when you are trapped inside an eight-hundred-year-old tomb?'

Hunter ignored him and grabbed Lauren by her shoulders. 'Keep talking to him while I try to find a way out of here.'

'Me? Why me? I don't know what to say!'

'Make it up as you go along. Riff. Freestyle. Try to be as casual and breezy as I just was.'

She rolled her eyes. 'You think an awful lot of yourself, don't you?'

'We can talk about my many virtues later, but only if we can get out of here. Do your thing, but stay out of their line of sight. The only reason they haven't used that rope and come down here yet is that they want to try the easy way first.'

'Which is?'

'We give up and throw the treasure chest up to

them.'

'Oh, that's a good idea! That would make them go away, right?'

'After they get rid of the witnesses, yes.'

'Witnesses?'

'Us, Lauren. We're the witnesses.'

Her face dropped. 'Oh.'

'Get talking! I need a distraction to give me time to find the other entrance.'

Hunter let go of her shoulders, gave her a confident wink and began searching the tomb for another way out. The rock was hewn by men's hands, smooth, cold, and black, but nowhere presented an obvious escape route like a hidden door or window or even a grate in the wall or floor. Above him, up in the abbey, he heard the man's voice grow colder.

'I'm going to give you one more minute to come to your senses and climb up out of that dismal little hole and bring the box you recently discovered with you. After that, I will send some men down in after you and they will take the items and kill you. Either way, I leave this place with that box, whatever the status of your vital signs.'

Lauren raised her voice. 'If you're trying to sweet talk me into dinner, you're falling pretty wide of the mark.'

'That's not bad,' Hunter muttered, hands all over the wall in his search. 'Not bad at all.'

'Thanks.'

The voice called down. 'Dinner is not such a bad idea. Why not forget about the loser who got you into that filthy little pit and join me for a long weekend in Prague? I know some beautiful restaurants there. We'll leave as soon as we bury Dr Hunter under a few tons of rubble.'

'Thanks, but no.'

'I'm giving you a chance to live, Lauren.'

She turned to Hunter, barely visible at the end of a short passageway at the back of the tomb. 'How does he know my name?'

'Can't think about that now,' Hunter said. 'This place must have another way out. Juliette told me they brought the treasure up into here from the sea. But where, damn it?'

'Are you turning down my offer of a date, Lauren?' the man said.

She ignored him. 'Dr Hunter, this guy's running out of patience. We don't have much longer.'

'That is the understatement of the year,' the man said from above. 'You have had all the chances I'm going to give you. Now my men are coming down. You will be shot and killed and they will bring the treasure chest back to me. You should have taken me up on Prague, Lauren. Instead, you're going to die in that hole like a rat.'

'Dr Hunter, they're coming down! Please tell me you've found a way out of here.'

'I found a way out of here.'

A second rappelling rope tumbled down through the aperture above her and came to rest a few feet from her face. Then she heard the man shouting orders. A moment later, two men in black fatigues stepped into view. They wore guns slung over their shoulders and what looked like some kind of utility belt packed with objects of various shapes and sizes.

'At least two of them, Max! One on each rope.' Almost frozen on the spot with fear, Lauren snapped back to reality when she heard Hunter shouting at her.

'Move, Lauren! Unless you want to go to Prague with Major Arsehole.'

Hunter swept the dust from some kind of trapdoor laid into the floor. Over his shoulder, he heard one of the men grunting as he made his way down the rope. The other man on the second rope was a metre behind him.

Lauren ran along the passageway and, reaching

Hunter, she looked at the trapdoor. 'There's no handle!'

'Sure there is,' Hunter said. 'The monks didn't go to the trouble of putting a trapdoor in here and then forget about the handle.'

'But you said there was a tunnel leading to his place from the sea.'

'And?'

'Maybe the trapdoor was only ever intended to be used from the other side.'

Hunter blew out a breath. 'Excellent. I never thought of that.'

'Are you kidding me?'

Hunter heard the first man's boots smack down on the tomb floor. When he turned and stared down the short passageway, he was relieved to see the man waiting for backup before venturing over to them.

'Yes, I'm kidding.' As he spoke, he continued to dig his fingers into the dusty trapdoor. 'Got it! A recessed handle, just as I thought there would be.'

He wasted no time in heaving the door open. It thudded down away in a cloud of dust to reveal a narrow tunnel descending away from them into pitch black, thick with cobwebs. Hunter turned to Lauren with a smile.

'Ladies first?'

Lauren turned from the cobwebs to the armed men making their way down the passageway towards them.

'Think I'll take you up on the chivalry, Dr Hunter. Filth and bugs over armed maniacs any day of the week.'

'You still have the treasure chest, right?' he asked.

She tapped the canvas bag she was carrying over her shoulder. 'Right here.'

Hunter had a thought. 'You'd better let me carry it. If we get split up, they'll come after the one with the goodies.'

As Lauren handed the canvas bag to him, a gun fired in the distance. A bright, angry muzzle flash lit the stone walls of the passageway behind them, followed by an explosive roar. Hunter pushed Lauren into the tunnel and covered his head as more bullets ricocheted noisily off one of the chamber walls. The men screamed for him to stay where he was.

Hunter decided against it and followed Lauren into the tunnel, slamming the trapdoor down as the gunmen opened fire and raked it with bullets.

4

When Juliette Bonnaire's face appeared on Amy's laptop screen, she looked like she was about to throw up. Pale and wide-eyed, the director of UNESCO's usually unflappable, calm exterior had given way to whatever horror she was about to explain.

'What's happening, Juliette?' Amy asked.

'When was the last time you heard from Max Hunter?'

'Not for weeks.' Amy's disappointment about what had happened between the two of them was quickly shelved when she realised the importance of what Juliette was asking. 'What's going on? Has something happened to Max?'

'I think this is possible, Amy. As you know, Max

left the United States and returned to France to do some fieldwork for UNESCO. The brief was confidential, as the significance of what may be found at the site stretches beyond the world of archaeology.'

Amy considered if this explained his lack of contact, but dismissed it. He didn't have to tell her the intricate details of his work to get in touch with her and let her know he was okay. He also didn't have to ignore the three voicemails she had left him since his departure.

'But now you say something's happened to him?' Amy asked.

Juliette gave a slow, sad nod. 'He called me just moments ago and told me they'd come under some kind of attack while working onsite. He said someone was shooting at them.'

Amy's heart began to beat like a war drum. She consciously slowed it down with a calm breath and let her professional head take charge of what was looking like a rapidly deteriorating situation involving someone she had started to think she was going to spend the rest of her life with. 'Slow down, Juliette. One thing at a time. You said they'd come under attack? Is he working in a large team?'

'*Non, pas de tout*. He was working with two doctoral students, Scott Wright and Lauren Lane. They are writing their theses at this time and trying to gain some field experience. Very bright students with great careers of discovery ahead of them, but...'

'What happened, Juliette?'

'Max called me and started to leave a voicemail. I was at dinner and had turned my phone off. I want to kick myself now for nearly having missed the call, but then we spoke and I really think he might be in trouble.'

'Juliette, you need to tell me what happened.'

'I told Max not to tell anyone what he was working on but now I think it's okay for me to brief you. He was following up with some fieldwork on research recently conducted concerning the missing crown jewels.'

Amy was confused. 'Wait, the crown jewels are missing? I thought they were kept under tight security in the Tower of London?'

'You are talking about the current crown jewels of the United Kingdom, the priceless collection that is indeed kept in the Tower of London. However, the original crown jewels, commonly referred to as the crown jewels of King John, went missing in the year 1216. These too would be priceless for both their historical value and their value in precious metals and gems. Max and Lauren were on the trail of finding these jewels after eight hundred years, working in the tomb of a Benedictine monk-knight named Xavier of Normandy. He is believed to have travelled on King John's baggage train.'

'But something happened today?'

'*Oui, ce soir*... this evening, at least it's evening here in France. Max told me they were under attack, that gunmen had injured Scott and one of the guards and that he feared they would also be shot. They shot Scott Wright, Amy! He was just twenty-four years old and under my care. He could have been killed!'

Amy felt her blood run cold. Hunter had been attacked by armed men out onsite and they had killed not only at least one security guard but also wounded one of Hunter's academic protégés. When she considered that the other student and Hunter may already be dead, she cancelled the thought and switched back to the distraught woman on the laptop screen.

'Where's the site?'

'On the island of Mont Saint-Michel in Normandy, here in France. I didn't know who else to call, not after what Max told me about the Illuminati having infiltrated so many institutions. What if I call the police and the matter ends up with one of them? It would make matters much worse – put Max and Lauren in even more danger than they already are. And... what if they're both already dead?'

'Don't go there, Juliette,' Amy said in a level tone. 'That's not how we approach a problem like this.'

'Then how?' Juliette asked, desperately lighting up a cigarette with trembling fingers, her eyes staring out at Amy like dark holes painted with pure fear. 'Can you help? I have a large discretionary budget and I can provide air support.'

'I'm already on it, Juliette. Now I need to make some calls. I'll be in touch.'

* * *

When Sal Blanco accepted Amy's third Zoom call of the last thirty minutes, she saw straight away that he was in his brother's Brooklyn Heights pizza restaurant. The place was already quite busy, as to be expected for the time of day, and it looked like her old friend was sitting in one of the elevated diner booths near the window. He had a mug of steaming coffee beside him and hadn't shaved for a few days. Behind him, out in the street, she heard someone angrily honking a car horn, and then she got right down to business.

'Sal. Hey.'

'How you doin', Amy?' He sipped some of his coffee. 'If you don't mind my saying, you look like crap.'

Amy dismissed his light-hearted opener and got

down to brass tacks. 'It's Max, Sal. I think something might have happened to him.'

Blanco's face fell and he set the mug down on the table. In the background, somewhere behind the laptop, she heard his brother calling out to him. Blanco waved him away. 'Not now, Angelo. I'm on a work call.'

Angelo laughed. 'Well, pardon me for breathing in my own place, brother.'

Some of the customers laughed. If she hadn't been so scared, Amy would have smiled.

'What makes you say something happened to Max?' Blanco asked.

'I just got off a Zoom with Juliette Bonnaire. She told me Hunter was working with two doctoral students on some kind of excavation in the abbey at Mont Saint-Michel when something went wrong. Very wrong.'

'What does "very wrong" mean, Amy?'

'They came under some kind of attack. Some armed men broke into the abbey and opened fire with automatic weapons. It's too early for more details, Sal, but she was able to confirm to me that one of Max's research assistants, a young man named Scott Wright, was shot and injured, and at least one of the abbey's security detail was killed. Juliette can't be sure, but it looks like Max and Lauren, the other assistant, are in grave danger. Max cut the call in the middle of the attack and there's been no contact since.'

Blanco's eyes widened in surprise and he leaned back in his chair, taking a second to absorb what she had just told him. He passed a hand over his face and blew out a deep breath.

'Did Juliette call the French police?' he asked.

'No, she didn't. Max has persuaded her the Illuminati may have infiltrated the French authorities and calling them could just make things worse. Frankly, I share her concerns that there's a good chance the French police may be compromised by the same people who just suspended HARPA.'

Blanco nearly fell off his chair. 'Wait, HARPA got suspended? When the hell did that happen?'

'Just a few hours ago. That was the next thing I was going to tell you.'

Blanco grabbed his mug and drank a good slug of coffee. 'Today is just full of surprises. First Angelo tells me he's opening a restaurant in Manhattan and he wants me to run it, and now I find out one of my buddies is in real trouble and my team just got suspended. And here was me thinking it was just another rainy day in New York City.'

Amy managed a smile, quietly stowing away what he had just said about the offer of a job running his brother's new restaurant for later consideration. 'Sorry to hit you with so much all at once.'

'They suspended us, huh?'

She nodded. 'And it came right from the top, Sal. The Office of the Deputy Director of the CIA got orders from on high to suspend HARPA pending further notice. We are officially trashed.'

He scratched his stubble. 'I guess we upset the wrong guys down in South America.'

'I think so too. Jim's also been suspended. He's at his place in the Rockies.'

Blanco stared off into the middle distance, deep in thought. 'I presume we're going straight out to rescue Max's ass, right?'

'We are.'

He nodded. 'He'd do the same for us.'

'He would.'

Blanco shifted in his seat and stretched his arms, already limbering up for the mission. 'But if we're not in HARPA, that makes things a little harder in terms of logistics.'

'We're not without contacts and resources outside of the agency, Sal. There's Juliette Bonnaire for one thing. UNESCO has most of what we need, and she's the director of UNESCO World Heritage. That comes with a lot of perks.'

'A friend with benefits.'

'Only in this case, it means we have access to a corporate jet and a substantial budget for the mission.'

Blanco paused for a moment, once again deep in thought. 'Have you spoken to the others?'

'Not yet. You're always my first port of call for new missions.'

'You think they'll want to get involved in a mission off the books?'

'Maybe, maybe not. I can't force them to come along, Sal. All I can do is ask for their help.'

'I think they'll all rise to the occasion. Ben's strong ethics leave him no choice, Quinn loves a new challenge and as for Jodie, we both know how much she loves Max.'

Amy knew he was trying to calm her nerves with humour, and she was grateful. He was old and wise enough to always know the right thing to say or do and she wasn't sure she'd want to continue in the team, should they be reinstated, if he left to work at his brother's new restaurant in Manhattan.

'Thanks, Sal.'

'Forget about it.' He smacked down his empty mug. 'You want me to call them?'

'No, I need to do it. They need to hear this from me, I think. I need to make the risks clear, not just to their personal safety but to their careers at the agency. It's possible we could get fired for working outside of our official remit.'

Blanco winced. 'If we're gonna do this, can we at least say we're going rogue?'

'You don't like the "working outside of our official remit" thing?'

'Not in any way. I'm an ex-army helicopter pilot. A tough guy. I don't work outside of remits, Amy. You know that. I go rogue.'

'Fine,' she said with her first genuine smile since speaking with Juliette. 'Then we'll say that instead. HARPA is about to go rogue.'

5

'Straight down the passageway,' Hunter said. 'As fast as you can.'

'You're kidding, right?' Lauren cried out as she ran through the tunnel, the only visible feature being small niches used for candles. 'They just shot Scott, Dr Hunter! I'm not about to let them do the same to me.'

'Whoever they are, I swear they'll pay for that.' Hunter's words were drowned out by the sound of ferocious gunfire back at the trapdoor. Then he heard boots smashing whatever was left of the wood out of the way. 'Looks like they got into the tunnel.'

'But you were expecting that.'

'Pretty much. See anything up ahead?'

'Just more tunnel, and lots of cobwebs.'

With the gunmen piling into the passageway, they continued along the rock-hewn tunnel. It grew narrower until their shoulders began scraping on the sides, but allowed just enough room for the two of them to speed along it in search of some kind of escape from the horror at their backs.

'You see anything yet?' he called out.

Ahead of him, Lauren decreased her speed. 'Problem.'

'I hate that word. What does it mean in the present context?'

'It means the passageway is turning into a tunnel. No more than a metre high.'

Hunter nearly crashed into Lauren's back when she slowed and came to a stop. She crushed herself up against the wall so he could see the tunnel. It was as she had described, around one metre in height and the same width as the passageway they had just used to get here. He raised his torch, shining it into the tunnel's entrance. Unlike the main passageway, which was mostly level, he saw the tunnel stretching into the darkness at a declining angle.

'It's going downhill,' he said.

'Makes sense. I'm guessing it's going down through

the rock the abbey's built on so it can take people out at sea level.'

'Making the secret passageway accessible by boat from the mainland,' Hunter said. 'Yeah, makes sense. Wanna go first?'

'You give me all the best jobs, Dr Hunter.'

'No one can say I'm not generous.'

Behind them, they heard men shouting for them to stop and the sound of boots pounding against the passageway's stone floor.

'We'd better make tracks,' Hunter said. 'Go!'

She dropped to her hands and knees and began to crawl through the tunnel. Hunter let her get a few feet in and then joined her, crawling through the narrow, cramped space as fast as he could with Xavier's wooden chest in his canvas bag, awkwardly hanging from his neck and scraping along a rough stone floor. Here and there, his knee would come down on a loose rock chip, making him grunt in pain. Crying out in agony was the appropriate response, but not with Lauren Lane right in front of him.

'C'mon, Dr Hunter!' she called out. 'You're falling behind.'

'Not everyone is twenty-two years old, Lauren.'

The seconds passed like minutes. Hunter heard the

sound of the gunmen clambering into the tunnel. They were still a good distance behind them, but the concern he was keeping from his young assistant, about if maybe another contingent of these men was already waiting for them at the other end of the tunnel, was growing worse.

'Please tell me you see something?' he said.

'You mean like the light at the end of the tunnel?'

'Sure, but this time I'm looking for something a little more than just proverbial light. Can you help me with that?'

'Why, running out of energy?'

'You could say that, yeah.'

'Then you're in luck. We're almost at the end of the tunnel.'

'How can you tell?'

'I can see light. Duh.'

Hunter's knees were killing him. 'What sort of light? Artificial, natural? Could it be torchlight?'

'It's moonlight,' she called back. 'And now I can hear the tide, too. We're almost free.'

'Let's hope so,' he muttered to himself. Against a wave of pain in his neck, he lifted his head and saw Lauren ahead of him, sliding out of the tunnel. He'd expected to hear a splash of water, presuming that the tunnel somehow opened out over the sea, but he heard nothing. When he reached the tunnel's mouth, he realised why. Lauren was standing on a natural ledge on the rock's north side, and she was surrounded by trees swaying in the wind. She looked down at him and grinned.

'Need a hand up, old man?'

Hunter gave her a look and then dusted himself off, slowly pulling himself up to full height and paying no attention at all to the creaking sound in his knees. 'No thanks, I've got it.'

She looked into the trees. 'Where are we, exactly?'

'Northwest side of the rock,' he said without hesitation. 'Look out to the channel. Nothing out there but seawater and the distant Normandy coastline. From all the other sides of this island, the coast is much closer and clearer. If we climb down through these woods, we'll get a better look at the estuary and see what the tide's doing.'

They ran along the slope in long zigzag angles to avoid falling, reaching the end of the steep forested slope a few minutes later. Here, they found themselves at the top of a high, almost vertical rockface descending away to the sea. Pausing to get his breath back, Hunter clung on to a tree trunk and stared out across the estuary. Then, he sighed.

'High tide. Bugger.'

'Up for a swim?' Lauren asked.

'These are some of the most unpredictable and dangerous tides anywhere in the world,' he said calmly. 'So, no.'

'Sure it's not just because you're knackered?'

'Very sure. Start walking along the top of the rock-face until you see a boat. There's plenty moored up around the other side, so just take it easy and keep your eyes peeled. First chance we get, we're out of here.'

'Wouldn't that be theft, Dr Hunter?'

'If you're that concerned about it, we can alert the authorities when we're safe and they can return it to its rightful owner. I wouldn't want anything inter-rupting your beauty sleep. After all, honesty is the best policy, right?'

'Absolutely. "If I lose mine honour, I lose myself."'

'Shakespeare again?'

'Am I that predictable?'

'You've been quoting the Bard all week, Lauren. It was the obvious guess, and—'

She interrupted him with a cry of joy. 'I see a boat! Look!'

He pulled up beside her and peeked through some trees, taking in the sight of the lonely Chapel of Saint-Aubert on the edge of the northwest coast. It seemed to sit precariously on a jumble of slate-grey rocks and boulders jutting out into the estuary. He had seen it many times before throughout their explorations here, but never once had it been flanked by boats.

'What sort of boats are they?' Lauren asked.

'RIBs,' he said. 'Stands for Rigid Inflatable Boats.'

'They don't look much like the ones on the other side of the island.'

'That's because those are regular boats used by the people who live on the island, and those belonging to people who visit from the mainland. These are lightweight, high-performance machines usually used as work boats and also by the militaries of the world.'

She turned to look at him, the moonlight brushing her cheek. 'Not tourist boats, then?'

'Sadly, no. I'll make a bet. Five gets you ten that these boats belong to the psychos who just took out their anger on the abbey back there.'

'So, we keep going until we find another boat?'

'No. We blow up one of theirs and then steal the other one. Let's go.'

This time, Hunter led the way, scrambling down the steep slope leading down to the chapel. Halfway down, Lauren slipped on some loose scree and nearly tumbled over, but Hunter caught her and pulled her up sharply to her feet. Seconds later, they were clambering over a final row of boulders before finally reaching the front of the tiny church. Hunter glanced up at the rock looming high above them for any sign of trouble.

'Take your jacket off.'

Her eyes flashed at him. 'Now is hardly the time, but—'

'I need it to make a sort of timer to blow up the other boat. I'd use mine but it's leather and too thick. It won't burn as fast. Yours is linen. It'll go up like a Roman candle.'

Lauren started to shake her jacket off. 'I must say, Dr Hunter, for a moment there I thought I was going to have to contact the department's HR division and make a formal complaint.'

He gave her a look as he took her jacket. 'You're all heart. Now, get in that first boat over there and tell me if there's a key in the ignition. If not, I'll have to pull it to pieces and hotwire it.'

She jumped into the boat. 'There's a key.'

'Idiots,' he said. 'Turn it on for me. I need to make sure we have power before doing what I'm about to do.'

She swivelled the key and the RIB's engine spluttered to life, making Lauren jump. 'It's on!'

'Good. Now, do as I say and keep your head down.'

'What are you going to do?'

'What I just said.'

He made his way around to the second boat and broke open the petrol tank. Then he ripped the lining out of Lauren's jacket and tore it into three lengths, which he tied together to make around two metres of fabric. Then he poked most of it down into the tank before pulling it back out again and stretching it across the hull of the boat.

Making his way off the boat, he stopped and reached for some matches. He struck one and tossed it down onto the end of the makeshift fuse. Soaked in petrol, it set alight immediately and flames started to race down the linen. Hunter jumped into the first boat, grabbed the controls and sent the boat surging forward in a sharp arc, spraying seawater up against the chapel's west wall. Just over the roar of the four-stroke outboard engine, he heard gunfire.

'Shit! I was kind of hoping to get clean away!' He glanced over his shoulder and saw black figures bursting out of the forest just above the chapel. 'It's the guys who chased us through the tunnel. Keep your head down, Lauren!'

'Are we going to be okay?'

He ignored her. 'Keep on coming, boys! All the way down to the chapel, and don't forget to say your prayers!'

He watched the men get closer to the chapel. Then, one of them noticed the burning linen fuse. He pointed and called out to the other gunmen. It was too late; the RIB exploded in a massive fireball, killing some of the men instantly and blasting others off the chapel rock and into the sea. Some were unharmed and now opened fire wildly at Hunter and Lauren and the fleeing boat, but they were too far out into the estuary. Seconds later, the rock was obscured by the dark, rainy night.

Lauren poked her head up from the back of the boat. 'Is it safe to come out now?'

'It's safe,' Hunter said, turning the boat around and aiming for a stretch of the Normandy coast at least a mile from Mont Saint-Michel.

She got up and walked to the front of the boat, linking her arm through his. Hunter glanced at it and then at her. 'To keep my balance,' she said. 'Don't get excited.'

'If you say so.'

After a pause, she said, 'Did any of that really just happen, Dr Hunter?'

'It sure did.'

'So, what do we do now?'

'We find somewhere nice and quiet and take a bloody good look at Xavier's little treasure chest. Men don't launch an assault like we just witnessed for some ancient knickknacks and trinkets. And I think it's time you started calling me Max. That okay with you?'

'I think so, Max.'

'Then let's get back to land. Something tells me we just opened Pandora's Box.'

6

A few hours after Amy's phone calls, the team was reunited at Washington Dulles Airport. Blanco flew in from New York, Quinn Mosley from an undisclosed location and Jodie Priest from California. Ben Lewis was already in DC with his wife Meg and their newborn son. She had already given them the bare bones about the team's suspension, to get their sense of shock out of the way and at least partially processed before the mission began. Now, gathered in the section for private jets, they made their hellos and walked briskly across the apron to a Cessna Longitude, privately chartered by UNESCO via Juliette Bonnaire's office in Paris.

On the jet, Amy discovered that the adrenaline created by driving across town to the airport had diminished some of the fear she was feeling about Hunter's plight. He was an accomplished and experienced soldier and knew how to handle himself in dangerous situations. She had tried to cling to that thought and stay positive, but now that the initial excitement was wearing off, she found her mind wandering back into dark places. The best way to ignore it was to get back to work, and right now, that meant briefing the team about the mission.

As the plane raced away from the runway, she said in earnest, 'Okay, listen up, people.'

Start as you mean to go on, her father always said. *Put your best foot forward.*

Blanco, Jodie, Lewis and Quinn stopped whatever they had been doing on the jet's climb out and turned to give her their full attention.

'First, I want to thank you all once again for getting over to the airport so fast. We're facing a real emergency on several fronts. First, as you now all know, someone around the level of the President of the United States, or maybe higher, ordered the full suspension of HARPA. Jim Gates is out, currently licking his wounds in Colorado. The rest of us are unemployed and frozen out of all the usual access to the various generous resources packages offered by Uncle Sam.'

'They're not that generous,' Quinn said. 'Considering we usually end up in three-star hotels.'

Jodie swiped at her phone and yawned. 'Maybe if you're that bothered about it you should just hack the system and elevate us to five-star hotels.'

'That's impressive,' Quinn said.

'That I think you're capable of that?'

'No, that you used the word "elevate".'

Without looking up from her phone, Jodie raised her middle finger. 'Elevate that.'

Lewis laughed. 'You crazy kids and your wild antics.'

Two ice-cold frowns made him slump back down into his seat.

'That's enough, everyone,' Amy said. 'You don't know how much it means to me to get you all back together, and to see your senses of humour are intact, but we have to get to business. You already know that HARPA has been suspended, and you also know something has happened to Max, that he may have been snatched. Now we're on the move, I'll go into everything in more detail. Earlier today, I took a call from Professor Juliette Bonnaire at UNESCO. She told me Max Hunter might be in big trouble, or maybe not. You know Juliette.'

'What exactly has happened to Max?' Lewis asked. 'Do we know anything more?'

'Not yet,' Amy said. 'Juliette called a few hours ago now after receiving a call from Max while he was under attack in the abbey on the island of Mont Saint-Michel in Normandy, France. As far as I'm aware, no one's heard anything since. I tried to call Juliette on the way over to the airport and there was no reply. We have to consider every possibility, however hard that might be. Max may have gotten away from the attackers, they may have killed him, or they may even have kidnapped him. Right now, we don't know why any of this is going on.'

'What was Max doing on Mont Saint-Michel?' Quinn asked.

'Yeah,' Jodie said. 'What was he looking for?'

'Juliette was panicked and kept things brief. She told me he was there with two research assistants working on something to do with the missing crown jewels of England.'

'Someone knocked off the Tower of London?' Jodie was impressed. 'Kudos to whoever did that. As a thief – I mean, as a reformed thief – that's kind of like my Holy Grail.'

'Except it's not the same jewels,' Amy said. 'Juliette told me that there was another set of crown jewels, the original set, which got lost in 1216 when King John was on the throne. She said that Max and his assistants were working from some information they'd gleaned from something to do with a monk-knight going by the name of Xavier of Normandy. I've done some research into this, but we'll get to that later.'

Blanco gave a sceptical frown. 'You think someone broke into the abbey and started killing people to get hold of these jewels?'

'Why not?' Jodie said. 'They'd be priceless. People have killed for much less than that, believe me. Especially thieves.'

'I guess,' Blanco said. 'Thing is, wouldn't it have been easier for regular thieves simply to follow Max and his researchers out of the abbey and then steal what it was they were looking for? Seems to me, going into a place like that, shooting everything up and killing people are not the actions of your average international jewel thieves.'

Jodie raised her eyebrows as she contemplated Blanco's point of view. 'You could have a point, Sal, I guess. Thieves usually try to be as quiet as possible, keep a low profile.'

'Then who attacked Max?' Quinn asked.

'We don't know,' Amy said. 'And it seems like the speculation isn't getting us very far. We have no idea what their motivation was, whether it was to kill or kidnap Max, but I agree with Sal on this one. I'm not convinced the gunmen were regular thieves. I think maybe Max got hold of something more than he bargained for and upset some very serious people. Whatever it is they're looking for, they must be desperate and that makes them dangerous.'

'They must be pretty desperate to want to kidnap Hunter,' Jodie said.

Quinn nodded. 'Is there a ransom? I'd pay good money for them to keep him.'

Blanco gave her a grim stare. 'Not funny, kid. He could already be dead.'

'I was kidding, Sal. You remember those weird things called jokes?'

'Yeah,' he said. 'I think I remember making one back in '76.' He chuckled. 'So thanks for the memory.'

'But Sal's right,' Amy said. 'I didn't want to be the one to say it out loud, but there's a chance something very bad already happened to Max. It's hard for me even to think about that, and I think you all know why. Max and I got close to each other recently, but we started to drift. Either way, this hurts, but I have a responsibility to everyone on the team and their families. Whatever's happening to him right now, or if he's been murdered, it's up to me to do all I can for him. We can't hide from any of this. With that out of the way, I want to move on and start working on a response. So, gather round and get your thinking caps on.'

Amy swivelled in her seat and opened up her laptop on the small foldout table. She typed in her password and pulled up some files. Then, after establishing a Wi-Fi link with the aircraft's plasma screen up on the bulkhead, the mission briefing plan appeared in glorious technicolour for all to see.

'As I have briefly alluded to, Max was at the abbey in search of the original crown jewels, so working from that basis, what we're getting involved with here began eight centuries ago. We're talking High Middle Ages here. Classic Max Hunter territory.' She felt her voice waver a little and pulled herself together before anyone noticed. It was probably too late to cover up her anxiety over Hunter's potential fate, but if anyone on the small plane noticed, they didn't make any comment about it.

She pressed on. 'It starts back in the fall of 1216 when King John of England was leading a military campaign against a group of rebel barons. On his journey, he was travelling across a tidal estuary in the east of England called the Wash. Halfway across, the royal baggage train got caught out by the rising tide. It's not hard to see why, because when the tides of the North Sea rise, they can flow faster than a person running. At least that's what I just learned.'

'You learn something every day,' Lewis said. 'I did not know that.'

'As fascinating as it is to learn about the habits of obscure English tidal systems,' Quinn said, 'I'm wondering what this has to do with Max's attack.'

Jodie smiled. 'We're getting to that, right?'

Amy nodded.

'Great,' Jodie said, turning to Quinn. 'But I do love the whole ten-second attention span of your cute little generation. Keep it up.'

Quinn gawped. 'My generation? We're almost the same age.'

'I don't think so.'

Amy softly clapped her hands together. 'Okay, let's go back to the briefing. To answer Quinn's question and satisfy her admirable speculation about how Max fits into all this, we need to go back eight hundred years once again. The royal baggage train King John was leading across the Wash just happened to contain, as I am sure you have already figured out, the original English crown jewels.'

'Which as we have also just learned are not the ones in the Tower of London,' Blanco said.

'More or less,' Amy continued. 'I'm not sure it's as clear-cut as that. While some of the jewels in the Tower of London date back to the time of King John, or even earlier in the case of St Edward's Sapphire, which dates back to 1163, most of the ones we can see today are around three hundred and fifty years old, from the middle 1600s.'

'Still pretty old,' Jodie said with a casual shrug.

Quinn smirked. 'Apparently as old as you are.'

Jodie flipped her off for the second time on the plane and returned the smirk, but said nothing.

'So let me get this straight,' Lewis said. 'We know nothing about what we're heading into. We don't know if Max and his PhD student are still alive or not and we also don't know exactly what they're looking for, except it has something to do with the missing crown jewels of England. This is shaping up to be the perfect storm.'

'And I'm glad you're along for the ride,' Amy said. 'I'm glad you're all along for the ride because everything Ben just said is true. We know next to nothing about what we're heading into or what we're up against.'

'But we know one thing well enough,' Blanco said.

'We know that if Max is alive, he's in trouble and he needs our help.'

'And that's why we're here,' Amy said. 'I need everyone to get everything squared away and then get some sleep. When we land in Rennes we have an hour's drive to get to Mont Saint-Michel and the abbey. After that, anything could happen.'

7

Hunter decided it was too risky to return to their hotel and booked into a new one in a nearby town. It was off the beaten track, and he checked in with a fake passport provided courtesy of the US government for his HARPA work. By the time they got up to the room, they'd read on the internet that a gas explosion had damaged part of the abbey on Mont Saint-Michel, killed some security guards and injured an American PhD student. Lauren was confused by the lie, but Hunter floated some theories to her about why the authorities might want to cover up the truth.

The main thing for both of them was the news that Scott was going to be okay, and would be returning to the United States to be with family as soon as he was strong enough to fly. More worrisome was how Hunter had tried to call Juliette a further three times, each time without success. It was late, but his boss was a night owl, plus she would be worried about what had happened earlier. He was concerned about the possibility of something having happened to her, but shared her suspicions about the French law authorities. At this level, any threat facing any of them had to be confronted by themselves. Keeping his worries to himself, he grabbed a quick shower and then decided to decompress by ravaging the minibar. After they'd shared a couple of drinks, it was pushing midnight.

'This bed is heaven,' Lauren said with a sigh as she stretched out on the fresh sheets.

'Seems like adequate compensation,' Hunter said, crashing down beside her. 'Considering what we just went through back at the abbey. Maybe we could call down to room service and have them bring up something to refresh ourselves. Say, some champagne and strawberries and cream.'

Lauren gave him a sly look. 'You're incorrigible, Dr Hunter.'

'It's Max, remember?'

'That doesn't feel right. You're my supervisor.'

'After what we just went through together, I think

we could drop the formalities.' Hunter ran his hand up her arm. 'After all, we have so much to explore.'

Lauren leaned in to kiss him, then stopped. 'No, not now.'

'The best time to explore is right now.'

'My thoughts exactly, starting with this.'

She produced the treasure chest they had extracted from the chamber back in the abbey and put it down on the bed between them. Hunter slumped back, then shifted his gaze from Lauren's full lips to the small wooden box sitting innocuously on the cream linen a few inches from his face. He gave her a wry look and made a quick study of the box. It was locked, but the key was long gone.

'Looks like the only way in is to break the lock.'

Lauren gasped. 'Surely we could take it to a professional locksmith and have it opened properly, without causing any damage to it.'

'That takes time, and I don't know if you noticed or not, but we just got shot at by a bunch of very angry men with automatic weapons. Men like that don't just give up because we gave them the slip. They'll be searching the area. We need to make this quick.'

'Is that what you tell all the ladies?'

He smiled. 'Glad to see you kept your sense of humour. Fleeing from a hail of bullets can sometimes have a neutralising effect on that.'

'But with you, there's just so much comedic material to work with.'

His smile faded. 'Maybe we should just get back to business.'

'I think so.'

He slid off the bed with the box in his hand and walked over to the window, holding it up in the light for a better examination. 'We can get in here without causing too much damage. Locks from this period were fairly rudimentary, especially ones of this small size. They were usually turned by keys with only one simple bit on them. I might be able to fashion a crude facsimile from something here in the hotel. You think you can manage without me for a few minutes while I take a look around and try to find something that can help us out?'

'I think I might just be able to handle it, Max.'

Hunter wasn't so sure. Experience working with the HARPA team had provided a clear picture of just how depraved and desperate some people in the world truly were, especially when it came to the hunt for relics from the deep past, or anything else that might lead to ancient treasures or doomsday weapons of antiquity. Maybe the gunmen were simply after the original crown jewels, or maybe they were after something else entirely – something that right now he knew nothing about. That possibility was even more alluring than the first. So he worked fast, turning on the full Hunter charm with the hotel staff to acquire a silver teaspoon from the kitchen.

When he returned, it took just a few moments to manipulate the handle in the keyway until the eight-hundred-year-old lock popped open, perfectly preserving the integrity of the wooden box.

'You did it!' Lauren said.

'I'd have forced it open with a knife if I had my way,' Hunter said.

'You're supposed to be a leading UNESCO archaeologist, Max. What sort of example would that be for me?'

He gave her a look. 'Out in the field, sometimes one must improvise.'

'That's what you just did with your little teaspoon trick, Max. It was clever. It impressed me.'

'I can see that,' he said. 'You just called me Max twice.'

They shared another moment, and then both broke away, ending the awkward silence.

'Let's take a look at what we have inside this little

box of delights,' Hunter said. 'And see if it's worth getting shot at by those loons back in the abbey.'

Hunter opened the lid. Inside the box was something wrapped in white cloth, a much purer white than the cream linen around the box's exterior, and made from what looked like satin. 'Here goes nothing.'

He lifted the object out of the box and carefully unwrapped it, producing a gasp from each of them.

'A crown!' Lauren said.

'It's not a crown,' Hunter said, lifting it to the light of the window and gazing at it in awe. 'It's a coronet.'

Lauren stared at the glistening gold in wonder. 'Aren't they the same thing?'

Hunter spoke without taking his eyes off the object, now turning it around to peer inside at the metal ring at its base. 'Crowns, coronets, tiaras, diadems. They all differ for various reasons. A coronet is usually simpler and used by lower ranks of the nobility, never the monarch. The monarch wears a crown.'

'So, this is a coronet. Got it.'

'More specifically Llywelyn's coronet.'

She gawped at him. 'You can't mean Llywelyn ap Gruffudd?'

He understood her shock. Llywelyn ap Gruffudd, the Lord of Aberffraw, had given the coronet to the monks of Cymer Abbey in the small north Welsh village of Llanelltyd near Dolgellau in Snowdonia in the year 1282, to protect it when he went into battle against King Edward I of England. Llywelyn, the last of the native princes of Wales, was killed later that year and Edward seized the coronet and other treasures from the monks in 1284 and took them to London as spoils of war where they were presented to Edward the Confessor's shrine in Westminster Abbey. At some point following that, the coronet disappeared from history forever.

'But it's been missing for eight hundred years!' Lauren said.

Hunter let her words hang in the air as he continued to study the golden coronet. 'Not any more, it seems.'

'Wait a minute, didn't the treasure Llywelyn ap Gruffudd left to the monks of Cymer Abbey also include the Cross of Neith, a relic believed to be part of the True Cross?'

Hunter felt a shiver go up his spine. 'So goes the legend.'

'This is amazing,' she said almost to herself. 'I can't believe we found something so incredible.'

'If you think this is incredible, you should come on a HARPA mission.'

'Ah yes, the mysterious HARPA. How does it feel being part of the world-team that raised the *Titanic*?'

Hunter was frowning now, peering inside the coronet's band. 'That was a hell of a job, for sure, but it's over now.'

'You're quitting HARPA?'

'I haven't decided, but it's not important. What do you make of this?'

Hunter handed Lauren the coronet.

'What am I looking at?' she asked.

'You tell me.'

'First thing that strikes me is it's not solid gold. This is gold plate, probably painted onto the iron.'

'Good. How else could you tell?'

'Its weight,' she said at once. 'If this were solid gold it would be much heavier.'

'Four times heavier, to be precise. What else do you notice?'

She squinted and turned the coronet over in her hands. 'Aside from the inscription, not much else.'

'And what do you make of the inscription?'

'It's nonsense.'

'It's not nonsense.'

'Well, it's not Latin, Middle Welsh or Middle English.'

'If you take a closer look, you can see it's in Latin.'

She frowned harder. Hunter saw she was growing frustrated. 'EUR RX SURAT: XX ARTEMUS QUOQUE UNDERFUR is not Latin.'

'It's an anagram. Re-arrange the letters and you get...'

She gasped. 'Oh, my heavens! Arturus Rex: Rex Quondam, Rexque Futurus. King Arthur: Former King and Future King.'

Hunter gave her his very best grin. 'And what do you deduce from this?'

'I'm holding the coronet of King Arthur! The mythical King Arthur.'

'You're so cynical. You're holding King Arthur's crown in your very own hands and yet still you disbelieve. You have so much to learn.'

'I thought you said it was a coronet?'

'Not if King Arthur wore it. Then it's a crown. Keep up.'

Lauren handed the coronet back to him with a look. 'Coronet, crown, whatever. It's an ornamental headpiece made from iron and covered in gold plate, worn by someone a very long time ago, who was certainly not King Arthur because there is no concrete archaeological evidence that King Arthur ever existed.'

'Until right now.'

She had opened her mouth to speak, but now she closed it again. Hunter saw he had given her pause for thought. 'But—'

'Miss Lane, you may just have made one of the greatest archaeological and historical discoveries of the decade, if not the century.'

She picked up the box and began fussing with it, totally absorbed by its beauty. 'But how the hell did Xavier get his hands on it?'

Hunter shrugged. 'We know Xavier knew something about the disappearance of the original crown jewels. We also know that King Henry II was rumoured to have discovered Excalibur. Just speculating, you could say that maybe Henry found Excalibur, and this coronet, and handed them down to his son Richard the Lionheart. After Richard died in France, this treasure was passed to his brother, King John. Then, when John's baggage train disappeared in the Wash, this particular item somehow fell into the arms of our warrior monk, Xavier.'

'Maybe...'

He looked at her sharply. 'What is it?'

'The coronet was on this satin cushion, right?'

'Yes, it's attached to the box.'

'But it's coming loose.'

Hunter walked over to her, excited and a little annoyed he hadn't thought of looking beneath the cushion before his protégé. 'Anything under there?'

She held up a piece of parchment, yellowed and crumbling, rolled up tight and held in place with a faded red ribbon. 'Only this.'

Hunter felt a shiver run up his spine. 'A parchment roll! I love parchment rolls.'

'Weirdo.'

'Sticks and stones may hurt my bones, but I know parchment rolls very often lead to nice, shiny things. Old, priceless things, perhaps even more amazing than the coronet.'

'Not to mention the glory of finding those things.'

'You have me all wrong,' Hunter said, plucking the parchment from her hand with a wink. 'I'm all about advancing the discipline of archaeological study. I'd never dream of chasing fame and glory.'

He slid the ribbon off with the greatest care and gently unfurled the roll of parchment. Pieces crumbled away and floated to the floor, making him stop and take a breath before resuming, each time a little slower. When it was fully unrolled, he saw a short verse in the same nonsense printed into the coronet.

'It's written in Latin again, like the inscription on the coronet.'

'Can you read it?'

'I can read it, but I can't understand it. Get a translation engine up on the internet and we'll plug it into that.'

'I love how you're teaching me all the timeworn, traditional methods.' Lauren gave him a sideways look as she got out her phone and searched for a Latin translation engine. Peering down at the parchment, she frowned. 'You can read that?'

'I'll spell it out.'

She typed in the words: Incipe coronam et sequere pugionem meum, custoditum a Lancelot, ad gladium. And hit the translate button. 'It says "Start with the crown and follow my dagger. Guarded by the servant, to the sword." What do you think that means? There's no dagger in the box.'

'My dagger,' Hunter said. 'It says follow my dagger. Xavier's dagger.'

'But like I say, there's nothing here... Wait a minute. Xavier was a Benedictine monk, and it was very common for them to carry a small blade. They used them for all kinds of things, from peeling vegetables to carving wood. They were the Middle Ages equivalent of a Swiss Army knife. My best guess is Xavier had his own dagger, presumably buried with him back up at the tomb. But follow my dagger to the sword? What sword?

Were there any swords in the original crown jewels?'

'The list of items lost back in 1216 isn't exactly comprehensive, so a sword may have been part of the collection, but I doubt it.'

She put her phone away and looked at him. 'What does he mean then?'

Hunter stared at her, thinking carefully about what the riddle meant. 'It's obvious. Look at the coronet and the inscription. King Arthur: Former King and Future King. Now, we have this parchment talking about following a dagger to the sword. As in the sword.'

Lauren gawped at him. 'Oh, no. That's insane. You can't seriously expect me to believe Xavier knew the location of—'

Hunter broke in. 'Turns out whoever wrote this parchment was under the impression King Arthur's sword, Excalibur, was very real and that his dagger is going to lead us to it.'

A minute of silence passed.

'Which is a very interesting development,' Lauren said.

'You could say that. Could we be on the trail of Excalibur?'

Lauren's face fell into a frown. 'I doubt it, at least if you think you're going to find a sword.'

'What do you mean?'

'You know I'm a sceptic, Max, but Xavier once wrote something about Excalibur. He said it was not what people thought it was, that they would be shocked by the reality of it, or something like that. I suspect Excalibur is something much more humdrum than what people think it is.'

'Or something much more powerful?'

'As I said, don't get excited. Xavier was a scholar and a man of God. A devotee of St John and a lifelong student of his gospel. I doubt he believed Excalibur was magical.'

Hunter's eyes were glazing over. 'Either way, we have to go back to the abbey.'

'Are you nuts?' she said. 'We almost got killed there this morning! Scott was nearly killed and is lying in hospital on a drip.'

'And?'

'And there's going to be cops all over the place!'

'And?'

She stared at him, a smile appearing on her face. 'And you want to go back?'

'You have to be driven by something powerful to

succeed in this game, Lauren.' As he spoke, he crouched down and pulled a bag out from under the bed. To Lauren's undisguised horror, he pulled out a handgun.

'What on earth is that?'

'It's a Glock 19,' he said, checking the mag. 'Just in case.'

'But why is it here?'

'Juliette lent it to me just in case we had trouble. This is trouble.'

'This is insane. I'm writing a doctorate. I'm not in a gang.'

'It could save your life, and it won't get used unless it's strictly necessary.' He got to his feet and clamped a hand on her shoulder. 'It's just in case. Relax. As I said, in this game, you need to be hungry. So hungry you'll risk your life not just once but many times.'

'Very philosophical, but you're just in it for the glory, right?'

Hunter's smile widened. 'Let's get to the car. We have a long night ahead of us.'

8

Hunter pulled the car over and came to a stop in a lonely coastal car park. The drive from their new hotel was uneventful but noisy with excited talk, brimming over with theories and speculation. They climbed out and looked around, scanning for any sign of trouble, but found none. Hours had passed since the attack. It was full night with dawn still an hour away, and a wild scattering of bright stars peppered the black vault above their heads like diamonds. Close by, the sound of waves lapping at the Normandy coast was calm and relaxing, but the awesome sight of the abbey perched atop Saint Michel's rocky island in the middle of the bay reminded them this was no holiday. Just a few hours ago, Scott Wright had been shot and wounded and rushed to Rennes by paramedics for emergency surgery. This was a dangerous place.

'How are we going in?' Lauren asked.

'Same way we came out.' Hunter stared up at the abbey. 'I've no doubt the place will be closed for weeks after what happened today, but I can't see much activity at the moment.'

'Except the police standing around at the head of the slipway.'

'We can get past them. C'mon.'

They walked along the coast towards a small village and then made their way down to the sea in search of a boat. They didn't have to look long. Moored in the bay were dozens of small boats bobbing up and down with the tide. Runabouts, dinghies, even a couple of cabin cruisers; Hunter studied them all.

'What about that one?' Lauren asked, pointing at a modest bow rider.

Hunter shook his head. 'I'm guessing you don't know how to hotwire an engine?'

'You guess right.'

'Then no. We were lucky before when we found the keys in the RIBs. If they hadn't been there, hotwiring was only an option until they found us and opened fire because it can take up a lot of time and patience. The owner of this boat is certain to have taken his keys away with him, plus starting up an engine that size at this time of night is too risky. We're too close to the village. Someone will hear us and call the police, and even if we get away with it, the police on the island will hear our engine when we approach. We need to go old-school. Follow me.'

Hunter led Lauren down a twisting path through some dunes until they reached a small rowboat. He helped Lauren in over the gunwale and took hold of the oars. 'Your job is to tell me if we need to go right or left.'

'Got it.'

He began rowing out across the bay. 'When we reach the rock, we secure the boat near the chapel.'

'What about the gunmen?'

'They'll be long gone by now. After we moor up, we can just go back to the tunnel we used to escape and reverse our journey. After that, we have some real work to do. Namely, we need to find Xavier's mysterious dagger so we can start looking for Excalibur.'

Her eyes widened, thrilled with the buzz of her first real adventure. 'You honestly think King Arthur was real, and not just a legend?'

'If you'd seen some of the things I'd seen, you'd have little problem believing King Arthur was a real man, trust me. For now, we're going to work on the assumption that not only was he a real flesh and blood person but also that there's a dagger somewhere inside the abbey on top of the bloody great rock behind me that might lead us to Excalibur. You're an expert on King Arthur. What do you think Xavier meant when he wrote about his dagger being guarded by the servant?'

'I'm not an expert on King Arthur, Max. I'm a medievalist writing a doctorate on Xavier. My interest in the Arthur legendarium is entirely personal.'

'Sure, but what do you think about it?'

'Lancelot,' she said crisply. 'Its original French meaning means servant. If Xavier hid his dagger in a tomb guarded by who he calls the servant, and that dagger has something to do with Excalibur, then in the current context, and I cannot believe I am saying this, the servant is most likely a reference to Lancelot.'

Hunter was unfazed. 'That's Sir Lancelot to you.'

'This whole thing is insane.' She told him to move direction a little to his left. As he corrected course, she said, 'You think the men who shot at us this morning already know about the dagger?'

Hunter shrugged. 'It's possible, or maybe they're just shooting in the dark and hoping for a result. One way or another, they know something, or they wouldn't have been here today, discharging firearms and murdering security officers. And I think it's more likely they came here looking for Excalibur than the crown jewels.'

'Who do you think they are?'

He shrugged. 'No idea, at least not yet. But don't forget they put Scott in hospital. I owe those bastards for that, and I'll pay back in kind if I ever run into them again.'

Lauren looked momentarily alarmed. 'You think that's likely?'

'What?'

'That we'll cross paths with those men again?'

'I think so, yes. Whatever we're looking for, it's got to be the same thing.' He turned and looked over his shoulders. 'Almost there, and then we can get to work.'

They rowed on, against the current, moonlight sparkling on the bay around them and stars brighter than ever above their heads. The only sound was Hunter driving the oars across the surface of the sea and heaving them through the cold water. In the far distance, the police mulled around on the slipway, smoking cigarettes and checking their watches, oblivious to the rowboat quietly making its way through the night.

'Why would Lancelot be buried here, Lauren?' Hunter asked. 'I thought he was an English legend.'

'His original name was Lancelot du Lac, which is French for Lancelot of the Lake. The reason his name is French is that the legend states that he originated from a region called Benoic, in north-eastern France near the German border.'

'I didn't know any of that. I thought the whole King Arthur legend was English.'

'British, if anything,' Lauren said. 'The whole Arthurian romance takes place long before the creation of what's now called England. Irish and Welsh folklore also claim Lancelot, so it's always been up for grabs, as has Arthur, with many places claiming him as a native of their own. But what we discovered inside Xavier's little box of delights may change all that. If we find the tomb of Lancelot tonight, here at the abbey, then we should be able to start building some proper concrete foundations to the story.'

'You mean, move it from legend to reality?'

She nodded. 'To history, even. I still can't believe this is real though. A little more to your left, Max.'

'Thanks. It's the damned tide pushing me off course.'

'If we find the tomb... if we find the body of Sir Lancelot and we can confirm at least his existence, that's going to be a major archaeological and historical discovery. A significant addition to the academic canon.'

Hunter blew out a deep breath. 'Correct. God, I'm knackered. Are we almost there?'

'Almost. But what I'm trying to say is, men who kill people with guns aren't interested in advancing our knowledge of history or archaeology, are they?'

'I've worked with some proper bastards in academia,' Hunter said. 'But no, I'd agree they never struck me as the type to gun down doctoral students and security guards.'

'Exactly. So maybe you're right. Maybe Arthur and Excalibur were real and that's what those men were hunting for.'

Hunter stopped rowing and fixed his eyes on her. 'You're dead right, Lauren. And that's precisely why we're rowing out here tonight and not waiting a few weeks while we refer the matter back to UNESCO. We don't know why they wanted Xavier's little treasure chest so badly that they were prepared to kill for it, but it wasn't so they could add to the literature in the kind of stunning paper you might expect from me, for example. Those guys are hunting for something much more dangerous, valuable, or both. Whether that's Excalibur or something else, it's our job to beat them to it.'

'Sounds risky.'

'Stopping evil usually is.'

'Look out! Rocks!'

Hunter spun around just in time to see the rocks at the bottom of the chapel racing up towards the bow of the rowing boat. He steered it away and then pulled in tight to the wrecked hulk of what was left of the other RIB. After lashing the boat to a rock, he helped Lauren out onto the shore and stared up at the abbey rising into the night sky.

'Let's hope we can get back inside without a hitch,' he said. 'In the meantime, you can finish telling me about Lancelot.'

9

They crawled back through the smaller tunnel and found themselves in the passageway, once more able to stand up to their full height. As they walked back to the trapdoor, Hunter led the way with his torch while Lauren talked. 'Lancelot doesn't appear in all legends about King Arthur. In any Arthurian romances where he features, it's usually as Arthur's most loyal lieutenant – hence the meaning of his name, "servant" – but in the French tradition, he has an affair with Queen Guinevere, which then leads to a series of battles mercilessly exploited by Mordred.'

'That's the guy from *Lord of the Rings*, right?' Hunter asked.

'I'm hoping that's one of your infamous jokes.'

'It is. I was referring to Morgoth. You're referring to someone else entirely, I hope.'

'I am. According to Geoffrey of Monmouth, a Welsh scholar and cleric living during the first half of the twelfth century who wrote extensive chronicles on British history, Mordred was the son of King Loth. The first mention of this is in his famous work, *Historia Regum Britanniae*, or *History of the Kings of Britain*. It's not strictly a history in the way we use the word today, but what we would call pseudohistory.'

'You mean a misrepresentation of history, like cryptohistory?'

'Exactly that. I'm impressed.'

'I'm an archaeologist, Lauren. Just because Arthurian legend isn't my field doesn't mean I'm a total idiot.'

'Are you saying there are other reasons you're a total idiot?'

Hunter stopped in the passageway and turned, lighting their faces with his torch. 'I can see I'm going to have trouble with you.'

She looked up into his eyes. 'Oh, I wouldn't say that.'

After an awkward pause, Hunter spun around and continued along the passageway. 'We still have a way to go until we get to Xavier's tomb. You might as well carry on with your gripping lecture on Arthurian pseudohistory.'

'Only if you're sure. I wouldn't want to keep you if you have somewhere more important to be.'

'Chop chop, Lauren. We'll be at the end soon. I might as well be properly briefed by the time I get there.'

'Very well. As I was saying before you so rudely interrupted, Mordred exploited the wars caused by Lancelot's affair and the kingdom was thrown into turmoil. If we fast-forward to a reimagining of Geoffrey's account by a twelfth-century Anglo-Norman historian from Lincoln named Henry of Huntingdon, we learn that Arthur fights Mordred and his entire army single-handedly and destroys them all, including beheading Mordred. A later retelling of the tale by Sir Thomas Mallory in the fifteenth century, called *Le Morte d'Arthur*, or the *Death of Arthur*, describes how Mordred savagely wounds Arthur in battle with one of his swords named Clarent, which he had the traitorous Guinevere steal for him to use against her husband.'

'If this is a passing interest, I guess it explains why your professional work is so good.'

'That's why I was assigned to work with you, Max.'

'Makes sense. When do we get Excalibur?'

'Patience, please. It didn't work out so great for the

traitors because Arthur was armed with Excalibur, which he proceeded to use to brutally skewer Mordred and kill him.'

'Shouldn't that be to skewer brutally?'

'Sorry, are you grading my grammar as I talk?'

'No, apologies. Please carry on.'

'Gee, thanks. Anyway, in a Welsh account named *Ymddiddan Arthur a'r Eryr*, or *Arthur's Dialogue with the Eagle*, the dying King Arthur tells Guinevere that he used Caledfwlch to strike Mordred nine times before killing him. Caledfwlch is the Welsh word for Excalibur.'

'But if Arthur used Excalibur to take out Mordred's entire army, I'm guessing it has some kind of scientific property that made it so dangerous.'

'It's a fable, Max.'

'Yeah, we'll see about that,' Hunter said as they continued their trudge along the passageway. 'After some of the stuff I've seen these last few years, stuff I just can't explain without sounding insane, I'm not ruling anything out. As we already said, those guys with guns aren't shooting people so they can write interesting new academic papers. Whatever they're looking for is connected in some way to the big two. Money, or power. If you ask me, getting their hands on Excalibur would fit into the last of those two possibilities very snugly. Tell me, where does the Holy Grail fit into all this exactly?'

'Why? Is finding out King Arthur was real and locating Excalibur not exciting enough for you?'

'It's just a simple question. I'm an archaeologist, not a religious scholar, or even less some kind of specialist on Arthurian legend, so give it to me straight. Could Xavier be leading us to the Holy Grail?'

'It's not going to be the Holy Grail, Max.'

'How can you be so sure?'

'First, because the grail is nothing more than legend.'

'But then, a few hours ago we would have said that about King Arthur.'

Lauren remained unconvinced. 'Fine. If we steelman your crazy hypothesis that anything is possible and presume the grail is a real object, we can still rule it out because there's no mention of the grail in the literature of any kind until the twelfth century. This is because that was when the Crusades occurred, and when, presuming it was real, it was discovered and brought, in this case, to Western Europe. If King Arthur was a real historical figure, he was living in the late fifth century and the early sixth century. How could he have had anything to do with the Holy Grail if it wasn't brought out of the Holy Lands for another six hundred years? That just doesn't make sense, not even in terms of a myth or a legend, never mind reality.'

'You sound kind of annoyed about that.'

'It just irritates me when people can't count centuries.'

Hunter laughed. 'All right, Lauren. Looks like we're getting closer to the tomb. Remember these niches used for candles? They were only at the tomb end of the passageway.'

'I remember.'

'This means we need to sharpen up our senses. At this time of night, the abbey would normally be empty, but we can't presume the only police are the ones guarding the place out on the slipway. We have to work on the assumption that there are going to be more security guards here than normal and they'll be on high alert after what happened earlier today. It's too bad I can't get in touch with Juliette. She might have been able to talk them into letting us back inside just to finish the job.'

'After what happened?'

'She has a lot of influence, plus there's a chance we might be able to help with the investigation.'

'Still sounds unlikely to me.'

'You're probably right.'

'We can always turn back,' she said. 'We'll just have to wait until the criminal investigation is completed and the damage to the abbey has been restored. Maybe that's fair enough.'

'Not in my book. It'll take way too long... Here's the trapdoor.'

Hunter reached up and pressed his palm against the wood. Wincing as it creaked open, he craned his neck until he was able to peer through the narrowest of slits and scan the tomb.

'You see anything?' Lauren asked.

'Nothing. C'mon – but be careful. If we get caught in here, we're going to be in deep shit. First, they'll probably demand that Juliette sacks me, and second, you'll probably get booted off your doctorate. These are not optimum outcomes, Lauren. You don't need me to tell you that.'

Inside the tomb, she drew alongside him and gave him a devilish smile. 'Then we'd better not get caught, right?'

10

Amy and the team touched down at Rennes in Normandy and quickly picked up an SUV from a company attached to the airport. The vehicle was a silver Toyota Hilux, spacious enough for the five of them and with plenty of room in the back for their gear. The entire process was slower than usual because they enjoyed none of the shortcuts afforded to them when working for the US government in the HARPA team. Now they were working off the books, with a little help from UNESCO. That meant doing things a different way.

As they drove north to the coast, Amy gazed out of her window and watched the rolling French countryside slide by in a gentle blur. It was just before dawn in

France, and the farmhouses and fields were starting to be lit by a pale, watery light. It was a beautiful, pastoral landscape that reminded her vaguely of somewhere she remembered in New England, but thoughts of Hunter in danger and her team working on a potentially perilous mission outside of the protection of HARPA nagged at her mind. Nearing the north coast, she saw the water of the bay sparkling as the sun finally broke the horizon, and then the imposing sight of the abbey, perched up on its rock.

'Keep rolling,' Quinn told Blanco, who was at the wheel. As was usual, the young goth had been managing navigation on her GPD Pocket laptop. The compact computer was fractionally larger than a smartphone but came equipped with a significantly faster Intel CPU. On top of that, it also offered a physical keyboard, which she preferred to use, especially when hacking, because of its greater speed and accuracy. 'You should see a parking lot up ahead in a few minutes.'

'I see it,' Blanco said. 'But it's some distance away from the abbey. I think we can get closer.'

Quinn removed a wireless earbud. 'Not a good idea. The police are all over that area. They've been there all night.'

'How do you know?' Lewis asked.

Quinn twirled the earbud. 'Because I hacked into their comms systems and have been listening to them for the last ten miles.'

'But you can't speak French,' Jodie said.

'No, but I'm running a real-time voice translator. Look, you wanna do this?'

'Thanks, Quinn,' Amy said, warning Jodie off with a look. 'We appreciate it.'

'Doesn't sound like it.'

'We do, and now the mission starts for real,' Amy said. 'When we get inside, the first thing I want to do is get to the tomb where Max and his student located the artefacts. I can't tell you what I expect to find in there because I don't know, but it's the last place we know Max and his research assistant were before they came under attack. So, that's where we start.'

'Maybe he left us some kind of clue,' Lewis said. 'I'd expect something like that from Max.'

'We're still presuming he's alive,' Quinn said, drawing a look from the others. 'What?'

Jodie rolled her eyes. 'I'm guessing if you disappeared, you'd want us to presume you were still alive, right?'

Quinn gave a petulant sigh, shrugged and pulled up her hoodie, highlighting in Amy's mind just how juvenile she could be sometimes. She let it slide for that very reason. Quinn didn't need a lecture in front of everyone else about how she was behaving like a silly child.

Blanco's deep voice ended the silence. 'We work on the assumption that Max is still alive because that's the only thing we can do. If we all thought he was dead, we wouldn't have raced across the Atlantic at the drop of a hat. It's the right thing to do. We don't leave anyone behind. If there's even the slightest chance he's in trouble and needs our help, then we're here to give him that help. He'd do it for us.'

'Changing the subject,' Amy said. 'Lewis, as the resident theological expert, have you got that briefing on the abbey ready? I think we need some context here before we dive right in.'

Lewis nodded and shifted in his seat as he pulled out his phone and navigated to his notes. 'Yes, I spent a good part of the flight looking into this. Mont Saint-Michel was made a UNESCO World Heritage Site in 1978. The literal translation into English is the Mount of Saint Michael, the archangel. Today, it's a major pilgrimage site for Christians, and its history stretches right back to the early eighth century when the Bishop of Avranches – Avranches is a nearby town – declared that Saint Michael had told him to build a church on top of the small rocky island that sits out in the bay.'

'Some kind of vision?' Blanco asked. 'This guy a drinker?'

Lewis laughed. 'Maybe, but that's what gave him the vision. Visions were not uncommon for the time or at least people who believed they had experienced one. Anyway, around a hundred and fifty years after the bishop had his vision, the local authority, which in this case were the same dukes of Normandy that ended up invading England in 1066, offered to support and fund the development of a full Benedictine abbey on the site. After power passed from the dukes to the French kings, they also continued to support the work of the monks here.'

'Generous,' Amy said.

Lewis continued. 'Thanks to the blessing of French royalty, the abbey went on to become not only a site of significant theological importance to pilgrims but also a prominent and esteemed place of education and learning. Manuscript illuminators came here to learn and then ply their trade, but it wasn't all champagne and strawberries. These were tough times and the site was attacked by English invaders on many occasions. The ramparts constructed around the base of the island were built to keep them out.'

'They certainly didn't keep one Englishman out,' Jodie said.

'Not much can keep Max at bay,' Blanco said, the corner of his mouth turning up slightly in fond memory of his old buddy.

Lewis was smiling too. 'Today, things are more peaceful. At least they were until Max turned up there and got kidnapped. The small community on the island includes around fifty monks and nuns and there are some amenities such as a restaurant, some shops and some hotels dotted around the tiny village, all tucked up behind the walled ramparts, and for much of the day, cut off from the mainland when the tide rises. And on that note, the bay has one of the highest tidal ranges in Europe, of roughly fifteen metres, or forty-five feet.'

'Thanks, Ben,' Amy said. 'That gives me a better picture of it. What about our ingress?'

Quinn interrupted. 'Hang on, Amy. You guys probably all presumed this, but the local police have suspended all traffic between the mainland and the island. Because of the attack last night, no one is allowed on or off.'

'Good to have it confirmed,' Amy said. 'Thanks. Given what Quinn has just said, it looks like we're going to have to forget about any regular forms of access. On that subject, Ben, you were saying something about the tides?'

He nodded. 'Normally, it's a straight-forward case of waiting until the tide goes out and then simply taking a walkway out to the rock. Problem is, thanks to the shooting there last night, as Quinn has just pointed out, the entire island has been cut off by the police until they're happy enough with their investigation to open it back up again. Several people were killed there, after all, and others seriously injured.'

Amy sighed. 'And we can forget about UNESCO greasing some palms and getting us in, too. Juliette already contacted me on the plane at the start of the journey and broke that particular piece of good news. Even though it's a UNESCO site, not even official staff members or researchers are allowed in until the police say so. And like Quinn says, the monks and nuns on the island are also not allowed to leave either. It's total lockdown.'

'Makes sense,' Blanco said. 'We're seeing this through a lens of HARPA missions and ancient relics, but from the point of view of law enforcement, they're looking at murder, attempted murder, assaults and thefts. Anyone on the island could have played a part in it, so you can understand their position.'

'Still makes our life more difficult,' Lewis said.

Amy agreed. 'Yes, it does, but we still need to get on that island and find out what happened to Max as soon as possible.'

'What about trying Juliette again?' Blanco asked. 'Any point?'

Amy frowned. 'I tried that on the drive up here after we landed. It's kinda weird, but she wasn't answering. I know it was before dawn, but I thought given what was going on she'd be on high alert and taking calls. I'll keep trying. In the meantime, any other ideas? Jodie? You're the expert in breaking and entering.'

'Which is why I'm already looking into the tides,' Jodie said.

'And what's the tide doing right now?' Amy asked.

'Low tide was an hour ago and right now it's shooting right up,' Jodie said. 'If we want to wait until it's safe to walk across then we're sitting here for another twelve hours.'

'At least it'll be dark by then,' Lewis said.

'I was thinking that,' Quinn said. 'We'd have a lot more options if it was night.'

Amy shook her head to dismiss the idea. 'But that's hours away. We haven't got that much time to waste, not now. We need a solution now.'

'This is not easy,' Jodie said. 'It's definitely not

helping that it's going to be broad daylight soon. The tide is in some ways a lesser problem.'

Blanco scratched his head. 'I was going to suggest we steal a boat. Too obvious?'

'Early morning in a small bay swarming with cops working a homicide case?' Amy said. 'I'm not sure that's such a great idea.'

'What then?' Quinn asked. 'We go hire some scuba gear and swim across the bay underwater like James Bond or something?'

Lewis smiled at the idea. 'Meg says I look like James Bond. That's kinda cool.'

'Which one?' Blanco asked immediately.

'I never asked her.'

'The tides are too strong for anything like scuba diving,' Jodie said, steering the conversation back to business. 'And there isn't a place to hire that sort of gear anywhere near here. And oh yeah, it's a ridiculous idea.'

Quinn flipped her off. 'What's your idea, then?'

'I like Sal's plan.'

Amy turned to her, frowning. 'Stealing a boat in daylight in a place swarming with cops?'

'Better than that. Much better than that.' A mischievous smile appeared on Jodie's face. Amy saw that she was hatching one of her great criminal enterprises.

'Okay, so what's much better?' Lewis asked.

'You took the words right out of my mouth,' Amy said. 'What is "much better" than stealing a boat?'

Jodie was staring out across the bay at the abbey. 'You'll see. Remember, the greatest plans are always the simplest.'

'If this is going to involve goddam paramotors or parachutes, I'm staying in the car,' Quinn said loudly. 'I'm not into that crap. I like my bones the way they are.'

'No, nothing like that,' Jodie said, her grin widening. 'Just some good old-fashioned deception and theft.'

'Just the way you like it,' Quinn said.

Blanco pulled up into a coastal car park and switched off the engine. 'Gotta say, Jodie. I'm officially intrigued.'

'So you should be,' Jodie said.

Amy was confused but began to smile. 'All right, let's have it. Spill the beans.'

Jodie opened her door and swung her legs outside. 'C'mon. Follow me.'

11

Hunter and Lauren had split up and were searching the tomb for something new. For Hunter, the job felt almost futile. He'd been working inside Xavier's tomb for weeks and thought he knew it inside out. When he'd discovered a secret compartment buried beneath Xavier's sarcophagus, and Scott Wright had gone down inside and found the treasure chest containing the coronet, he was sure that was all there was to the place. Now, it looked like Xavier had left one last surprise behind.

'But where?' he muttered.

Lauren stopped her search. She was on her hands and knees at the base of the sarcophagus and now looked up at Hunter. 'You say something?'

Hunter shook his head, despondent and running out of patience as he stared out at the poky tomb. 'This is hopeless. We've turned this place inside out looking for something, anything that might lead us to his mysterious dagger. Maybe we got something wrong.'

'You give up too easily, Dr Hunter. Think of things from Xavier's point of view. After all, the legend of Xavier of Normandy is notorious. He was much more than a Benedictine monk; he was a warrior monk, or what was sometimes called a soldier saint. He ranged across Europe on horseback, staying at abbeys and monasteries when he was able, or just camping out under the stars when he was in the countryside. He was on a mission not only to spread the word of God but also to humble himself before God.'

Hunter was staring at her now. 'And your point?'

Still deep in her search, fingertips pushing into the crack where the sarcophagus met the stone floor, she turned and looked at him, her hair rolling down over her shoulder. 'My point is, he's not going to make this easy. He doesn't want just any old idiot finding his dagger. Keep looking.'

'Shush!' Hunter whispered. 'I hear footsteps! Take cover.'

Hunter pushed himself up into the shadows, just

out of sight of the hole in the floor above, while Lauren slithered around the back of the sarcophagus. Memories of hiding inside the tombs under the Gates of Nineveh flooded back to him, of Brodie McCabe and his mercenaries hunting him under the hot, Iraqi sands. McCabe was now a dead man, a fate Hunter was working assiduously to avoid.

'Who is it?' she whispered.

'I'll ask them when they come over,' Hunter said with an eye roll. 'In the meantime, be quiet!'

He listened as the footsteps grew closer to the hole above him. They stopped and a torch shone down inside the tomb. He heard someone speaking in French and then they walked away, the footsteps receding into a blur as they echoed inside the giant abbey.

'Must be more security,' Hunter said. 'They've gone. Keep looking.'

He turned and helped Lauren look. She was still working on the area around the base of the sarcophagus. Hunter looked up to the heavens, in this case, the vaulted ceiling, but saw nothing suspicious, nothing that indicated a hidden weapon. Lauren stood up and dusted her hands off.

'Maybe you're right,' she said. 'We've been through this place like a dose of salts. The only sodding dagger around here is the stone one on the statue of Xavier.'

Hunter looked over at the monk's reclining statue, stretched out on top of the sarcophagus as if in deep sleep. It was an effigy of Xavier, but they had seen it before when they opened the lid and examined the contents of the sarcophagus. They'd found nothing inside, but now a thought struck them both at the same time.

'Dr Hunter!'

'I know,' he said. 'The stone dagger in Xavier's hand. It's slightly larger than life, wouldn't you agree?'

'I would. I'm familiar with Benedictine knives and this is bigger than one might expect.'

'Indicating that perhaps it might be concealing something.' He walked closer and reached out to touch the stone dagger gently held by the effigy. 'Something like a real blade, maybe? Pass me one of Scott's rock hammers from his bag.'

Lauren rummaged around in the bag, sitting exactly where Scott had left it the previous day before getting shot. 'Here.'

'Thanks.'

Hunter swung the hammer down and struck the carved stone dagger, shattering the tip into fragments. They fell to the floor. Hunter leaned forward and blew a thick coating of dust away to reveal a shiny metal point gleaming dully in the low light of their torches.

'It's steel,' he said coolly.

'The tip of a blade?'

Hunter smacked the hammer down again and broke the rest of the carved stone away until he was able to gently pry the dagger out of the statue's hand. Holding it up to the light, he saw at once a lengthy inscription along one side of the blade. On closer inspection, he saw it was unusual compared with the handful of others he'd come across in his work. The back of the knife's blade was a strange shape and contained a lengthy inscription. Further, he observed a tiny gold-embossed arrow on its handle that intrigued him even more.

'Lauren Lane,' he said calmly. 'It looks like we're in business.'

She peered forward, standing on tiptoes to get a better look. 'An inscription! I love inscriptions. What does it say?'

'That's what we're about to find out.'

* * *

'You were right about them coming back.'

From the pilot's seat of his helicopter, Lars Lundquist stared out through the glass at the beautiful sight of Mont Saint-Michel abbey. He had been here just a few hours ago, giving pursuit to the former Grenadier Guards officer and UNESCO archaeologist Maximilian Hunter. He turned to Stig, who had just spoken, and smiled. 'I'm always right. That's why we tracked them back to their hotel and waited, rather than killing them as you suggested.'

Stig shrugged. 'We could've beat it out of them.'

Lundquist winced. 'This is the approach of the thug and that is fine because that is why I employ you. But sometimes a more subtle art is required. I have researched Hunter fully. I knew he would never give up information. Far better simply to place a tracker on their car before we attacked the abbey. To allow for all contingencies. This way, we are guaranteed to get the whole truth, so to speak.'

Berg yawned and rubbed his eyes. He'd been smoking a Stogie. It was currently unlit and jammed in the corner of his mouth. 'So there's whatever they found in the box they ran away with, and then something else. Something even more precious.'

'Things so precious and ancient and dangerous, they will shock an unsuspecting world,' Lundquist said.

Kjell cracked his knuckles and belched. 'Weird to think they've been hidden in that abbey for nearly one thousand years?'

Eklund nodded. 'At least, that is my hypothesis. And it's eight hundred and six years.'

'That's what I said,' Kjell growled.

'No, you said nearly one thousand years.'

The big man from Gothenburg turned in his seat and narrowed his eyes when he addressed the professor at the rear of the SUV. 'Are you trying to be funny with me? Eight hundred and six is nearly a thousand.'

'It depends on how you look at it. I would argue that it's only 80 per cent of the way there.'

Berg started squeezing his hand into a tight fist. If Kjell had looked down, he would have seen all the blood being pushed out of his knuckles with the force of the squeeze. 'And I would argue that I could punch your head through the window you're sitting beside.'

'But if you did that, whose head would you use to work out what we have to do next? Not yours because yours is full of shit.'

Berg unbuckled his seatbelt and twisted his upper body until he was almost facing Eklund in the back seat. 'Say that one more time and see what happens.'

'Fine. I said your head is full of—'

'Enough!'

When Lars Lundquist finally spoke, everyone fell silent. He went on. 'I don't want to hear any more from anyone unless I ask a question. Is that clear? That is a question.'

They all nodded.

'Good. This is much better. Silence is golden. Everyone here has a role to play, so you will all respect each other. Professor Eklund is a genius researcher and historian. Stig is an expert in firearms and explosives. Kjell is a master thief. Berg, you are the strongest man any of us have ever met and your fighting skills are second-to-none. But Eklund is right. Your head is full of shit.'

Berg turned his square head on his big, broad neck and stared at Lundquist with hate on his face, then, when Lundquist began to laugh, the rest of the vehicle joined in. Berg was last to laugh but he laughed loudest. Lundquist looked back out through the windshield. Like everyone else in the aircraft, his eyes had been fixed on Mont Saint-Michel out in the cold bay. The magnificent abbey was a sight to behold, poking up from behind circles of rocks and then trees growing around its base protecting the ancient building and the dead inside it from the bitter English Channel winds that scoured the landscape across the winter months.

Outside the abbey, on the slipway, a man in his early seventies appeared on a black bicycle. He was as thin as a rake and his wispy silver hair flicked up in the air as he pedalled down the lane leading from the small settlement on the island up to the abbey. He wore a tweed jacket and a black shirt with a pristine white dog collar.

'A religious fellow,' Lundquist said. 'Will the police let him in after our fun and games yesterday?' The police waved him through. 'Being a son of God has its compensations. If only I had been inclined to... Wait! Who is that?' Lundquist asked, handing Berg the binoculars.

Berg scanned the coast. 'It looks like another team. Whoever it is, they're stealing a police boat. I think things are about to get interesting around here. Everyone needs to shut up, load up and buckle up. We're about to go hunting.'

12

'Can you even read it?'

Lauren was squinting at Xavier's tiny inscription, carved in intricate letters onto his blade eight hundred years ago. 'It doesn't make any sense to me.'

'Me neither,' Hunter said with a frustrated frown. 'Looks like it's almost Greek, not even Latin, but that's not right. I've read enough ancient and modern Greek. Bugger, I thought we had it, but now we have to wait again until we can regroup and go over this in more detail. C'mon, let's get out of here and maybe I'll try Juliette again and see if she's around.'

They retraced their footsteps, going down through the trapdoor and then along the passageway until finally reaching the tunnel. Hunter found the experience of kneeling through the tunnel much easier without armed men in pursuit, but it still felt good to get outside in the fresh air. Down through the trees, they walked, making good progress towards the rowing boat they had stolen from the mainland coast before dawn. At the shore, he patted his pocket to ensure Xavier's dagger was still in his possession, then climbed into the boat.

'Like before, you need to be my eyes, Lauren.'

'Got it. Sure you're up to the rowing?'

'Hey, I'm in pretty good nick for...'

'For a man of your age?'

His smile faded. 'I was going to say for an archaeologist.'

They made their way out into the bay to avoid the scrutiny of the police on the slipway. In broad daylight, they couldn't avoid being seen by them, but the least they could do was look like they had come from another direction and had been nowhere near the island. Hunter was confident of his plan until he saw Lauren's face fall.

'What's up?' he said. 'Seasick?'

'Not a bit of it. The problem is the massive police boat a few hundred metres behind you.'

Hunter felt his world fall away. 'Damn it! I thought we were going to get away with this. The sodding dagger is in my pocket, Lauren! We can't just throw it over the side. They're going to get hold of it and that's the end of our journey.'

She sighed. 'I don't see what we can do. They're slowing down.'

'They're preparing to pull aside us. It's over.'

He heard the low rumble of the boat's diesel engine and then turned to look up at the wheelhouse looming above him. A figure stepped out, silhouetted by the sun.

'Bonjour!' Hunter said. 'We're just out fishing for some delicious cod.'

'Atlantic cod, in this estuary and without fishing rods?'

Hunter recognised the voice immediately. 'Salvatore Blanco! Could that be you? If it's not, it's a hell of a convincing impression.'

'Yeah,' Blanco said, stepping out of the sun to reveal a big grin. 'And a hell of a lot more convincing than fishing for Atlantic cod in this water. What the hell has been going on, Max? We heard you got kidnapped or shot or stabbed.'

'And yet here you are,' Jodie said, emerging from the wheelhouse. 'Being a smartass.'

'Great to see you, Jodie. Great to see all of you. Can we climb aboard?'

'Be my guest,' Amy said, also stepping into view. 'You and your new friend are more than welcome.'

Hunter helped Lauren aboard and then climbed up after her. 'This is Lauren Lane, everyone. Lauren, this is the HARPA Team.'

'There is no more HARPA Team,' Quinn said. 'And I feel sick. Can we get back to land?'

Hunter was shocked. 'No more HARPA? What the hell happened? I was only away a few weeks and everything's fallen apart.'

'Don't flatter yourself, Max,' Amy said. 'It has nothing to do with you, but we can talk about it later.'

'How the hell did you get this boat?' Hunter asked.

'It's a long story,' Amy said. 'Let's just say a combination of Quinn's communications hacking skills, Jodie's hotwiring skills and Sal's boat piloting skills turned out to be lethal. But we can talk about that later, too, when...'

'Amy?' Hunter asked, looking at her. 'You look like you've seen a ghost.'

'Not a ghost,' she said, pointing out to see just above the island. 'A helicopter, and it's coming this way.'

Hunter instinctively felt his pocket to make sure the dagger was safe. 'I think I know who that might be.'

'The police, looking for their stolen boat?' Lauren said.

'No, I don't think so,' Hunter said.

The young historian looked at him, horror quickly clouding her face. 'Not the men who tried to kill us before?'

'I think so, yes, and they're nearly right on top of us.'

The chopper swooped down over the water so low its downwash blasted a series of ripples across its surface. When it was less than fifty metres off their bow, it pulled to a stop and performed a grim formation in the sky, revealing an open side door occupied by a large man in black crouching behind what looked to Hunter like an FN MAG Belgian GPMG.

'This is a very unfortunate development,' he said. 'That thing will perforate this boat and everyone on it like a teabag and we can't outrun it either.'

'They're opening fire!'

Amy's cry of alarm could do nothing except warn them. Seconds later, the surface of the water just a few metres away burst into a chaotic explosion. As the gunner improved and adjusted his aim, the hell ripped closer to the boat.

'What do we do?' Lauren asked, her voice filled with terror.

'I see another chopper!' Blanco said. 'Over there to the south. It's approaching from the mainland.'

As it grew nearer, Hunter saw this time it was a police helicopter. The chopper firing on them now stopped and turned to face the police helicopter. 'This could get interesting.'

'Not for us,' Amy said. 'Sal, get us out of here, yesterday!'

Blanco needed no further encouragement. He was already inside the wheelhouse. By the time Hunter joined him, he was slamming the throttles forward as far as they would go and spinning the wheel hard to port. 'We're gone. What's going down outside?'

'Whoever they are, they're firing on the police!' Lewis said. 'And the police are firing back!'

Hunter regained his balance as the boat swayed and bobbed up and down, slowly making its way from the chaos. The first chopper fired a savage volley of rounds at the police, but the pilot was superior and performed an impressive evasive manoeuvre. The other chopper fired on the police again, this time with some kind of air-to-air missile. It ripped away from the aircraft and headed towards the police helicopter. Again, the police pilot manoeuvred out of the way with seconds to spare. The missile tore past the police chopper and smashed into the abbey's roof, blasting a massive explosion into the air.

'My God!' Lauren said. 'That is an unspeakable crime!'

'And may have killed someone,' Amy said. 'Bastards.'

The police fired back. Hunter saw a line of rounds streak up the side of the first chopper, punching holes in the tail boom.

'They're hit!'

'But they're not giving up!' Amy said.

The first chopper fired back, this time hitting the gas tank. Hunter shielded his eyes from the savage explosion that blasted pieces of the police helicopter all over the estuary. As what remained of its wrecked fuselage crashed down into the water, they all prepared for the worst – a renewed attack from the first chopper. Instead, he was pleased to see smoke billowing up from its tail boom. After a moment of hesitation, the chopper turned in the sky and flew out of sight over the island.

'They've got too much damage to give pursuit,' Blanco said. 'We just got very lucky.'

'But it won't last for long after what just happened here,' Amy said. 'There'll be hundreds of cops here in minutes. Sal, get us as far away as you can. We need time to get our heads together and work out who those psychos are.'

'I got a picture of one of them,' Hunter said. 'They're not great but they might yield something. I'll send it to you and you can forward it to Jim. Maybe he can help.'

'Will do,' Amy confirmed. 'And good work. Let's get somewhere safe. We need to figure out what we're going to do next.'

'Including working out what the inscription on this Benedictine dagger means,' Hunter said, pulling Xavier's blade from his pocket. Noticing everyone's shocked faces, he couldn't resist one of his famous smiles. 'Because I think it might just be about to take us on our greatest adventure yet.'

13

'Now we're away from that chaos, it's time to get some serious work done,' Lauren said.

The team was gathered around a table in a small bistro in central Rennes, a short drive from the airport where the UNESCO jet was already refuelled and waiting to take them wherever they needed to go.

'Agreed,' Amy said. 'But make sure you don't forget to eat something as well. That dagger could lead us anywhere and I guarantee wherever that place is, we're going to need to get there at breakneck speed.'

'Just as always,' Blanco repeated with a chuckle. 'Life's never boring in HARPA.'

'We're not in HARPA,' Amy reminded him with a cautious glance.

'What is that all about?' Hunter asked. 'I couldn't believe it when you told me.'

'It's not a long story,' Amy said. 'It's really rather simple. I got a call from a guy named Brent Reed who hangs out in the upper echelons of the CIA and he told me we'd been suspended pending further enquiries. Jim got dumped too. I can't tell you any more than that because it's all I know.'

'Sounds to me like someone wants to stop us poking our noses around,' Hunter said.

'That's what I think too, but Jim's still on the fence. Don't take this the wrong way, Max, but I really don't want to talk about it now. It's too much to take in. You've got the UNESCO gig, but the rest of us are screwed. If some shadow elite just erased HARPA, then that's because of what we were doing in it. That means we're not getting work anywhere else on the inside.'

'Hey, we'll be fine,' Blanco said. 'We look out for each other.'

After a pause, Hunter said, 'Amy's right. Let's talk about something else.'

'I am right,' Amy said. 'Now, everyone, eat!'

'Eating is not going to be a problem,' Lewis said, hungrily tucking into a warm bowl of coq au vin and mashed potatoes. As he ate, he was continuing to study the strange Latin inscription on Xavier's blade as he had been doing since Hunter handed it to him on the boat. 'This is the best-damned chicken I ever ate.'

'It's purple,' Jodie said with a sneer.

'That's because it was marinaded in red wine overnight,' Lauren said casually. 'Conforming to tradition.'

'How lovely,' Jodie said, her voice dripping with sarcasm. 'I'm just grateful they served steak and fries. That's my kind of food.'

'Mine too,' Hunter said, almost drooling as he watched a waiter bring his lunch over. 'I'd have opted for a burger, but a great big, fat juicy steak will do just fine, not to mention that beautiful pile of chips.'

'Fries,' Amy said.

'Chips.' Hunter pulled one from his plate, glistening in duck fat. 'Big, fat chips.'

Amy rolled her eyes as Hunter devoured the crunchy fried potato, then turned to her own meal, a more modest bowl of French onion soup. Lauren and Quinn had chosen the same thing, caramelised onions, chicken stock, cider vinegar, croutons and melted cheese. Blanco had pushed UNESCO's budget out a little further and selected crispy duck confit with juniper berries, orange rind and sprigs of fresh thyme.

Jodie peered over at his side dish. 'Nice fries.'

'According to the menu, they are pommes de terre à la Sarladaise,' he said.

'And what does that mean exactly?' she asked, chewing her steak.

He winked at her. 'Slices of potato cooked in duck fat.'

'Fries, then. Fancy French fries with a chunky price tag.'

Blanco forked one and raised it to his mouth. 'Whatever you want to call them, they look pretty damn good to me and I bet they taste even better.'

Hunter laughed and glanced out of the bistro's window over Blanco's shoulder. Since joining HARPA, checking for people who shouldn't be in the vicinity had become an instinct. HARPA might be suspended, but life-saving habits die hard. The view was not special. Just the plastered wall of a quiet alleyway with the added interest of some graffiti tags sprayed here and there. It was the middle of a normal sunny day and shoppers walked back and forth occasionally, carrying bags stuffed with vegetables and baguettes.

'On the way into town, Amy, you said Jim had already got back to us.' Hunter returned his attention to the table and cut off a nice, thick slice of his steak. He slipped the meat into his mouth and started chewing. 'What little gems does he have for us?'

'Yeah, Jim came through for us, as we all knew he would. He might be in self-imposed exile up in the Rockies, but he's well-connected to many trusted sources and he knows how to make things happen. He sent the pictures we gave him of the man's face around to some of his old intel buddies, making sure only to pick ones who are retired and are now outside the government. He told me most of them were unable to help, but one guy, a former DIA operative called Vito, now living it up in the Florida Keys, is in touch with a trusted source on the inside. This unnamed source ran the picture through the system and came up with an answer.'

'Should I do a drum roll on the side of the table?' Jodie said. 'Maybe with those breadsticks.'

'In France,' Hunter said, 'we call them *gressins*.'

Jodie nodded, her eyes widening with gratitude for the new information. 'Thanks, Hunter. What are they called if I ram them up your ass?'

'And back to the mission,' Amy said, setting down her spoon beside her soup bowl. 'The unnamed source passed a short briefing document back to Vito who sent it to Jim within minutes. That document is now on my cell phone.'

'I can't stand the tension,' Quinn said. 'Oh, and I

think if you rammed them up Hunter's ass, they would be called *Gressins à la Coq*.'

Jodie agreed and the two women shared a high-five.

'That would be *Gressins au Coq*,' Hunter said with a cheerful smile. 'Coq is masculine. Obviously.'

Lauren laughed out loud, but Quinn disappeared into the world between her hoodie and her onion soup. 'Just sayin'.'

'And again, back to the mission.' Amy's voice sounded more frustrated. 'The man Max photographed in the abbey is named Stefan Eklund, which for a while was a bit of a head-scratcher.'

'How so?' Blanco asked.

'Because his full name is Professor Stefan Eklund, and he's an academic working out of the University of Gothenburg, in Sweden.'

'I think I heard them speaking Swedish,' Hunter said. 'So, that makes sense.'

Amy continued. 'Turns out Eklund has published several papers on medieval romance poems and other literature of the era and is not the sort of person one would normally expect to be part of a team of relic hunters and killers. Except, of late he's been associating with some very unsavoury people.'

'So, who are his new friends?' Hunter asked.

'This is where it gets more interesting. His new friends are a team of ex-cons and relic smugglers led by a man called Lars Lundquist.'

'Not heard of him,' Hunter said. 'Anyone else?'

'Not me,' Lewis said, enjoying his meal with gusto. 'And I have to get the recipe for this. Meg's going to love it.'

Hunter saw no one else had heard of Lundquist. 'What else do we know about this guy?'

'After a short period as a soldier in the Swedish Army, including the Special Forces, he was dishonourably discharged after stabbing a sergeant. Following this, he essentially became a lifelong criminal, but more of the mastermind variety than out on the streets,' Amy said. 'His speciality is white-collar crime, and he's defrauded banks and various business consortiums all over the world from Hanoi to Houston to Hong Kong. He has a real reputation for getting away with it. Think *Catch Me If You Can* but with considerably more violence and ruthlessness. His last masterpiece was setting up an enormous scammer farm in India where his minions spent their days stealing what added up to millions of dollars from ordinary customers, mostly the elderly, with fake calls demanding their banking details.'

'What a piece of shit,' Jodie said.

'Like I said, Max,' Lauren said. 'An inheritance may be gotten hastily at the beginning; but the end thereof shall not be blessed.'

'You did indeed say that.' Hunter finished his steak and leaned back in his chair, watching a fat streak of sunlight slide down the alley wall opposite the bistro. 'But why would a man like that be blundering around Mont Saint-Michel trying to murder me for a medieval monk's treasure chest? Why engage the services of Professor Eklund?'

Amy shrugged. 'That is what we're here to find out.'

'Sounds like he's branching out into archaeology for some reason,' Lauren said.

Lewis asked, 'Do we know anything about the other men on Lundquist's team?'

Amy referred back to the briefing document on her phone. 'Not much, no. It's Lundquist at the top, then another man known only as Stig whom we believe may be an expert in explosives. The other two are called Kjell and Berg. The DIA source suggests Kjell is some kind of master thief and Berg is their strongman. Lundquist is heavily international, but this new team is based entirely out of Stockholm, his hometown. There's an address and maybe we can get the local authorities there to get inside and go over it, but I'm not sure these guys are stupid enough to leave anything that might incriminate them just lying around and waiting for the cops to pick up.'

Blanco nodded. 'I think you're probably right, but it wouldn't hurt.'

'It might hurt,' Hunter said. 'Especially if anyone high up in the Stockholm police department just happens to be on the same team as the guys who just got HARPA's arse canned.'

'You mean the Illuminati?' It was the first thing Quinn had said since the breadstick joke.

Lauren turned to her, gawping. 'What did you just say?'

'Ah yes, about that,' Hunter said to Lauren. 'The Illuminati are trying to kill us all. How's your soup?'

The young student was horrified. 'The soup is just fine, thanks. And what was that other thing? Oh yeah, that's right. The Illuminati are trying to kill us! What the hell is that all about? Are they even a thing?'

'First,' Amy said patiently, 'the Illuminati are trying to kill *us*, not you. Second, yes, they are a thing. It all started when we collided with a secret society called the Creed. They were a very dangerous group of people whom we believed controlled much of the world behind the scenes. As it turns out, we were wrong. There was another group even more powerful and higher up than the Creed, and for want of a better word, we shall call this group the Illuminati. It's a long story, but that is the abridged version, just for you.'

Lauren was stunned. 'I can't believe I'm having this conversation.'

'It's not a conversation,' Quinn said tartly. 'It's more of a lecture. Amy knows a shitload more than you do about nearly everything and she's imparting some of this information to you right now as you slurp your little onion soup.'

Lewis finished his dinner and pushed the plate out of his way to focus solely on his translation efforts. He looked up at Quinn and frowned. 'That's not a nice thing to say, Quinn.'

'Question,' Lauren said to Amy, pointing at Quinn. 'Why is that little creature such a bitch?'

Quinn's face was hidden once again in the shadows between her hood and her soup, but everyone heard her laughing as she ate more soup. 'Little creature. Love that.'

'Lauren, it's not personal,' Amy said.

'Yeah, it is,' Quinn said.

'No, it's not.' Amy sighed deeply. 'Because I don't tolerate personal abuse and bullshit on my team. That's why it's not. Lauren, you need to understand that we work out on the edge. We banter. Things can get a little close to the bone sometimes.'

Jodie wiped her mouth and tossed down her napkin. 'And no one likes you because you're obviously trying to steal Amy's boyfriend.'

Hunter feigned offence. 'First, I am not Amy's boyfriend, and second, Lauren is not trying to steal me.'

'I've seen the way she looks at you, Hunter,' Jodie said.

Hunter shook his head. 'You make me feel like a piece of meat. A worthless sex object.'

'Give it a rest, Max,' Amy said wearily. 'Your little charmer routine ain't working today, got it?'

Jodie winced. 'He's not that charming.'

Blanco looked at Hunter with a certain degree of sympathy, but Hunter saw the majority of the Brooklynite's sympathy lay with Amy. As it should.

'Listen,' Hunter said more seriously now. 'My and Amy's private life is just that, private. It's not to be slung around a dinner table in a public restaurant and used to intimidate Lauren. Everyone got that?'

'No one's intimidating anyone,' Amy said. 'Quinn and Jodie, please apologise to Lauren for what you both just said.'

Quinn grunted something unintelligible and Jodie

offered a grudging apology, then changed the subject. 'So, tell me more about what you two found in the abbey, Hunter.'

Hunter explained about the coronet and what he thought it might be connected to, then Lauren took over and spoke about the dagger, which they both agreed looked more promising as a clue to Xavier's hidden treasure.

'It's part of a Benedictine way of life called the Rule of Benedict,' she said. 'It's like a code of conduct, a way to live life properly in the eyes of God. For a monk like Xavier, this required many things, but one of them was to carry a blade. They wore these daggers "at the belt" and they were multipurpose tools for eating, working and even for defence if necessary. Another word for them is lunellum, named after the shape of the blade resembling a crescent moon, and others were called a scramasax. But Xavier's is unique, at least among the ones I've seen because of the inscription.'

Jodie thanked her and turned to Lewis. 'Talking of which, what's that blade inscription say, Ben? You translated it yet?'

He looked up from his work and gave the team a proud smile. 'I think so, and it's pretty amazing. Want to hear it?'

14

'But it's not just a case of translating it,' Lewis said. 'It was also ciphered. In this case, he'd turned the original Latin into almost a completely different language consisting of strange letters. Luckily for us, it wasn't a different language but just the Latin letters disguised by extra lines. While you guys were arguing and eating and joking, I just finished cracking the code. If I'm right, it says "To Find What is Not There but Should Be, the Pilgrim must cut the Thief's throat and speak to the Man with the name of the Rock at his first Refuge."'

Everyone stopped eating and talking and simply stared at each other in silence, all instantly vexed by Xavier's enigmatic riddle.

'That clears that up then,' Jodie said. 'Anyone else feel like a strong drink?'

'Can I see it?' Amy asked, taking Xavier's dagger from Lewis and examining the blade. 'Incredible that he carved this into the blade so many centuries ago. The problem is, what does that riddle mean?'

Hunter had the same problem and was already deep in thought. 'We're the pilgrims, that much is obvious.'

'Well, duh,' Jodie said.

Hunter gave her a wry smile. 'Any ideas of your own?'

She shrugged. 'You mean, besides the strong drink?'

'Yes,' Hunter said. 'You being a thief and all.'

'A thief who saved your ass more than once.'

He smiled. 'Touché.'

'I think I know,' Lauren said quietly. 'Max, remember what we talked about earlier, about where Xavier may have come across the coronet?'

Hunter's smile widened. 'Of course – that thief!'

Blanco frowned. 'Wait, how can Xavier be the thief if he's leaving us a clue on his dagger telling us to cut the thief's throat? Does he mean we have to go back to his sarcophagus again?'

'Xavier's not the thief, Sal,' Hunter explained. 'It's just speculation at this point, but Lauren and I were trying to hypothesise where a Benedictine monk like Xavier got his hands on Arthur's coronet. Like we talked about on the boat back to the mainland, we think he found a lot more than the coronet, and by this we of course mean Excalibur. Maybe he found them, but I think it's more likely they were found by someone else who Xavier calls the "thief". After this, it's possible he dedicated his entire life to returning them to Arthur after they were stolen. I'm guessing the riddle on the dagger was his way of leaving a clue about the location for posterity, for the future. There are likely other clues, making a sort of trail.'

'What makes you think that?' Amy asked.

'I've been thinking about this,' Lauren said. 'I know Xavier better than anyone, and I know his personality. He was in the Cult of St Michael, an order who built churches in the name of the Archangel Michael, and they typically built those places in very remote places or locations that were very hard to reach, like mountain strongholds or islands. All of these places were built along a direct, perfectly straight ley line called St Michael's Line running between Mount Carmel in Israel, right through Gargano and Mont Saint-Michel to St Michael's Mount in

Cornwall. Ending at Skellig Michael off the Irish coast, which is a little weird, no?'

Hunter raised an eyebrow. 'You're full of surprises.'

'Just because I didn't believe in things like Excalibur and ley lines doesn't mean I'm ignorant of them. These things were much more important to people hundreds of years ago. And when you think about it, it's more than a little odd, especially when you consider when most of the religious buildings built to honour Michael in those places were built. Freakier still is the legend that says the straight line drawn between these places represents the slash mark that Michael inflicted on the Devil when he sent him to Hell. Xavier would have known all this when he was considering his clue trail. The whole thing is fascinating.'

Hunter sighed. 'Or the whole thing is a load of bollocks because those locations don't line up as exactly as you say and in some cases deviate by up to forty kilometres from it.'

'Shame though,' Jodie said. 'It would have been a lot easier just visiting everywhere along a nice, neat little line instead of having to work out Xavier's riddles.'

Lauren gave her a look. 'I know Xavier went on a pilgrimage to many of these sites around Europe, over many years. As I say, I'm starting to think he used that pilgrimage not only to show devotion to God but to lay down a clue trail full of riddles that would lead other pilgrims, those with enough dedication, to Excalibur itself. I was a sceptic at first, but after what's happened in the last few hours I think I can believe almost anything.'

'You can't think this has anything to do with ley lines?' Quinn asked. 'I never heard such a load of crap in all my life!'

'I'm not saying there's a definite connection,' Lauren said. 'Just that the Line of St Michael would have been known by Xavier. I've looked at all of this stuff for a long time, albeit as a sceptic. As part of my studies, I came across an amateur British archaeologist called Alfred Watkins who kicked off the whole ley lines phenomenon back in the twenties in a book called *The Old Straight Track*. It was in this book that he presented his complex theory of ley lines to the world.'

'It was trashed by professional archaeologists,' Hunter said. 'Dismissed as New Age tripe because there are so many sites of archaeological interest in Britain, particularly from the prehistoric period, that anyone can join at least some of them up in straight lines.'

Lewis said, 'But maybe Xavier used these lines as a

sort of guide to follow when he was leaving the clue trail to Excalibur?'

'That's what I was thinking!' Lauren said. 'At least the Line of St Michael, if not something specifically to do with regular ley line lore.'

Amy frowned. 'Wait. Back up a bit. You'd got onto something about a thief that Xavier mentioned. Someone who may have stolen Excalibur, and the person whose throat we have to cut to find it again. Who is this thief?'

Lauren replied. 'There's an old legend that King Henry II somehow came into possession of Excalibur.'

'So he was who Xavier called a thief?' Lewis asked.

She nodded. 'But like everything else in the legendarium, it's nothing but ancient and weak speculation, but it's all we have. We know Xavier was on King John's baggage train when he was crossing the Wash, and we think that he was there specifically to find Excalibur and return it to its rightful resting place. The reason it was on the baggage train in the first place is that it was part of the original crown jewels, belonging to King John, as handed down to him by his older brother King Richard the Lionheart.'

'And he got them from his father, King Henry II,' Lauren said. 'Who possibly, and as we say, this is nothing but a theory with no evidence at all, so I stress *possibly*, discovered Arthur's tomb and helped himself to Excalibur. As the King of England, he would have felt like he had a right to it, after all.'

Amy was still frowning. 'So, if King Henry II is the thief, how do we cut his throat?'

'Yeah,' Jodie said. 'Dude's been dead for centuries, right?'

'Think about where we found the dagger,' Lauren said, her voice almost a whisper as her mind raced. 'It was being held not in Xavier's hand, but the hand on his sarcophagus effigy. Seems to me that we need to go and see the sarcophagus statue of King Henry.'

'Which is where?' Blanco asked. 'In England?'

'No,' Lauren said. 'King Henry II was a Plantagenet, so even though he was the King of England, he was buried in France at Fontevraud Abbey, in the Loire region.'

'Never heard of it,' Amy said with a shrug. 'Sorry.'

'I have,' Hunter said.

'Don't tell me,' Quinn said. 'It's a UNESCO site?'

'It surely is,' Hunter replied. 'Fontevraud has been a UNESCO World Heritage Site since the year 2000, right back when you were toddling around in a nappy.'

'Diaper,' Amy said.

'And,' Hunter continued, 'Lauren is of course completely right about Henry. They call Fontevraud the Necropolis of the Plantagenets because so many of them were buried there.'

Amy slid her phone into her pocket and pushed her chair back. 'Okay, how far is this place from here?'

'Less than thirty minutes to Angers-Loire Airport and then an hour by car,' Quinn said. 'Already looked it up, slowpokes.'

Amy was now on her feet. 'Quinn, book a car from the airport to the abbey. I'll call Rennes Airport and get the pilot to fuel up and file a flight plan. We're out of here.'

15

After a short flight, they arrived in the small commune of Fontevraud-Abbaye, deep in the rich and verdant vine-streaked Loire valley, and picked up the car Quinn had organised. A short drive through a village jumbled with a mix of old and new buildings led them to the abbey itself. Not even its full name, the Royal Abbey of Our Lady of Fontevraud, began to do justice to its vast and majestic beauty, as they saw when they drove inside its high outer walls and took it in for the first time. They parked up in the rear car park and walked with a small group of other tourists towards the abbey's high cream-coloured walls, shining radiantly in the sun. Stepping inside the perfectly manicured heart of the complex, they reached a beautiful cloister of neatly trimmed box hedges and flowers, open in the sun and swaying in a gentle breeze.

'This place is kinda like paradise,' Jodie said. 'I think I'm gonna stay.'

'Max, maybe you could give us a rough guide,' Amy said. 'You're the UNESCO rep.'

Quinn peeked out from behind her hoodie. 'Which you could have done on the airplane had you not been asleep the entire way.'

Hunter gave her a sideways look. 'Just topping up my energy levels. Remember, I was up all night being shot at by Lundquist's team of Swedish mercenaries.'

'Does that also explain the snoring?' Jodie said with a smile.

'Moving on to the abbey,' Hunter said. 'Long story short, it was founded in 1101 by a preacher named Robert d'Arbrissel. He'd lived as a hermit in a forest in western France for many years before deciding to start the abbey here. He was a very popular figure who enjoyed a large following and many men wished to emulate him, so it was these men he used to populate the abbey in its earliest days.'

'Shorter than that,' Jodie said.

Hunter gave her a withering stare. 'Then, women

came, and they lived together in what some called the "ideal city" because that was not standard practice for the time. Robert put a woman in charge of the entire place as an abbess, also not normal. The monks had to serve the nuns as a form of penance, eating their leftovers and being given only half their rations, including of drink.'

'I'm kinda digging this place,' Jodie said. 'Maybe that's how we should run HARPA?'

'I'm not voting for that,' Lewis said with a laugh.

Amy looked at Jodie. 'There is no HARPA, remember?'

Hunter continued. 'Anyway, a couple of hundred years after Robert d'Arbrissel, the abbey fell on hard times when the Plantagenets collapsed and its funding disappeared, then the place got trashed during the French Revolution. Then it was a prison. Now it's this. Short enough for you?'

'Getting there,' Jodie said. 'Keep working on it.'

Amy gave Jodie a passing glance of disapproval. 'Where's King Henry's body, Max?'

'His body isn't here,' Hunter said. 'Did I not mention that?'

Amy furrowed her brow. 'No, you did not. Why, then, are we here?'

'Have some faith. Henry's body is not here and neither are those of the other royals. Like a lot of the bodies of the kings and queens of France in the Basilica of St Denis, they were probably destroyed during the French Revolution. It was a very violent and destructive time. During the revolution, over thirty abbeys were either partially or completely destroyed, in some cases wiping out hundreds of years of history and architecture, sometimes in just a few days.'

'If Henry isn't here, what was Xavier talking about?' Blanco asked.

Lauren began to explain as they walked along the chequered black-and-white tiles of the cloister, but now Hunter led them off to the left and directed them inside the main part of the abbey itself, a vast and open space of white stone built in the twelfth century. Ahead of them, a smooth flat floor dropped away into a lower area at the bottom of some steps.

Hunter pointed down to the lower floor. 'See those four recumbent statues?'

Jodie looked confused.

'Recumbent. Statues that are lying down,' Hunter said. 'As Lauren was about to explain, they're what we're looking for. Each of them is an important figure in the Plantagenet Dynasty. Richard the First, better known as Richard the Lionheart, Eleanor of

Aquitaine, Henry the Second of England and Isabella of Angoulême.'

They made their way down the steps and walked over to the four Plantagenet royal statues, protected from unwanted touching and damage by a waist-high stainless-steel rail. Hunter leapt over the rail without even so much as a glance over his shoulder and headed straight for the statue of Henry II.

'So, here it is,' he said, giving the king's crown a gentle pat. 'All good, Your Majesty?'

'Max!' Amy said. 'For God's sake, you'll get us thrown out!'

'This is a UNESCO World Heritage Site,' Hunter said casually. 'And I'm a senior field archaeologist with UNESCO. If I can't abuse the rules around here, who can?'

'That is a great attitude right there,' Jodie said. 'You bring such a unique blend of dedication and professionalism to your discipline. I am in awe.'

'What can I say? I'm a maverick,' Hunter said. 'A radical. A wild horse. Normal rules don't apply to people like me.'

Quinn rolled her eyes. 'Good God almighty.'

'You see anything of note down there, Max?' Amy asked.

Looking around, Hunter shook his head. 'That's

the problem, I see nothing except an eight-hundred-year-old recumbent statue of a Plantagenet monarch.'

Without warning, he pulled out Xavier's blade from his pocket and tapped it against the stone carving of Henry's throat. 'Seems solid, sorry. With Xavier's hand, the blade was hidden inside the stone carving of his hand. Which was a hollowed-out shell. Unfortunately, Henry's throat sounds like solid stone. Xavier didn't pull the same trick twice.'

'Damn it,' Amy said. 'Any other ideas?'

'Just one.'

Hunter crouched down and held the blade against the king's throat as if cutting it.

Quinn blew out a breath and pulled her hood up. 'What the hell is he doing now?'

'He's cutting the king's throat,' Lauren said with a scowl at the young goth. 'Don't you remember the riddle? "To Find What is Not There but Should Be, the Pilgrim must cut the Thief's throat and speak to the Man with the name of the Rock at his first Refuge." It's not hard to work out what he's doing, Emo.'

Quinn narrowed her eyes and then turned to gaze around the nave. 'I see nothing.'

'No,' Hunter said, jumping back up to his feet. 'Me neither, at least nothing that one could say constitutes anything that might help us in our— Wait a minute.'

'Max?' Amy asked. 'What is it?'

Everyone turned to look at him except Blanco, who was already looking at what Hunter had just noticed. When Hunter raised his finger and pointed high across the abbey, they all turned and saw what they were looking at.

'The stained-glass window!' Amy said. 'When he tries to cut the king's throat, the blade reflects the light up to a specific part of the stained-glass window.'

'Exactly,' Hunter said, crouching down behind Henry's head. 'It's got to be the window. If you pretend to cut his throat, the light from the blade is reflected onto the wall. I can direct the light by changing the angle of the blade, but there's nothing else in that area of note except the stained-glass window. What's going on in that window, Ben?'

Lewis was already wandering over to the immense window on the ethereal nave's far wall.

'It's beautiful,' Lauren said. 'Whatever it's saying.'

'Sure,' Jodie said. 'But when you've seen one stained-glass window, you've kinda seen them all.'

'That's not true at all, Jodie,' Lewis said, transfixed by the impressive kaleidoscope of colours sparkling above his head in the giant window. 'They're practically all unique in some way. What we're looking at right now is classic Christian iconography. It's called

Christ Pantocrator, deriving from the Greek word for Almighty. It's a specific way to depict Christ. Pantocrator is not a word used lightly in the Bible, occurring only to describe the Lord of Hosts and El Shaddai, one of the earliest names for the God of Israel.'

Hunter leapt back over the security barrier running around the four statues and made his way briskly over to Lewis, slipping Xavier's dagger into his pocket as he approached him. 'Don't want to miss the party, and it looks like this is where it's at right now.'

Lewis continued. 'Note the way the top of the window is a smooth arch. This is to represent the half-dome shape usually used for Pantocrator imagery. The oldest image like this we have is around fourteen hundred years old, preserved in St Catherine's Monastery in the Sinai.'

'Now you say it, it looks kind of Greek,' Lauren said.

Lewis nodded in silent agreement. 'It's an image more often associated with the Eastern Orthodox Church. The dominant halo behind Christ's head, the open book in his hand and his fingers posed to depict the Greek letters IC, X and then C... These are all classic parts of the imagery. Those Roman numerals portrayed in that way are what theological scholars would call a Christogram, a kind of symbol used in this case to represent the name Jesus Christ.'

'Those four winged creatures flying around him?' Amy asked. 'Are they the Lion, Ox, Man and Eagle we encountered during the hunt for the Revelation relic?'

Lewis turned now, smiling. 'You remember that detail?'

She shrugged, her bright eyes still staring up at the brilliant array of multicoloured lights streaming in through the window. 'It was kind of a big thing in my life, Ben.'

Lewis turned back to face the window. 'Mine too. And you're 100 per cent right. The four winged creatures we see here are what we call a tetramorph, which just means a depiction of four elements. In this case, it's a representation of the Four Living Creatures. Matthew the Man, Mark the Lion, Luke the Ox and John the Eagle.'

'But the tetramorph predates Christianity,' Hunter added. 'We have archaeological evidence showing that some of the very earliest civilisations divided space into four quarters and then gave each one a specific religious trait. The ancient Babylonians incorporated these concepts into their sphinxes in elaborate carvings. Sorry, just didn't want Ben to hog all the limelight.'

Lewis laughed and patted Hunter on the back. 'I'm no hog, brother. Our knowledge is only strengthened when we bring it together.'

'Is the tetramorph relevant to our current mission?' Amy asked. 'Is that what Xavier wanted us to see?'

'It could be,' Lewis said. 'But I don't think so. I think we're supposed to be looking at that little book in Christ's left hand.'

'With the Greek letters in it?' Amy asked.

Blanco said, 'What did you call that?'

'A Christogram,' Lewis said. 'And yes, I think this is precisely what Xavier wanted us to see. Those Greek letters are Alpha and Omega, the first and last letters of the classical Greek alphabet. They're part of the famous phrase "I am the alpha and omega", or "I am the beginning and the end". That's Revelation 21:6, 22:13, for anyone taking notes.'

'But what's the relevance of Greek letters here, Ben?' Lauren asked. 'I thought the Bible was originally in Hebrew.'

'The Old Testament, sure. But the New Testament was first written in Koine Greek and that's why we use alpha and omega and not, say, alef and tav, the first and last letters of the Hebrew alphabet.'

'We're making some progress, right?' Jodie asked

with a glance at the time on her phone. 'Because this all sounds like Greek to me. No pun intended.'

'I think we're making progress, yes,' Lewis said with a smile. 'Alpha and Omega lead us to the Revelation quotation "I am the beginning and the end". Maybe this could tell us a great deal.'

Quinn, hands stuffed in her hoodie pockets, had been twirling around on her heels, yawning. Now she stopped and looked at Lewis. 'Really? What the hell does that tell us?'

'Take it easy, Quinn,' Amy said. 'Ben's working on it, and he doesn't lose his cool when you're working on computer problems.'

Quinn huffed and turned her back on them, stomping away across the smooth white flagstones and disappearing out of sight into another part of the nave.

'Is someone going to pick up her dummy?' Hunter said. 'She seems to have spat it out of her pram.'

'If you mean she just spat her pacifier out of her stroller, that's quite amusing,' Jodie said.

'I do indeed mean that,' Hunter said. 'Thanks for the translation.'

Blanco chuckled at the banter and folded his arms over his big barrel chest. 'How did my life ever come to this? It's totally nuts.'

'Let her be,' Lewis said. 'She's young and frustrated. She doesn't get this stuff. She's on the team for another reason, an important reason. We all need each other. I don't hold anything against her at all, so let's get back to the clues.'

'Could this be about water?' Lauren asked. 'Maybe it's water and not the alpha-omega thing.'

'Water?' Amy asked. 'I don't see any representation of water in that stained-glass window.'

'Me neither,' Hunter said.

Blanco scratched his stubble, a frown appearing on his face. 'And I make three. So what gives, old friend?'

'The riddle on the blade told us to cut the thief's throat to find what is not there but should be,' Lauren said. 'Is that what he meant? There's no water in the window, after all.'

Lewis broke away from the window and turned to his teammates. '"And he said unto me, It is done. I am Alpha and Omega, the beginning and the end. I will give unto him that is athirst of the fountain of the water of life freely."'

'Damn it, I hate it when you do this!' Jodie said.

'The verse I just quoted is the full King James version of the bit I just said a second ago, from Revelation 21:6.'

Jodie frowned. 'Wait a second. The water of life? I thought we literally just found the goddam fountain of eternal youth in the jungle? Please tell me we're not going back into that.'

'We are not going anywhere near that,' Lewis said. 'Because we're not looking for the fountain of eternal youth or anything else to do with water. Sorry, Lauren, but I don't think this is about water. Or the alpha-omega thing. Xavier was a shrewd scholar, and he just sent me all around the houses for nothing. That's the bad news. There is also good news.'

'Religious guys,' Jodie said with a shrug. 'In riddles, they speak.'

'It's no riddle, not this time,' Lewis said. 'And it's definitely not about water.'

Blanco grinned at him. 'You know something then?'

A big smile appeared on Lewis's face. 'I think I know what Xavier was alluding to in this window, but that's only the beginning. I've still got some serious thinking to do before I can figure out the exact location. I need more time, but if my theory is right, then it's kinda obvious when you think about our journey so far. No disrespect to Xavier.'

'I'm sure there's none taken,' Amy said. 'But where is the old monk telling us to go?'

Lewis took one last look at the enigmatic window and then turned to her. 'That's what's so exciting. To find what is not there but should be! If I'm right, you're not going to believe it!'

'But it's going to have to wait,' Quinn said, returning from her travels. 'Because we have a problem. A big problem.'

16

The big problem had arrived in two black Mercedes SUVs. Hunter stood just inside the abbey's entrance and watched the bright French sunshine flash angrily on their polished coachwork. In their interiors, obscured by shadow, sat a full complement of men, all of them still and passive and staring dead ahead. A third vehicle now turned into the abbey car park, its wide tyres crunching on the gravel as it pulled to a stop alongside the other two.

'Looks like our friends from Mont Saint-Michel want to have another go,' Hunter said.

Jodie frowned. 'Are you sure they didn't get a chance to put some kind of tracker on either of you two, Hunter?'

'Pretty sure,' he said. 'Lauren?'

She shook her head. 'They never got that close.'

Jodie gave her an accusatory glance. 'You don't know those guys, do ya, Lauren?'

Lauren was mortified. 'Take that back!'

'Listen, everyone, just relax,' Blanco said. 'They could have got here any number of ways. Followed us somehow, but just hung back so we never saw them. A tracker. Friends in high places, and by high places I mean satellites. You name it. No more accusations.'

'We'll need to figure it out one way or another,' Hunter said. 'Because if we get away from them this time, then they're just going to turn up all over again like the proverbial bad penny.'

'But Sal's right,' Amy said. 'There's no time for speculation. We need to get going, right now. There must be a hundred tourists in this place, not to mention all the staff. If those guys open fire, innocent people are going to get hurt, or worse. Thank God we used the parking lot around the back. Everyone just turn around and walk calmly back inside. Then head straight to the car. With some luck, we might be able to get away from them completely, and if not, at least we can get them away from here and deal with them someplace less populated.'

They turned and made their way back inside the

abbey, passing the confused staff in the visitors' lobby with cheery smiles. Quinn was at the rear, a step behind Blanco. When she glanced over her shoulder, she delivered more good news to the team.

'They're getting out of the SUVs,' she said, speeding up her step.

Blanco turned around and peered over Quinn's shoulder through the door. 'Shades and earpieces. Trendy.'

'Through the nave,' Amy said. 'Then out to the car. Quickly.'

Amy led them across the nave, passing the four Plantagenet royals and the stained-glass window of Christ Pantocrator. When the men stepped into the abbey at the other end of the nave, they heard a woman scream. Hunter turned and saw the woman shielding her young son. A few yards from them, the man leading the team drew a concealed weapon from a holster under his jacket. He casually raised it at arm's length and fired a single shot. The sound filled the previously silent nave like a hand grenade exploding, and a second later the bullet drilled into the wall a few feet behind Quinn's head.

'And now we break into a run, right?' Jodie said.

'I think so!' Amy said. 'They're after us, not the people in here. If we have to turn ourselves into bait to get those bastards out of here, then so be it. Go, go, go!'

They broke into a run, sprinting through the nearest door and leaving the nave behind them and stumbling out into the rear car park. Jodie ran ahead to the SUV and blipped open the locks as she jogged across the gravel. Then she was inside and firing up the engine. It roared to life as Hunter and the others grabbed hold of the door handles, opened the doors and swung themselves inside in short order. Lewis was last in. Jodie had selected reverse and stamped her foot on the gas, sending the car surging backwards through the car park before he'd even had a chance to close his door.

'Location,' Jodie said, spinning the wheel and throwing the chunky gear stick into drive. 'Where am I driving?'

'The hell outta here is my vote!' Quinn yelled.

'Away from people,' Amy said. 'Get out into the countryside. We have to draw their fire away from as many people as possible.'

'It's what UNESCO would want,' Hunter threw in. 'If not HARPA.'

'Damn it, Max!' Amy said. 'Just for once, take something seriously.'

Hunter perceived not an ounce of warmth in

Amy's voice and understood his interest in Lauren had irritated her. He understood that. Deciding it was time to show her just how serious he could be, he reached into his jacket and pulled out a Glock 19.

'Where the hell did you get that?' Amy asked.

'Juliette gave it to me. Her sister lives in Geneva and guns are not hard to come by in Switzerland at all. She asked if she could lend it to me for a little while in case things got a little out of hand during the dig.'

'And you didn't get a shot off during the attack at Mont Saint-Michel?' Jodie said.

Hunter mumbled a reply.

'I didn't catch that,' Jodie said over her shoulder.

'I said I left it in my hotel room,' he said.

'Great.'

'Hey, call me old-fashioned, but I never anticipated a terror attack on a tomb in Mont Saint-Michel. As it happens, I used it on the return trip. Now, how about you get us the hell out of here?'

Jodie caught a glance of his eyes in the mirror, then tore out of the car park, swerving violently into the road running parallel to the abbey's south wall. Behind her in the middle row, Amy was still gawping at the gun.

'And you never thought to tell me you were armed?'

'This is not a HARPA mission, Amy,' Hunter said coolly, pushing down his window behind Jodie. 'It's UNESCO unless I am very much mistaken. That means you're not the boss of me and I don't have to inform you of jack. All right, dear?'

She glared at him, shook her head and turned to face the front. 'Whatever.'

'I'm glad he has it,' Jodie said. 'Those guys are catching up behind us, all three of them.'

'And we've used guns before,' Lewis said. 'A lot.'

'That is not the point,' Amy muttered. 'We work as a team. Everyone should be upfront with everyone else about stuff like that.'

Hunter had no reply. He'd already unbuckled himself and was twisting around in his seat, trying to manoeuvre himself into a rear-facing position from where he was able to take a clear shot at the pursuing vehicles. The air rushed around him, whipping at his hair and flapping his collar wildly as he extended his right arm and aimed at the first Mercedes.

The first shot was on target, punching a hold in the driver's front tyre and instantly blowing it to shreds. What would normally be a controllable problem was rendered lethal because of the high-speed and aggressive driving of the man behind the SUV's wheel. As the tyre disintegrated into a thousand pieces of shredded rubber, the SUV slammed down on its wheel, grinding the two metal flanges on its outer edges into the tarmac and triggering a wild shower of sparks up into the wheel arch. That didn't last long. The extra friction of the wheel cutting its way into the tarmac slowed the front left corner of the car too quickly and turned the wheel into a kind of fulcrum over which the vehicle now turned, flipping into the air and crunching down on its roof. But the mass of the heavy car was moving too fast and had too much energy for a sudden stop. It flipped again, crashing down on its tyres and then flipped a final time, landing upside down in the ditch at the side of the road before exploding into flames.

Hunter, still outside of the car, felt the shockwave blast over his face and then they were clear of the chaos. Looking back, he saw the second Mercedes SUV burst through a thick cloud of smoke generated by the crash. It was bearing down on them with even more anger than before, the engine revving and roaring. Behind it, the third SUV was only a few yards further away.

'Good shooting, Max!' Blanco called out, reaching forward from his seat and punching his old friend on the back.

'Thanks, mate,' Hunter called out. 'They're returning fire! Everyone down!'

Hunter struggled to get back inside in time to avoid being hit by the returning fire, scraping and bruising his ribcage as he hauled himself through the window and then cradling his head in his arms with a second to spare. Bullets peppered the rear window until it was completely shattered. Jodie swerved from left to right to avoid another wave of bullets, throwing Hunter down into the rear footwell. He looked up at Amy and smiled.

'What do you think of me now?' he said. 'Hero or villain?'

'You're maybe halfway to redemption is what I think of you now, Max. Get your ass out of there and do some more damage with the gun!'

'Fair enough.'

He clambered out of the footwell and returned to his window. As he moved, he heard more rounds punching through the rear tailgate panel of the SUV. 'Jodie! They're gonna hit the petrol tank!'

'Nuh-uh,' she said, violently swinging the SUV to the right at a small rural crossroads and heading out in a new direction towards a large wooded area. Gesturing ahead at the trees, she increased speed hard.

'We're going into that forest. Let's see if we can lose them in there.'

'Quinn!' Amy said. 'How fast can you get a map of that woodland up on your—'

A bullet pinged off the rear panel next to Lauren, making her scream in terror.

Hunter climbed outside again and returned fire.

'Already done it,' said the young goth, sliding a piece of chewing gum casually into her mouth as if she were on a normal drive in the country. 'Looks like there are lots of little nooks and crannies up there we can use to give these assholes the slip. Keep going ahead, Jodie. I'll programme you with directions when we get a little closer to the trees like the good bot you are.'

Jodie met her eyes in the rearview mirror. 'Screw yourself, Quinn.'

'More incoming!' Hunter screamed.

Just as they crossed into the woods, another shot rang out, exploding their rear tyre and ripping it to pieces. Hunter felt the SUV crash down on its rear end and saw the sparks flying out into the air behind them. 'We're hit!'

Jodie was struggling with the wheel. 'No kidding. Everyone, hold on... This is going to get rough but maybe I can save it. Hang on!'

17

'The car's done, Jodie!' Hunter cried out. 'Get us as far into these trees as you can. We're on foot from then on!'

Jodie had felt the tyre go and was already well on the case, spinning the wheel and sending the SUV down a steep, leaf-covered embankment between two enormous horse chestnut trees. At the bottom of the slope, she turned the wheel again, steering the ill-fated SUV neatly through a small maze of tree trunks and bushes before finally bringing them to a stop in a gloomy thicket.

'Everyone out,' she said.

As Amy climbed out of the car, she turned to Quinn. 'You have that map up, right?'

The goth nodded. 'Sure. We're in some kind of recreational forest. There are amenities for public hiking and camping.'

'Wonderful,' Hunter said. 'Maybe you could book us into a gite for a few nights while you're at it. Or tell us the way out so we can get away from the psychopaths currently hunting us down with automatic weapons?'

'Stop being an asshole, Hunter,' Jodie said.

As they staggered deeper into the thicket, Hunter looked at Quinn's face and felt a surge of guilt for his comment. 'Sorry, Quinn. That was uncalled for. You're doing a great job.'

The goth simply shrugged and said nothing. Returning to her computer, she said, 'As I was saying, there are amenities here for campers, so I was thinking we could use one of the gites to hide in, use as cover. I already looked on their website and most of them are available, which means empty.'

'What a good idea,' Amy said, glancing at Hunter. 'If only we had a former professional soldier on the team who might have thought of something like that instead of leaving it to you.'

Hunter returned her smirk. 'We have one gun, Amy. Hiding in a place that can be surrounded by a team of heavily armed nutcases when you only have one weapon and a handful of bullets is not generally considered sound tactics. Fish and barrels and all that.'

They heard the other vehicles revving and roaring as they turned off the road and drove down the slope towards the thicket.

'They're closing on us,' Lewis said.

Blanco scratched his head. 'And we have one gun.'

'I've an idea,' Hunter said. 'Everyone else, head over to Quinn's gite and take cover.'

Amy stared at him, confusion on her face. 'I don't understand. What about you?'

'I'll be along in a second or two. First I want to give our friends a little surprise.'

He watched them vanish in the vegetation as they headed towards the gite, and then he made his way back along the way they had just come until he was able to see their own hired SUV. The two remaining Mercedes SUVs pulled into view, now joined by a new third one Hunter hadn't seen before, and came to a stop on either side of it. One of the men climbed out of the lead Merc and walked over to the SUV. The doors were all open, just as they had left them, and now he craned his neck to get a better view inside the driver's side.

He called back to the others in Swedish. Hunter

knew the language well thanks to an old flame named Hanna Vikander, who had helped HARPA locate the fountain of youth in South America and joined them on their famous voyage to raise the *Titanic*. None of which mattered right now. Hanna was back in Stockholm working at the university there, and he was in a French forest, less than sixty feet away from at least a dozen armed men who seemed intent on taking his life.

The man looking in the SUV now came back outside and started fussing around the vehicle, taking particular interest in the leaves and mud. He was trying to find their tracks. Hunter knew this wasn't going to take long. Seven people clambering out of an SUV and running in a pack churned up a lot of mess and left easy tracks to follow. The man soon found them. Then, he pointed in the direction where they had run, almost fixing his finger directly on Hunter's current location. When he started to make his way back to the Mercedes, Hunter knew it was now or never.

He raised his gun and fired three shots into his own SUV's petrol tank, instantly igniting the highly flammable fuel inside and triggering a wild explosion inside, blowing up the tank and then the entire SUV. The blast blew the SUV several feet into the air and tore it to pieces, firing lethal projectiles all over the clearing. The man died at once, peppered with steel shrapnel from the devastated SUV, and his Mercedes, parked closest to the SUV, was tipped on its side. When more flying shrapnel chewed into its base, it broke the fuel line and ignited. The second explosion was just as overwhelming, instantly trapping and killing its inhabitants in a raging inferno.

When the two remaining Mercedes reversed and then separated, driving in two directions on either side of him, Hunter turned tail and ran. He'd only a handful of bullets left and his work here was done. He sprinted through the thicket to the gite where he found Amy and Blanco on a low decking behind a wooden balustrade. The gite was in a row of three along a narrow, gravelled track winding through the woods. Everyone else was inside, taking cover.

'Get inside!' he yelled. 'We've got company and they're not happy bunnies.'

'We heard the action,' Blanco called out just as Hunter rounded the steps and leapt up onto the decking. 'What the hell happened?'

'I blew up our SUV,' Hunter gasped. 'And took out one of their Merckie-Benzes along the way. We still have the other two to deal with and they just lost a lot of friends.'

'I thought there were only three,' Amy said. 'If you took one out on the way over here and then another one in the woods, that leaves one.'

'Another one turned up. I can count, Amy.'

'All right! Sorry.'

'Listen,' Hunter said. 'The two SUVs split up but both headed roughly in this direction, following our tracks. We need to be inside. We're not losing anyone here today, so we're going to need to get smart because we're massively outgunned.'

They went inside and closed the door and Hunter was immediately mobbed.

'What happened?' Lewis asked.

Lauren's eyes were full of fear. 'Are you okay?'

'Stay out of sight, everyone,' Amy said, assuming command once again. 'Max took out one of the Mercs and its passengers, but the others are following our tracks and he thinks they'll be here in seconds. They were joined by another vehicle, so we're looking at two more SUVs. These guys are serious and they know how to get backup when they need it.'

'Hunter was right,' Jodie said, peering through one of the windows. 'Two SUVs, each approaching from a different direction. They're in the trees and driving cautiously, but they'll be at this row of vacation rentals in less than thirty seconds.'

'What are we going to do?' Lauren asked, terrified.

'They don't know which one we're in,' Blanco said. 'So they'll probably split up and check all three before moving on. Maybe we could do something with that.'

'Should we arm ourselves?' Lauren said.

'Yeah,' Quinn said. 'Go in the kitchen and bring us all back some teaspoons.'

'C'mon, Quinn,' Blanco said. 'Don't be like that.'

'She's just trying to help, Quinn,' Hunter said.

'Damn it all.' Lewis sighed and slammed his fist down on the back of a chair. 'Quinn's right, though! I don't like to be Mr Negativity, but we know from the lovely drive over here that those guys are armed with automatic weapons. There's not gonna be much in here that can defend us against that sort of firepower.'

'We're sitting ducks,' Lauren said.

'I'd say fish in a barrel was more apposite,' Quinn said. 'And sorry about the spoon thing.'

Lauren gave her a weak, frightened smile. 'Forget about it.'

Amy looked at Hunter. 'I don't suppose Juliette could arrange a helicopter airlift in, say, less than a minute?'

'Not this time, sorry,' Hunter said. 'She's dropped off the radar. We can worry about that later if we're still alive. Right now, we have to get out of this little hole we find ourselves in.'

'Run further into the forest?' Lauren asked. 'It goes out behind the gite.'

Amy shook her head. 'Not a good idea. They'd hunt us down like wild dogs.'

'They're pulling up out front.' Jodie was still peering cautiously through a slit in the curtains. 'And climbing out of the cars. They're all outside now. Four in each vehicle makes eight. Looks like they all have sidearms and some of them have MP7s.'

Lauren looked at Hunter. 'What's one of those?'

'They're what's called a personal defence weapon. Compact, mobile and able to fire armour-piercing cartridges at nearly a thousand rounds per minute. Highly lethal in the wrong hands, and right now they're in very wrong hands.'

'Oh my God...' Lauren reached out for a chair and slumped down in it. 'We're dead.'

'Not if you hurry up and get those spoons,' Hunter said with a smile.

'How can you make jokes at a time like this?' Lauren asked. 'We have one handgun against a small army.'

'But we have the element of surprise, and we're

holding a defensive position.' Hunter stepped over to Jodie. 'What's up? Any news?'

'They're splitting up again, just like Sal said they would. Four in the first place at the end of the lane and four in the second.'

Lauren groaned. 'And by second, you mean the one we're in right now?'

'Yes.'

'Can you fire on them now and try to take some out?' Lauren asked.

'Not smart,' Hunter said. 'Then they'll know which one we're in and redirect the entire complement of arseholes into this house.'

'So what then?' Lauren asked.

Hunter paused a beat, thinking through his plan. 'Sal and Jodie, stay with me. Amy, you take everyone else out the back while you still have a chance and move along to the third gite.'

'What are you thinking?' Amy asked.

He threw his canvas bag. 'You take the coronet and Xavier's knife, get out of here and get along to the last house. When the team heading into this place gets inside, the three of us will jump them, neutralise them and take their weapons. Then we'll move next door and take out the other team. Then we'll ride in style in one of their Mercedes SUVs right the hell out of this forest.'

Amy considered the plan. 'Okay, I can work with that. C'mon, guys. You heard what he said.'

Hunter watched Amy lead the rest of the team out through the living area and along to the back door. When it slammed shut, Hunter turned to Blanco and Jodie.

'We drew the short straw,' he said.

Jodie fixed her eyes on him and gave him one of her best unamused looks. 'It was more like you just gave us shitty short straws, Hunter.'

Blanco laughed and stepped away into the kitchen.

'You should be flattered,' Hunter told Jodie. 'I picked you because you're so good at kicking arse.'

'Now you're just trying to butter me up.'

'Whatever are you suggesting?' Hunter said. 'At a time like this?'

She shook her head but couldn't resist a smile. 'Your ass is first in the firing line, Hunter. You have the only weapon, after all.'

Blanco returned and handed Jodie a ten-inch carving knife. 'That's just not true. We have something to work with, too. Lauren's idea wasn't so stupid, you know? I was thinking along the same lines as soon as we got in here.'

Jodie weighed the substantial knife in her hand and winced. 'I'm a thief, Sal. I break and enter. I'm a specialist in burglarising complex properties and relieving their owners of valuable objects. I can shoot a gun at someone from a distance, but I'm not so sure about ramming a knife into someone in close-quarter combat.'

'It's for self-defence,' Blanco said. 'Just in case. As soon as Max takes these guys out with the gun, we take their weapons and then nothing can stop us. Okay?'

She nodded reluctantly, showing Hunter once again that somewhere under the bluff and bravado was a decent young woman with ethics and principles who just wanted to do the right thing.

'All right, buckle up,' Hunter said, peering through the curtains. 'They're stepping onto the decking.'

18

Hunter watched the window next to the front door, gun raised at arm's length. When the first gunman stepped into view, he opened fire, punching a hole through the glass and the man's head in less than a heartbeat. The gunman fell to the decking, dead on arrival. Behind him, Hunter heard the other men react to the brutal death. Screams of fear and rage, boots trampling on the wood and then, at last, the sound of gunfire as they peppered the window with rounds.

Hunter escaped the gunfire by retreating to the sunken living area and taking up a cover position behind the large stone chimney of a central fire. He clocked Blanco in his periphery, tucked down behind the staircase. Jodie was to his left, hiding behind the alcove leading into the kitchen and holding the knife close to her chest.

The men burst in through the door. Hunter hadn't seen any more of them cross the window but had already presumed they would either crawl across the deck or regroup and approach from another direction. He fired on them, but a hail of bullets from their ferocious machine pistols streaked across the room and blew apart everything in sight, keeping him pinned down behind the stone chimney. As bullets blasted away chunks of rustic masonry from the stack and slammed into the wooden panels all over the room, Hunter again tried to fire on the men but was unable to get a clean shot in all the chaos.

'I count four of them,' Blanco called out, a knife gripped in his hand too. He was tucked down behind an L-shaped staircase, safe for now but with poor long-term prospects.

Adrenaline pumped through Hunter's body like lava, and his senses were working overtime. He heard the men shouting in Swedish. Their riot boots crunched on the glass they had blown out of the front window in their first assault. The smell of gun smoke and masonry dust from the smashed chimney stones stung his nose. He saw Jodie's terrified eyes as she cowered in the kitchen with nothing but a carving knife to protect her life.

Hunter realised he could still hear boots but no more crunching. This meant they had stepped off the wooden hall floor and down into the sunken, carpeted area. They were closer but more vulnerable. He had to make a quick decision. Did he swing around and take another shot with the Glock, blowing his cover, or stay in the position for longer and allow them to come closer, allowing Blanco and Jodie to attack them from behind?

It was too dangerous for either of his friends to attack men armed with weapons like these with nothing but knives. The only way it might work was if they could pull off a surprise attack, and right now, that was impossible. Hunter swung around the chimney and opened fire again, this time hitting two more of the men. He saw the shock on their faces as he appeared from nowhere and fired his weapon, pumping them full of lead and dropping them dead on the floor. The other two men fell to the floor and rolled into the closest cover they could find. One went behind a couch and the other ended up wedged in between a bookcase and the kitchen door. Both then returned fire with their weapons, once again tearing the fireplace to pieces in a matter of seconds. The glass casing around the firebox was instantly reduced to shards, spraying out all over the floor around Hunter's boots. Bullets nipped at the marble hearth, chipping pieces off and sending little puffs of dust into the air.

Hunter fell to the floor, gun gripped in his hand as he tried to shield his eyes from the flying glass and stonework. The situation was going about as well as expected, given the wide disparity in the two sides' firepower, but then he saw something moving out of the corner of his eye. He raised his head slightly and was shocked to see Jodie, just a few inches from one of the gunmen on the other side of the archway. She was gripping the knife in her right hand and sidling up against the plaster wall, back pressed up against it and her lips open. She seemed to be taking a deep breath and muttering to herself.

Hunter flicked his eyes to Blanco. He was still behind the bottom of the L-shape staircase where it bent around to the right into the room. He only had the height of five steps to hide behind before the steps bent around to a landing and it headed up to the next floor. Now, he was staring through the bannisters and watching Jodie, his eyes filled with concern. Neither man could give her any support as this would alert the gunman, but Hunter did what he could. He opened fire on the other man behind the couch, keeping him pinned down and unaware of what was unfolding on the other side of the room.

Then Jodie struck. She spun round the arch's narrow intrados and lunged at the gunman, slashing the blade forward and plunging it into his chest. Hunter saw the man's face register the horror. It had all happened so fast. He dropped the gun and looked up at her. His face was coloured more with confusion than fear, but then his eyes closed and his head slumped down onto his chest. Jodie was standing still, exposed in the archway, just staring at the dead man.

'Gun!' Hunter yelled. 'Jodie, get the bloody gun!'

Startled, she reached down just as the man behind the couch worked out what had happened. He pivoted around in the tight space behind the couch and fired on her, just as she grabbed the machine pistol and rolled out of sight into the kitchen. Hunter turned his gun on the man and aimed for his back. He fired, but nothing happened. Not unless you counted a dry click as something. Hunter did not. The Glock was finally out of rounds. With no clear shot at Jodie, the gunman spun around and aimed his weapon at Hunter. A grin appeared on his face as he moved to pull the trigger, but then a carving knife spun across the room and buried itself in his heart.

Hunter was stunned. Then he felt a heavy hand on

his shoulder and turned and saw Blanco standing right behind him. They both watched the man die right before their eyes, the same way his associate had died up near the kitchen. Then, Blanco called out to Jodie and told her it was safe to come out.

Struck silent by what he had just seen, Hunter stepped over to the man and checked he was dead. Jodie walked through the arch, wet blood still on her hands from her knife attack on the gunman.

'I killed him with the knife,' she said, almost to herself.

Blanco outstretched his arms and beckoned for her to come over. She walked over to him, machine pistol hanging loosely from her hand, and let him give her one of his big bearhugs. 'You did what you had to do,' he said quietly, patting her back. 'You saved your life, and ours too.'

Hunter was still staring at the knife embedded in the gunman's heart. 'Tell me, Sal. Is there a part of your life you're keeping from the rest of us, like how you were a knife thrower in a circus?'

'Sadly no,' he said. 'But I'm an old guy. You pick up skills along the way, right?'

Hunter's eyes widened. 'That's some skill. You were thirty feet away.'

'What can I say? I'm not past it yet.'

'You bet you're not,' Jodie said, breaking free from the hug. 'Thanks, Sal.'

Hunter saw her eyes were wet with tears, and he realised just how deep she'd had to dig to kill the man with the knife. He was also reminded of just how close she was to Blanco.

'You did the right thing,' Hunter said to her. 'He would have killed you without a second thought. You know that.'

'I know,' she muttered. 'I'm already over it.'

'We have to stick to the plan,' Hunter said, stepping over to the man he had killed out on the front decking. He picked up his gun and walked back inside the gite, boots crunching over the bloody glass all over the floor. 'There are still four of the bastards left and after all the noise we just made in here, they'll be heading this way right now.'

The shootout had taken less than three minutes, and Hunter knew he was right about the other team when he heard men's boots pounding up to the rear door.

'They're coming in from the back!'

'We can't surprise them this time,' Jodie said.

'Sure we can,' Blanco said. 'We have these lovely new weapons.'

'My mag's almost empty,' Hunter said. 'What about you two?'

They checked. 'Almost all out,' Blanco said. 'Didn't think that guy fired so many rounds.'

Jodie smacked her mag inside the receiver. 'I'm almost out too.'

'Then we're out of here,' Hunter said. 'Now.'

19

Forced back, Hunter led the small team out through the front door, across the decking and down the steps onto the ground. Their boots crunched on leaves and twigs as they made their way over to the two Merc SUVs. Then, the inside of the gite erupted once again with screams and gunshots.

'Call Amy on your cell phone, Jodie,' Hunter said. 'Get her out to the Mercs, now.'

'No need.' Blanco raised a hand and pointed at the last gite in the row. 'She already sees us.'

Hunter looked over his shoulder as he jogged down to the SUVs and saw Amy's face in one of the front windows. She knew what to do. She disappeared out of sight and then he saw the door swing open.

Then Amy led her team out of the gite and down the slope towards the two Mercedes SUVs.

'Get in that one,' Hunter cried out, pointing the barrel of his MP7 to the car on the right. Within a second of his order, the gunmen appeared at the door of the second gite and immediately opened fire.

Hunter turned and fired on them. He was exposed, standing in front of the SUV, but he had little choice. His aim was good and he drove them back inside the gite. Blanco and Jodie, both around the safe side of the Merc, joined in the attack and gave Hunter the cover fire he needed to turn and use his last rounds on the other SUV. His preference was to take out the vehicle in the same way he had done to their own, but he was unable to get a clean shot of the petrol tank from the angle he was standing at. Instead, he settled for blowing out the tyres and ripping the grille to pieces, bursting the radiator. It wasn't as final as the petrol tank option, but it still rendered the vehicle inoperable.

'Get in, Max!'

It was Amy's voice. He turned and ran back to the one remaining SUV, tossing the MP7 into the footwell as he clambered into the front passenger seat. This time Blanco was at the wheel and the engine was already on. Before he had even slammed his door,

Blanco stamped his foot on the accelerator pedal and spun the steering wheel, sending the Mercedes surging forward into the forest and spraying up two giant arcs of mud and dead leaves in a cloud in their wake.

The men streamed back out of the gite and opened fire on them. Inside the SUV, they all heard their rounds thudding into the steel coachwork at the rear of the vehicle, but it was too late. The sun had gone down behind the trees, darkness was wrapping around the forest and Blanco turned hard to the left and drove down a slope, quickly ending the line of sight and putting the mayhem behind them, at least for now.

'That was quite close enough for me!' Amy said.

'And me,' Lauren said, still visibly terrified. 'I'm way out of my league right now.'

'You'll be fine when we find somewhere to eat, shower and sleep,' Hunter said. 'But first, we need to make sure we lose this car as fast as we can. They may be tracking it in any number of ways and the last thing we want is to lead them right to where we're sleeping tonight.'

'What do you suggest?' Amy asked.

Hunter thought about that. They were still deep in

the French countryside without the faintest idea where the trail was leading them next.

'We could stay in a gite,' Jodie said. 'I think there's still one or two those guys didn't destroy.'

'Funny,' Hunter said. 'But no thanks. Quinn, options?'

The goth was already on her computer. 'Right now we seem to be roughly equidistant to three main locations. Angers to the northwest, Tours to the northeast and Poitiers to the south. As we have no way of knowing where to go next, we have a one in three chance of ending up in the right direction if we stay the night at one of those places.'

'I say we go to Angers,' Lauren said. 'This mission is about Excalibur and King Arthur. The places most closely associated with these legends are northwest France and Britain. Angers will start us off in the right direction tomorrow morning when we know what we're doing.'

'It's a bit of a leap,' Hunter said. 'After all, the information we uncovered in Fontevraud Abbey was directly connected to Jesus Christ. That might indicate we're going to the Holy Lands in the morning.'

'Which means we should head to Tours,' Lauren said. 'That's on the way to several airports around Paris.'

Amy scratched her head. 'Ben – you said you knew what the clue in the stained-glass window was telling us.'

'That's not exactly what I said,' Lewis responded. 'I said I have a theory. Right now, it's just not enough for me to be sure about. I'm not comfortable committing the team to anything unless I'm sure I'm reading Xavier's riddle correctly. I still need more time.'

'Then we go to Tours,' Amy said. 'If Jodie is right about us needing to go to Britain, then we can still fly from Paris, or anywhere else in Europe if it's required. Going northwest to Angers boxes us in. It's Tours, Sal. Head to Tours.'

'Got it,' Blanco said. 'And that's marginally closer than Angers anyway, so we'll all get a shower and something to eat just that little bit faster.'

'Now you're talking my language,' Jodie said, stretching out in her seat and closing her eyes.

'Me too,' Lauren said. 'I'm starving. I've never had a day like that in my entire life.'

In the dark of the cab, Hunter smiled to himself. When he'd first met Lauren, he'd wondered how she'd handle herself on one of the HARPA missions. Now, unexpectedly, he'd seen how.

'You did all right,' he said at last.

But she had fallen asleep, like everyone else except Blanco, steadfast at the wheel.

'Looks like it's just you and me, Sal.'

Blanco huffed out a polite laugh. 'You got it, brother.'

After a long pause and a mile or so of cruising through the night, Hunter spoke again, his voice low and level. 'I'm not sleeping with her, by the way.'

'With Lauren?' Blanco turned his head for a second, to show he was interested, then eyes back to the oncoming glare of the traffic's headlights. 'Ain't none of my business, Max.'

'I know. I'm just saying. Because of Amy and everything. I love her.'

Another pregnant pause as the man from Brooklyn deftly overtook a dawdling truck. 'Maybe you should think about telling Amy that.'

Hunter heard his words, the unique Brooklyn accent, but the gentle swaying motion of the comfortable Mercedes was lulling him to sleep. He thought about replying, but the effort of thinking of something to say pushed him over the edge, and then he was gone.

20

No one knew his real name. Everyone called him Sathanas because those were his orders and no one dared question or challenge them. And nothing was known about the man behind the name either, not even if he was the true leader of the Illuminati or if he answered to someone higher. Not even Pedro Razquin, his most loyal lieutenant, enjoyed his master's confidence. When Razquin had searched covertly for details about his master on the internet, he'd found nothing except that the name Sathanas was the name of a demon associated with the emotion wrath.

Knowing what he knew about his master, that made perfect sense to Razquin, who had allowed his mind to wonder if the Devil himself had given him the name. That too would correlate perfectly with some of the horrors he'd seen the master commit in the name of what he called the Dark Lord. Was the Dark Lord a man above the master, or something from the supernatural world? It was pointless to speculate.

Razquin knew his place and he knew how to survive. Asking such questions of the master would be most foolish. He had pleased the master greatly after successfully taking the manuscript of the famous Spanish explorer Francisco de Gama right out of the hands of Agent Amy Fox in the South American jungles and bringing it safely into Illuminati custody. How much credit this had bought him, he had no idea, but for now, at least, he seemed secure. As the master had put it, his power inside the society had been greatly enhanced.

When Sathanas ended his phone call and beckoned him forwards with a simple gesture of his fingertips, Razquin stepped into the vast office and closed the door behind him. He always hated it in here. Dark wooden panels, dust motes floating in the air, the smell of leather and something else, something he could never put his finger on. Something that smelt like old, burning coal.

'That was the CIA director, Razquin,' Sathanas said coolly.

'About your orders to suspend HARPA?'

'Indeed. Their suspension is now permanent.'

'This is excellent news, Master. Life will be considerably easier with them out of the way.'

Sathanas paused. He was still holding the old-fashioned black telephone receiver in his hand. Long, crooked yellow fingernails at the end of pale, bony fingers. Now he set it down in the cradle with a gentle click. 'I said their suspension was permanent, Razquin. This is not to be confused with them being out of the way. I have recently been informed that Fox and the rest of the newly redundant Team HARPA are operating outside of the United States as we speak.'

'Independently, Master?'

Sathanas nodded. 'They're working on a mission loosely associated with UNESCO, Dr Max Hunter's old stomping ground.'

'A mission, Master?'

'Details are at this time vague. It has something to do with a UNESCO dig in Normandy. I'm waiting for more information. Perhaps Professor Bonnaire will be able to help us with that. I take it her kidnapping went according to plan?'

'Yes, Master. She is on an aircraft as we speak. When she gets here, she'll tell us whatever we need to know.'

'Certainly. HARPA has been terminated officially by the United States government, but as we have seen with their latest escapades in France, the team members themselves seem to show no sign of slowing down or bowing out. I want the entire team, from Director Gates down to Mosley and her little pocket computer, brought to me here and then taken out permanently. I want to see the life being drained from their eyes.'

'Yes, Master.'

A long, rusty sigh escaped from Sathanas's old, dry lips. 'Perhaps you should have killed them in the jungles of Colombia.'

'But those were not your orders, Master. You ordered me to retrieve the manuscript.'

Talking to the master like this was a risky business, but Razquin knew how far he could push and decided to see just how much credit that recent victory had bought him. The flash of contempt soon faded from the master's eyes, and then he nodded.

'True, loyal servant. True. The fault lies with me. I was too generous to them. This is not a mistake I intend to repeat. You are to organise a team, and I mean the very best we have. When we determine their precise location, you will be dispatched to snatch them all. If what this latest mission is about has any merit, then you will bring whatever they find back to our inner sanctum. Is all this clear?'

'Yes, Master. I will do my duty with pleasure in loyal service to the Society.'

Sathanas gave a vague nod but had already lost interest in the conversation. Up on the wall above the fireplace was the most grotesque painting Razquin had ever seen. The image was of something very hard to describe. It was painted in oils, mostly in shades of red and with lots of black and grey, and looked like a room of some kind, perhaps a depraved torture chamber, but when he stared at it, nothing at all made sense in it. No object was discernible. What looked like a chair was something else, something odd that fooled him into believing it was a chair, when it resembled nothing at all. It was almost as if the painting changed the longer he stared at it. Only one thing remained recognisable no matter how long he stared at it, and that was the face of a demon, its face contorted in depraved laughter, looking into the painting from the other side. Looking right back at the viewer. Whenever he looked at it, Razquin felt a shiver run up his spine, followed by a sense of deep foreboding. Who had painted this monstrosity? And how? What did it mean?

Sathanas now turned and stared at the image, a

broad smile slowly appearing on his face, then without warning, he ushered Razquin out of the office with another gesture, this time more dismissive. 'Get out, now.'

Razquin took one look at the painting, felt a wave of nausea, and happily retreated from the office. After giving a deep, respectful bow, he closed the door behind him with a profound sigh of relief.

21

Hunter was last to arrive in the dining room the following morning. After tracking down a suitable hotel to spend the night in, they had dumped the Mercedes across town and booked a minibus taxi to drive them the final stretch. Now, the rest of the team was sitting at a table near the window on the far side of the room. Warm low sun. Crisp white tablecloth, sparkling glasses full of freshly squeezed orange juice and a big, stainless steel coffee jug in the middle of an array of breakfast foods.

'Nice of you to join us,' Amy said. 'I was going to send Jodie up to kick your ass out of bed, so thanks for saving us both the effort.'

'Just a coffee, thanks,' Hunter said, sliding down at the end of the table a safe distance from them both.

Lewis poured the coffee for him, and as the first sip hit Hunter's lips, he sighed and then smiled with satisfaction. 'French coffee. Straight from heaven.'

'Just like the latest addition to our little riddle,' Lauren said with an excited smile.

Hunter stared at her, cup an inch from his mouth. 'Wait, you guys already worked out the next part?'

'Yes,' Quinn said tartly. 'While you were sweating it out in your little fartsack upstairs.'

Amy winced. 'Quinn!'

'You have a beautiful way with words,' Lauren said. 'Now all those things Max told me about you make so much more sense.'

Quinn scoffed. 'Like I give a damn about any of that.'

'Take it easy, you two,' Blanco said. 'We're a team. Act like it.'

'She's not on the team.' Quinn gave Lauren an accusatory look.

'She is for this mission,' Amy put in.

Jodie poured more coffee. 'Yeah, she knows more about King Arthur and Excalibur than even the legendary Dr Max Hunter. Isn't that right, Hunter?'

'I'm happy to admit it,' Hunter said. 'Who worked out the riddle and what does it say?'

'It was a team effort led by Ben,' Amy said. 'Everyone helped except for you.'

Hunter looked at her and thought about what Blanco had suggested to him in the car last night when everyone was asleep. 'What does it say, Amy?'

'Over to you, Ben,' she said. 'This is your forte.'

Lewis was in the middle of eating a big forkful of scrambled eggs and buttered toast. He finished eating them and set his fork down. After dabbing at his mouth with a cloth napkin, he opened up his notebook and turned to the relevant page.

'It should be just about here. Yeah, got it. Okay, Max – here we go. Remember when we were driving away from the abbey and we were trying to work out which direction to go in? Turns out Jodie was wrong and you were right about that.'

'As is so often the case,' Hunter said with a sideways glance at Jodie. She raised her middle finger in response and then smiled and went back to her coffee.

'Anyway,' Lewis continued with a smirk of his own. 'Now we have a little more time to talk about this, I can give you a fuller briefing. Turns out I needed to sleep on it, but that's better than sending us a thousand miles in the wrong direction, right? So, to the clue. Remember when I told you that there are two main versions of Christ Pantocrator? The first is known by researchers as Christ in Glory and the second is called Diesis. Christ in Glory shows him sitting on a throne, gesturing with his hand and surrounded by heavenly creatures, such as the four beings of the tetramorph that I talked about.'

'So the one we saw in Fontevraud Abbey was Christ in Glory?' Amy asked.

Lewis nodded. 'Right. This version also often has depictions of various angels, seraphim and the archangels Michael and Gabriel. The other version, Diesis, is different. It usually depicts Christ, once again enthroned but this time flanked by the Virgin Mary and John the Baptist.'

'Which is not what we saw,' Blanco said.

'Right again,' Lewis continued. 'The problem is, the riddle on Xavier's blade told us to cut the thief's throat to find what is not there but should be.'

Hunter's eyes darted up to the young American. 'Wait, you just said the Christ in Glory Pantocrator usually featured the tetramorph and then angels and seraphim, including the archangels Michael and Gabriel.'

'I did indeed.'

'None of that was in the stained-glass window we saw in Fontevraud,' Amy said, stealing Hunter's thunder. 'Only the tetramorph.'

'And Xavier's riddle asked to find what was not there but should be,' Lewis said, his smile broadening.

Hunter opened his mouth, but Jodie got there first. 'And the seraphim, angels and archangels were all missing. So we're looking for something to do with those.'

'You took the words right out of my mouth,' Hunter said.

Lauren frowned. 'But the missing images cover a lot of ground. Seraphim, angels, archangels. What part of all that should we be looking at?'

Lewis grinned again. 'That's why I needed some extra time to think about it, even though I had a hunch early on. Xavier's riddle didn't just tell us to cut the thief's throat to find what is not there but should be.' He pulled the blade from his bag, made some room on the table and set the blade down. 'That was only the first part. The second part says... "and speak to the man with the name of rock at his first refuge".'

'Still not getting it,' Jodie said.

Quinn was searching around inside a box of cereal. 'Do they still put little toys in these things? I remember little plastic toys in sealed bags when I was a kid.'

'Or, maybe you could pay attention to what Ben is saying?' Lauren said.

Quinn looked up, annoyed. 'It's Archangel Michael. Obvs.'

Lauren was astonished. 'What do you mean?'

Quinn sighed as if irritated at having to explain. 'Speak to the man with the name of rock? As in, the great big rock the abbey at Mont Saint-Michel sits on? Saint-Michel? The man with the name of the rock is Archangel Michael. Jeez. And this is what a PhD gets you? And all I want is one of the little toys. The pack says there's a toy in here. It's in French, but I used the little translator app on my computer. Those things are sick.'

Hunter saw Lauren, like everyone else and even himself, not that he would ever admit it, was dumbstruck by what Quinn had said, and even more so by the casual way she had said it. Leaving the goth rummaging around inside the cereal box, he turned to Lewis. 'You already had all that, right, Ben?'

'I did indeed,' Lewis said. 'But great work, Quinn. You're a genius.'

'Tell me something I don't already know, Ben.'

'All right, I will. After breakfast, we're going to Italy.'

They all stared at him.

'Italy?' Amy asked. 'For why?'

'Yeah,' Jodie said. 'Italy doesn't sound very King Arthur.'

'But it sounds very Archangel Michael,' Hunter said. 'Am I right, Ben?'

'You are. The end of the riddle tells us to speak to the man with the name of rock at his first refuge. Quinn just eloquently explained what the rock reference means, but the first refuge part is what's sending us to Italy because that's where the Sanctuary of Monte Sant'Angelo, or if you prefer in English, the Sanctuary of Saint Michael, the Archangel is. Mount Gargano on the south-eastern coast. It's a refuge or a shrine, and not only a shrine, but—'

'But the oldest in Europe,' Hunter put in.

'Do not tell me it's a UNESCO site,' Jodie said. 'I will scream.'

Hunter looked sympathetic. 'Sorry, but UNESCO made it a World Heritage Site back in 2011, so I'm aware of the place, although I've never been there. Sorry, Ben. One doesn't like to steal someone else's thunder in the gleeful way Jodie did to me earlier.'

'No problem,' Lewis said, snapping his notebook

shut. 'I'm just pleased we know where we're going next. Old Xavier is a hard taskmaster, but we've already shown we're up to the challenge.'

'Yay!' Quinn said, pulling her hand out of the cereal box. 'I got a little jumping frog!' When her jubilation ended, she pocketed the plastic toy and looked at the rest of the group. 'Okay, I'm ready to go now.'

22

As they walked down a sun-bleached road running along the northern slope of Mount Gargano, the stark beauty of Monte Sant'Angelo Castle rising behind them, Lauren Lane was almost able to see how the others enjoyed what they did. Most of her experience of archaeological field trips was limited to remote sites on the outskirts of ancient towns and cities, usually overseen by focused and often humourless professors working hard to compete with their contemporaries.

But this was very different. First, there was danger. She had never been shot at before, for one thing. That part was not something she could ever get used to. But there was also excitement and a sense of never-ending adventure. When she had woken up in the hotel back at Tours and rolled over to check the time, she had no idea where in the world she would go to bed that night. That part was something she could learn to live with. As it turned out, the next stop was southern Italy. A more beautiful location she found hard to imagine.

Then again, as her father sometimes said, it wasn't all beer and skittles. She was an outsider, and some of the others had done little to veil the irritation that her inclusion in the mission caused them. Also, there were mutterings. Clipped sentences she was not meant to hear involving words she didn't understand. She knew about HARPA and had worked out the team had been suspended. As for why the word Illuminati had been mentioned now and again, she chose not to ask too many questions about that. It frightened her too much.

She was ignoring that side of the team's life, knowing her adventure with them would be over in a matter of days and then she would likely never see any of them again. She had a career to pursue and wanted one day to start a family. She didn't need to be checking over her shoulder every minute for masked gunmen and secret society assassins. But other aspects of their life intrigued her.

She fought away the envy she felt when thinking about the team's jet-set life and all the interesting sites they got to explore and decided to consider her temporary status as a team member a blessing. As for Hunter, what was there to say? He liked her and she liked him. It was hard not to. He was successful and brave and good-looking and charming, but those assets were tempered by a cocky arrogance, and never knowing if he was joking or being serious with some of the things he said. But then there was the formidable Agent Fox. The cool, measured American woman was clearly from a serious and moneyed background, and to say she didn't suffer fools gladly was the understatement of the century.

Lauren was young and inexperienced, but she knew enough to realise it was a bad idea to get caught up in whatever the hell was going on between Max Hunter and Amy Fox, no matter how flattered she was by the attention. This was another reason to go back to university the second all this was over. Goodbye HARPA, or whatever they were called since the suspension.

'Earth to Lauren.'

She realised they'd almost made the end of the road and had nearly reached the church's perimeter wall, a sturdy blend of stone columns and black iron bars that had stood the test of time over hundreds of years.

'Sorry, Max. I was thinking about where all this was heading.'

She didn't like lying to him, but it was better than telling him what she had been thinking about.

'With a bit of luck, it's heading towards us finding Xavier's next riddle and getting one step closer to finding out the truth about Excalibur. Whatever that may be.'

She felt a shiver go up her spine. Her private time had not all been spent idly mulling over the virtues of Hunter's impressive physique and courage. She had also devoted considerable mental energy to contemplate the very subject he had just mentioned. Her entire university career, from her undergraduate degree up to this final year of her doctorate, had been spent studying the period in English history, including the myth of King Arthur.

The myth.

The rest of the team had shown no problem readily accepting the premise that Excalibur was real and then set about hunting it down. She'd harboured reservations, but as the mission wore on, she had come to accept the idea it could be a real object. The obvious corollary to this was that King Arthur and the entire legend surrounding him was also real. This raised significant questions for European history. Xavier's enigmatic historical intervention added fuel to the fire. She was expected not only to believe that all of these myths were real, but that King Arthur's Excalibur might be real and perhaps something more than merely a sword.

It was a lot to take in.

Up ahead, Amy and Blanco rounded the corner of the church fence and stepped through an open gate into a courtyard. Lauren and Hunter then followed the rest of the team into the courtyard's small, neat space of smooth white tiles, dazzlingly reflecting the hot Italian sun back up into the bright blue sky above their heads.

'Do you think Excalibur is more than a sword?' Lauren asked Hunter.

He stopped to scan the courtyard, lifting his chin to take in the famous octagonal tower at the corner of the yard. 'What makes you ask that?'

She shrugged. 'Just a hunch... maybe based on how much those armed men seem to want it.'

'You're the expert, Lauren. You tell me.'

'I'm an expert in the myth, Max. The myth states that both Excalibur and its scabbard had magical powers inherently linked in some way to the true king of Britain. Some say those magical powers were given to the sword by the mysterious Avalon blacksmith who forged the sword; others say the Lady of the Lake imbued the sword with its powers, which make the sword unbreakable, or undefeatable. But this is all myth, Max. We're talking myth, legend, magical fairy tales.'

Hunter lifted his sunglasses momentarily to get a better view of some of the masonry detail on the octagonal tower. 'What's your point?'

'We both know myth, legend and fairy tales are not real. If what Xavier said is true and Excalibur is real, it's not going to have been forged by an elf in the caves of Avalon until it was unbreakable. Excalibur must be something else; it must have some other quality we haven't thought of yet.'

He approved of her enquiring mind, then couldn't resist a leftfield question. 'Fancy coming out to dinner with me tonight? According to Tripadvisor, there's a bloody great pizza restaurant just around the corner from here.'

'I know you're not being serious,' she said.

'How so?'

'Because I was awake in the car the other night and heard what you told Sal about Amy.'

Hunter opened his mouth to reply, then paused

and shut it again. She turned on her heel and followed the others into the church, feeling pretty good about finally getting one over on Hunter and rendering him speechless.

'Are you coming along, Romeo?' she said. 'Or do I have to do all the heavy lifting around here?'

23

Hunter paused at the entrance to read a plaque written in Latin. *Terribilis est locus iste. Hic Domus Dei est et Porta Coeli.* Working in archaeology for so many years, his Latin was nowhere near Lewis's level, but still good enough to make a translation, which he muttered to himself in the heat as he stared up at the carved words.

'This is a terrifying place. It is the House of God and the Gateway to Heaven... an odd welcome, I'll give them that.'

He stepped aside at the entrance to allow a small group of tourists out of the church. When they were out of the way, he continued inside. Lauren had already caught up with the others, all standing together in a small, cool vestibule. To his right, tourists browsed in a little shop for postcards and other souvenirs. He saw his team waiting beyond the shop at the top of a flight of smooth stone steps leading down to a subterranean level.

'Exactly eighty-six steps leading down to the holy cavern,' Lewis said, visibly excited.

As he spoke, Hunter joined him and the others. Making their way down the steps together, he asked Lewis about the plaque he had observed at the church's entrance.

'It's from *Genesis*,' Lewis said casually. 'Chapter 28, Verse 17. It describes Abraham's grandson Jacob when he wakes from a dream in which God promised to be with him.'

'But a terrible place?' Hunter asked. 'Seems like an odd choice of words for a church.'

'A better English translation of *terribilis* would be "awesome", as in, the House of God is awesome. It's not as terrifying as it sounds. Not really, not when you think about it.'

'I'll take your word for that, Ben, but thanks.'

Electric lights shone up the walls, lighting up smooth white plaster walls and casting eerie shadows onto the recessed arches and alcoves that punctuated the descent. At the bottom of the steps, Hunter was surprised to see an underground nave, complete with several rows of pews and a new tiled floor. Above the people sitting in silence on the pews, the ceiling was carved out of solid rock. Ahead to his right, he saw a small raised area at the top of three steps, tucked away behind a traditional church balustrade of beautifully carved stone.

Behind the balustrade, a man was standing at a lectern, reading in soft Italian what Hunter presumed was a passage from the Bible to the gathered pilgrims. It was behind this man that Hunter saw what they had flown to Italy for – the shrine of the Archangel Michael.

'So, this is it,' he whispered to Amy.

'I guess so,' she said. 'Not sure we can break up the service just to go fumbling around up in the shrine.'

'I'm an archaeologist. I explore, I don't fumble.'

'So, quite different from when you're in bed, then?'

Hunter knew he'd had that coming too, so he let it slide. 'It's not complicated. We simply wait until the service ends and then I'll present my UNESCO credentials and request a few moments to look around the shrine. I'm sure they'll be more than co-operative.'

Amy made no reply to him but turned to Lewis. 'How long do you think he'll read for, Ben?'

In the background, the man's quiet voice continued the sermon.

'*Confidati nell'Eterno con tutto il cuore, e non t'appoggiare sul tuo discernimento. Riconoscilo in tutte le tue vie, ed egli appianerà i tuoi sentieri.*'

'Whatever he's saying, it's from the Bible,' Blanco said. 'Mom was Italian.'

'He's reading from *Proverbs*,' Lewis said. '"Trust in the Lord with all thine heart; and lean not unto thine own understanding. In all thy ways acknowledge him, and he shall direct thy paths." A very beautiful reading. It's hard to say how much longer, but I'd say less than ten minutes.'

'Great,' Quinn huffed out, causing some of the older people on the pews to turn and scowl at her. 'That's all we need. Hanging around in a damp cave for thirty minutes.'

'Quinn!' Amy said tersely. 'Take it easy. You're making a scene.'

'Whatever.'

'Maybe someone should get her a strawberry lollipop,' Lauren said. 'To occupy her mind while we wait.'

Quinn once again returned to form and retreated inside her hoodie, turning away and walking over to the rear pew where she slumped down with her hands in her pockets. She tipped her head down until her chin was touching her chest and only the tip of her nose was visible to the world. Blanco walked over, sat down next to her and began whispering to her.

'That's one problem stowed away for a bit,' Lauren said.

'Quinn's unique, Lauren,' Jodie said. 'You can't handle her in the way you're used to dealing with...'

Lauren raised an eyebrow. 'Normal people?'

'Just don't push her too far,' Jodie said. 'Believe me, you'll regret it big time. She'll have you evicted from your own life in less than fifteen minutes. You just won't exist any more.'

'What the hell does that even mean?' Lauren said, working hard to keep her voice to a whisper.

Amy gave a long, weary sigh. 'It means, everyone, get your minds back on the task at hand. We know Lundquist's gang of thugs are on our tail, but we have no way of knowing if or when they'll rock up to this shrine. We need to be getting out of this place as fast as possible.'

'Then it's just as well our friend has finished his sermon,' Hunter said, gesturing to the man up on the raised shrine. He had finished talking and was now making his way down the steps towards the main congregation.

'You're on, Max,' Amy said. 'Make it good.'

Hunter walked over to the man and asked in English if he could spare a moment.

'Of course,' the man replied in English. 'How may I help?'

Hunter got out his phone, pulled up his picture on the UNESCO website and began to explain. He worked for UNESCO as a senior field archaeologist and this was part of an ongoing research project concerning the discovery of some personal effects belonging to a Benedictine monk who had once lived and worked on Mont Saint-Michel. He apologised for not telephoning ahead and making a formal request, but explained about Lundquist's men, describing them as relic thieves and smugglers who couldn't be permitted to get ahead of UNESCO in the search for the monk's ancient clues.

The man, who now introduced himself as Guido Santoro, the local priest, was only too happy to allow him to take as much time as he needed in the shrine on the condition nothing was taken and no damage was made. He also cautioned Hunter that he thought it most unlikely he would find anything of use in the shrine, as he had spent years working here and seen every square inch of it. There was nothing unusual to be found here, except, as he put it, its exquisite beauty.

Hunter readily agreed to the priest's reasonable terms and then made his way up into the shrine, followed by Amy, Lewis and Lauren as Jodie made her way over to Blanco and Quinn and took the weight off her feet.

On the raised area, inside the shrine, the cave roof was lower, creating a sort of nook out of the bedrock. Vases of beautifully arranged lilies and roses, all white, surrounded a marble plinth, which supported a large man-sized glass case containing a statue of the Archangel Michael. The scent of fresh blossom filled the small, sacred space, its cool air a welcome relief after the heat out on the streets.

As they made a preliminary search of the shrine, Lewis began to speak. 'It's great to be here, from my per-spective. Just thinking about how long the devotion to St Michael has been given in this place is mind-boggling.'

Amy was kneeling now, peering beneath an alcove on the wall at the back of the shrine. 'And how long is that?'

'It all started when a local man named Garganus lost one of his bulls. After it became separated from his herd, he tracked it up here into these mountains, to the mouth of this very cave. He was so enraged by the bull causing him so much inconvenience he shot it with an arrow, but then a miracle happened. The arrow turned in the air and flew back into him, instead of hitting the bull.'

Hunter stopped his search and looked over at Lewis. 'How is that a miracle?'

'Because Garganus then went to the local bishop of this area, a man named Lorenzo of Siponto, and told him all about it. Lorenzo, who later became an Italian saint, then witnessed an apparition of the archangel here after three days of fasting.'

Hunter shook his side and sighed loudly. 'These guys should write soap operas.'

Lewis smiled but ignored him. 'After the bishop asked the archangel for help converting local pagans to Christianity, Archangel Michael told him that the cave we're standing in right now was a special, sacred place and that whenever anyone prayed in this place, it would be heard by God.'

'So, what you're saying is,' Hunter drawled, 'be very careful what you wish for down here?'

Lauren laughed. 'You can say that again.'

'Praying is not wishing, Max,' Lewis said. 'But I think you already know that.'

'Maybe.'

Lewis pressed on, undeterred. 'Because this place was consecrated not by a man but by the archangel himself, it's what we call a heavenly basilica. It's a very special place.'

'Xavier certainly thought so,' Amy said, still searching around the shrine.

'As holy grottoes go, we're very lucky,' Lewis said. 'Over two million pilgrims come here every year. This is an honour and a privilege. I can't wait to tell Meg all about it.'

Hunter perked up. 'Two million visitors? Maybe I should open up another giftshop.'

'Thanks for the valuable contribution, Max,' Amy said. 'You find anything yet?'

Hunter was now behind the plinth on his hands and knees, where Amy had been a few moments ago. Now he reversed out of the gap and jumped up to his feet, mobile phone in his hand. 'As a matter of fact, I think I have.'

Amy and Lewis stopped what they were doing and faced him, stunned.

'Well, what?' Lauren asked. 'What have you found?'

Lewis stepped towards him, beaming with excitement. 'Yeah, spill the beans, Doc!'

Hunter turned the phone around so they could both see the screen. 'Witness, if you will, a small, faint inscription carved into the rock at the base of the plinth.'

'But I looked there!' Amy said. 'I never saw that.'

'That's because you don't know the dark ways of professionally trained epigraphists like me.'

Lauren chuckled and looked at Hunter with an almost starstruck expression on her face.

Amy looked confused. 'Damn it, Max! How did you find it?'

'I'll tell you later, but what's more important is *what* I found, not how I found it.'

Amy was peering into the screen now, squinting. 'And what did you find? Just looks like scratches to me.'

'Oh, ye of little faith, Agent Fox. Ye of little faith, because what you are looking at is telling you exactly what you want to know. What we all want to know. It's telling us where Xavier travelled to next, and where we are going to find his next mischievous little riddle.'

24

'But whatever it says and however you found it, we can't just leave it there, on the plinth,' Amy said. 'Lundquist's men will find it and use it to follow Xavier's trail.'

'Not going to happen.'

Lauren looked like she was about to burst into tears. 'Please tell me you didn't scratch off the stonework?'

'I promise.'

Amy stared at him, narrowing her eyes with confusion. 'Then how can you be so sure they won't use it to find the next place on Xavier's pilgrimage?'

'I think that's for later,' Hunter said, pocketing the phone. 'A man has to have his little secrets, after all.

For now, we need to get out of this place before Lundquist and more of his thugs show up. It's a UN-ESCO World Heritage Site for the very good reasons Ben here has so eloquently pointed out. We can't risk those nutters coming down here and trashing the place in search of this.' As Hunter spoke, he tapped the phone in his pocket with a cheeky grin on his face.

'You're right,' Amy said, stepping down off the shrine and back into the main nave of the church. 'Let's go.'

By the time they reached the back of the room, Blanco, Jodie and Quinn were already on their feet and ready to leave.

'All good?' Jodie said.

Blanco looked at Amy. 'Yeah, get what we wanted?'

Amy nodded. 'Apparently, yes.'

'Apparently?' Blanco asked. 'What does that mean?'

'It means Max is playing stupid games,' she replied. 'But he says we have it and that Lundquist's men can't get it... so I guess we have it.'

'We have it,' Hunter said with a shrug. 'When I say we have it, we have it.'

'Then I guess we have it,' Quinn said, her voice melting with boredom. 'So, can we please join the land of the living and get the fu—'

'Quinn, please,' Lewis said, wincing. 'Not in here.'

The young goth was visibly apologetic. 'Sorry, Ben.'

Hunter shook his head. 'How come she never says sorry to me?'

'You're not as likeable,' Jodie said, deadpan.

They were lost in conversation as they made their way up the main steps towards the ground-level vestibule. When they reached the top, they saw the area was now much busier with tourists. Some were milling in the giftshop while others were beginning to descend the steps on their way down into the cave. Soft, respectful chatter, faces glowing with the sun or excitement. Hunter was enjoying the atmosphere, and his mind turned to lunch at one of the many excellent local restaurants.

'Looks like we got lucky,' Lewis said, glancing around at the new wave of pilgrims. 'It must be about time for another sermon.'

'I'll call us lucky if we get out of here with our lives,' Amy said, glancing at her watch.

They stepped outside and crossed the courtyard, the bright dazzling sun making them all reach for their sunglasses as the hot, dry Italian sun blew over them like a hair dryer.

'What an amazing day,' Lauren said, gazing up at

the sky. 'I forgot about how beautiful it was up here while we were in the sanctuary. You must be sad, Quinn, leaving your natural vampire habitat and being exposed to all this vitamin D.'

'Get lost, Lauren.' Quinn turned to Lewis. 'I'm not inside any more. I can say what I want.'

As they passed the gate and stepped out into the cobblestone road, Hunter noticed some men in black shirts and jeans. They were all wearing sunglasses and leaning up against the shaded wall of a building a little further down the street. As he and the team walked away from them, the men pushed off the wall and began to follow them.

'Don't turn around, but I think we're being followed.'

Lauren turned and looked over her shoulder. 'Those guys in black?'

'Yes,' Hunter sighed. 'But luckily no one turned around, so they don't know we're aware of their presence behind us.'

Lauren winced. 'Sorry, Max.'

'Forget about it. If it's Lundquist's men, they'd have had to make their move eventually.'

'So what are we going to do?' Lauren asked him.

'This first right turn up ahead is no good. When we make it, they can still see us through the iron bars of the church courtyard wall. But the next left, on the way back to the car, that's behind a solid wall. When we make that turn, we make a break for it. Run for the car as fast as we can, and if they start shooting before we reach it, then everyone scatters and find cover wherever you can.'

'Got it,' Lauren said. 'Run for the car, then if they start shooting, run for cover. Got it.'

Hunter checked his watch. 'It's just after three o'clock. If we're forced to split up, we'll meet at the top of the castle. If that falls apart, we rendezvous again tonight at the pizza place. Say, eight o'clock.'

'What if these guys like pizza?' Jodie said from the back.

Amy said, 'Don't worry about that. If these guys start a hot war in the middle of a little town like this, this afternoon, they're not going to be hanging around for margaritas tonight. So, is everyone clear on what Max just said?'

'We are,' Blanco said. 'I'm just hoping these old legs can make the car before those maniacs turn the corner and start shooting at me. I'm not as young as you guys.'

'You'll be fine, Sal,' Amy said as they made the right turn and walked along the courtyard wall. 'It's not that far.'

'But we left our guns in the car,' Jodie said. 'That makes it way too far for all of us.'

'We could hardly take the mercenaries' stolen machine pistols into the church,' Amy said.

Blanco's concern grew. 'Wait, if we get back to the car before they get a chance to open fire on us, we still get to have pizza tonight, right?'

Amy smiled. 'Tonight we can all have as much pizza as we want and it's all on UNESCO, right, Max?'

Hunter's smile was not convincing. 'I'm sure my department will be only too happy to ensure the team gets a proper meal after such a hard day assisting me with my research.'

Jodie scoffed. 'Assisting you my ass. I'm not your assistant, Hunter. I'm your teammate.'

Hunter ignored her. 'I still can't get in touch with Juliette, though.'

'Maybe she went away,' Jodie said. 'Since working with you, I also feel a strange need to get away.'

'As hilarious as that is,' Hunter said, 'I'm now officially worried about her. When things settle down I'm asking questions.'

Turning left onto the road where they had parked their car, Hunter hung back and made a glance over his shoulder just before they moved out of sight. 'You want the good news or the bad news?'

They were breaking into a sprint now, all eyes fixed on their SUV at the end of the sunny road.

'The bad news first,' Lewis yelled.

'There are more of them than we thought. They must have been joined by some others who were waiting down the other end of the road in case we went back to the car that way instead.'

Jodie glanced back as she ran, then called out to Hunter. 'So what's the good news?'

'We're having pizza tonight. Now, run!'

25

None of them made the car. Jodie was closest, so Blanco threw her the key. She caught it and unlocked the doors but was still five metres short of it by the time the men rounded the corner and opened fire on them.

The team's reaction was instinctive and instant. Some ducked, some dived, and others rolled or ran. Hunter was closest to Lauren, so he wrapped his arm around her shoulders and wheeled her quickly to the relative safety of a wall jutting out at the base of the Monte Sant'Angelo Castle. Lewis and Jodie had leapt over the wall on the other side of the car. The others had run around to the back of the vehicle and were using it as cover as they made their way along the street to the castle's main access road.

The men continued to pound down the road in the blazing sun, guns raised and sporadically firing on them.

'What now?' Lauren asked Hunter. 'It looks like we're trapped and they'll be here any minute.'

He scanned the area, finding a slope running up towards the castle as their only option. 'This way. Fast!'

He grabbed her by the wrist and pulled her up the slope. It was grassed, narrow and, as they got higher, dangerous with a drop of at least forty feet and a hard landing on the car park's tarmac far below.

Lauren shielded her eyes from the sun as she stared up the slope. 'Is this leading anywhere?'

They passed several iron doors built into the castle's stone foundations as they moved up the slope towards the top. Hunter hurriedly tried all of them, but they were locked, as he had expected. No matter. They reached the end of the slope and found themselves at the base of the castle's northern perimeter wall, nestled inside a small, wooded area. Small progress.

Lauren breathed hard as she tried to catch her breath after having raced up the slope. Now she stared up at the stone wall. 'You don't expect me to climb that?'

'I surely do,' Hunter said, also trying to control his breathing. 'It's that or die.'

'When you put it like that, it doesn't seem so dangerous.'

'It's not dangerous at all. See where those two walls meet, forming that corner? We can easily get up that and then we run back on ourselves along another grassy slope, the one running above our heads right now. See it?'

She nodded. 'But aren't you forgetting about the maniacs with the guns?'

'No. We'll tuck down inside this undergrowth and wait for them to pass. Then we go up.'

Crouched down in the thick vegetation growing around the base of the wall, the two of them sat in silence and watched as the men scrambled down the street. One of them looked up and scanned the slope and the castle's north wall. He yelled something in Swedish and some others turned and looked, then another gunman pointed ahead and called back and then they went on in the direction of Amy's team.

Lauren looked at Hunter and spoke in a scared whisper. 'Didn't you say you can understand some Swedish?'

He nodded his head as he watched the men streaming away. 'A little, but mostly stuff like "why are you back so late?" and "why do you smell of strong liquor?" Stuff like that. Oh, and "get out and don't come back." I heard that one a few times. It sounds much angrier in the original Swedish, believe me.' He shook his head, smiling at the memories. 'Good old Hanna. She gave as good as she got and then some.'

She shook her head in disbelief. 'As fascinating as that was, what did that guy with the big gun just say, Max?'

'He asked where we went. The one who called back told him we must have climbed back down and joined our team. He said it was too dangerous for anyone to climb up and that we'd have to be idiots to try.'

'So why don't we just go back down and go back the way we came? They've moved on now.'

'We have no idea how many more of them are back there and this is the way to rendezvous with the rest of our team. As a bonus, you'll also get to tell people you escaped from armed Swedish terrorists by climbing up the wall of a ninth-century Italian castle. Tell me that's not gonna get some free drinks, right?'

'You're unbelievable.'

'Thanks. You want me to take a picture for proof?'

'Get up the damned wall, Max!'

'Sure. Now, just copy what I do with my hands and feet. It's only another twenty feet and we're clear.'

'If you say so.'

Hunter made it to the top in short order, then lay down and hung his hand over the edge, guiding Lauren up towards him. At the top, she slipped with her foot and started to fall, but Hunter strained to reach her and grabbed her hand, arresting the fall.

'Up you come,' he said, trying to sound calm as he pulled her up and over the edge to safety. When she was up on the grassy ledge, she was shaking with fear.

'I nearly fell!'

Hunter leered down at the drop. 'It's not that far. You probably would have landed in those bushes and got away with a few scratches and maybe a bruised arse.'

'Sorry, are you talking about my fate had I fallen down the wall, or about a typical Max Hunter dating experience?'

He looked at her and grinned. 'I like you, Lauren. You can keep up with my urbane if slightly sardonic sense of humour, like the best of them.'

'Keep up? I could run rings around you. Watch me.'

Gunfire ended the banter. Hunter made his way along the second grassy slope until he was at its peak and then clambered over a broken stone wall before making the final stage of the climb and pulling himself through a metre-wide gap in the castle's ancient crenelated wall. Below him, Lauren was running up the slope and then attacking the same broken wall with vigour. He rallied her with a cry of support, all the while scanning south of their position for any sign of Amy and the team. There was no sign of either her or the gunmen, but when he looked out to the north, he saw Lewis and Jodie climbing back over the wall they had used as cover and heading back to their SUV. Beyond them, a vast wooded valley making up part of the Gargano National Park stretched away to the horizon.

'Maybe we should have hidden in there,' Lauren said, pointing to the wilderness as she climbed up beside Hunter. 'Instead of climbing up this stupid castle.'

Hunter looked behind him across the castle ruins and counted a dozen or so tourists. Then he looked at Lauren. 'It's a lot further away than it looks, and they don't call it the Umbra Forest for no reason. That means Forest of Shadows. It's notorious for how dark it gets in there. I think you'd be frightened.'

'Get real. How do you know so much about it anyway?'

'This place is a UNESCO site. I read internal

memos and then do my research. It's all part of being a sensible adult with a responsible job. You'll get there one day.'

'Get lost, Max,' she said, hiding a smile.

'Wait, I see Amy.'

She and the rest of her team had run into view just to their left, on the southern side of the castle ruins. The main entrance road had snaked around to the west and led them to the lower part of the castle, fifty feet below Hunter and Lauren, who were in the main part of the complex inside the inner curtain wall.

'And they've got company!' Lauren pointed along the snaking pathway behind Amy to the armed men, now closing in on them with their weapons raised.

Hunter watched, horrified as the men opened fire on his friends, but they were close enough to the castle's main gate to scramble inside and get out of the line of fire before anyone got hurt.

'C'mon, let's get down to them!' he said.

They made a break for it, vaulting over an internal wall and then climbing their way down a series of stone fortifications until they were on the same level as Amy. The hot sun beat down on Hunter's back as he called out to her, waving to alert her of their location.

'Over here!'

Amy and the others reached them in seconds,

breathless and shaken. 'They're right behind us, Max. Please tell me there's another way out of here!'

'I'm not a tour guide.'

'You got here first. Have you had a chance to look around?'

'A little,' he said. 'If we can get inside the main castle keep, the place is like a rabbit warren. I studied it briefly when it was in the process of being classed as a World Heritage Site. It's this way, come on. We'll stand a much better chance if we can get there without being seen. If we can draw them away from the entrance, we can get back outside and meet up with Ben. He and Jodie are already back at the car.'

'They're all right?' she asked, wide-eyed. 'You saw them?'

'Yeah, they're fine.'

'But we won't be if we don't shake our asses,' Quinn said. 'I hear them coming. They can't be more than thirty seconds behind us.'

They broke into another run, weaving through a thin scattering of tourists and then leaping over another low wall. After scrambling along a wide stony path, they finally made the main castle keep and ducked inside one of the stone-arched entrances. They found a cool, shaded interior of beautiful white masonry, vaulted ceilings and gothic arches. Across a wide, smooth flagstone floor, a security guard was waking from a light afternoon snooze in a chair behind a wooden desk, the only piece of furniture in the room. When they burst in, they had disturbed his slumber. He looked up at them with a confused expression and began to talk in Italian.

'We have no time for this,' Amy said. 'Sal, say something! Your mother was Italian!'

'True,' Blanco said. 'Spanish father, but my mother was Italian.'

The old Brooklyn boy raised his hands to calm the guard and began speaking in soft, fluent Italian. Hunter watched Blanco point to the door they had used to come in and heard the word *terroristi*. They all heard that word, but the guard's reaction was the most acute. He was unarmed and carried only a small two-way radio. He reached for it as he walked over to the entrance door to take a look outside, verifying what the crazy strangers had just alerted him to.

'No! *Allontanati dalla porta!*' Blanco called out.

It was too late. Three shots roared outside in the blazing heat. Their sound seemed to split open the day, like an axe splitting wood. The tourists screamed and ran like frightened sheep. Hunter heard men once again shouting in Swedish. The guard clutched his stomach and fell to his knees, blood instantly blooming on his crisp white shirt. He looked at Blanco, blinked and then slumped down dead inside one of the gothic arches.

'They're here in ten seconds!' Lewis yelled.

Amy scanned the room. 'Then we need to be out of here in five.'

26

'This way!' Quinn yelled.

Hunter turned, wanting to contradict her. Then he saw she had swiped a paper map off one of the tourist stands. 'You're certain? I only know this place vaguely.'

'I can read a map, damn it!' She pointed to the opposite side of the room from the dead security guard to a staircase descending to a lower floor. 'We go this way!'

'Let's go!' Amy said.

Hunter followed along with everyone else and ran for the staircase. Thinking on the fly, the best way out of this mess was to get back down to ground level, find an exit, maybe something with a panic bar, and then move outside. They could use the castle walls as cover until they met up with Lewis and Jodie and got the hell out of the place in the SUV as fast as modern automotive technology would carry them.

At the top of the stairs, Hunter pulled to a stop and made sure everyone was out of sight in the stairwell before turning and making his way down. About six steps down, when his head was at the same height as the floor they had been on, he saw the gunmen charging into the room. The lead man leapt over the dead security guard's legs and scanned the room. He was holding what looked like the same model of Heckler & Koch submachine gun that the other men had used on them back in the French forest.

Catching the sight of Hunter's head out of the corner of his eye, the gunman whirled around and opened fire, screaming at the top of his voice as he unleashed a wild volley of fire all over the entrance to the stairwell. Bullets blasted the wooden banister rail into chunks and raked into the ancient stones above him, blasting pieces of them into plaster, now raining down on the heads of Hunter and the team as they leapt down the steps three at a time.

'You think they saw us?' Lauren yelled.

'I'm the funny one, Lauren,' Hunter said. 'Remember that and you'll fit right in!'

Without waiting for the Swedes to reach the top of

the stairs, they sprinted down a broad tiled corridor lined with glass exhibit cases and information boards covered in writing and images about the castle's long and venerable history. The stone walls were lit by amber spotlights, creating a warm, modern feel to the place, but an appreciation of its charms would have to wait. Spotting an open archway with what looked like daylight spilling from it at the far end of the corridor, Amy ran towards it and led her team back out into the searing Italian heat.

Blinking to adjust their eyes, they heard sirens in the distance.

'Someone called the cops,' Quinn said.

'Keep running!' Amy ordered from the rear. 'We're not out of this nightmare yet!'

With the main keep towering high above them, they made their way across a stone courtyard and leapt over a low wall to where a path led down to the grass-covered ward below. As they ran down the path, Quinn reached for her phone and called Lewis.

'Get the car round the front, Ben! We're in a big heap of shit and we need an emergency airlift right now!' She slipped the phone away. 'They're on their way! Head out to the road at the front!'

They heard a scream.

Hunter turned and saw Lauren cartwheeling down

the path. It looked like she had lost her footing on some loose gravel and stumbled. Falling over at such speed sent her into an uncontrollable roll. He turned to run back to her, but Amy was already there, leaning down and reaching for Lauren's hand.

'Go!' Amy screamed.

Hunter ignored her, heading back along the path towards Amy and Lauren as the others obeyed Amy's order and continued down to the ward.

'I said go, Max!' Amy screamed. 'Just for once will you do as you are damn well told! I've got this, okay?'

Both women were on their feet. Then the Swedes appeared from behind the wall they had hidden behind. Seeing them making their way along the slope, the men turned their guns on them and resumed firing.

'Holy crap!' Hunter cried out. 'Take cover!'

It was a vicious, endless fusillade of heavy automatic fire deployed by the Swedish team from a defensive position at the top of the path. Bullets flew everywhere, ricocheting off stone walls and the path, chewing into the hard, baked earth and blasting grass and dirt and stone chips up into the air in a nightmarish maelstrom.

Still at least fifteen metres from his teammates, Hunter had little choice but to dive for cover behind a low wall jutting out of the castle wall beside the path lower down the slope. When he peered over the edge, he saw Amy take a bullet in the arm. He felt sick when he saw it, and nearly threw up when he heard her terrified scream echoing out of the castle grounds and fading somewhere in the hot blue sky. She spun around and hit the deck, grabbing at the top of her arm, her hand quickly reddening with blood. Lauren was on her backside and now scrambled back like a crab, staring wide-eyed in horror at the sight of Amy in so much pain.

The firing stopped. Hunter was stunned. He'd seen much worse during his time as a British Guards officer, but this was Amy. This was different, something much harder to process. He needed to get out of the cover position and make his way up to her. He needed to grab a hold of her, probably a fireman's lift, he calculated, and then somehow run with Lauren back to this position. That was what he needed to do, but he couldn't. The Swedish team unleashed a second volley, but this time over the heads of Amy and Lauren, redirecting their fire purely at Hunter.

Hunter ducked again, cursing the day. He flicked his head around and saw Blanco leading the rest of the team to the safety of a high wall running around the outside of the grassy ward. They were in the range of the gunmen's weapons but out of their line of sight. So was he unless they advanced further on the path. He heard more shouting and then boots crunching on the dry earth and gravel. When he peered over the top of the wall, it was just in time to see four members of the Swedish team, dressed in black and armed to the teeth, scrambling down the path towards Amy and Lauren. He knew what came next.

The men grabbed the two women and pulled them roughly to their feet. Amy screamed and tried to push them away from Lauren. One of them back-slapped her hard enough to knock her out. She collapsed back into another of the men who now scooped her up and threw her over his shoulder, carrying her in the same fireman's lift Hunter had visualised himself doing. Only this time, it wasn't him rescuing her, but the enemy kidnapping her. He cursed again, wiping sweat from his brow. Up the path, Lauren obeyed without resisting, and the figures slowly ran back into the castle.

Hunter had only one play. Exploiting the gap in hostilities, he ran down the path and crashed into Blanco's team behind the lower wall in the ward.

'I blew it,' he said, slamming his fist against the wall and splitting open his knuckles. 'I had a chance to save them and I blew it.'

Blanco ignored it, eyes crawling all over the top of the castle, just visible from their position behind the wall. 'Where are they now, Max? Where did they go?'

'Back inside the castle. I let them down, Sal. Amy and Lauren.'

'Quit bleating about it,' Quinn said, 'and do something about it.'

Hunter looked at her and saw something more than the usual petulant goth girl. The indifference that usually dwelled in her wary eyes was gone. He saw anger, hate, and desperation. Eyes full of emotion.

'We're outgunned and outnumbered,' he said. 'And now they have two hostages. We have no play here, Quinn. They won this battle.'

Their SUV zoomed around the bend to the south of the castle and up the access road. At the wheel, Lewis, and beside him Jodie, hope on their faces. They screeched to a halt and both jumped out, racing across the ward until they were at the group.

'Amy?' Jodie said, gazing around. 'Where is she?'

'She's gone,' Quinn said. 'They snatched her and the other one.'

'Lauren,' Hunter said, giving Quinn a look. 'They took Amy and Lauren. I could have stopped it, but I stayed under cover.'

Blanco grabbed his shoulder and shook him.

'Enough, Max. You were too far away. I saw the whole thing. If you'd broken cover, they'd have cut you in half with gunfire.'

In the background, they all heard the distinct whomping of a helicopter's rotor blades.

'Cops?' Jodie asked.

'Maybe,' Blanco replied. 'But I think we all know different.'

Lewis pointed at the sky to the east of the mountain ridge. 'There. I see it.'

Hunter shielded his eyes from the glare of the sun and soon found it. A black helicopter was approaching at a low altitude, the sun reflecting on its smooth metallic sides and flashing in his eyes.

'This isn't over.' Lewis ran back to the car and returned with the two machine pistols they'd stolen from the mercenaries back in Fontevraud. He threw one at Hunter. 'Make it count, Max.'

'Looks like it's redemption time, Hunter,' Jodie said.

'Everyone else in the car,' Blanco said. 'Jodie's at the wheel.'

'We can't keep up with them!' Jodie protested.

Blanco began to walk back over to the car. 'We're not going to. We're going to get the hell out of here before the cops turn up.'

'And what about Ben and Hunter?' Jodie asked.

Blanco's look was grave. 'They're going to try and repel the chopper and stop it landing, giving the cops a fighting chance to take those guys out and stop them kidnapping Amy and Lauren. After that, we all meet together at the pizza place and tell jokes about this great day we're all having.'

Hunter looked at his old friend and clapped him on the back. 'Get them out of here, Sal. Leave the rest to me and Ben.'

27

When Hunter and Lewis reached the higher castle, they sprinted inside and took up cover positions on top of one of the towers. From here, they had a good line of sight across most of the ruins. Far below, they could hear the Swedish team's radios squawking and crackling as they waited impatiently for their rescue, but there was no sight of them.

'We haven't got enough rounds to finish the team,' Hunter said. 'But we can stop that damned helicopter from landing.'

'Just so long as nothing else goes wrong,' Lewis threw in.

'It can't go wrong, Ben. If it goes wrong, we lose them both.'

Lewis nodded and wiped the sweat from his eyes. 'Their ride is almost here. Look.'

Hunter scanned the sky. He could hear it, but not see it. 'Where is it?'

'Coming in low. Remember, we're up on a mountain.'

Then Hunter saw it. Rising above the outline of the castle's western ruins, blades whirring, and then the main body, flashing in the sun. It rode above them like a spectre, before hovering one hundred feet in the air.

'Pilot's scanning for somewhere safe to land,' Hunter said.

'There!' Lewis said. 'I see the Swedes.'

Hunter saw them too. They had been hiding inside a recess beneath them and were now walking out into the middle of a flat expanse of grass at the castle's north. The area was encased on three sides by ancient stone walls, but the wall on its northern side had crumbled away across the centuries and was now almost completely gone. In its place, the castle's authorities had erected a steel barrier to stop tourists from getting too close to the edge and falling. Beyond it, the great wide valley he and Lauren had seen earlier stretched away towards the horizon, shimmering in a heat haze.

'They're coming in right there,' Hunter said, noting how the narrow and long grassy landing area they had chosen was on the opposite side of the castle as the imminent police presence. 'They'll have to turn the helicopter to get it down. That's when we fire.'

'Got it.'

They waited patiently as the aircraft began to descend. Then they unleashed their limited firepower, reeling off a few carefully timed bursts of fire as the chopper rotated and prepared to land on the narrow strip. Below them, the Swedes bolted. Turning on their heels and running back into cover, they grabbed Amy and Lauren and pulled them along as they went.

The chopper responded by moving over to the Swedes' new position and remaining in a hover half a metre above the ground while the men below forced Amy and Lauren to board the aircraft. When they were all inside, it immediately climbed back into the sky and turned fully around, revealing an open side door. Inside, two men with AK417 battle rifles had climbed into position and now opened fire on Hunter and Lewis with a vengeance.

'Here it comes!' Lewis yelled. 'Take cover!'

They ducked down behind the wall, but the chopper flew forwards until it was almost above them, exposing them to the gunmen inside who now opened fire a second time.

Lewis fired, the crack of his shot echoing across the ruins and out into the valley to the north. One of the gunmen inside the helicopter screamed and dropped his weapon, clutching his fatal throat wound as he tumbled out of the aircraft cabin and smashed down onto the ruins below, instantly dying. In the chaos, Hunter just caught the familiar sound of the Swedish team's radios and then their boots pounding on stone.

'The pilot must have radioed down and told them our position,' he said. 'Which puts us in deep shit. We're about to be surrounded.'

Lewis was calm as he took another potshot at the helicopter, aiming for the surviving gunman up inside the cabin. This time, he wasn't so lucky. The shot missed and then the man inside the aircraft opened fire again, pouring fire all over their position.

'We have to jump!' Lewis yelled.

Hunter fired next, striking the body of the heli-copter and punching a line of holes through its metal skin. The pilot responded by gaining more altitude and pulling back a few hundred feet. 'Are you crazy?'

'Not over the side!' Lewis called back. 'We jump down inside the castle on the other side of the tower.

It's less than twenty feet. You've done jump training, right?'

Hunter looked over the side, estimating the height. Then he looked up at the chopper, returning for another firefight. 'That means letting them take Amy and Lauren, Ben.'

'It's our only chance, Max! Live to fight another day, yeah?'

Hunter took a deep breath. He knew Lewis was right. He had to let go of the thought of rescuing Amy and Lauren here and now and let the other team take them. If they wanted to kill them they would have already done it. He had no fears about that. They were being snatched either to grill for information, to use as bait or to barter some kind of trade with. Either way, they were safe for now. He knew what to do.

'Fine, then we go. On the count of three!'

'Screw that, I'm going now!'

Hunter watched Lewis leap over the side and land with a perfect roll. He was back up on his feet and running towards the safety of an internal doorway on the other side of the grass. Hunter was suddenly aware of the downwash from the descending chopper's massive rotors. It was closing in on him again, as were the rest of the Swedish team, who were now smashing their way through the door at the top of the tower. The airborne gunman opened fire on him and then the rest of the team joined in another barrage of gunfire. As the rounds nipped along the tower's roof towards him, he saw Amy and Lauren inside the helicopter. Locking eyes with Amy, he had no time to talk. He turned and leapt over the wall, landing and rolling exactly where Lewis had moments earlier. By the time he reached the internal door, Lewis was shaking his head and pointing to the sky above the ruins. Hunter looked up and just caught the helicopter rising above Monte Sant'Angelo. Amy and Lauren and the Swedish team were now safely aboard. It rotated smoothly in the sky and flew out across the valley to the north. It was rapidly out of sight, and then the sound of its engine was gone too. The only sound was the police sirens blaring to the castle's south where they would be screeching their cars to a halt right about now.

'I don't know about you, Max,' Lewis said, 'but I'm not digging the idea of police custody, getting charged with criminal damage of a historical monument and then maybe a few years in an Italian prison. How do you like the idea of another chance to practise your jump training?'

Hunter managed the ghost of a smile, unable to resist his friend's turn of phrase. 'Let's do it.'

28

Hunter's aching ankles and sore shoulder were numbed by the time he'd assailed his third bottle of cold Italian lager. When he thought about it, he hadn't done jump training for so many years he couldn't even be sure of the exact number. Plus he was much older and, dare he think it, slightly heavier than way back then. The two parachute landings and rolls had impacted him more than he cared to say, especially in front of the younger and fitter Ben Lewis, who seemed to be largely unaffected by the afternoon's adventures. When their evening meal was finally in front of them, he decided to wash it down with a fourth and final beer and call it a day.

After the two men had made their second jump

and fled the castle, they'd used their phones to rendezvous with the SUV on a backstreet in the middle of
the old town. From there they'd beat a hasty retreat
from the police and drive on rural back roads until
reaching the main road south, figuring they were
probably going to need to fly somewhere, and Bari
was the closest place with an international airport.
The drive along the coast to Bari was beautiful, but no
one noticed; their minds were too heavily occupied by
the kidnap of two of their own.

'Now we have two problems,' Hunter said. 'The
clock's still ticking on cracking the Excalibur code before Lundquist does, and now we have to rescue Amy
and Lauren.'

'From Lundquist,' Jodie said.

Hunter nodded. 'Looks that way.'

'Which could be a good thing,' Lewis threw in.
'Killing two birds with one stone and all that jazz.'

'Unless they took them some other place, away
from the clue trail,' Quinn said through a mouthful of
pizza. 'Which could throw a serious wrench in our
little plans, am I right?'

Lewis swallowed some pizza and shook his head.
'We'd just have to split the team in two.'

Hunter considered this. 'Quinn, is there any way

you can hack into air traffic control records for this part of the world?'

She gave a sloppy shrug and drank some Coke. 'Sure.'

'Neither Amy nor Lauren had their passports on them when Lundquist's men snatched them. Those and the rest of their things are in their bags in the SUV. This means any attempt to get them out of the country would have to be covert...'

'But they'd still have to file a flight plan and activate their transponders,' Blanco said. 'Even if they were going entirely privately and somehow smuggled Amy and Lauren aboard their plane.'

Lewis nodded enthusiastically. 'And you know what else?'

'What?' Jodie asked.

'I never had a pizza with a fried egg in the middle of it, but damn, this thing is great.'

'Florentine pizza,' Blanco said with authority. 'And it ain't too shabby, either.'

Jodie washed the crust down with a glug of lager. 'You going to put those on the menu of your Manhattan restaurant, Sal?'

The table fell silent. Hunter spoke first.

'You're going to start a restaurant?'

Jodie flushed red. 'Sorry, Sal.'

'Forget about it. It's nothing.' Blanco shrugged and took a second out to sip his beer before explaining to the others. 'As you all know, my brother Angelo runs a pizza place in Brooklyn Heights. He talked to me not so long ago and made me an offer.'

'An offer you can't refuse?' Quinn said. 'You are Italian, after all.'

Blanco smiled. 'Half Italian, and no, it wasn't one of those offers. I can refuse it if I want.'

'Tell us more about this offer,' Lewis asked. 'I'm officially intrigued, especially if it means I get free pizza whenever I'm in New York.'

'It's nothing. Angelo wants to expand the business, start up like maybe a franchise model or something like that and use me as some kind of guinea pig. See if it all works out. I don't know much about running a restaurant. He has the business head. Knows he can trust me, see? He also knows I care about the family name.'

Jodie smiled. 'I think it's a great idea. I can see it now, in pink neon: "Sal's Pizza".'

Blanco frowned. 'First, it would be "Blanco's" because it's Angelo's business. Second, the neon thing isn't happening. I have my pride to think about.'

'But is this a thing?' Hunter said. 'Or just some kind of pipe dream?'

Blanco thought long and hard about the question. Hunter could see he was trying to respond in a way that kept everyone happy. Typical Blanco.

'It's a thing, I guess,' he said at last. 'I'm not getting any younger, guys. I'm not as fit as I used to be. I can't work out anywhere near like I did even ten years ago. And what do I give the team, anyway? I can fly helicopters? Amy could find any number of rotorheads to replace me.'

Quinn took a few bites from a fresh slice before shocking everyone with what she said next. 'You're more than that, Sal. You're like the team's father or something. At least, you're like my father. The one I never had.'

Blanco stopped chewing and thought about what she had said. He swallowed his pizza and smiled. 'Thanks, Quinn. Appreciate that. I think of you like a daughter, too.'

Now it was Quinn's turn to blush. 'I'm not getting you a card or nothin' on Father's Day.'

'Fine with me.'

She pulled up her hood to hide her face and then slipped her computer out of her pocket, hurriedly typing into the keyboard. 'I'm gonna look at the flight plans now. I don't want anyone to talk to me.'

'I think I can restrain myself,' Hunter said, swigging his beer. 'But the rest of us need to talk about the business at hand. Sal's new business venture into Italian cuisine in Manhattan might be a nicer subject, but we have a code to crack and two friends to save.'

'I second that,' Blanco said.

'So, where do we start?' Jodie asked.

Hunter said, 'We can't work out a plan to rescue Amy and Lauren until Quinn can tell us where the Swedish team took them after they flew away from us on Mont Sant'Angelo. So, in the meantime, I suggest we go right back to basics and think about the clue Xavier left for us in the sanctuary.'

'About that,' Blanco said. 'After we broke away from you by the castle, Amy told me she'd searched behind the Archangel Michael's plinth in the shrine but found nothing. Then she told me you looked in the same place after her and found it. I know Amy, and if she's one thing it's thorough. There's no way she would have missed something like that. How'd you find it, Max?'

'That doesn't matter for now,' Hunter said, working hard to hide a grin. 'What matters is what our old friend Xavier was trying to tell us about the next stop on his little European Tour.'

'And what did he tell us?' Jodie asked.

With the sound of Quinn's fingers flying over the

computer keyboard in the background, Hunter pulled his phone out and swiped to the image he had taken. 'The message is simple enough, but just like the last one, the meaning hidden within it is much more complex.'

Blanco slipped on his glasses and peered at the phone. 'Just looks like scratches to me. I guess I'd better stick to making pizzas.'

'And flying helicopters,' Quinn said from behind her hood.

'I knew you were listening to us!' Hunter said.

Quinn sighed heavily. 'I thought I said I didn't want anyone to talk to me?'

'Sorry,' Hunter muttered with a smile.

Jodie swigged her beer. 'So, what does it say?'

'I don't know that,' Hunter said, his smile fading. 'That's what we're about to find out.'

'Damn it, Max,' Jodie said with a shake of her head. 'I thought you had it already.'

'Hardly, darling. You might remember that a few minutes after expertly uncovering the hidden message behind the plinth, we were set upon by a team of psychopathic gunmen, chased around an ancient castle, shot at some more, and then strafed by a machinegun-wielding nutcase in a helicopter. It all adds up.'

She ate more pizza. 'Especially at your age, right?'

Hunter shut his mouth when he caught the way she ended her barb with a cheeky wink. 'So that is why I haven't solved the sodding riddle yet. Okay?'

'Sounds reasonable,' she muttered with a shrug.

'So, get your phone out,' he said. 'We can't use Quinn's computer because she's otherwise engaged trying to track down where Amy and Lauren went on Psycho Air.'

'Why not use yours?' she asked.

'Because we're using it to look at the pretty little picture of Xavier's calligraphy I took back in the sanctuary. Do keep up, darling.'

Jodie smiled and got an anagram solver up on her phone. 'Hit me, Hunter.'

Hunter resisted the obvious reply and showed her his phone. The inscription was faint, but legible: *ZCXTGECPED PYMT PODAPRO YPLCP*.

'What the hell is that?' Jodie said.

'Our ticket to Excalibur,' Hunter said. 'So get typing.'

29

Jodie typed it into the anagram solver, but the search returned nothing but gibberish. 'This mean anything to anyone else?'

They all looked.

'Not to me,' Blanco said. 'But then, that's hardly surprising. I'm not educated.'

Quinn shook her head. 'Me neither.'

'Nor me,' Hunter said with a sigh. 'At least not in this area. Ben? You're the closest we have to a linguistics expert. What do you make of it?'

Lewis stared at the jumbled letters on the screen. 'Nothing. I was hoping for some Latin, I guess. Looks like Xavier is upping his game as his pilgrims draw closer to the treasure.'

'Then we're back to where we started,' Jodie said, slumping down in her chair.

'No, wait.' Hunter clicked his fingers and smiled. 'I have an idea, and if I'm right, it seems Ben is right and our old monk friend has decided to up the riddle ante a few notches. I think he's using some kind of cypher, most likely the Caesar Cipher.'

'And that is what, exactly?' Blanco asked.

'It's a retarded code for kids.' Quinn shifted in her seat. 'And can you guys keep it the hell down? I'm trying to do some serious, adult work here.'

The others shared a parental 'what can you do?' look, then Hunter spoke again. 'It's not a retarded code for kids. It might seem simple now, but two thousand years ago it was considered a pretty nifty little piece of deception. As the name implies, it was named after the Roman emperor Caesar and involves shifting letters along the alphabet to any agreed number. This produces a simple but effective code. So, if we agreed to a shift value of two letters, then "cat" would become "ecv" and so on. It's simple enough, although it might have been considered more complicated all those centuries ago, especially if you think about how illiterate most of the population was back then. Anyway, the user simply shifts the letters along however many he wants and then tells the receiver of the message how many letters he moved along. So, maybe A is now a B, and B is a C, and so on.'

'Like I said,' Quinn mumbled. 'Retarded.'

Hunter turned on her. 'Yeah, well, maybe to a twenty-first-century emo fluent in Malbolge, it is, but to a first-century scribe it was pretty damned sneaky.'

Quinn poked her face around the hood. 'You know about Malbolge?'

'I can read, Quinn.'

She disappeared again. 'Weird.'

'Maybe we can get back to Xavier's riddle?' Blanco said with a chuckle. 'I like that Caesar kind of stuff because I think I might just have a first-century mind.'

Hunter carried on, more excitedly than before. 'As I was saying, looking at the anagram returns, we can see they're all nonsense, but I think this is just a case of garbage-in, garbage-out. If Xavier was using a cypher first, then turned them into an anagram, we'd have to reverse that process to get back to the original message.'

'I get it,' Lewis said. 'We need to know the shift value first, then run that through the anagram solver. Then we get our goodies.'

'That's the theory,' Hunter said.

Jodie drummed her fingers on the edge of the table. 'But how do we know the shift value? If it's just a case of moving the letters along, then there could be twenty-six possible ways to find it.'

'Twenty-three,' Hunter said. 'Xavier would have been using the classical Latin alphabet which had twenty-three letters. No J, U or W.'

'Yay,' she replied with mock happiness. 'We just have to sit here and try out twenty-three possible shifts.'

'Exactly,' Hunter said. 'So, you get on with that while I go and clear my head. Great work, guys.'

'Huh?' Jodie said. 'Why do we have to do the donkey work?'

'In your case, I'll resist the obvious reply.'

'On second thoughts,' she said, 'it's probably better if you go.'

He blew out a breath. 'Sorry, I didn't mean that, Jodie. It's just that I blame myself for what happened to Amy and Lauren and I need a few minutes to clear my head. Amy got shot, remember? I'm sure it was just a flesh wound, but it's on my mind. Now, it's looking like we might be making progress and I want to be at my best before moving on. We have a lot to do.'

Before anyone could object, Hunter rose from his chair and walked out of the restaurant, the sound of Blanco laughing at his exit in the background. Outside, the sunset had painted the sky in a dozen reds and oranges, and the night was bringing a welcoming cool breeze, blowing in from the Adriatic Sea off the eastern shore. Somewhere in the air, he caught the delightful smell of barbecue smoke, mingling with soft laughter.

Hunter checked for oncoming traffic and then stepped across the road, making his way down past a children's playground and across a park bordered with mature palm trees until finally reaching a long, golden sandy beach. The sun sank out of sight behind him, over the city, as he stared out across the water. Any other time, he would have talked Amy into coming for a walk with him and they would joke and laugh. But not this time. Even if she were here tonight, she wouldn't be walking with him along any beach. She would be back in the restaurant, eating pizza and dutifully ignoring him for his indiscretions with Lauren, just as he deserved.

When the sunlight was gone and the sky turned to night, he checked his watch and saw twenty minutes had gone. He guessed they'd had time to go through the alphabet by now, and he made his way back up to the restaurant. When he got back, his friends were on another bottle of wine and hunched over their phones, talking and laughing.

'Any luck?' he asked as he took a seat back at the table.

'Not so far,' Jodie said, lifting her glass to her lips and taking a sip. 'But this wine is helping.'

Then Lewis startled everyone by crying out. 'I think I have something!'

All eyes turned to him.

'What have you got?' Blanco asked.

Lewis was beaming. 'Ah, I decided to try to think laterally instead of just hacking my way through the alphabet.'

'Think laterally?' Hunter asked.

'It just occurred to me that Lauren said Xavier was particularly devoted to the Gospel of John, remember?'

Hunter poured himself some of the wine. 'No, but do go on, please.'

'Thing is, the Gospel of John specifically details eleven promises concerning what true believers can expect from God if they have faith and devote themselves to the Lord. I tried to think like Xavier might have done all those centuries ago and figured that if I were him, I wouldn't have just used any old random number, but something special, with meaning.'

'So you tried a shift value of eleven and it worked?' Hunter asked.

'I think so, but it could just produce more non-sense like all the other ones we just tried. Let me see if it works.'

Hunter joined the others in the silent hope their teammate's speculation had been right. When Lewis cried out again and punched the air, they knew he'd been right.

'What have you got, Ben?' Jodie asked.

Lewis turned his phone around and showed them all. 'This: *ORMIVTRETS ENBI EDSPEGD NEARE.*'

As she typed the words into the anagram solver, Jodie said, 'Is that Latin or something?'

'It is and it isn't,' Hunter said. 'As I said earlier, it's an anagram, but if Ben's right about the shift value, it should now turn into a Latin sentence. Run it through the engine.'

'What do you think I'm typing?' she asked.

'Wait,' Lewis put in. 'When you type it in, change the V in the first word to a U.'

Jodie looked at him, her index finger hovering over the virtual keyboard on the phone's screen. 'Why?'

'Good idea, Ben,' Hunter said.

'I'm sure it is,' Jodie repeated. 'But why?'

Lewis answered. 'Because back in Xavier's day, they used the classical Latin alphabet which had no letter U. They used V for sounds made with a U, so today, any modern Latin that comes up in a search we do is most likely going to be using a U, so we're not going to find it if we use V. Type U.'

'I need another beer,' Blanco said with a long sigh.

Jodie nodded as she typed. 'V to U. Done.'

'What does it say?' Lewis asked.

They all peered closer at her phone.

'Er, there's about a thousand possible meanings.'

Lewis shook his head, gently plucking her phone from her hands as he spoke. He ran his eyes down the list. 'No, most of this isn't Latin. It's just gobbledegook. There are some Latin words here and there. Let me go down the entire list.'

'Good work, Ben,' Hunter said. 'We're looking for a phrase of purely Latin words. That's what Xavier would have started with.'

Blanco finished his beer and rubbed his stomach in satisfaction. 'That was a good meal. I just wish Amy and Lauren could have enjoyed it with us.'

'Me too,' Jodie said. 'I hope they're all right.'

'They'll be fine,' Hunter said. 'But not forever. I'm guessing Lundquist sees them as an asset right now, either for pumping information out of, or using to blackmail, us in some way, but when they're no longer useful to him, we can all guess what he might do. The name of the game right now is working out what

Xavier hid behind his encrypted handiwork and praying Quinn can find what we need. Any progress, Quinn?'

A deep sigh from the goth, this time expressing genuine annoyance. 'I won't say it again, Max.'

'Sorry.'

With Quinn's fingers still clattering over the keys, Hunter turned from her to Lewis just in time to see the former US Marine's eyes light up.

'You have something?' Hunter asked. 'Don't say you don't, because I can see in your eyes that you have something.'

'I surely do,' Lewis said, holding Jodie's phone up for everyone to see a specific, short sentence he had highlighted about halfway down the long list. 'This is the only sentence I can find that is composed purely of Latin words. It reads *AD MONTES IRE DEBET PEREGRINUS.*'

30

'You know what that means or do you want me to run it through a translation engine?' Jodie asked as he handed her back the phone.

'No need,' Lewis said. 'It's not difficult Latin. It says, "The pilgrim must go to the mountains."'

Blanco sighed with frustration, a rare thing, driven by the kidnapping of Amy and Lauren. 'And just what the hell does that mean?'

'We're the pilgrims,' Hunter said. 'Remember?'

Jodie rolled her eyes. 'Yeah, I think Sal got that much, Hunter.'

'I got that much, Max,' Blanco confirmed. 'And there is a hell of a lot of mountains in this world. It seems a little thin on detail to me, but then maybe that's just me.'

Sensing the rising dissatisfaction at the table, Hunter pushed his chair back and walked over to the restaurant's main window. Staring outside at the light evening traffic trundling back and forth in the night, he thought about what Xavier had written, a short riddle inscribed so long ago with the intention not of confounding someone in the far future, but of enlightening him.

The pilgrim must go to the mountains.

He imagined Amy and Lauren, probably bound and gagged and in some darkened room somewhere. Lauren would be terrified, naturally. Amy would be calm and measured, coolly taking stock of their situation and calculating options. Hopefully, those bastards had dressed her wound properly and administered some safe painkillers. She would know that the main option would be waiting for him and the rest of the team to rescue them. He knew she would be thinking that, counting on it.

We are the pilgrims.

Maybe Lundquist might figure out that Lauren was the academic expert and Amy was ex-FBI, with little to offer his quest. If he thought she was essentially disposable, then he might decide he didn't need the extra baggage. The thought made his blood run cold, but he dismissed it as insane paranoia. Amy knew how to talk to men like Lars Lundquist. She knew what to say to keep herself alive, no matter what it took. But still, she would be relying heavily on him to come and pull her out of whatever hell she was trapped in.

Yeah, I think Sal got that much, Hunter, he thought, hearing Jodie's voice in his head. As usual, she was right. But the problem was, which mountains was Xavier talking about? As Lewis was studying the Latin, he meandered back over and drank some more wine.

'Damn it if old Xavier wasn't a serious little cryptographer,' Hunter said. 'He hid his message behind four layers of code. Those trying to follow his pilgrimage must first find the inscription, then they must decipher a Caesar shift, then they must unravel an anagram, and if they do all that, they are then left with a cryptic clue.'

'Which now I think I know,' Lewis said.

Everyone turned to him once again. Hunter felt a strange mix of excitement, relief and disappointment. He wanted to get there first, but this was the American's speciality subject, after all. He slumped back down into his chair, hands in his pockets. 'All right, what have you got, Ben?'

'*AD MONTES IRE DEBET PEREGRINUS*,' Lewis began. 'We already know that the literal meaning of this is the pilgrim must go to the mountains, but this is cryptic.'

'As we also already know,' Jodie said.

'But then again, is it? I don't think so. I think it's literal, not cryptic. Put yourself in the place of Xavier and think like him. He was a highly religious man, devoted to the Lord. He was on a pilgrimage across Europe when such a thing was difficult and dangerous. He was doing this not only to humble himself before the Lord but also to leave this amazing trail of clues behind him, leaving it for the ages like a permanently unanswered question. But if you think like him, it gets easier.'

'Tell us how he thinks, Ben,' Blanco said.

'He thinks about the Lord God and his pilgrimage, and what he sees as his sacred duty to both protect Excalibur, but also to ensure it's not lost forever. And most importantly, he is, remember, on a pilgrimage, so that narrows things down.'

'He left Gargano for another religious site,' Hunter said.

'Exactly,' Lewis said.

'On the line of St Michael?' Jodie asked.

Lewis shook his head. 'I don't think so, not this

time. That would just be too obvious to nefarious types like Lundquist. This time, Xavier gives us a curveball. *Ad Montes* means "To the mountains", but we were wrong to think it was a cryptic clue. It also means something else, very literally, or more to the point, somewhere else. Xavier was telling us where he was going. Not cryptically, but literally. *Ad Montes* means Admont, as in Admont Abbey. When Xavier left this place, he went north to Admont Abbey.'

Jodie was the first to speak. 'You're sure?'

He shrugged. 'As sure as any of us ever can be.'

'And where is this place?' Blanco asked.

'In Austria,' Lewis asked. 'I know about it because it has the largest monastery library in the entire world.'

'Let's hope his next clue isn't inside a sodding book, then,' Hunter said.

Blanco finished his beer. 'In that case, it looks like we're off to Austria.'

'Wrong.' Quinn switched her computer off and pulled her hood down. 'That is unless you want to forget all about Amy and Lauren.'

Hunter's eyes flicked from Lewis to Quinn. 'You know where they are?'

Quinn linked her fingers together and slid petulantly down in her chair. 'Sure do, and it ain't Austria.'

After a long silence, Hunter spoke. 'So where is it? Where are they?'

'After leaving Mont Sant Angelo in the helicopter, Lundquist's team flew here, to Bari. From here, they took off on a private jet and flew to Ljubljana in Slovenia. From there they took off in another helicopter and flew into the Triglav National Park, a very mountainous area on the Slovenian-Austrian border. They landed at a private compound in forested foothills in a valley to the east of a small town called Bovec. Looks like Lundquist likes his privacy because it's about as remote a little nook as you can get.'

'Do we split in two?' Jodie asked. 'Three go to rescue Amy and Lauren and two go to the abbey?'

Hunter shook his head. 'I don't think so. That's inviting trouble. Quinn, are you sure they're all still there?'

'I can't be sure they're still there, but I can say they haven't filed any flight plans to leave the area by air.'

'How far is Bovec from Admont Abbey?' Blanco asked. 'You said this place was on the Slovenian-Austrian border.'

'Wait,' Quinn said, opening her computer back up. Less than thirty seconds later, she was back in the conversation. 'It's a four-hour drive across a lot of mountains and valleys.'

Blanco sighed. 'Meaning that if they already worked out what we now know about Admont Abbey, they could decide to drive there. They might already be on the road.'

'How can they know?' Jodie asked. 'Hunter said they'd never find the clue in the shrine.'

'That's right,' Hunter said. 'They don't have the clue.'

'Are you sure about that, Max?' Blanco asked.

'Yes, I'm sure. We go to Slovenia,' Hunter said firmly, trying his best to sound as authoritative and decisive as Amy. 'We go there and rescue Amy and Lauren. It's en route to the abbey, after all. If we get there and they already worked out about the abbey – and I still think that's impossible – then we just keep on going till we catch them up. One way or another, we're getting Amy and Lauren back and then we're finding whatever the hell old Xavier hid for us at Admont Abbey.'

31

Hunter felt a deep responsibility to get Amy and Lauren away from Lundquist and his men as fast as possible, and that meant prioritising their rescue over the trip to the abbey. For him, there had never been any question of chasing after Xavier's secrets before saving their friends. If they played their cards right, they could get their teammates back from Lundquist's Slovenian compound and somehow sabotage his mission too, stopping him from going to the abbey even after they had raided the compound for Amy and Lauren.

Everyone else had been on the same page. Their flight north to Slovenia's Julian Alps was spent planning the assault on the castle and working out the most effective way to break Lauren and Amy out while disabling Lundquist's capacity to continue his quest at the same time. That was optimal. After some private speculation about Excalibur's ancient provenance and the tremendous powers it may possess, he felt more acutely than ever that the Swedish relic smuggler had to be kept as far away as possible from any potential 'Avalon treasure cache', or anything else once belonging to King Arthur.

After a brief pitstop in Bovec to eat and drink and purchase some basic climbing gear at an outdoor sports shop, the team hired a car and drove east into the mountains. Chatter was muted and sleep came and went on the meandering drive, with Blanco at the wheel. He carefully navigated steep climbs and alpine switchbacks with the diligence and patience for which he was so well-known. Hunter watched the landscape glide past, sometimes with scrutinous eyes as he pondered an escape route from Lundquist's compound, other times in a blur as his mind drifted to his life, specifically his love life and the bottom-drawer mess he was currently making of it.

They pulled up at a site meticulously selected by Quinn and Jodie after a consultation involving the hacked blueprints of the compound and much debate over Google Earth maps. Jodie's input was focused primarily on her interest in ingress and egress strategies, and after some deliberation and a long examination of the blueprints and various online maps, she chose what looked to the others like the hardest route: right up the rockface to the compound's west.

Hunter knew why. Any guards Lundquist had stationed up there would be primarily focused on the main approach road, some lanes leading up to the place from the south, and also to a certain extent on some goat tracks trailing away up the slope to the north. No one in their right mind would select the western approach, but after a rigorous inspection of the topography, they had decided the ascent was possible, but only to experienced climbers.

'Which means Quinn stays in the car,' Hunter said.

'Like usual,' she said. 'Maybe I should learn to climb and then I'd get to do some of the exciting stuff.'

'Climbing takes experience,' Hunter said. 'And that comes after the initial learning.'

'And what's your experience?' Quinn asked.

'I've built up some time on the Swiss and French Alps over the years. Just a little hobby, but it keeps me in shape. Point is, you don't start that experience on a climb like the one we're going to do today. There's some rope work involved and some dangerous falls. I'm not happy with you attempting any of that without much more basic training under your belt. So yeah, like usual, you get to stay warm and cosy and monitor operations from the safety of a locked car.'

Quinn looked up at the mountain. The peak was obscured by thick grey clouds, and icy winds scoured the slopes sliding down beneath it. 'On second thoughts, I guess I can live with that arrangement.'

'I knew you'd see it my way,' Hunter said with a smile, which quickly faded when he turned and studied the climb Quinn had just looked at. To say conditions were not optimal was the understatement of the century. No sane climber would attempt this approach in weather like this, but the destination was nowhere near the notorious Death Zone where oxygen became an issue. From his estimation, it wasn't going to be what the army had taught him was a Class 5 climb or a technical rock climb. This was going to be somewhere between a Class 3 and a Class 4, which meant some intermediate scrambling on exposed terrain and some knife-edge ridges. Like Blanco and Lewis, Hunter had been trained by the military in the techniques required to make the ascent, and while Jodie had no such experience, he had no fears or doubts about her. Some of the urban climbs she had made to access locked buildings made his hairs stand on end.

'And it beats getting shot to pieces by Lundquist's team halfway up the approach road,' Blanco said, deadly serious.

Lewis nodded and smacked his hands together with anticipation. 'Looking forward to the workout.'

'And getting Amy and Lauren back,' Jodie said, pulling some rope from the back of the car.

Hunter joined her, grabbing a pre-packed backpack full of gear from the car. 'They're our priority. After they're safe, we can resume our search for Excalibur.'

'Whatever the hell that might be,' Quinn said with a shudder, turning to go back into the car.

Hunter slammed the car's boot down and stared up at the swirling clouds, hefting his pack over his shoulder. 'Yeah, whatever the hell that might be. Let's go.'

The lower slope was Class 1 level climbing, which meant simple walking on straight-forward terrain with no surprises. Ahead and high above, a quick scan through portable binoculars was still able to reveal the compound, but as they got closer to steeper ground, it began to slip from sight. It wasn't somewhere they would easily forget. Built in the traditional

Slovenian style, it was a large jumble of white buildings and red roofs with a round tower at each corner and completely protected by high, turreted walls. As the steepness increased and they moved through Class 2 into Class 3 terrain, the clouds swirling around the castle compound increased and then it was gone completely.

'Time for some rope work,' Hunter said, setting about breaking a trail up the rocks for the others to follow.

'This is already getting a little challenging,' Blanco said with a puff. 'Hope I can make it.'

'You can make it, Sal,' Jodie said. 'We need you up there. Amy needs you.'

'And look at it this way,' Hunter called down over his shoulder. 'Now you can slap breaking and entering an armed Slovenian castle via a Class 4 rock climb on your CV.'

'Resume,' Jodie said.

Hunter worked his fingers into a cleft in the rock and pulled himself up another two feet before fixing a cam into place and threading his rope through it. The spring-loaded camming device allowed him to slide it into the split in the rock and then release a trigger, causing it to expand and fix firmly in place. When the job was done, he called down to Jodie. 'Fine, resume.

I'm outnumbered three to one by Americans. I give in. I surrender. I'll do it your way.'

She laughed, whipping her hair from her face as she followed him up the face. 'There's a good boy. I knew you'd come round in the end.'

'And you'll be outnumbered five to one when Amy's back with us and we're down with Quinn,' Lewis said.

'Five to two,' Hunter said. 'Don't forget about Lauren.'

'Lauren ain't on the team, Chief,' Jodie said. 'She doesn't count.'

Hunter let it slide. If HARPA was ever unsuspended and put back to work, someone like Lauren had a lot to offer them, but he had his doubts she even wanted to join them. Going on the road with a team like this would upend her entire life. It wasn't her age. He knew Lauren was older than Quinn, so age wasn't the problem. It was more that she was building a serious career and had a future. He had no right to ask her to give that up to join an outfit that could get shut down by someone in the shadows at the drop of a hat.

And the truth, the truth he hadn't talked to the team about, was that right now he was more concerned about getting Amy and Lauren out alive. Worrying about any kind of future beyond that was pointless. Lauren was a passing interest and at her age, he should know better, but he had loved Amy and maybe he still did. Losing her to a psychopath like Lars Lundquist would be a crushing blow, from which he wasn't sure he could recover. It would certainly utterly break Jodie and Quinn, and of course, Blanco and Lewis would also be badly impacted, although, unlike Jodie and Quinn, the two men both had large, loving families to nurse them through the grief.

When Hunter reached the top of the rockface and saw the castle hove back into view, still partially obscured by snow clouds, he gave a silent prayer of thanks. After climbing over onto a safe ledge, he helped the rest of the team up. They drank water and ate some high-calorie snack bars and then checked their weapons. There wouldn't be another chance when they broke cover to make the final part of their journey and breach the castle via the southwestern tower. It was another climb, but this time only fifty feet and using grappling hooks, which was much less hazardous than what they had all just achieved by coming this far.

Blanco poked his head above the ridge line and took the castle in. 'Looks quiet enough.'

'As we suspected,' Hunter said. 'I'm expecting most of the guards to be on the other approaches, but that doesn't mean to say this section of the castle is going to be unguarded. This place is Lundquist's nerve centre, the little inner sanctum from where he runs his criminal enterprises, including buying and selling all his stolen and smuggled artefacts and relics. It's not just us coming to rescue Amy and Lauren he has to worry about. Imagine some of the kind of scum he's crossed to accumulate the sort of wealth that allowed him to live in a place like this. He'll have armed men all over the place, it's just that this approach will be the least protected. Unfortunately, that's the best deal we can hope for.'

'Thanks for the pep talk, Hunter,' Jodie drawled. 'I don't know about everyone else, but I know I feel a hell of a lot better after that.'

'Thanks for your input, Agent Priest,' Hunter said with a sarcastic smile. 'But I'm just trying to make sure we don't get too blasé about things when we get in there. Amy and Lauren are relying on us. So let's get on with it.'

With his words still hanging in the air, Hunter pulled a grapnel from his bag, fixed it to a length of climbing rope and began to swing it in an arc around his shoulder. When he'd built up the requisite momentum, he released the hook and watched it sail up into the air and over the wall. A second later it fell, and he heard its hooks scraping on stone. He tugged at it and felt it move a few inches towards him before coming to a firm stop. He pulled again to ensure it was safe.

'Looks like we're ready to rumble,' he said and began climbing up the wall.

When he reached the top, he cautiously poked his head over the battlement. Looking down, he was able to see the inner courtyard of the castle. He'd been in places like this before and presumed most of the guards stationed actually inside the castle would be sheltering from the storm inside the towers. Placing a hand on the crumbling merlon to his left, he swung around and beckoned for the others to join him. Then he pulled himself through the narrow embrasure in the turret and landed with a light thud on a walkway just inside the castle wall.

He used the time when the others were climbing the wall to assess the situation inside the castle in more detail. Opposite his position looked like the main part of the castle, a long rectangular building with a red tiled roof, whose white plaster walls were punctuated with small square windows, most of them dark. A handful were lit, and warm yellow light spilt out onto the snowy courtyard below. He saw a shadow pass across one of the windows. When the others were gathered around him, he briefed them on his findings.

'If Amy and Lauren are anywhere, it's got to be in there,' he said. 'It's right in the centre of the compound, so it's the most secure location, Second, there are no other lights on anywhere else around here except the watchtowers. Lundquist might be happy to keep his prisoners and hostages in the dark, but on a night like this, whoever guards them is going to want light and warmth.'

'Sound logic,' Blanco said, still out of breath from the climb up the wall. 'But between us and that main building, we have a courtyard overlooked by two watchtowers, not to mention any number of other rooms harbouring Lundquist's men.'

'Which are all hidden by the cloister,' Lewis said. 'Sal's right, we'll be walking right through the hornets' nest.'

Jodie shook her head, eyes all over the compound, scanning and assessing. 'Only if we do the dumb thing and walk right across the damned courtyard like a bunch of idiots. So yeah, we could do it the stupid way as Hunter suggests, or we could do it my way.'

'I don't see another way,' Hunter said.

She turned on him. 'That's because you don't know everything, and you're not the best at everything. It's because you look at things through the eyes of a soldier and an archaeologist. I look at things through the eyes of a thief, a cat burglar. I see different things, different options, including a better way over to that main building.'

Hunter sighed. 'Here we go again.'

'What do you see, Jodie?' Blanco asked.

She pointed out her proposed route to the main building with her hand as she spoke. 'First, we go along this wall to the southwest watchtower. When we're there, we have to fight our way past some of Lundquist's men. I get that. Nothing's perfect. But then, we go along the western wall until we're parallel with the main building. Notice that the height of the wall is lower than the main building's roof but higher than the balcony on its second floor. So we take the grapnel with us and when we're there, we throw it across the yard until it hooks on the balcony, secure our end of it and use it like a zipline.'

Blanco smiled and gave her a playful punch on the shoulder. 'And then we put the window in and we're inside. Do we know what's behind that window?'

She nodded. 'Yes. We know what's inside the window from the blueprints Quinn pulled up. It's a stairwell running up three floors, right there at the western end of the building. It literally couldn't be a better place to break in.'

'Great work, Jodie!' Lewis said.

'What do you think, Hunter?' Jodie asked. 'Does that kick the ass out of your plan or what?'

Hunter picked up the grapnel and gave her a sideways look. 'Let's get moving. Lundquist's out of here the second he finds out about Admont Abbey.'

32

Hunter led them along the top of the southern wall, crouching down behind the battlements where they had to stay out of sight until they approached the southwest tower. There was a door in the tower, flanked on either side by what was once two arrow slits, but today these had been converted into narrow windows. Amber light shone through them and lit the end of the walkway.

Hunter approached the one on the left and saw what he was looking for. He turned to the others as he waved them forward.

'Two guys playing cards,' he said. 'We have to take them both out at the same time to stop them from alerting anyone else. After we take them both out, we should be able to make our way along the western wall just like Jodie described.'

'Shit's looking up, right?' Jodie said.

Hunter surprised everyone by scratching the tip of one of the grapnel's hooks on the door.

'Max?' Lewis asked.

Blanco smiled. 'Stand aside, everyone, and let the good Dr Hunter work his magic.'

Hunter saw the men stop their card game and share a confused glance. Then he scratched the door again. One of the men laid his cards down and stood up from the table.

'One of them is coming,' Hunter said quietly.

'What are you going to do?' Jodie whispered.

'Have a heart-to-heart conversation with him about his poor decisions in life.'

The man opened the door and Hunter plunged the grapnel into his chest. It happened in less than a second, shocking Jodie and making her take a step back, clasping her hands over her mouth. Blood pumped from the man's heart and poured down his clothes. The other man pushed back from the table and reached for his gun. Hunter pushed the wounded man backwards with the grapnel and used him for cover as the other man fired on him. The rounds punched into his colleague's back, finishing him off.

As he slipped off the hook and fell to the floor, Hunter pulled the dead man's sidearm from a holster around his belt and fired into the other man's chest, knocking him backwards over his chair where he landed with a crunch in a tangle of broken chair pieces.

'Inside, now!' Hunter called out.

Blanco was last in, closing the door behind him. 'That was quick thinking for an unarmed man.'

'It was...' Jodie's eyes were fixed on the bloodstained grapnel hook. 'I don't know what it was.'

'It was a good job done,' Lewis said. 'Don't forget those bastards were part of the team holding Amy and Lauren hostage against their will.'

Hunter peered through the narrow windows. 'You think anyone heard those shots?'

Blanco shook his head. 'Storm's pretty strong tonight, Max. Maybe the sound of the wind covered them up.'

Hunter passed a hand over his face and sighed. 'Let's hope so, mate. A lot's riding on this one. Ben, grab one of their radios and listen out for what the rest of the bastards are up to.'

'On it.'

Hunter reached down and picked up the grapnel, wiping the bloody hook on the man's black combat jacket. 'It's time to move on. Follow me.'

'No, follow me,' Jodie said. 'This is my route from now on. My plan.'

Hunter yielded. 'That's fair enough. Here, take the hook.'

She looked at it and paused, then snatched it from his hand. 'I'm not afraid of holding this thing, Hunter, if that's what you thought. As Ben said, these assholes were on Lundquist's team, holding Amy against her will.'

'And Lauren,' Hunter said.

'Yeah, sure. Let's go.'

Hunter followed Jodie out of the tower's other door and stepped back outside into the stormy night. With Blanco and Lewis a few steps behind him, he tracked her path along the western wall until they were adjacent to the main building. By the time Blanco pulled up beside them, Jodie had already cal-culated the distance to the balcony and was swinging the grapnel rope around her shoulder, just as Hunter had done at the base of the castle's outer wall.

When she released the hook, it flew silently through the air, but she had misjudged the distance and the hook smashed the window and then flew right back out again, falling to the bottom of the western wall. Jodie ducked down behind the battlement, cursed herself and pulled the rope up as fast as she could.

'Damn it! You think anyone heard that?' she said.

'We wait and see,' Hunter said, crouching down beside her, as did Blanco and Lewis.

After a few seconds, Blanco spoke. 'I think we're good. Try again, Jodie.'

'You want me to do it this time?' Hunter asked.

'I do not,' Jodie said. 'I can do it.'

And she did. The second time, the grapnel landed on target, its hooks grabbing a firm hold of the balcony's ironwork. When she tugged on the rope, it pulled tight. Then she tied the other end of the rope around the top of the nearest merlon. 'Safe as houses, right?'

'If you say so,' Hunter said, casting a doubtful eye along the rope. 'That balcony looks a lot further away now I'm standing here looking at it.'

'You want Mommy to hold your hand when we go over?' Jodie asked.

'Just lead the way, Mum,' he said sarcastically. 'And after Ben and Sal have tested it out with their heavier weight, I'll be right across.'

Blanco laughed. 'I think I'd better go first, considering how long it's going to take me.'

'I'm going first,' Hunter said, serious this time. 'No

arguments from anyone. It's my fault Amy and Lauren are in there in the first place. If there's any problem with this rope or whatever the hell's on the other side of it, then it's my problem, not anyone else's.'

'I can live with that,' Jodie said. 'Where are we heading when we get inside?'

'They're probably hiding Amy and Lauren in the dungeon,' Hunter said.

'A dungeon?' Jodie asked. 'There was nothing like that on the blueprints.'

'It's a castle, Jodie. It's going to have a dungeon. Think of its resale value without one.'

Hunter didn't wait for any other replies and climbed out over the battlement. Giving the rope one last tug, he swung his legs over the edge until he was able to climb out onto it and make his way along it with a monkey-crawl. A few metres along, the height above the ground made itself known to him. Any slip, any fall, would be fatal. The balcony was on the second floor, but the main building was enormous, and the second floor was at least fifty feet above the ground. Worse, the ground in this part of the castle was a stone yard. If he fell, he'd land with a splash, breaking every bone in his body and exploding every organ. It was not what Hunter considered an optimum ending to his life.

The wind rocked the rope. He clung on, closing his eyes as the bitter, cold air howled around his neck and ears, clawing at his hands and whipping his hair around. He took a deep breath and continued his crawl along the rope. Halfway across, there was more give. He felt it as he bounced up and down more each time he moved. The extra give made this the hardest part of the journey, right over the centre of the western courtyard. The space between the castle and the wall where Hunter was clinging on for his life was like a corridor, channelling the icy wind against him and scratching at his face like razor blades. He paused to get his breath. Staring up into a freezing night rent by icy gusts, he caught sight of the silhouette of a man on the main building's roof. One of Lundquist's men was on guard.

Calling out would alert the others in the team, but it would also draw the guard's attention to his some-what precarious position on the rope, dangling help-lessly above the yard. He strained his neck to look behind him, checking if anyone else on the team had seen the guard, but no one was in sight. Maybe that meant they'd seen the man and had taken cover. Maybe not. Hunter knew he had no choice but to act. But before he could do anything, he heard the guard shouting down at him. He had seen the moonlight lighting up the long line of rope below him, turning it into a fine silver thread connecting the outer wall to the main building. Exactly where there should be nothing but darkness.

'*Vad händer där nere?*'

Hunter recognised the question. The man was asking what was happening down there. He decided to ignore him.

'*Är det du, Kjell?*'

Now he wanted to know if he was Kjell. Hunter remembered that name from the briefing. Then he called out again and Hunter craned his neck just in time to see him slope his shoulder and let his submachine gun slide down into his hands. Hunter acted fast. He had been on top of the rope in the traditional position used when monkey-crawling, but now he gently released some of his grip and let gravity swing him around like a pendulum until he was suspended under the rope, hanging on by both his ankles and the crooks of his elbows. Now he moved one arm down and reached for his weapon, the old SIG Sauer he'd stolen from the dead guard back in the watchtower. As the man cautiously made his way to the edge of the roof and switched on a powerful torch for a better look at what was transpiring beneath him on his watch tonight, Hunter brought the gun up above his head and prepared to fire.

His position under the rope meant the target was upside down now, and the angle of his arm and neck meant there was no way to aim properly through the sights. Instead, Hunter had to go by nothing but instincts and pray to the heavens there was only one armed man on that part of the roof. The man called out again, this time in English. This meant his suspicions were growing, and he no longer believed it had something to do with one of his colleagues.

'Who is that down there? Answer me or I'll open fire!'

Hunter went first, squeezing off three rounds in what he hoped was the right direction to hit the man. He was wrong. The rounds all went wide and gave the man time to crouch down in the darkness behind a chimney stack. Hunter heard a radio crackle and the man speaking in rapid Swedish. Then searchlights lit up the castle compound like a cross between Times Square and the Blackpool Illuminations. A klaxon began wailing in the stark, bright artificial light and the sound of slamming doors and boots crunching on gravel around the front of the castle filled every inch of the previous silence.

Hunter had little choice but to expedite his

journey across the gap. Pulling himself up from his position beneath the rope back into the monkey-crawl position was no easy thing to do. Special Forces and commandos trained hard to do it, and usually with a heavy pack on their packs. Hunter had also trained to do it back in the army when he was a Guards officer, but he'd been out of the game too long and no longer had the strength and stamina to pull himself around, at least not in the few seconds he knew he had left before the fireworks display started. Instead, he yanked himself painfully along the rope upside down, staring at the balcony as it inched closer to him in the bright, artificial searchlights.

Then the fireworks display started.

33

Amy stared at Lars Lundquist with hate burning in her eyes.

'Don't look at me like that, Agent Fox,' he said, reaching out for her hair and brushing it gently away from her face, where it was clinging to a cheek slick with sweat and blood. 'Anyone would think you no longer love me.'

She and Lauren were each lashed to a stone pillar in the castle's dungeon, wrapped deeply in the ancient building's gloomy, damp darkness. The only light was that of a large open fire, flickering in a gothic fireplace on the other side of the grimy cell. The only sound was that of the crackling flames in the hearth. Lauren was unconscious, her head limply hanging forward, blood congealed on her lip. Amy had not seen them do this to the young historian. It had happened earlier when they were in different cells. Now, the young historian seemed almost unconscious. Despite Eklund's attempt to clean and dress the flesh wound they had inflicted on Amy's arm, it still burned like hell.

'No one could ever love a creature like you, Lundquist,' Amy said coldly.

Lundquist nodded sagely as if perhaps there was some truth in the words she had just uttered, her voice thin and tremulous with fear.

'You might have a point, but then again, my love life is not the subject we are here to discuss tonight, as I am sure you know only too well. We are here to talk about the little competition we seem to have got into, your team and mine. The little treasure hunt that is proving to be so dangerous and difficult. And now, boring.'

'Tell me,' Amy said, working hard to control her voice and sound calm and in control. 'What could a disgusting piece of slime such as yourself possibly want with King Arthur's sword? If it's real, then Excalibur is a historic artefact, an archaeological wonder. Those things couldn't possibly interest a man like you.'

The men behind Lundquist shared an uneasy

glance. Their boss was unfazed by the question, so Amy deduced it was the subject matter that had caused their strange response and not the way she had just spoken to him.

'Is that what you think this is all about? History and archaeology?' He laughed out loud and walked over to the fire where he picked up a long, iron fireplace poker and began to rummage around in the hearth with it, jabbing sloppily at the chunks of half-carbonised wood and sending plumes of sparks and fresh smoke up into the chimney. Then, with some force, he rammed the poker deep into the hottest part of the fire and dusted his hands off, returning to Amy with a smile on his face.

'If not history or archaeology, then what?' she asked. Lundquist was standing right in front of her now but over his shoulder, she saw that same look on his men's faces once again.

'I wonder, I wonder...' he began, his voice softening to the point where it had almost a dreamy quality. 'Are you playing games with me, Agent Fox? Do you know more than I do? Or are you fishing for knowledge I possess and you do not? I wonder.'

Amy guessed it was probably about time to shut the hell up.

Lundquist looked over his shoulder at the poker,

mulling, judging, then he turned his head back and fixed his ice-blue eyes on hers. He frowned as he studied her, desperately trying to find the truth in her frightened eyes. 'Yes, I do believe I have you at some disadvantage, at least as far as what we are looking for is concerned. And yet, somewhat ironically, I believe that even though you don't know what this little treasure hunt will lead to, you are further along the path of clues than I am. This is amusing but frustrating, would you not agree?'

Amy's thirst for knowledge overpowered her tactical mind, the part of her telling her to keep her mouth shut. Instead, she asked another question of her captor. 'If not merely a historic artefact, then what is Excalibur?'

Lundquist nodded. 'A woman with a craving for knowledge is impressive, but what turns me on is a woman who desires power. Do you desire power, Agent Fox?'

'I desire justice, honesty, and decency.'

Lundquist stared deep into her soul before letting out a long sigh and clicking his fingers in disappointment. 'Wrong answer. And just when you were doing so well, too.'

'Go to hell, Lundquist.'

He nodded again and stepped over to the fire. He

pulled out the poker and was pleased to see the way its tip glowed bright orange in the darkness. Then he walked back over to Amy, the poker hanging almost effortlessly at his side.

'Tell me, are you in possession of a literary education?'

'I'm not answering any more of your questions, Lundquist.' When Amy spoke, she found it impossible to keep her eyes from wandering down to the red-hot poker in his hands. 'This is a law enforcement situation. You're a relic smuggler and a thief and a murderer. One way or another, you're going to spend the rest of your sad little life in jail.'

The men all burst out laughing. Lundquist quietened them and then lowered his voice to a creepy whisper. When he spoke, she felt his breath on her face. '"But the sword of Michael from the armoury of God was giv'n him tempered so, that neither keen, nor solid might resist that edge: it met the sword of Satan, with steep force to smite descending, and in half cut sheer; nor stayed, but with swift wheel reverse, deep ent'ring, shared all his right side: Then Satan first knew pain."'

Silence now descended over the dungeon. Amy felt the temperature drop about fifty degrees.

'What is that?' she asked. 'It wasn't you, that's for sure.'

'"Paradise Lost", by John Milton,' he said. 'To be precise, Book VI, Lines 320 to 327. Beautiful, is it not?'

'That's how come I knew it wasn't anything you came up with.'

'Quite so, quite so. Milton was a genius, and "Paradise Lost" was his magnum opus. I would never dare to keep company with such artistic and literary brilliance. My genius resides in an altogether different realm.'

The fire crackled. 'Why did you recite those lines to me?' Amy asked.

Lundquist grinned. 'You know why. You are a smart woman.'

'It began with a reference to the Sword of Michael? You meant the Archangel Michael?'

'I meant nothing. As I just told you, the poem was written by Milton, not me.'

Amy glanced once again at the poker. 'Then Milton was referring to the Archangel Michael?'

'Yes, of course. I see you're slowly putting two and two together. Perhaps with the right encouragement and guidance from me, you might even make four.'

Amy felt her stomach turn over. 'My God, you can't mean that Excalibur was...'

'That it was originally the sword of the Archangel Michael as given to him by God to drive Satan out of Heaven during the rebel war?' His face turned into a grisly smile. 'But oh yes, I think I can mean that. What's making four out of two and two doing for you? Hitting the right spot?'

Amy felt a shiver run up her spine. 'I can't believe it.'

'Ever wonder why King Arthur was so powerful? Ever wonder how come a regular sixth-century tribal chieftain who slept in a place made of animal dung every night ended up upstream of so many incredible legends, specifically concerning his amazing powers and strength? Legends that still light the world ablaze fourteen centuries later? You think that was because of a special kind of steel used to make his fighting blade? You think it was because he could bust some special moves on the battlefield?'

'This is insane. You're lying to me.'

'Take it or leave it,' he said sharply. 'But the truth is always so much weirder than fiction, don't you find? No one knows how, exactly, because the legends are so ancient and vague and diverse, but one way or another Excalibur was once the sword of the Archangel Michael. The very same blade he used to fight and cut Satan in the War in Heaven. Somehow, that sword came down through the ages until it ended up in the hands of King Arthur. And soon, it will be in my hands.'

'Like I said, insane.'

Lundquist's smile faded fast as he drew the poker up and held it in front of Amy's face, just inches away from her cheek. 'So, now you know what I know, but I still don't know what you know. This seems unfair and yet a moment ago you talked about the virtues of justice, honesty and decency. Does it seem decent and fair that I told you my secret and yet you're still keeping yours to yourself?'

'What secret?' Amy felt fear and frustration rise equally inside her. 'What are you talking about?'

'The secret of whatever the good Brother Xavier hid inside the shrine at Gargano, of course! Despite the best efforts of my men, we were unable to work out what he left there. For us, the trail runs cold at Gargano and yet as you may now appreciate, this is not acceptable. There is too much at stake. So you will tell me where the trail leads from Gargano or you will learn what it's like to be melted to death, starting with that pretty little face of yours.'

Amy flinched in terror as he raised the poker and slowly brought it closer to her skin. 'Get away from me!'

He grinned. 'But shall we start with your cheek, your lips, your nose or your eyes?'

Things changed fast when everyone's radios crackled, jumping to life in a burst of static, and then panicked voices. Then a klaxon sounded.

Lundquist whirled around to his men, still wielding the poker in his hand. 'What the hell is that?'

A man was on his radio. When he finished, he turned to his boss. 'We've got trouble.'

34

Hunter was under heavy fire by the time he reached the balcony. Only his team's cover fire, blasting at the guards from their position on the outer wall, saved his life. That was one way of finding out they were still alive. Grabbing hold of the balcony's iron bars, he was able to release his legs from the rope and hang down beneath it. Then he heaved himself up inside the small ledge on the inside of the balcony. Overhanging iron gutters above blocked the guards' view of him and gave him the time he needed to smash in the rest of the window and climb inside the building.

Quinn's blueprint analysis was on point. He was standing inside a giant stairwell, lit now only by the powerful external searchlights out in the yard. He looked outside, into the chaos. He caught a glimpse of Lewis's head as he returned fire on the men on the roof. Then he heard boots pounding on the stairs above him. The guards had seen the rope and calculated where he had broken into the castle. A deep explosion rocked the yard outside. Another look through the window revealed an enormous cloud of smoke spewing into the air above his team's position. Masonry and dust had been sent flying in every direction by the blast and were now raining down over the courtyard like a re-enactment of Mount Vesuvius. The other end of the rope he had used now fell limply away from the outer wall and tumbled down to the ground, useless.

He cried out to his friends, but there was no response. He felt sick. Had he just watched almost his entire team get killed by a well-aimed grenade explosion? The boots smashing into the steps above him got louder and were joined now by the angry voices of men screaming and shouting orders for him to stay where he was.

Hunter thought that was a bad idea. He turned and fled down the stairs, pistol in hand, leaping three steps at a time until he reached the ground floor. The place looked how he'd imagined it. Greystone tiles on the floor, grubby plaster walls that were once white but now more of a stained brown colour. Its long history was all around him in everything from the old-fashioned electric switches to the smell of damp pervading the air he breathed. When he tried to make contact with the team outside, there was nothing but static on his radio. With the fate of his team still clawing at his mind, he pushed on in search of Amy and Lauren.

Thanks to Quinn's research, he knew where to make that start. The blueprints hadn't specified a dungeon, but there had been some kind of basement or cellar and that was where he wanted to start his search. Recalling the image of the blueprints in his mind, he made his way along the corridor and made a left halfway along it, turning into a narrow flight of stairs leading down into darkness. Gun in hand, he used the silent darkness to take out his radio and call the team. The only response he got was Quinn's quiet voice, outside in the forest in the car.

'Is that you, Max?' she asked.

'The one and only. Quinn, the team got hit. Try and get hold of them, see if they're okay. I'm on my way down into the basement, alone.'

'What do you mean they got hit?'

'One of Lundquist's men got lucky with a grenade. I didn't see the moment of the explosion, but I was just quick enough to see the results. They're not answering the radio.'

'I'll try and get through. I can also check to see if their cell phone signals are still active and if so, where they are.'

'Thanks, Quinn. For now, we have to work on the assumption it's just me and you.'

'Find Amy.' She cut the line, in true Quinn style. Hunter pocketed the radio and continued down the stone steps leading into the basement. He had been right in his speculation that this place had once been used as a cellar, noting empty wine racks lined up against the far wall. To their right, in the corner, was a small wooden door. He saw it was ajar and decided it was where he needed to go. He crossed the cellar and headed towards what he presumed was the castle's dungeon, fighting hard to push away thoughts of the grenade explosion. It was safe to say things were not going to plan. His team were possibly injured or worse, his only method of escape – the rope – was well and truly busted, and the only chance Amy and Lauren had, if they were still alive, rested on him, as if he could single-handedly take on a small army of Swedish special ops guys.

Oh, happy days.

He moved on, pushing open the door and

checking behind it. A set of stone steps vanished into the darkness ahead of him. He switched on his torch and stepped down inside, acutely aware of the responsibility resting on his shoulders. He made the bottom of the steps and felt a noticeable drop in temperature. This was subterranean, he knew it in his heart. This was the dungeon. He crept along, staying close to the wall on his left, the naked lightbulbs dangling from black wires here and there in the ceiling throwing his shadow out along the corridor like something out of a horror movie.

He heard a woman scream. It sounded like Amy. At once, his mind was flooded with conflicting emotions. He felt fear and rage at the thought of her being tortured by Lundquist and his men, but at least he knew she was alive. That was a much better feeling. It also told him where to head, like some kind of homing beacon.

As the scream faded, he heard men's boots smacking on the stone tiles, and he pulled up to a stop in a dark section of the corridor, equidistant from two of the lightbulbs. He never saw the men, but heard a door open and shut and then the sound of their boots receding into silence as they clambered up another staircase somewhere ahead of him to his right. He breathed out a sigh of relief. The longer it took these guys to rumble his location, the better. Staying quiet and still tucked in tight next to the wall, he moved forwards, forging ever closer to his fear-stricken friends and their demented captors.

He waited in the corridor until certain the coast was clear. Then more voices, subdued and tense, came from up ahead. He moved on and came to a room on his right. It was in darkness, but he crossed the corridor and checked it out all the same. Seeing nothing except a cold fireplace and some old furniture, he resumed his trek forwards, ever deeper into the castle's dungeon.

Ahead, he stumbled across the staircase he'd heard the men using. He was surprised to see it went not only up to ground level, but also further down. The dungeon had at least two levels. When he heard another scream echoing up the steps from below, he gauged more precisely where Amy and Lauren were being kept and instantly made his way down the circular staircase. The cramped, dusty space was lit not by lightbulbs but by candles set inside tiny alcoves punched into the stone wall as it curved its way down ever deeper into the castle's darkest recesses.

The voices were louder now, discernible even over the klaxons. He heard Amy's voice as clear as day. She was talking to Lundquist but there was no sign of Lauren. Lundquist being down there also meant his immediate protection officers were as well. Stig, maybe. Berg. No way of knowing. Hunter knew he was going to have to take them all on if he were to rescue his friends, and that meant freeing Amy and Lauren as a priority and getting at least one of them armed. That would even up the fight a little.

The men's boots faded on the staircase and he knew it was time to go on. There was no point trying Quinn. Two-way radios and cell phones couldn't work down here, deep underground. There was no signal. It was up to him now. Out of nowhere, the sound of a slap resounded sharply up the stairwell followed by Amy screaming again and then men laughing.

That just about did it for Max Hunter.

'Brace for action, Max,' he whispered to himself. 'You're going in.'

35

Hunter approached the bottom of the stairs, a torch in one hand and a gun in the other. He knew how many bullets he had in the weapon. He'd counted them in the magazine when he'd liberated it from the man in the watchtower and counted off how many he'd used since then. The answer was nine. That was the limit of his firepower at the current time. It didn't fill him with confidence, but at least he had the element of surprise. The klaxons and searchlights told Lundquist he was inside the compound, but it was a big place. No one knew he was right on top of them, so now was the time to unleash hell.

Peering inside the open door at the base of the steps, he saw a large room, made entirely of stone, with an ornate fireplace in the wall to his left. He was disturbed to see carvings of demons' faces decorating the mantelpiece. Their evil, twisted little faces stared back at him and sent a shiver down his spine. Beside the fire hung a large tapestry depicting some hideous scene of beasts eating humans. Even worse than the demon gargoyles, Hunter decided.

Across the chamber, several stone pillars were supporting the ceiling, and tied to two of those pillars were Amy and Lauren. Lauren was unconscious, her head slumped down against her chest. Amy was alert but wounded. He saw blood on her face and what looked like a bruise forming around her right eye. There was a bandage around her upper arm. Someone on the Swedish team had at least dressed her gunshot wound.

Standing in front of Amy, he saw Lars Lundquist from behind. It looked like he was holding a hot poker. Closer to the fire, he saw Berg and Stig, as he had thought, but no sign of anyone else. He guessed Lundquist's other guards had been down here enjoying the show until the klaxon went off and then he'd ordered them up top to find the intruders. That was who he'd heard clambering up the stairs like a herd of wildebeest.

Three-on-one. He could handle that.

Hunter charged into the room, raising his gun and firing on Stig, who was closest. From such a close range and assured of a hit, only one shot was necessary. That shot tore through Stig's head and killed him on the spot. Lundquist and Berg immediately bolted, whirling around and reaching for their weapons. Lundquist simultaneously hurled the poker at Hunter and scrambled for cover behind the pillar to which he'd lashed Amy. Hunter sidestepped the poker, which clanged on the stone floor and slid to a halt by the wall, its hot tip igniting the tapestry.

Berg was behind Lauren's pillar, leaning out and firing on Hunter, who now scrambled for the cover of another pillar. He couldn't fire back in case he hit Amy or Lauren, but neither of the men could stay hidden behind those pillars forever. Flames were now racing up the tapestry, producing a thick cloud of noxious smoke, which began to fill the dingy cell. The fumes brought Lauren back to life in a wild coughing fit, but like Amy, she was too far away from Hunter for him to be able to untie her hands. Smoke inhalation was a problem for everyone now, but the cloud of smoke was also providing some cover. It was a fog of war Hunter was determined to use to his advantage.

He crouched, filled his lungs with air and rolled into the smoke on his right. The heat from the burning tapestry seared his face as he came to a stop and oriented himself. Lauren was closest, coming around with a raspy cough just as he had predicted. Amy was obscured by smoke. Berg was behind Lauren's pillar, but still firing in the same direction at Hunter's previous position nearer the entrance. Hunter fired through the smoke and flames, striking Berg in the shoulder and dropping him to the stone floor. He landed with a thud and a cry of pain but swivelled around and fired at Hunter's new position.

The archaeologist was ready, shifting further to his right and returning fire, this time ending the Swedish Special Forces sergeant with a bullet in the brain. The big man slumped on his back, an anti-climactic end to a twenty-year career, Hunter considered. Lundquist had fallen silent and could be anywhere in the smoky dungeon. It didn't matter, Lauren was beginning to pass out again, her renewed state of unconsciousness certainly induced by smoke inhalation. Hunter jumped to his feet and ran to her, tearing at the knotted rope lashing her to the stone pillar.

'You're going to be all right, Lauren. It's me, Max.'

She tried to smile. 'Better late than never, right?'

'There, you're free.'

She rubbed her wrists as the rope fell away to the floor. 'Thanks.'

'One down, one to go.'

Hunter weaved across the room, using the pillars for cover until he reached Amy. 'What's a nice girl like you doing in a place like this?'

She managed a confused smile, almost not believing he was there. 'Max? How did you find us?'

Hunter fumbled at the rope, scanning the dungeon for any sign of Lundquist. 'How do you think?'

Amy smiled more broadly. 'She's pretty amazing, isn't she? Is she safe?'

'Quinn's outside in the car. She's fine.' Hunter paused as Amy's hands broke free from the rope. 'The others are waiting for us at her position.' It was a lie, but there was nothing else he could say to her. If the team were injured or worse, she didn't know about it in here. Not now.

Amy frowned. 'They sent you in here alone?'

A savage impact of a bullet striking the stone pillar inches from her face shook them out of their conversation and into action.

'We can talk about it later,' Hunter said. 'Right now, we have to get the hell out of here. Back into the smoke.'

There were no arguments as the three of them ran back into the burning smoke, once again vanishing from sight. They heard gunshots roaring in the darkness as Lundquist opened fire on them from somewhere across the darkened dungeon. His bullets punched into the smoky cloud but missed their mark.

'The door's over here!' Hunter said. 'I think.'

At the entrance, he heard Lauren screaming. When he turned, he saw Lundquist had somehow tripped her up in the smoke and she was on the floor at his feet. He was training his gun at her head and laughing insanely in the hot smoke, his face smeared with sweat. Amy screamed, but with no weapon, she was helpless and had no way to protect Lauren. Hunter raised his gun and fired, hitting Lundquist in the lower arm and knocking him off-balance. He fell to the floor and dropped his gun. Amy knew what to do. She ran forward, snatched up the weapon and pulled Lauren to her feet.

'We're gone, now!' Amy cried out.

Hunter had reached the door and now called out to them like some kind of beacon. When they were outside in the corridor, they strained and heaved to get their breath back. Lauren's cough was deep and ugly, but she managed a shaky thumbs-up when Amy asked her if she was going to be all right.

'Which way?' Lauren asked through the coughing.

'This way!' Hunter said, leading them to the staircase he had heard the Swedish team use earlier when he was on his way to the dungeon. 'It goes back up to ground level. C'mon!'

For a few moments, they enjoyed being alone and not being under attack, but their silent reprieve didn't last long. Within a few seconds of running up the stone steps, they heard men screaming from both below them and above them.

'Looks like we're in deep shit,' Hunter said. 'Again.'

Lauren looked from Hunter to Amy. 'Which way do we go?'

'We're going up,' Amy said firmly. 'No more screwing around. Down means a dungeon but up means out. Everyone clear?'

Hunter nodded. 'You've got your boss hat back on again, haven't you?'

'You bet your ass I do,' she said. 'Move!'

Hunter decided against telling Amy this was technically a UNESCO mission and that he was the lead officer. Something about the look in her eyes told him to keep his mouth shut. And then there was the fact she was a better leader than he was, more dependable and less prone to flighty, off-the-wall decisions.

'You got it!' he said. 'C'mon, Lauren! We're out of here.'

Fear filled the staircase as they ran upwards, knowing they would soon meet whatever contingent of the Swedish team had been sent down to protect Lundquist and extinguish the fire in the dungeon. Amy was up ahead, and she saw it first – shadows bobbing on the wall as the enemy descended the steps on their way down towards them. She raised Lundquist's gun into the aim and pointed it up at the candlelit void ahead. The first man ran into view and she fired, punching a hole in his stomach. He grunted in pain, dropped his weapon and fell to his knees with a look of shocked horror on his face.

Another man charged forward, bravely leaping over his fallen comrade before unleashing a wild fusillade of gunfire from an automatic weapon. Hunter thought it sounded like a Steyr but didn't care enough to think about it. He tucked himself into the internal curving wall for cover and returned fire. Amy fired too. Their first shots streaked up the wall in a shower of sparks and masonry dust, and then they heard muted, meaty thwacks as their rounds drilled into the man. The next thing they knew, he was tumbling forward past them on the steps, his face covered in blood.

Hunter stuck his boot out and arrested his fall. Then he picked up the Steyr and tossed Lauren his handgun. 'Here, for self-defence if things get tricky.'

The young historian reached out but fumbled for the gun. It slipped through her fingers and smacked on the stone step at her feet. She grinned awkwardly and reached down, snatching it up and holding it loosely in her hand, barrel pointing right at Hunter.

'Lower the gun, Lauren,' he said. 'Keep the business end pointed to the ground at all times and your finger outside the trigger guard unless you're in real trouble. The last thing we need is one of us taking a bullet in the back from friendly fire.'

'Sorry,' she said with a nervous smile as she pointed it to the ground. 'It's safe now.'

'But we're not,' Amy said. 'We still have a good way to go if we're going to get out of this madhouse.'

They started back up the stairs, their options rapidly running out. At ground level, Hunter knew he could reach Quinn on the radio but decided against it. If the team had been killed in the grenade explosion, he didn't want Amy and Lauren to know about it until they were out of danger and away from the castle. At the top of the steps, he saw a door and reached out to yank it open. He raised the Steyr at the same time and prepared to open fire, but there was no one ahead of them, just another empty corridor.

Tension rose like poison in their veins as they walked slowly down the passageway, the klaxon still blaring all around them. Behind them, they heard the anguished screams of Lars Lundquist as he cried out for his men to help him. The arrogant, sinister tone of his voice had gone and was replaced with a hollow-sounding terror as he faced a hideous and painful death down in the smoky dungeon.

'Should we go back and get him?' Lauren said. 'I mean, hand him over to the police or something?'

'No!' Hunter and Amy said together.

They carried on down the corridor. 'Is that ethical?' the young woman asked.

'If you want to live, it's ethical,' Hunter said. 'The smoke is already spewing out of the top of the staircase. Getting him out of there would mean going back down those steps, in thick smoke, and under heavy fire from his soldiers. There's no way to do it without proper breathing equipment. When we get out of here, we'll call the emergency services anyway – police, fire, paramedics. They can sort it out. We have somewhere else to be.'

Amy looked at him. 'You know where Xavier went next?'

'We do, but first let's just focus on getting out of here, agreed?'

Hunter reached the end of the corridor and opened another door. It was an outside door and when he opened it, a blast of icy air whipped across them from what looked like another courtyard. This time, two men were running towards them, guns at their sides.

Hunter swung the Steyr up and opened fire, raking them with a wild volley of rounds and killing both instantly. Their bloody corpses fell onto the slick flagstones. Lauren screamed again, and almost dropped her gun.

'Anyone else around here?' Hunter asked, peering into the yard. The klaxon blared and searchlights crisscrossed over the castle walls looming high above the yard.

'Not that I can see,' Amy said.

'But which way is out?' Lauren asked. 'I was unconscious when we arrived.'

Amy turned to her and smiled. 'I'm glad you asked that because I was wide awake. Follow me.'

Hunter and Lauren followed Amy across the yard to another door. She opened it and ran inside. Hunter was a step behind her and followed her into a darkened room. 'What is this place?'

'It's some kind of a cross between a warehouse and an office,' Amy said, opening a cabinet on the wall behind a desk. 'When they brought me here, they dropped off the keys to the car and handed it to someone working at that desk. Lundquist is former

Special Forces, remember? This entire castle compound is run exactly like an army base.'

'So this place is the QM?' Hunter asked.

She looked at him. 'Huh?'

'The Quartermaster,' he said, looking down the
long line of shelves full of tinned food and blankets
and other goods. 'They control the acquisition and
distribution of supplies to an army base. By the looks
of it, this guy's also controlling the vehicles... checking
them in and out.'

'Got it!' Amy said, pulling a set of keys from a hook
in the cabinet. 'Follow me. The garage is down here, at
the far end of this room.'

Hunter ran after Amy, Lauren at his side. They ran
down the long room, past rows of dull, perforated
metal shelves filled with basic goods – coffee, tea,
flour, blankets and batteries. Now, up at ground level,
he saw through the windows that the sky had broken a
little and moonlight was pouring in, leaving ghostly
stripes along one of the walls.

'Where are we meeting the others?' Amy said,
speedily moving down the aisle. 'Did you say they
were out with Quinn?'

'Yeah,' Hunter said after a short pause. 'That's the
plan.'

Amy reached a door at the far end. She paused,

took a breath and kicked it open, gun raised into the aim. 'Clear!'

Hunter followed her into the garage. Their shoes smacked on the polished concrete floor as Amy made her way over to a Humvee. She turned and winked at Hunter. 'The obvious choice, right?'

Hunter returned her smile. 'It's certainly obvious to me, at least.'

'Everyone inside!' Amy said, swinging open the driver's door. 'Lauren, you're up-front with me. Max, you take the rear.'

'Really, Amy. Not in front of Lauren.'

Both women rolled their eyes in perfect synchronicity. Hunter feigned innocence. 'What? Really, what?'

'Get in and buckle up, Max!' Amy said. 'And get ready for the fight of your life.'

36

Amy hit the gas and sent the Humvee surging backwards towards a double wooden door. The six-thousand-pound metal beast tore the doors from their hinges and shredded what was left into matchwood. As the explosion of dust and splinters blasted out into the air, the Hummer finished its exit from the garage and spun around in a tight circle.

Hunter turned in the back seat and blew out the rear window with the Steyr. Shooters were firing at them from more than one direction, but the exact number was impossible to know. Searchlights streaked across the castle and its grounds. The klaxon roared. He spun the Steyr and smashed out the re-maining glass with the gun's stock, then glanced outside across the moonlit yard for a clue. It came when he saw a muzzle flashing up on the southeast watch-tower, the same one he had attacked earlier on their way in. He spun around until he was pressed into the rear door of the Hummer and then fired through the broken rear window at the tower. The rounds traced across the darkness, chewing into the stonework around the watchtower and driving the armed guards back inside.

A moment's respite.

'Max, where's Quinn parked up?'

It was Amy. She was calling out from the front, the wheel spinning through her fingers as she slammed her foot on the gas pedal and sent the Humvee racing towards the castle's main entrance. The courtyard doors were old and wooden and fortified with thick, decorative iron hinges stretching across each panel. Hunter watched it approach at speed through the gap in the two front seats. He also watched Lauren shield her eyes at the last moment before impact. He did the same thing just as another shooter fired on the Humvee, punching holes in the rear panel and shat-tering the side window behind his head, scaring the hell out of him.

'Just get out of here!' he called back.

Amy piled the Humvee through the gates, blasting

them into long chunks like surfboards as the heavy vehicle powered through them and into the outside world. She spun the wheel again, barely keeping the driver's side wheels on the ground as she steered sharply to the right and headed down a winding track lined on both sides with tall black fir trees.

'Max?'

'Keep going, Amy,' he said. 'She's parked up halfway down this road, I think.'

'We'd better hope so,' Lauren put in, staring out of her window in horror. 'Because I see trouble, guys. Two motorbikes riding at speed through the trees off to our right.'

'What the hell?' Hunter turned and looked through the smashed side window. As he squinted into the moonlit forest, a maze of moonlit trunks and shadows, it took a few seconds to find what she had described. Then he saw them. Two men riding off-road motocross bikes. They were hard to make out, wearing black, including their helmets, and both had compact machine pistols slung over their shoulders. Hunter saw the moonlight glinting on the guns' metal bodies as they tore through a clearing and turned to head down the slope towards the Humvee.

'They're heading towards us!' Lauren said.

'Who is it?' Amy cried out. 'Can you see them?'

'No,' Hunter said. 'They're wearing crash helmets, but it sure ain't Stig or Berg.'

Hunter twisted in his seat and pushed himself back until he was able to get a good shot through the smashed window. 'This is not a good development! Can you get a shot at them, Lauren?'

She shook her head and looked at the bikes racing towards them. 'I don't think so! They're moving too fast.'

The rider at the rear deftly pulled his gun from his shoulder and with one hand still gripping the handlebars, he extended his arm fully and opened fire on the Humvee.

'Down!' Hunter yelled. 'Take cover!'

The last thing he saw before cradling his head in his hands and ducking down below the window was Lauren crouching down in her seat, just out of the line of fire. Amy hunched up instinctively, but her job at the wheel stopped her from taking full cover. Bullets flew everywhere, some pinging off the coachwork, others punching holes in the metal. Sparks flew. Lauren screamed. Amy spun the wheel and turned away from the riders, so now the Hummer's rear was facing them, giving Hunter a clearer shot, but the change in direction had taken them off the track and out into the forest.

Amy struggled to avoid tree trunks as they zoomed up to her in the darkness, her headlights flashing on the trunks and boughs. In the rear, Hunter fired on the riders with the Steyr, almost cutting one in half and sending him tumbling out of his saddle and smashing into the trunk of a giant fir tree. The riderless bike revved wildly as it drove over a fallen trunk and then left the ground, flying through the air for a few seconds before crashing down in a crumpled heap on the forest floor.

'Way to go, Max!' Amy yelled, spinning the wheel and weaving the Humvee through the dense woodland. 'One down, one to go!'

'If I could see him, maybe,' Hunter called back.

Lauren rose from her crouching position and took a look around. 'Is it over?'

'Not yet,' Hunter said. 'I got one of them, but the other one has gone free range. You see him?'

She shook her head. 'No, sorry.'

Amy gasped. 'There! He's up ahead, heading right for us!'

Hunter climbed back over the back seat and began to pull his upper body outside. When he was out in the night, he pulled the Steyr up into position, the lower branches of the firs whipping at his face as he tried to get a clear shot at the rogue rider up ahead of them. Seeing the rider weaving in and out of the trunks like a ghost, he struggled to aim the Steyr. It was a compact weapon, but heavier than a handgun, and its weight and recoil made it harder to fire at arm's length. He took a shot, a short burst, but missed. The rider whipped out his machine pistol and unleashed a longer burst of bullets, firing indiscriminately at the Humvee. Rounds tore up the bonnet and raked into the windshield, punching another line of holes across the glass.

He heard Amy and Lauren cry out in response and felt the vehicle sway wildly from side to side, its front right bumper just clipping the trunk of a tree and tearing off into the night. For a second he feared Amy had been hit, but then she called out and asked him if he was okay.

The rider zoomed past them, firing up the side of the Humvee before vanishing into the woods behind them.

'I'm okay!' Hunter slid back inside the car. 'I'm all good, I think. You two?'

'We're fine,' Amy said.

'Speak for yourself,' Lauren mumbled. 'Are we any closer to Quinn?'

Hunter craned his neck and stared out at the forest

ripping past in a blur outside the Hummer. 'Bugger knows if I'm being honest.'

Another burst of gunfire, this time blasting out the rear lights and shredding one of the tyres, sending Hunter tumbling down into the footwell and dropping the Steyr.

'Bollocking hell!' he cried out.

'What's up, Max?' Amy turned for a second and saw he was missing. 'Max?'

'Dropped the gun,' he said, fumbling around for it in the dark.

'Tree!' Lauren cried out.

Amy's eyes were back up front, just giving her hands time to spin the wheel hard to the left and clip the trunk with the side of the Hummer. The violent change of course knocked Hunter back down into the footwell.

'Ditch!' Amy yelled. 'Hold on tight!'

Lauren screamed as the Humvee ploughed down a steep slope covered in pinecones and dead branches. When the front tyre rammed up against a boulder, the front axle nearly broke and sent Hunter surging forward in between the two front seats. He grabbed hold of the headrests just in time to stop himself from flying through the shattered windscreen.

'Hello, ladies!'

'Damn it, Max,' Amy said. 'Can't you get this ass-hole off our tail?'

He climbed into the back, gun in hand. 'It's not like you to use bad language, darling.'

Amy ignored him, vigorously handling the steering wheel to avoid another trunk. Down below them, they saw moonlight flashing on the water.

'The river!' Hunter said. 'Quinn's parked up by a river. Keep going.'

Amy turned. 'Keep going? Are you sure? I was going to pull up so we could enjoy a moment in the moonlight.'

Before Hunter could find an apposite reply, Amy drove the Humvee out of the forest and skidded across a slope of scree before scrambling down the last few yards and hitting the river. The passengers were tossed around like dolls but fared better than the motocross rider, who tried to swerve to a halt before losing control on loose scree. As the bike raced out from under him, he fell and rolled head over heels until landing headfirst among a jumble of boulders jutting out from the surface of the river.

Amy grabbed Lauren's gun and poked it out of the window, but Hunter called out, 'Wait – I think he's already dead!'

The Englishman kicked open his door and made

his way over to the rider, the Steyr gripped firmly in his hands. Wading through the knee-high water, Hunter called out to the man.

'Get out of the river and put your hands up.'

Nothing.

Hunter went closer and saw why. He turned his head and shouted over his shoulder, 'He broke his neck in the fall!'

'Then let's get out of here,' Amy said. 'Where's Quinn?'

Hunter looked up at the sky and saw a narrow line of stars hemmed into place by the firs on the banks on either side of the river. Finding the pole star, he worked out which way was west. 'I think we parked up over here, on the north side of the river. A hundred yards or so up the slope. Let me just check the depth of the river.'

After seeing it was shallow enough for the Humvee, he joined Amy and Lauren and they drove across the water and then made the last few yards up the slope on the opposite bank.

'Max?' Amy said.

Hunter had been gazing out of the window, still wondering what he was going to say to Amy if Quinn was alone and there was no sign of the others. Now, he looked up, concerned about something in the tone of Amy's voice.

'What's up?' he asked.

She didn't need to reply. When he looked at her, his eyes moved naturally to what she had seen up ahead of them, parked up at the side of the road. 'Bloody hell.'

Lauren stared at the sight, speechless.

'Pull over!' Hunter said and opened the rear door. When the Humvee was parallel with the smoking, burned-out wreck of their SUV, Hunter jumped out and ran over to the back window, staring inside through the broken glass into a carbonised void. His blood had turned to ice when he first saw the wreck, but the absence of Quinn's skeleton calmed him down again. Slowed his heart, which had been quickened by the thought of seeing her dead inside. When the wave of relief had washed away, he turned to the Humvee. Amy and Lauren were outside now, walking over to him.

'Max?' Amy's voice was weak, trembling. 'Please tell me that—'

'She's not inside.' It was all he had to say.

Amy's eyes teared up, and Lauren comforted her. Hunter didn't know what to think at first, but his indecision was ended by the crackling of his radio. He fumbled for it and barked into the microphone. 'Jodie, is that you?'

'It ain't the Easter Bunny, Hunter.'

Another wave of relief. 'Thank God you're okay. What about everyone else?'

'We're all good. After the grenade, we broke into two teams and gave them all the hell we could, to give you time to get in and save Amy and Lauren. You did that, right?'

'I did. They're both safe and with me now.'

'Finally, some good news. Where's your current position?'

Hunter explained that they were where they had parked earlier. 'But there's a problem.'

'What kind of problem?' Jodie asked, her voice darkening.

'Just get over here, and then we'll talk.'

37

The drive to the border was hard. No one had wanted to leave Quinn behind, but however much they argued, they all knew they had no choice.

'If only we knew what had happened,' Amy said, her hand balled into a tight fist. 'That's half the goddamn problem. Not knowing.'

'We know someone got to her and then torched the car,' Hunter said. 'That's more than enough for now.'

Blanco was at the wheel, cruising a hired Toyota Highlander along the forested main road to the Austrian border. 'Whoever did it wanted her alive. That's what is keeping me going right now. She's all right, I can feel it in my heart.'

'Yeah,' Jodie drawled. 'Until Lundquist pulls her out of his top hat to blackmail us with.'

'That's presuming he's still alive,' Hunter said. 'He got shot in the dungeon and there was a hell of a lot of smoke down there when we left. I never saw him in the chaos outside when we broke out of there, either.'

Jodie stared out of the window at the cars on the other side of the motorway. 'There are others on his team, Hunter. Others who'll carry on his work. If Lundquist isn't alive, then one of his other psychos has still got his hands on Quinn. All I'm saying is maybe they'll try and use her to blackmail us.'

'We'll cross that bridge when we come to it,' Hunter said.

After a pause, Lewis spoke up. 'You're presuming it was Lundquist who took her.'

Hunter rubbed his shoulder, still injured from being thrown around in the Humvee. 'What are you getting at, Ben?'

'Nothing. Just thinking out loud, but it seems to me that the Swedish team were up to their necks in trouble trying to stop you from rescuing Amy and Lauren, and also fighting a rear-guard action against the rest of us at the same time. Not sure when they had the time to spare to go out to the forest, make a search for the SUV, drag Quinn out and set fire to it.'

'Then who?' Blanco asked.

Amy said what everyone was thinking. 'You think the Illuminati took her?'

'Maybe.'

Hunter wasn't so sure. 'Wait a minute. Let's think this through. If that's true, it would require the Illuminati not only to have been stalking us across Europe but also to have made the decision just to snatch Quinn and leave the rest of us alone. Why would they do that?'

The car fell silent and no one spoke for a long time. Hunter drifted in and out of sleep with Amy's words echoing in his head. It was nothing more than speculation, but maybe she had a point. It was very unlike Juliette not to return a call, especially during an emergency. And Lewis had made a good point about Lundquist's men being stretched too thin during the attack to be able to spare the men needed to comb the forest and find Quinn. With these thoughts haunting his mind, he pushed his head back and tried to sleep, but it was no good. Instead, he just stared ahead and tried to make sense of what was fast becoming the most confusing and chaotic mission they had undertaken.

In the driver's seat, Blanco kept the wheel steady as they crossed the border and headed into the Austrian dawn. The Benedictine abbey was just over the eastern reaches of the Alps and drawing closer by the second. Their journey seemed to take forever, but eventually, Hunter's tortured mind gave him some respite. He felt his eyelids getting heavy and decided to give in to it. When he woke, the landscape of forests and mountains had transformed into a pastoral, rolling terrain of wooden farm buildings and soft, un-dulating meadows. Dawn light had painted everything a fat, buttery colour and turned the entire scene into something like a dream.

'Ah, we're in the *Sound of Music*,' Hunter said with a yawn. 'How lovely.'

Jodie pulled a cigarette from a crumpled packet and slipped it in her mouth. When she spoke, it wob-bled up and down. 'Another classic Max Hunter aphorism.'

'Just saying,' Hunter said. 'I'm full of wisdom, after all.'

'Yeah?' she drawled. 'That ain't all you're full of.'

'And try this for size,' he said, ignoring her. 'Ever thought about giving up those things? You're a long-time dead, Jodie.'

'They help with my anxiety levels,' she said bluntly, sparking it up. 'I'll quit when I leave this team. For now, they stay.'

'Can they stay away from me?' Lauren said, winding down the window. 'They smell like shit.'

Jodie ignored her completely, closing her eyes and tipping her head back against the headrest.

'When can I get out of here?' Lauren asked, waving the smoke away from her face.

'Not long,' Amy said. 'I hope Professor Hofbauer can be of some assistance when we get there.'

Hunter turned and frowned at her. 'Professor Whobauer?'

'You were sleeping,' Amy said. 'I called ahead and told her we were a UNESCO team researching Xavier of Normandy. She wasn't too happy about the wake-up call, but when I explained the urgency she seemed interested and keen to help. She's the head librarian but also the on-site historian. She just finished writing a history book about Admont Abbey, so if she can't help us, then no one can.'

'Excellent work,' Hunter said. 'I was going to suggest calling ahead and arranging something like that, but I wanted to see which one of you would come up with it. You win, Amy.'

'Gee, thanks.'

Lauren coughed again, waving more smoke from her face. 'Am I getting some oxygen any time soon?'

'You sure are,' Blanco said. 'Because we're here.'

Hunter gazed through the windscreen and saw the road they were on sloping down towards a chocolate-box town surrounded by forested mountains. 'Nice.'

'Wilkommen nach Admont,' Amy said. 'Where's the abbey?'

'Up ahead in the middle of the town,' Lauren said, staring at her phone. 'It's not far.'

Blanco reduced the speed a little further as they cruised through the sunny town and crossed a junction onto a tree-lined road.

'I see it,' Amy said. 'It's the next right, Sal.'

'Got it.'

Hunter's eyes caught a red and white sign on his right: Benediktinerstift Admont. 'This is it, all right. Get ready, everyone.'

'There's that observational genius of yours again, Hunter,' Jodie said. 'I don't know how you do it but I'm sure as hell glad you're on our team.'

Blanco smirked as he drove the Toyota through the gates and into the car park at the front of the abbey. He killed the engine and sighed with relief after the long drive through the night. 'All right, folks. Looks like Max was right. This is the abbey. Let's get on with it. The sooner we get this done, the sooner we're going to find Quinn.'

'And Xavier's Arthurian treasure,' Lauren said, her eyes glinting.

'Quinn first, dear,' Amy said. 'Quinn first.'

The Turning Seit

And Sophia Arthurian feared her Hunter and her eyes glaring.

'Don't understand,' Amy said. Quinn the

38

With Amy's words about Quinn still echoing in his mind, Hunter climbed out of the car and slammed his door. The car park was a sun trap and even the sun's early rays felt warm and good on his back as he stared up at the abbey's twin towers, looming high above the ancient compound that sprawled around them in various buildings and quads and tree-peppered gardens.

'The very definition of a sanctuary,' he said.

'It's just a shame we're not all here to see it,' Amy said quietly.

'We'll get her back,' Blanco said. 'We got you and Lauren back, didn't we?'

She looked up at the sky and sighed. 'I guess so,

but she's more vulnerable and we're not even sure who took her.'

'As I said, we'll get her back. C'mon, let's get into the library. That's the best thing we can do right now if we want to help Quinn.'

Hunter remembered the burnt-out wreck back in the black Slovenian forest. The smell of charcoal, burnt metal and melted plastic. The paint, peeled and pocked all over the destroyed SUV and the blackened foliage and scorched tree trunks around the car. He imagined what Quinn must have gone through while he was inside rescuing Amy and Lauren from Lundquist. His mind also wandered onto the subject of exactly who was responsible for burning the car and snatching the young goth. With all of this whirling in his mind, he'd barely had time to consider what Amy had told him about Lundquist's cryptic reference to John Milton, to the Archangel Michael and the provenance of Excalibur, far more ancient and holy than anything ever written in traditional Arthurian lore. It seemed to match up with some of the things Xavier had written about it. If even a shred of it was true, they could be playing with the most dangerous fire any of them could ever imagine.

Putting it aside, he followed Amy inside the abbey and after buying their entrance tickets, they made their way into the world-famous library. Dating from the 1700s, the physical building was constructed many centuries after Xavier had lived and worked at the abbey. Sunlight streamed in through high windows and shone on its intricate baroque interior. Finding Professor Frida Hofbauer working on some cataloguing at the end of the library, where the front desk had told them she would be, Amy made the introductions.

'I was surprised when you called,' Hofbauer said. 'I must say, working with UNESCO is a first for me, so I'm excited to be of any assistance if I can be.'

'We're very grateful for your time,' Amy said.

Hofbauer looked at the bandage on her arm and frowned. 'What happened to your arm? It looks serious.'

'Oh, it's nothing,' Amy replied. 'Just a scratch.'

Amy changed the subject and explained a little more about their mission, carefully avoiding too much detail concerning what Lundquist had told her back in the castle. 'We're on the trail of a Benedictine monk named Xavier of Normandy. We believe he came to the abbey in the thirteenth century and spent some time here, living and working and writing.'

Hunter spoke up. 'We believe he may have left a message here, something very specific concerning his pilgrimage across Europe during that time. We think the message he left, if indeed he did leave such a thing, will be cryptic, or encoded in some way.'

'In other words,' Amy continued, 'we're asking where might Xavier have been able to leave a message, especially one that could stand the test of time and still be readable so many centuries later?'

Hofbauer's eyes widened with excitement. 'Well, certainly not in the library here. This place is famous for being the largest library inside a monastery anywhere in the world, with over two hundred thousand items in various collections, seventy thousand items of which are carefully kept right here, inside the main hall we're gathered in right now... But it was built in 1776, so it wasn't even here when your mysterious monk was passing through.'

Hunter stared up at the ceiling mosaics and then over to a large bronze statue depicting four strange figures of various sizes. 'Shame he never saw that.'

'It was created by the Austrian sculptor Joseph Stammel,' Hofbauer said with pride. 'The four figures represent the final four chapters in life – Death, Judgement Day, Hell or Purgatory and then finally Heaven. It's a baroque masterpiece, naturally. But as you point out, Xavier never saw it, or anything else in here.'

'We want to know where he wrote his little clue,

not where he didn't write it,' Jodie mumbled under her breath.

Hofbauer never heard the comment and continued talking with a pleasant smile on her face. 'Do you have anywhere in mind that your monk may have left his clue?'

'The last place he left a clue was in a shrine,' Lewis said.

Hofbauer turned and pulled on a section of the bookshelf to reveal a hidden staircase.

'Whoa, secret tunnels,' Jodie said. 'I like it.'

'There are four of these hidden around this main section of the library,' Hofbauer explained, picking up a small box of papers. 'I must put these on the first floor, and then I have something to show you. Follow me, please.'

Hunter and Amy exchanged a sly glance and then joined the rest of the team now following Hofbauer up the secret steps. At the top, they found themselves standing behind a balcony rail with an elevated view across the library. From up here, the entire place seemed larger and brighter, almost as if it were outside. Daylight shone in through the ornate windows and illuminated the baroque frescoes stretching over the ceilings, giving the place a serene, almost heavenly atmosphere.

'This place is truly amazing,' Lewis said. 'Almost like a heaven on Earth.'

'It has a long and rich history.' Hofbauer deposited her papers on a shelf and turned to face them. 'Originally founded in 1074, it has seen its fair share of disasters, including wars and even a devastating fire that destroyed much of the original buildings. However, many of the oldest papers were saved and kept in a special archive. This is not normally open to the general public, but in your case, I think we can make an exception. I don't want to disappoint you, but I don't recall seeing anything there written by anyone of the name Xavier of Normandy, but as you say, he may have left some sort of cryptic message that flew right past my eyes. Perhaps this would be the best place for you to start.'

'Sounds like a plan to me,' Hunter said. 'Please, lead the way.'

The short journey took them along the upper floor, down a second hidden staircase and then through another door, which Hofbauer opened with a key card. They followed her along a narrow, windowless corridor and then down a short flight of steps into the archives. The Austrian academic walked along the shelves, each one loaded with bundles of paperwork and sorted by age until they reached the oldest section in the room.

'Here,' she said. 'This part of the collection was gathered together from the very earliest days of the abbey. Some of the manuscripts go back before the abbey to the eighth century. There is a great deal of material here, as you can see. There is not so much written by monks specifically during the thirteenth century, which is, of course, what you are hoping to find. This small section contains everything we have from the monks here from the abbey's founding until the fourteenth century. Having said that, if there is any trace of Xavier here, it will be in this section.'

'Thank you so much,' Amy said. 'We'll be as quick as we can.'

'Don't we need some of those groovy white gloves when we handle this stuff?' Jodie asked.

'Not at all,' Hofbauer said. 'It's not the abbey's policy to use cloth gloves when handling these ancient documents. It's a myth that they're better for old texts. They reduce dexterity and increase the likelihood of a document's page being bent or torn, and they also soak up sweat and oils from the hand and transfer them to the page. Our only policy is washed hands, which you can do in the sink in the room behind you, and then, of course, a great deal of care. I'm afraid you cannot take anything with you, and you will be searched on the way out. You may take photos of what you find here.'

'Again, many thanks,' Amy said.

Hunter saw Hofbauer to the door and then closed it after her with a gentle click. Then he turned. 'All right, let's get going. We'll divide up everything from the relevant era and go through it with a fine-tooth comb. Whoever finds anything written by Xavier of Normandy gets a warm congratulations from me and maybe even a vague mention in a footnote when I write up my paper on this mission for UNESCO.'

'But that's too generous, Hunter,' Jodie said. 'Really.'

'Just start looking,' he replied. 'We want to be out of this place as fast as possible. Quinn is still out there somewhere.'

Amy nodded. 'All the more reason to get going.'

The search lasted an hour. Each member of the team went through their section of papers carefully and methodically, but nearly everything still had to be referred to Hunter or Lauren for verification that it was or was not Xavier's handiwork. After a break, they went back to work, and it was half an hour after that that Lauren cried out excitedly.

'I got it,' she said. 'This is Xavier's work, right here.

I recognise the handwriting from his journal back on Mont Saint-Michel.'

'Are you sure?' Amy asked. 'His name's nowhere to be seen.'

'It's not signed by him,' Lauren said. 'But remember what Professor Hofbauer said? She had no recollection of anything written by a man called Xavier. But even if not signed, I know in my heart this is him. I've studied him for a long time.'

'But what is it?' Hunter asked, moving over to her and taking a look for himself.

She angled it for him to view. 'See?'

He frowned. 'Doesn't look like his writing to me.'

'No, not the main text. This is the work of another monk, a man named Brother Olbrecht. See his name here?'

He squinted. 'That says Olbrecht?'

She laughed. 'Yes, it says Olbrecht. It's in gothic script and this is a ledger he kept – a ledger of transactions between the abbey and the local population. Fruit, vegetables, honey, that sort of thing. But look in the margins.'

Hunter followed her finger as it went down the page and stopped in the margin to tap on a different kind of handwriting. 'Xavier?'

She gave an enthusiastic nod. 'Right, our old

friend Xavier of Normandy also kept himself busy by checking over Olbrecht's work. And yet here, he seems to have written something quite different from the general business of the ledger.'

'It looks cryptic again.'

Blanco spoke up. 'I read about some kind of cypher monks used back in the day. Something to do with writing a code in a special kind of numeral. Is it that?'

Lauren shook her head. 'That was Cistercian monks. Xavier was a Benedictine monk. But good thinking.'

Blanco shrugged. 'I should stick to pizzas, I guess.'

'And it's not cryptic,' Lauren said. 'Look again, Max.'

He leaned in closer until Lauren's head brushed against his shoulder, drawing an eyebrow raise from Amy across the room. 'You're right! It's written backwards, that's all. We need a mirror.'

'Surely you of all people have a vanity mirror, Hunter?' Jodie asked, making Amy laugh.

'I do not,' he said.

'Use my phone,' Lauren said. 'If we angle it the right way in the light, it can act as a mirror.'

Lauren held the phone as Hunter angled the document until he could see its reflection on the small screen. 'It reads, "*Salve iterum, viator commilito! Ibimus ad insulam vitream bibendam?*"' He turned to Lewis.

'Ben, looks like it's your time to shine again.'

The young American walked over and looked at the reflection. Then he chuckled. 'This Xavier guy had a good sense of humour. I think I'm getting to like him.'

'What does it say?' Amy asked.

'It says, "Greetings, fellow traveller! Shall we go to Drinking Glass Island?"'

'And what's the meaning of that?' Jodie asked.

Lewis shrugged. 'Sorry, I'm Bibles and Latin.'

Everyone looked confused, except Lauren.

'I think I know what this means!' she said. 'It's a reference to a Welsh place name.'

Hunter looked at her, smiling. 'Lauren, didn't you study Welsh as part of your undergraduate degree?'

'Literary Welsh so I could read ancient poems and mythologies, yes. It's a little different from modern spoken Welsh, but that's not relevant here. I believe this is a reference to a Welsh place name, but it's written in Latin. Either way, I think I know what it's about, but I'm no expert.'

'You're as close as we're going to get to one around here,' Amy said. 'What does this mean?'

'If I'm right, then Drinking Glass Island is a reference to Glastonbury.'

Hunter frowned. 'I thought the Welsh name for Glastonbury is normally translated as "Isle of Glass".'

Lauren frowned. 'Yeah, if you're getting your material from Wikipedia, which I sincerely hope you are not, Dr Hunter!'

'Moi? Never.'

She gave him a sceptical look. 'The cheap translation is the Isle of Glass, sure, but that's not exactly right. The Welsh word for glass is gwydr. The Welsh name for Glastonbury was Ynys Wydryn, which means Island of the Drinking Glass. In the Welsh language, there's a grammatical function called mutations in which the first letter of a word can change depending on the context, and in the case of the letter "g" it can disappear altogether. This is why Gwydryn means drinking glass, but it's Ynys Wydryn.'

'That's as clear as glass,' Jodie said.

Hunter looked at Lauren. 'You think Xavier knew about the Glastonbury Labyrinth?'

Her eyes lit up. 'Just imagine! What if he returned Excalibur to King Arthur's burial place... and remember, the tower at the church there is St Michael's Tower.'

'There's that name again,' Amy said.

Jodie sighed. 'Old Xavier sure liked to keep things consistent.'

'Wait,' Lewis said. 'What's the Glastonbury Labyrinth?'

'We'll talk about it later,' Hunter said. 'Right now all we need to know is that it looks like Xavier's next stop after Admont Abbey was Glastonbury.'

'And that means it's our next stop,' Amy said. 'We need a plane to England. Now.'

39

When Quinn finally came around from unconsciousness, the first thing she experienced was a heavy and violent wave of nausea. She fought it hard, but then gave into it and threw up all over the floor. Her head was spinning, but she already felt better. She knew the worst of it was over.

After cleaning up her mouth with her hoodie sleeve, she blinked in bewilderment at her new surroundings and tried to work out where she was. She was sitting on a low-cut carpet. There was no furniture and no windows. Maybe she was on a boat. No, a plane. Whatever it was, something was moving. A gentle hum that grew louder and clearer when she pressed her head up against the wall. Engines. Turbulence. The pressure felt wrong and she quickly satisfied herself she must be on an aircraft.

Her mouth was dry and she tasted copper. She badly craved water. In the hazy dizziness, she tried to claw at her shredded memory and retrace what had happened. The last thing she remembered was sitting in the car out in the woods in Slovenia. The rest of the team had gone into the castle. She was waiting back at base, which in this case meant the SUV. She was on her computer, trying to hack into Lundquist's database inside the castle, seeing if she could glean anything further that might help the others.

Then what happened?

She closed her eyes, felt a headache slowly building.

A shadow moved in the trees. Then it was right beside her, a few inches from the side of the car. It was all coming flooding back. The figure of a man, dressed in black. He swung a rock at the window and smashed it, showering her in fragments of broken glass. She screamed as he reached into the car and opened the locks. Big, heavy hands, black leather gloves. Then he swung the door open. She swung her legs up to kick him. He grabbed one of her ankles and yanked her out of the car like a rag doll. Her head cracked against the car door sill and nearly knocked her out.

She remembered another figure, stalking out of the trees and across the narrow track towards the car. Still firmly gripping her ankle, the first man dragged her further away from the vehicle. The second guy raised a machine pistol and opened fire at the petrol tank, detonating the fuel inside and triggering a massive explosion that instantly wrecked the car. Then she felt cloth move over her mouth. The noxious smell of some kind of chemical overwhelmed her memory and she came jumping back to the aircraft. The here and now.

Her heart was racing at the mere recollection of what had happened.

She looked around and took more in. Her hands were not tied but her computer was nowhere to be seen. The plane rocked in the sky, almost rolling her over and momentarily inducing another wave of nausea. Then, the door opened.

'Agent Mosley, you're awake at last.'

Quinn blinked. The light in the corridor behind the man was bright and reduced him for the time being to a mere silhouette.

'Who are you?' she croaked, her voice as dry as brittle kindling.

She saw now that he was holding his hands behind his back, calm and relaxed. He stepped into the room and she saw his face for the first time. He was in his late fifties, clean-shaven and well-groomed. Short, grey hair with a perfect parting. Nothing remarkable about him at all.

'You can call me Jophiel.'

'You piss your parents off or something?'

He smiled warmly. 'My parents did not give me that name, Agent Mosley. Jophiel is my Society name. It was given to me by the master. It is a great honour.'

She let the comment pass. The truth was, she wasn't sure what to say or do without the others around her. She had never been in a situation like this before and she knew only two things. One, she was scared, and two, she was never going to let this guy or anyone else responsible for kidnapping her know it.

'Where are we?'

'Forty-thousand feet above the North Atlantic. Yes, you are very far away from your friends. And no, no one is coming to rescue you.'

'Why have you done this?' she asked at last. 'Why did you kidnap me?'

He frowned. 'Alas, I fear I have greatly disappointed the master. You see, my orders were to seize the entire team, but we were a little late to the party. By the time we located your presence in Slovenia, the others had already engaged with Mr Lundquist's little army. I made an executive decision on the ground to extract only you, as you were, well, all alone out there in that dangerous forest. The others will surrender when they know we have you and then they will turn themselves over without a fight. Was it not Sun Tzu who once wrote that the supreme art of war is to subdue the enemy without fighting? I think it was.'

When he smirked, Quinn felt a shiver run up her spine. 'Who is the master?'

'When you ask such a question, you automatically supply yourself with the answer. The master is the master. He is the High Lord of our Society.'

She rubbed her temple, the pain behind her eyes growing fiercer. 'What do you mean when you keep saying that? Are you talking about the Illuminati?'

Jophiel took a deep breath and looked as though he wanted to clear the air. 'Such a lowbrow term to describe what we are. But yes, I suspect we are what you would call the Illuminati. Sadly, the word cannot even begin to describe what we are and what we do. I suspect the next few days of your life will disabuse you of any previous preconceptions you may hold in that regard.'

'I'm not afraid of you.' It took everything Quinn had in her to bring the words out, but she did it with an even and level voice.

'But what is fear?' Jophiel said quietly. 'There are things in this world which would terrify you so much, you would no longer wish to live just to avoid the smallest chance of ever having to face them. But if you don't know of these travesties and horrors, how could you fear them?'

Before Quinn could reply, Jophiel rose to his feet and walked to the door.

'We land in less than an hour. If I were you, I would take that time to give sincere thanks you got this far in your life without knowing of these things, because that innocence is soon to be speared like a ripe fruit. You will never be the same again.'

When he closed the door of the tiny cabin, Quinn felt the nausea return, but this time it was caused by fear, not the drugs or turbulence.

Outright, rank fear.

40

Glastonbury Tor rose out of a morning mist like an ethereal apparition. At the top of the terraced, grassy hill, standing in perfect isolation on the Somerset Levels, was the ghostly St Michael's Tower, the only remaining ruins of a fourteenth-century church destroyed in 1539 during King Henry VIII's Reformation.

Lauren stared up at the enigmatic hill through the windscreen of their car as they approached via a road to the east. 'The original church was built way back in the eleventh century, but it was destroyed by an earthquake in September 1275. The hill is generally believed to be manmade, and some say that deep inside it is a maze called the Glastonbury Labyrinth. They say the site was chosen because it's on a ley line.'

'Why does it look like the tower is floating?' Jodie asked.

'It's a phenomenon caused by the mist called Fata Morgana, which is an Italian term deriving from Morgan le Fay, or Morgên y Dylwythen Deg in Welsh. Both mean Morgan the Fairy. She was a powerful enchantress from the legendarium of King Arthur. But in reality, the floating effect is caused by the bending of light rays as they pass through various levels of air at different temperatures.'

'Kinda wish it was floating,' Jodie said, lifting her phone to snap a picture. 'It's cool.'

'Everything to do with the Arthurian legend is cool,' Lauren said. 'That's why I study it.'

Amy said, 'On the drive down here, I was reading about someone named William of Malmesbury who wrote all about Glastonbury in the fourteenth century. I never found any reference to Xavier though.'

Lauren gave her a look, her eyes slightly frowning suspiciously. 'I don't think so, Amy. William of Malmesbury was a twelfth-century historian who wrote a work called *On the Antiquity of the Glastonbury Church*.'

Amy fixed her eyes on Lauren, unblinking, and

looked annoyed at having her research challenged by Hunter's student protégé. 'This article says it was written in the fourteenth century.'

'Then that article is wrong,' Lauren said with a cold smile. 'William was born around 1095 and he died around 1143, which is considerably earlier than the fourteenth century. He spent his life worshipping God as a monk in Malmesbury Abbey and wrote the work for an old friend of his, the Bishop of Winchester, Henry of Blois. Correct dating of historical figures and works is a pretty basic skill for my discipline and a very important one. Otherwise, you're just working with rubbish.'

Amy switched her computer off and sighed. 'Normally, Quinn would be looking into this. Sal, you got any vacancies at that restaurant of yours?'

Blanco smiled warmly. 'Sometimes it starts to sound great, doesn't it? No more 5 a.m. wake-up calls. No more getting shot at. Just the best ingredients in town and the smell of freshly baked margaritas. Tell me I'm crazy.'

'You're not crazy,' Amy said. 'Would Angelo let us call it Blanco & Fox?'

'I like that. It has a nice ring to it.'

'We could sell cocktails.'

He laughed. 'There go the profits.'

After a short silence, Jodie cleared her throat. 'I have a question. If the whole damn hill is a manmade construction to fit in with the ley line theory, that's cool. But you're telling me a site of this level of conspiratorial theory interest exists and no one ever thought about blasting it with ground-penetrating radar? I find that hard to believe.'

'That's because ground-penetrating radar has been used on the hill,' Lauren said. 'But only in specific locations. One team carried out such an exploration around twenty years ago, but focused their search on two areas just to the east and west of the tower as part of an investigation into the tower's stability.'

'They find anything interesting?' Lewis asked.

'Yeah, like gold?' Jodie said.

'No gold, but they did locate a fissure in the rock which was filled with masonry before the tower was built.'

Jodie started flipping through her phone. 'Gripping stuff.'

Lauren smiled thinly. 'Gripping or not, the point is that as far as I know, there has never been a comprehensive exploration of the entire local topography with ground-penetrating radar.'

'Even though the "Glastonbury Labyrinth" was

built by man?' Jodie said with an eye roll. 'Archaeologists, right?'

'Mainstream archaeologists, Jodie,' Hunter said, coming to Lauren's defence. 'You have to remember the way academia works. The Glastonbury Labyrinth, if it's really inside this hill, is no more than a theory, and a conspiracy theory at that. If you want to fund a nice three-month field trip, you don't go to your boss and talk about sh— I mean, stuff like that. You talk about safe stuff, and the bottom line is the Glastonbury Labyrinth is a theory based on the terraces you can see right now, running down the side of the hill. To the guy who's going to rubber stamp your funding request, Glastonbury Tor is a natural hill that was shaped artificially on the outside, and that's the end of it. They're not buying any sh— I mean, stuff about labyrinths and mazes and underground bunkers and tombs holding the remains of mythical leaders like King Arthur.'

A frown formed on Jodie's face. 'What are we talking about again?'

'Max is trying to explain why teams of academics haven't comprehensively covered the entire tor with ground-penetrating radar,' Lauren said. 'And he's right.'

'Naturally,' Hunter said, with an exaggerated head wobble.

Lewis spoke up. 'You said back in Austria, and again on the plane, that Arthur might be buried here. Now we're here, I'd like to hear a little more about it.'

'Sure thing,' Lauren said. 'I'm always only too happy to speak history with a fellow nerd.'

Lewis laughed. 'Thanks, I think.'

'In terms of the legendarium surrounding King Arthur, the significance of this site cannot be underestimated. It's a key part of the entire myth.'

'Except it's not a myth, not any more,' Hunter said.

'No, I keep forgetting that. It's a lot to take in. Anyway, as we discussed briefly back in Austria and on the plane, this place here is essentially the Isle of Avalon, Avalon coming from *afalau*, the Welsh word for apples.'

'So, it's the Isle of Apples?' Jodie asked.

'Right, and this entire area is one of the best places in England to grow fruit, so I guess there were a lot of apple orchards here back in Arthur's day. Just thinking about this place when it was an island in the middle of a vast lake takes my breath away.'

'Lake, as in Lady of the Lake?' Blanco asked.

Lauren gave a little shrug. 'Maybe, but there are

other contenders for that coveted place, including Dozmary Pool on Bodmin Moor in Cornwall, two lakes in Snowdonia – Llyn Lydaw and Llyn Ogwen – the River Brue in Somerset and even some locations in France. But since all this turned from myth to reality for me back in Mont Saint-Michel, my heart tells me it's right here in Avalon.'

'What happened to Drinking Glass Island?' Jodie asked.

'It's an old story,' Lauren said. 'It's been called many things over the centuries. Anyway, back to Ben's question. Arthur's association with this place is very well-known, coming as it did right at the end of his life. There's a debate here. Some scholars have argued that Arthur died at the Battle of Camlann in the year AD 542, which is believed to have been at a site called Slaughterbridge near the River Camel in Cornwall. The etymological base there is kamm, which means crooked in Cornish.'

'Wait while I make a note of that on my phone,' Jodie said sarcastically.

'Please go on, Lauren,' Lewis said, glancing at Jodie. 'It's fascinating. Really.'

'I think so! Thanks to the work of Geoffrey of Monmouth, legend holds that it was at Camlann that

Arthur was fatally wounded in a desperate fight with Sir Mordred, also known as Modredus, who fell at the same battle too. After the battle, the king's body was moved for burial. Like anything else relating to Arthur, there are competing theories about where this place may have been, including at Camlann itself where today there is a dolmen burial site with a Roman inscription declaring it to be the tomb of Arthur, but the most accepted theory has always been Glastonbury. Right here on the Isle of Avalon... or Drinking Glass Island. Whatever you prefer.'

'How can you be sure that the Camlann tomb is not the right place?' Amy asked.

'Because when it was dug up in 1586 it was found to contain the remains of soldiers who most likely died fighting for King Egbert of Wessex when he was attacking Cornwall way back in AD 825.'

'Decisive?' Blanco asked.

Lauren nodded. 'Camlann was never the burial site of Arthur. I've always favoured Glastonbury as the burial site. There is a theory that the monks at Glastonbury cooked up the entire story to raise funds for their abbey after a devastating fire in 1184, but I'm not buying it. First of all, monks of that period were especially devout and solemn. It's not likely they perpetrated fraud on this scale just to raise the cash needed for their abbey. Add to that the scandal that would break out if their lies were ever to be discovered. It would be enough to end their vocation as monks and see them packing. On the flip side of the argument, there's much more tipping the scales in the other direction.'

'You mean, advocating that Glastonbury is the site of the tomb?' Lewis asked.

'Yeah. It starts with a manuscript called the *Chronicon Anglicanum*, which you can read on the Magna Carta section of the British Library's website.'

'Oh, somebody stop me,' Jodie said.

Lauren ignored her. 'The *Chronicon Anglicanum*, which is Latin for the Chronicle of England, was written by a Cistercian monk chronicler from Essex named Ralph of Coggeshall, as in Coggeshall Abbey. In the year 1225, he described Glastonbury in the chronicle with the words: "Here lies the famous King Arthur, buried in the Isle of Avalon." He wasn't the first historian, or chronicler if I'm to be accurate, who used this phrase. I believe that honour goes to Gerald of Wales who wrote his *Liber de Principis instructione*, or *Instruction Book for a Ruler*, in 1193. In that document, he writes of Glastonbury: "Here lies buried the famous

King Arthur with Guinevere his second wife in the Isle of Avalon." After that, the phrase was borrowed and rehashed many times by later writers, including the monks of Margam Abbey in Wales, the monks of St Albans at the end of the thirteenth century, and John Leland in 1542.'

'So these dudes were just copying each other then?' Jodie asked.

'We prefer to say they were disseminating a common message,' Lauren replied coolly. 'Either way, the generally accepted view is that as far as the myth of King Arthur goes, he was buried at Glastonbury after being killed by Mordred at the Battle of Camlann in Cornwall. The downside to the story is that the lead plaque found at the gravesite in 1191 is typical of such things from that era, and not at all from six hundred years earlier when Arthur was supposed to have died.'

'Rocking stuff, Lauren,' Lewis said. 'Thanks a lot. If I get the time away from my normal studies, I think I could get lost in a rabbit hole like King Arthur.'

'I think you easily could,' Lauren said with a smile. 'I know I did.'

'Consider me learned,' Jodie said with a yawn. 'Are we even there yet? My ass aches sitting in this goddam car for so long.'

'Yes, we're here,' Blanco said, pulling off the main

road and turning into the small Somerset town of Glastonbury. 'I'll pull up and then we can try to find something interesting to do like maybe discover the burial site of King Arthur and the final resting place of Excalibur.'

41

Blanco brought the SUV to a stop in a small parking area in the middle of town and they climbed out, grabbed a couple of their packs and walked through a housing estate until the tor once again became visible a few hundred yards to the east. They continued up the hill, stopping in the mists halfway up to take a breath. The cool, damp air was refreshing after the controlled atmosphere of the jet from Austria and the long heated car drive from the airport.

'Nearly there, everyone,' Amy said. 'Keep going. According to Xavier, we should be almost at the site of the tomb.'

As they trudged up the wet hill, Hunter pointed off

to the right. 'I don't know what the hell we're supposed to do now. All that damned clue said back in Austria was... What the hell did it say, Ben?'

'Greetings, fellow traveller! Shall we go to Drinking Glass Island?'

Hunter held his arms up and turned around three-sixty degrees in the misty air. 'Yeah, and a fat lot of good that does us!' He raised his voice to a shout. 'What the hell do I do now, Brother Xavier?'

'Tell me, Lauren,' Amy said. 'While Dr Hunter is having some kind of mental breakdown over there, are we looking for a Christian burial site or a pagan one?'

Lauren smiled at the comment regarding Hunter. 'It's hard to know, because Christianity came to Wales in the fourth century, two hundred years before Rome sent missionaries to England to convert the Anglo-Saxons. Arthur is generally accepted as being a Briton and not an Anglo-Saxon, so I would argue he could have been a Christian. Fingers crossed his tomb sheds a little light on that. Damn, this is going to blow my career into the stratosphere.'

Amy gave her a sideways look. 'Yeah, about that – and it's bad news.'

'What does that mean?'

Hunter had returned to normal. He said, 'It means

if we find Arthur's tomb, the discovery will be kept from the public for however long it takes for the powers that be to make sure there's nothing too shocking in there, nothing that might put the frighteners on the plebs.'

'You have a real way with words,' Amy said in a disapproving tone.

Lauren looked confused. 'I don't understand. We're talking about an archaeological discovery that will rock Britain and the world! People have a right to know. And what do you mean when you say they need to make sure nothing is shocking in there?'

Hunter shrugged. 'Lauren, listen. As you know, after I left the army I began a new career in archaeology. After I completed my doctorate, I enjoyed a short but illustrious career at UNESCO before starting a little, ahem, consultancy work for the US government as part of the HARPA team. Up till HARPA, I held a fairly orthodox view of the world we live in, but no longer. My work with HARPA opened my eyes to some stuff.'

'A lot of batshit crazy stuff,' Jodie said. 'And you can take that to the bank, girl.'

The team continued to search around the misty tor for any sign of King Arthur's tomb, but as the minutes slipped by and with nothing to show for their efforts, even Amy's optimism began to wane. 'This is starting to feel a little hopeless,' she said. 'There's nothing here to help us. Nothing to give any kind of clue about what we need to do next. Are you sure you got the translation of Xavier's last clue right, Ben?'

'Very sure.'

As the mist cleared and gave way to a persistent drizzle, the team gave a collective sigh of defeat. Then, Hunter snapped into life. 'Wait, who's got Xavier's dagger?'

Blanco raised his hand. 'Me.'

'Give it over, mate.' Hunter waved his hand at him hungrily.

Blanco rummaged in his backpack and handed him Xavier's knife. 'Here it is.'

'What is it, Max?' Amy asked.

'I just had a thought.'

Jodie looked serious. 'It had to happen eventually. What does it feel like, Hunter?'

Hunter heard her talking but ignored her. Instead, his mind was focused on the blade, which he now held up at arm's length directly in front of the tower. 'Both the strange shape of the back of the knife and the gold embossed arrow on the blade's handle. They've been bothering me since we found it back in

France, but now I think I know why it's there. They're another clue.'

Lauren's eyes widened. 'In what way?'

'We're too close. We need to get further back and move around to the north.'

'What's this all about, Max?' Lewis looked curious. 'Gonna spill the beans?'

Hunter was already marching forward to the ruined church tower, a cold wind driving the rain against his face. He drew up and raised the knife again, looking at the tower. When everyone else had caught up and gathered around him, he sighed and shook his head. 'Further away.'

He carried on down the hill, then stopped again to raise Xavier's blade, holding it up against the silhouette of the tower. Unhappy with the result, he continued down the hill until the journey took him inside a secluded, wooded area where they stopped in a small clearing. The tower was barely visible through the trees, but when he held the blade up once again, a smile appeared on his face.

'How are those features of the dagger a clue, Max?' Amy asked.

'I wondered if the shape of the blade was forged to tesselate with the tower, and it looks like I'm right. When you hold the knife up, the weird shape on the back of the blade fits perfectly with the north side of the tower fitting together like pieces in a jigsaw puzzle, but only when you're exactly at the right angle and distance from the tower. Then the gold embossed arrow points directly to the ground. I think the entrance to the labyrinth is right here beneath our feet, in this woodland.'

'Good job I brought these,' Blanco said, pulling two folding camping shovels from his pack.

'You're sure this is the right place to dig?' Lauren asked.

Hunter nodded. 'Look for yourself. Hold up the knife until the blade aligns perfectly with the east side of the tower. If you move even a few feet to the right or left, you lose the alignment. If you move a few feet closer or further away, the blade no longer matches the height of the tower. It has to be right here. This was the location of the entrance Xavier used to access the Glastonbury Labyrinth. It's his last clue. It has to be.'

'Let's just get in there before we say that,' Amy said.

Jodie scraped at the topsoil with the toe of her boot. 'Hard. That's too bad. You better get digging, Hunter.'

Hunter took one of the shovels and he and Blanco

got stuck in. The work started hard and got harder with every inch. Tree roots and rocks slowed progress considerably, but after thirty minutes of digging, they struck something solid three feet below ground level. Something manmade.

'Looks like we might be in business,' Hunter said, dropping down into the hole and holding the shovel with his hands to scrape away excess dirt.

'What have we got, Max?' Amy asked.

'Looks like some kind of trapdoor. Iron.'

'Looks like we found it!' Blanco said, mud on his cheek.

Amy and Lewis high-fived. 'Great work, team!'

Lauren looked excited. 'Is it locked?'

Hunter was still clearing the dirt away from the iron door, now with his hands. 'I don't know yet, hang on.' He finished the job and turned his grinning face up to the team. 'No locks, just a latch. It's covered in filth, but it's unlocked.'

In the excited hubbub, Hunter grabbed the latch and awkwardly manoeuvred out of the hole until he was standing above it, bent forward with one hand on the latch and with a foot on each side. He pulled on the trapdoor with all his strength, grunting with the effort until it clicked free, and then he pulled it up on its hinges until it was vertical, revealing a staircase receding into the darkness of the earth.

'Ladies and gentlemen,' he said, wiping the mud from his hands on his trousers. 'Looks like we just found the Glastonbury Labyrinth.'

Amy turned on her torch and handed it to him. 'Let's go make history, team.'

42

Hunter shone the torch down the steps. Seeing they were free of detritus or another obstacle that might cause someone to trip and fall, he slowly made his way down into the earth. The team followed him, with Blanco at the rear. The way was filthy and cold and strewn with thick blankets of cobwebs, but the steps ended soon enough to reveal a passageway disappearing into darkness to the south, the direction of Glastonbury Tor.

'Is it safe, Max?'

Lauren's voice. She was standing right next to him, inches from his elbow. 'Sure it is. Check the construction. Limestone bricks on either side of the tunnel and a solid ceiling of what looks like slate slabs. This place was built to last.'

'I'll take your word for it,' she whispered. 'But I'll still be glad when we get to wherever the hell we're going.'

Hunter was still walking forward, checking the way with the torch at every step. When he saw the beam shine up against a flat limestone slab, his heart sank. 'Damn it, looks like the way is blocked. That's all we need...'

'Wait, Max.'

Amy was at his side now, gently nudging Lauren away. She angled her torch at the slab. 'Look again! It's not the end of the tunnel, it's more like a T-junction. See?'

He stepped forward, neck craned forward in anticipation. 'Damn it, you're right! I hate it when that happens.'

'Yeah, I bet you do, too,' Jodie said.

They were at the T-junction. At their backs, the long tunnel they had just walked down; to their right and left, two more passageways.

'Which way now?' Lewis asked.

'We split up,' Amy said. 'It's the best thing to do. That way, we can cover a greater area in less time. Either we meet up further ahead somewhere, or we rendezvous back here in fifteen minutes.'

'There's a third option,' Hunter said.

'Which is?' Amy asked.

'That one of these tunnels is a trap that will lead whoever goes down it to die in painful and undignified circumstances.'

'Now then, Hunter,' Jodie said with a finger waggle. 'No more of your infamous pep talks. Time is running out.'

'Lauren should go with Amy's team,' Lewis said. 'Each team should have an archaeologist.'

'I'm more of a historian,' Lauren said.

'But you have the greatest knowledge of Arthur,' Lewis said.

'Agreed,' Hunter said. 'Lauren, go with Amy, please.'

'Sal, you're with me, too,' Amy said.

Hunter looked at Lewis and Jodie. 'Looks like you guys are with me.'

'The shortest straw, huh?' Jodie said.

Amy's look said it all. 'See you on the other side, guys.'

Hunter watched her lead her sub-team away into the dark and then looked at Jodie and Lewis before taking off down the other tunnel. 'C'mon! The very least we can do is get there first.'

The cold air inside the damp passageway brushed against Hunter's face as he jogged through the dark, torch gripped in his hand. Turning a corner with caution, he was confronted with another thick mass of cobwebs blocking the path ahead. He pulled himself up to a stop and angled the torch beam around the outside of the tunnel to check for traps or any other dangers. Seeing none, he carefully breached the web with the LED housing at the front of the torch, by which time, Jodie and Lewis had caught up with him.

'Snoozing on the job?' Jodie asked.

'I was just checking for boobytraps.'

'I'll let you off,' she said with a wink. 'But just this once.'

Hunter paused and smiled at her. 'Are you finally warming to me, Agent Priest?'

'As if. Let's go.'

Lewis put his arms around their shoulders and squeezed. 'Aw, you two are gonna be just fine.'

They each shook him off and Hunter resumed his journey down the tunnel, the reassuring sound of his friends' footsteps just a few yards to his rear. Another corner approached, but this time he saw light spilling out from around it onto the path in front of them.

'Wait,' he said, pushing his arm out to stop them from going forward. 'We have light.'

'You think Lundquist's men somehow got in here first?' Lewis asked.

'Is that you, Max?'

Amy's voice. Hunter sighed in relief. 'Yeah, I don't think so. C'mon.'

When they turned the corner, they were in a passageway running parallel to the one they had started on. Ahead, he saw Amy and the others standing in the tunnel in a tight huddle, just in front of a doorway. It was Amy's torch he had seen on the floor, presumably shining it over to their location when they had heard their footsteps. Now, she swung it around to the doorway ahead of her. Hunter drew up alongside them.

'You beat me to it,' Hunter said.

'But beat us to what?' Lewis said.

'It's made of stone,' Sal said, running his hands down the door in front of them. 'And it has these weird carvings inside these three raised squares.'

'I think they're like some kind of ancient keycode,' Lauren told Hunter. 'Like those you told me about in that Burmese temple.'

Hunter smiled at the memory. 'You remembered that story?'

'You're my mentor.'

Amy rolled her eyes. 'Can we get out of the goddam Burmese jungle and back to this? Time is not on our side.'

'Amy's right,' Blanco said. 'What do you mean when you say like a keycode?'

Hunter was studying the three raised squares on the stone door. 'Exactly like you're imagining, Sal. Like a modern keycode security unit on any one of a million doors. Enter the correct sequence and gain entry, enter the wrong sequence and get—'

'Skewered or crushed?' Jodie angled her torch up at the ceiling and illuminated dozens of metal spikes embedded in flagstones, their tips just protruding from perfectly sized holes.

Hunter also raised his torch. 'Skewered, by the looks of it.'

'Nice touch,' Blanco said. 'Any way we can block these things before we try to get in, just in case we get the sequence wrong?'

Amy looked at the spikes and winced. 'I don't think so – there must be dozens of them and there's nothing in here we can use to block the holes.'

'Plus we don't know how much downward pressure will be exerted on them when Hunter screws up the sequence,' Jodie said. 'Sorry, I meant *if* he screws it up.'

Hunter nodded at the barb. 'I love you too, Jodie, but I'm going to have to insist everyone walks back along the tunnel until they're in the section without any spikes in the ceiling. I'll stay here and try to figure this out. That way, only one of us gets skewered if I screw it up.'

'I'm not happy with anyone standing under those things while we try to open the door,' Amy said, looking up at the spikes and wincing. 'Not at all.'

'But we have no choice,' Hunter said. 'Look around, and remember the clock's ticking. Lundquist could turn up at any moment.'

Amy wrestled with it. 'Damn it, Max.'

'It's the only way.'

'I'm staying with you,' Lauren said. 'You need my help, Max. I know more about this subject than you do.'

'And me,' Lewis said. 'A lot of what Xavier left behind relied on my knowledge of Latin. This keycode thing might be the same.'

'Absolutely not,' Amy said. 'Ben can go, but not Lauren.'

'Why not?' Lauren asked.

'Because you're not even in HARPA.'

Lauren looked at her in disbelief. 'You mean I'm not, like, insured or something?'

Amy sighed. 'No, not that. I mean you've been out of school for about two weeks and I'm responsible for your safety.'

'I'm writing a doctorate, Agent Fox,' Lauren shot back. 'I left school years ago. And last time I heard, there is no more HARPA. And you're not responsible for me. I work for UNESCO. Copy that?'

Amy looked away but had no response. 'Fine, don't blame me if you get a spike through your head.'

'I'm not likely to, am I?' Lauren said with a smile.

'She's right though,' added Hunter. 'I do need her.'

'Then let's stop arguing about this and get going,' Amy said. 'Max, Ben and Lauren – stay here and get that door open. The rest of us will wait back where it's safe... And good luck.'

Hunter watched them walk back, stopping a few yards to his left. They were still in sight, lit like eerie ghosts in the beams of their torches, all staring at him and Lauren as they turned back to the door.

'What have we got?' Hunter asked.

Lewis answered first. 'I see Latin again, in two inscriptions, but no surprises there. The first one at the top says "*spiritus et materia convenient*" and the second one beneath it says "*Acolythus illuminationem quaerenda est.*"'

Lauren said, 'And I see three raised squares, each with its own haut-relief carving. Working from left to right, we'll number them one, two and three.'

'A good start.'

'Number one has one circle, number two has two circles, and number three has three circles.'

'So far, so obvious.'

Lauren frowned. 'They also each have a little slit beneath them. I'm confused.'

Hunter was also having trouble. 'What does the Latin say, Ben?'

'Number one says "spirit and matter must come together" and inscription number two says "The Acolyte must seek enlightenment."'

'That's interesting,' Hunter said. 'All the way through this journey, Xavier used the word "pilgrim" but now all of a sudden he's using the word "acolyte".'

'I've got it!' Lewis said. 'An acolyte is the name of an assistant in a church who helps to light the candles before a service. The name comes from ancient Greek – bearers of light. They're telling us not to follow them religiously, in the normal way the meaning of the word acolyte is understood, but to be literally the bearer of light. They want us to light candles. There must be candles inside those slits that we can't see from here.'

Hunter peered inside and saw three candles, corresponding with the three squares. Above each candle was a thin piece of twine, each one disappearing into the darkness beyond. He patted his pockets down and cursed. Then he called back along the passage. 'Hey, Jodie! Throw me your lighter.'

'You want some cigarettes too?' she said with a laugh.

'Yes,' he said, surprising them all. 'Throw me the pack.' Hunter caught the cigarettes and lighter. 'Thanks.'

'What now?' Lauren asked.

'I'm guessing when lit, their flames are beneath twine or ropes,' Hunter said. 'When the right one is burned through, the door opens. When the wrong ones are burned through, some kind of mechanism releases the spikes.'

'And it's kebab time?' Lewis said.

Hunter laughed nervously. 'Yeah, you could put it like that. I'd rather you didn't though. The imagery it invokes upsets me.'

'Sorry.'

'I'm kidding. I like kebabs.' Hunter looked at Lauren. 'Can you make any sense of the images on the raised squares? I need to know which one to ignite.'

'I think so,' she said uncertainly, taking another lingering look at the haut relief carvings on the squares. 'The middle one.'

'The one with two circles?' Hunter asked. 'You're certain?'

'Yes.'

'Why? A lot is riding on this, Lauren.'

She looked up. 'You don't have to tell me that, Max. I'm standing right next to you!'

'Why the second one?' he repeated.

'Two circles interlocked,' she said. 'It's called the vesica piscis.'

Lewis clicked his fingers. 'Of course, the vesica piscis! It means fish bladder in Latin.'

Lauren shrugged. 'I never knew that, but I do know that it's an ancient symbol associated with Arthurian legend that symbolises Heaven and Earth joined together. One circle generally symbolises eternity; three circles represent the Holy Trinity. The Latin inscription above the three squares tells us that spirit and matter must come together. Heaven and Earth, spirit and matter.'

Hunter winced. 'A little tenuous, no?'

'It makes perfect sense,' she said.

Hunter looked up at the spikes poking down through the holes in the stone ceiling, winced and said a silent prayer. 'Here goes nothing.'

Lighting one of the cigarettes, he poked it through the slit beneath the second stone square and angled it until the lit tip was touching the wick of the second candle. When it ignited, he pulled out the cigarette and stuffed it in his mouth, taking a long drag with another glance up at the spikes. There was no time to move to the safe section of the tunnel. The candle's flame was already wrapped around the twine just above it, turning it black. When the flame burnt through it and the twine snapped, Hunter heard a loud bang and nearly jumped out of his skin. Lauren gasped and jumped over to him, grabbing hold of his arm. Lewis closed his eyes and muttered a prayer.

Then the stone door began to slowly grind open.

'We did it,' Lauren said.

Hunter felt a palpable wave of relief wash over him. Dropping the cigarette and crushing it out with his boot, he looked over to Lauren and Lewis. 'Good work, both of you. We're in!'

43

Jim Gates peered into the trees at the end of his garden and tried to see his dog in the gloom. A thick mist had descended over Telluride this evening, and now its wispy tendrils were coiling around the trunks and boughs of the trees demarking the end of his property. Lucy, his faithful golden retriever of many years, was curled up by the fire inside the lodge, but his black Labrador Zack, a much newer and younger addition to the family, had vanished into the mist a few seconds ago.

'Jim, dinner's nearly ready.'

His wife's voice, calling from the kitchen.

'Just a second, honey,' he called back. 'Going to find Zack.'

He clicked the door shut, pushed his hands into his fleece jacket and blew out a deep breath as he stepped off the deck and made his way down the sloping garden to the trees.

'Zack! You out there, boy?'

He stopped at the tree line and turned to look back up to the lodge. Three floors of traditional hardwood, mezzanines and big windows reflected the dull evening light right back out to the Rockies. In the kitchen window, he saw his wife. It looked like she was draining the pasta, but hard to see exactly thanks to the steamy window. He turned around and went into the forest.

'Zack? C'mon, boy!'

No sign of Zack. The light faded further and the mist thickened into a fog. The night was on the way and he wanted to get back inside and lock up. He was hungry. He'd asked his wife for spaghetti pie but she wanted to surprise him with something different. He had a bet with himself that meant spaghetti and meatballs because that was what she usually made when she said it was going to be a surprise. He smiled at that and couldn't wait to start eating.

'C'mon, Zack. It's gonna be meatballs.'

Still no Zack, not even a bark or whimper. Gates's suspicion stirred inside him. Zack was a young dog but already well-trained. It wasn't like him to ignore commands, especially when beef was on the menu. Gates walked deeper into the woods and felt the chill air envelop him like an icy shroud.

'Zack! You're one second away from losing all privileges, soldier.'

Silence. Gates began to grow concerned now. He was sure something had happened to Zack, but it was too dark to start looking for him. He called out one more time and made a brief search of the woods. Then he decided to go inside and grab a flashlight and take a proper look around the woods. There was no way he was going to abandon Zack without a full-scale search of the area.

He reached the lodge and went inside.

'Good timing,' his wife said. 'Dinner's on the table. It's meatballs!'

He looked at her and smiled.

'You guessed?' she said.

'Not at all. It's a great surprise and I can't wait to eat. But listen, something's up with Zack. He won't come when I call him and it's getting dark.'

She frowned. 'Is he okay?'

'I'm sure he's just chased after a rabbit or something. You know Zack. Open a bottle of wine and get started. I won't be long.'

She looked outside. 'But it's almost night, Jim. You're not going to see much out there.'

'I'm taking a flashlight down. If I can't find him tonight, we'll have to wait till morning. I don't want to do that.'

He took a torch from a kitchen drawer and kissed his wife. Then he went back outside and jogged down the garden to the woods, flashlight beam bobbing about on the grass ahead of him. When he reached the trees, he pulled up and angled the beam down onto the forest floor. He swept it from side to side, squinting as the bright beam reflected at him off a trunk. Still no sign of Zack.

He went deeper into the trees and continued his search, this time assisted by the bright flashlight beam. But it was no use. He almost made it to the far side of the woods, far enough to look out across the valley and see the airport lights in the distance. Zack was nowhere to be seen.

With a heavy heart, Gates returned through the woods to the lodge. He took his shoes off at the back door and then stepped inside, slipping his feet into his slippers and closing the door behind him. 'Damn it,' he muttered. 'Where the hell is he?'

He went back into the kitchen. His wife was gone. On the table, he saw two steaming plates of spaghetti and meatballs and two glasses of red wine. She was in the bathroom, he thought. He set the flashlight down on the table and took a sip of the wine. Zack's disappearance was nagging at him, yet he knew he'd probably be all right. Dogs wandered off sometimes, and either they wandered right back a few hours later or you got a call from the local pound. Zack was chipped. As soon as someone in the business of dog collecting found him, he'd be identified and returned to the lodge in a matter of hours.

'Now whose dinner is getting cold?' he called out with a chuckle. He sat down and started to eat. Dinner was great, as always. His wife was a fantastic cook. Beautiful, tender beef meatballs with just the right amount of garlic and seasoning, and spaghetti with a light coating of olive oil. The whole thing was topped off with freshly grated parmesan cheese. The only problem was Lucy's empty dog basket over in the corner. Lucy was getting on in years, a grand old dame who rarely moved unless strictly necessary, and certainly not to follow his wife to the bathroom.

Something was wrong. First Zack and now Susanna and Lucy. All vanished into thin air.

Gates felt his hackles rise and quietly set his fork down on the side of his plate. Then he pushed back his chair and walked over to the knife block and pulled out a carving knife. Stepping over to the wall, and tucking himself against it, knife in hand, he called out cheerily. 'C'mon, darling! This is great. Don't make me eat it all alone!'

He peered around the wall and saw the corridor connecting the kitchen and the main hall was clear. Stealthily, he made his way along it, slippers soft and silent on the old Persian runner they'd been given as a gift by an Iranian diplomat many years ago. Pausing at the phone on the hall table, an antique affair Susanna had arranged to be converted to digital, he lifted the receiver off the cradle and checked. As he thought, the line was dead.

He decided to check the ground floor was clear before venturing upstairs. Right now, he had no idea what was going on. It was possible they were thieves and still in the house, or the kidnapping of his wife was also possible, for blackmailing purposes. He was an important man with contacts in the US government as high as they were deep. If there was a better way to gain leverage over him than snatching his wife and threatening to hurt her, or worse, he couldn't think what it was.

Checking the coast was clear, he slipped across the hall and into the main living room. This was a formal place, at his wife's insistence. Expensive leather couches were arranged in a horseshoe shape around a beautiful bespoke fireplace. He'd wanted to dress the place up with the skull of a deer he'd shot, but that was a major no-no. The skull was eventually mounted on the wall of the informal space they jokingly called the man cave.

Gates had now checked the kitchen, hall and living room and they were all clear. On this floor, that only left the man cave. He went towards it, knife in hand and wishing he had a gun. He had guns on the property, but they were locked in a cabinet in the man cave. For now, the carving knife was his only option.

The man cave door was ajar. Not how he had left it earlier this evening. It was possible Susanna had been in there for some reason, but unlikely. She disliked the deer skull staring down at her, all bare teeth and antlers, and she rarely ventured inside. He tensed. Checked his grip on the blade. It was eight inches long and more than up to the job of reaching deep inside a man and slashing his organs. Most would prefer a bullet, he knew.

Outside the door, he took a breath and listened but heard nothing. He had to move. If she'd been taken from the property, he needed to get to his cell phone upstairs and raise the alarm as soon as possible. Whoever had taken her may have forced her to get her passport and keep quiet at the airport. They might even have a long-range chopper. Beyond the town, this was a wild and enormous landscape, sparsely populated and easy to get lost in. If he didn't act fast, she could be gone forever.

He resolved to fight and kicked the door open.

What he saw stopped him in his tracks.

44

Hunter's uncertainty about what they might have discovered soon faded when he saw what was inside the chamber behind the stone door. It was without doubt a tomb and the treasure inside it took his breath away. As he swept his torch around the enclosed space, the beam illuminated piles of sparkling gold and silver. Jewel-encrusted plates and goblets. Sceptres. Orbs. Ornamental daggers. Even canvas bags, open at the top and bursting with coins. At the back, behind it all, a stone sarcophagus with a statue of a sleeping man on top of it. A man in a simple crown.

'Bingo,' Lauren said. 'I think we just hit the jackpot. Right, Max?'

Hunter nodded, almost rendered speechless by their discovery. 'Either I'm about to wake up, or we just found not only the English crown jewels, missing since the year 1216, but also the tomb containing the body of King Arthur.'

'You're not sleeping, Max.' Lauren was standing by the sarcophagus, and wiping away dust from the top with her fingers to reveal a carved inscription. When she read aloud, her voice was pure, and even trembling slightly with the realisation of what she was saying. '*Hic Jacet Arthurus Rex Quondam, Rexque Futurus.*'

As the team's best Latin speaker, Lewis responded before anyone asked the obvious question. 'Here Lies Arthur, King Once, and King in the Future.'

The silence was so profound, Hunter could almost hear the dust motes drifting past his ears.

'Anyone want to open it up?'

Jodie's voice startled Hunter back to reality. He already knew this was a moment in his career to rank right up there with the very best, if not the very greatest of all his discoveries. 'Yes, we need to get it open and see what's inside. Clearly, people have been in here since the sarcophagus was placed here because the crown jewels weren't stolen for six hundred years after Arthur died, and we know Xavier came in here at some point after that, too. Someone may have robbed the sarcophagus of the body.'

'And left all this?' Blanco said, nudging a bag of silver coins with the toecap of his boot.

'There could have been more in here,' Jodie said. 'More that was stolen.'

'She makes a good point,' Amy said.

'Always thinking like a thief,' Lauren said.

Amy glared at her. 'That's not fair, Lauren.'

'Anyone see a giant sword made in heaven?' Jodie said.

'Not yet.' Lewis was going through the jewels, carefully pushing them aside and looking in every nook and cranny.

Jodie had been looking through some of the gold plates and piles of goblets stacked up against the far wall. Now she stood up and shook her head. 'Nor me. Sorry.'

Amy sighed. 'It's not in here, Max. The room's not that big and there's nowhere to conceal a full-sized sword.'

'Damn it,' Blanco said, the frustration clear in his voice for all to hear. 'What did we do wrong?'

'Let's just get the sarcophagus open,' Hunter said, making his way over to Lauren. 'Sal and Ben, a hand please.'

The three men and Lauren began to heave the heavy lid, reclining statue and all, off the main sarcophagus. After a series of grunts, they carefully set it down on the floor and then returned to their full height to look inside. Hunter spoke first.

'We have a body, severely decomposed almost back to nothing more than a skeleton with leathery skin over it. It's wearing a crown and there is no sword, but it's holding a piece of rolled parchment in its right hand.' His words hung in the air for seconds before anyone spoke.

'They'll run DNA tests, I guess,' Amy said.

'And match it to what?' said Lauren. 'Up until one minute ago, he was mythical.'

'I'm going to take the parchment out,' Hunter said. 'If the sword isn't in here, then maybe Xavier left something about its location written down for his pilgrims to follow.'

'Good luck with that,' Jodie said. 'I'm starting to think good old Xavier of Normandy was the original troll and he's had us running all over Europe for nothing.'

Lewis laughed. 'I think you might be right.'

Hunter took the parchment from King Arthur's hand and gently unfurled it. Then he cursed.

Everyone stared at him. Lauren took the parchment. She cursed too.

'Max?' Amy asked. 'Problem?'

Lauren handed the parchment to Lewis. 'It's in Latin.'

Lewis took the crumbling parchment as gently as if he were holding his newborn baby back in Washington DC. Squinting at the ancient, faded calligraphy, a smile appeared on his face. He turned to face the others, their expectant faces looking back at him, eyes full of hope. 'You want the good news or the bad news?'

Amy sighed. 'Can't there ever just be good news?'

'Not this time,' Lewis said. 'But I can give the good news first if that helps. I was able to translate this note, and it was written by Xavier because I recognise the handwriting from the example that we saw in Austria. Also, he directly mentions Excalibur. This is all of the good news.'

Jodie swept her hair back away from her face and gave a long, frustrated sigh. 'And now we get all of the bad news, right?'

Lewis's bright, young face looked back at her, lit up by a beaming smile. 'Right.'

'Let's have it, Ben,' Blanco said. 'I'm too old to be

standing in a place this dark and damp. You're a long time dead, right?'

'And I quote,' Lewis said, reading straight from the parchment. '"Weary pilgrims have found a King but not his Power. I brought not the Great Sword to the Royal Tomb, for this place was too obvious. Instead, weary men, I returned Excalibur to the mountain village place where it all began."'

'What the hell does that mean?' Jodie screamed and kicked over a bag of coins. 'And there's weary women on this goddam team, too, Xavier! Take it from me because I'm one of 'em!'

'I'm not sure too many women partook of treasure hunts in the thirteenth century,' Hunter said.

'Partook?' Jodie replied. 'You've been reading too much Xavier of Normandy, you know that?'

Hunter ignored her on purpose and turned to Lewis. 'You're certain of the translation?'

The former US Marine nodded once. 'Completely. Xavier says he took the sword not to King Arthur's tomb here at Glastonbury, as that would be too obvious. He says he returned Excalibur to the mountain village place where it all began.'

Hunter cursed again. 'That's it?'

'That's all of it.'

'Another setback, then,' Amy said. 'Damn you, Xavier!'

'Where it all began?' Lewis said, thinking aloud. 'If we accept what Lundquist told Amy, and Excalibur is the sword of the Archangel Michael, I guess it began somewhere in the Middle East. St Michael is closely associated with Mount Carmel in Israel. Maybe that's the mountain Xavier was talking about.'

Jodie sighed. 'You cannot be serious? You mean to say after all this, we now have to fly to Israel?'

'If that's what it takes, then that's what we do,' Hunter said. 'I'm starting to doubt if your heart is truly in this mission.'

'Are you kidding me?' Jodie said, rounding on him.

'Everyone, just calm down,' Amy said.

'No,' Lewis said. 'It can't be Mount Carmel. The church dedicated to Michael there wasn't built until the nineteenth century. Xavier couldn't have left any messages there.'

The team burst into an animated row, but Lauren raised her hand and brought it all crashing down. 'I don't think that's what Xavier meant.'

'Huh?' Jodie asked.

Lauren took a deep breath before explaining. 'When he wrote about going back to where it all began, I don't think Xavier was referring to Archangel Michael and the Holy Lands. Remember, Xavier was a scholar and a student not only of the Bible but also of King Arthur. So when he describes how he returned St Michael's sword to the mountain village, the place where it all began, he wasn't talking about Mount Carmel or Israel, or anything else connected with the Archangel Michael at all. He was talking about where it all began for King Arthur. It's so obvious, I can't believe I've been so stupid.'

Hunter could see from her eyes that she was onto something, that she believed she had the answer they were all looking for. He recognised that look. He'd seen it in the mirror more times than he could remember. 'So where then, Lauren? Where did Xavier hide Excalibur?'

'To where it all began for Arthur,' she said, checking her watch. 'C'mon. We need to get back to the car. We have another drive ahead of us and we need to get there before Lundquist.'

'To where?' Amy asked.

'Tintagel,' Lauren said.

Blanco scratched his head. 'I don't understand how you get Tintagel from the clue.'

'Trevena comes from the Cornish *tre war venydh*, which means the "village on a mountain",' Lauren explained. 'The modern English name for the place is Tintagel.'

'Of course,' Hunter said with a click of his fingers. 'Arthur was conceived at Tintagel. Even I know that. And King Arthur's Castle is at Tintagel Haven. Good work, Lauren.'

'Thanks, Max.'

'Conceived but not born?' Jodie asked. 'Is that difference important?'

Lewis spoke. 'Many religions, including Catholicism, consider conception as the start of life, not birth. You can bet a thirteenth-century Benedictine monk like Xavier would believe that too. When he writes about where it all began, he would be talking in this context about conception and not birth.'

'So this place is a big part of the Arthurian legend?' Blanco asked.

'It certainly is,' Lauren replied. 'It's one of the main locations in his story. As Max says, he was conceived there, and some say it's where Camelot is, although...'

'Don't tell me,' Jodie said. 'That's up for debate.'

'It's up for debate, yeah. Another strong contender is Caerleon in South Wales, where the circular ruins of an old Roman amphitheatre there kindled ancient stories about it being Arthur's round table.'

'C'mon, let's get back outside. I need to call UN-

ESCO,' Hunter said grimly. 'We can't just leave a place like this open for anyone to wander into and poke around, and I don't trust anyone except the people in Juliette's office at UNESCO. She might be absent without leave, but she works with a strong team. One of them will send a team out to guard the tomb and start cataloguing its contents.'

As they made their way back out of the labyrinth, Amy reached for her phone. 'I'm calling Jim. Maybe he can get some people to start looking into it.'

She dialled his number and waited patiently for him to answer.

'Any luck?' Blanco asked.

She shook her head. 'No answer.'

'Maybe they're out,' Lewis said.

'He always takes his phone when he goes out, Ben. You know that. He's the director of HARPA. He can't afford to miss a call. You hear from Juliette yet, Max?'

'I haven't tried her for a few hours for obvious reasons,' he said. 'But no, she's not answering.'

'I'm starting to get a very bad feeling about this,' Amy said coldly. 'First Juliette drops off the radar, then Jim and now Quinn. Someone's taking us out one by one.'

'You don't know that,' Blanco said. 'Just take a breath.'

Amy reluctantly agreed. 'Fine, but the British authorities will have to be told about this finding. One way or another it's going to get back to them.'

Hunter wasn't sure. 'Why?'

She was astonished. 'Er, because not only is this the tomb of King Arthur, but it also contains the missing crown jewels! You think maybe, just maybe, the British government might be interested in a discovery like this?'

'Bugger the British government,' Hunter said crisply as they climbed the steps and emerged into the gloomy daylight. 'We already know our old friends who prance around under their calling card of the "Illuminati" have infiltrated just about every institution in the world. If we call the local police to guard this place, news of this discovery will travel upstream like a randy salmon. The next thing any of us knows, it's all gone for good and our enemies have taken the lot off somewhere, never to be seen again.'

'You could say the same about UNESCO,' Jodie said. 'The Illuminati wouldn't be much damn good if they forget to infiltrate that, surely.'

'I don't disagree with you,' Hunter said. 'But not Juliette or her office. I know them personally and have done so for years. We can trust them. We have to trust them. It's all we have.'

One of Juliette Bonnaire's assistants answered, and after confirming that she had not come into work or called anyone, Hunter explained what had happened. The conversation was short and clipped. Yes, they understood the need for secrecy. Yes, they would dispatch a team of trusted colleagues immediately who would protect the site and begin taking an inventory of the entire cache. No, they did not agree about keeping the site a secret long-term. They would be forced to follow protocol and law and alert the UK authorities of the discovery at some point. They agreed to make sure they had a full inventory and suite of photographs of the entire site and its treasures before alerting the British authorities. Yes, they accepted Hunter's argument to leave the search for Juliette to him and his team.

Hunter hung up and reported the conversation to the rest of the team. 'So, after we've concealed the entrance, we can get on to Tintagel as fast as possible. We're nearly there.'

'Great news,' Amy said, looking at Hunter. 'But we're going to need some backup. We can't presume we gave Lundquist the slip. He's a skilled and determined man, and his team have shown us how lethal they can be. They tracked us down once; they can do it again.'

'What about Director Gates?' Lauren asked.

Amy shook her head. 'He's not answering his phone. I'm not sure why. I'm worried something's not right. Jim's a close friend.'

'I'm sure he's all right," Jodie said.

'Any other options?' Blanco asked. 'Ben?'

Lewis also rejected the idea. 'All of my contacts in the Marines are all stateside, Sal. Even if I can get hold of them and they agree to help out, which they would, we're still looking at a transatlantic flight until they're here. Factor in traffic and airports at both ends of the flight and we're probably looking at a twenty-hour delay at the very least.'

'Nearly a full day,' Jodie said. 'Not optimal. What about you, Lauren? You know any old soldiers or mercenaries? Maybe some sailors?'

'I don't think now is the time for humour,' Lauren said with a frown. 'Do you?'

Amy looked at Hunter. 'Max?'

He considered the question, then smiled. 'There might be someone. My old CO, Lieutenant-Colonel Sam Bodie. He's out of the game now, but let's say he kept his hand in.'

'Don't tell me,' Lewis said. 'He can pull more strings than Geppetto?'

'He's very well connected, yes,' Hunter said with a

smile. 'In the worrying absence of Juliette and Jim Gates, he should be able to step in and get us some help. Ex-soldiers and weapons, too.'

Blanco whistled. 'Sounds useful. Can he do it at short notice?'

Hunter activated his phone again. 'We're about to find out.'

'In that case, let's get moving.' Amy turned to Hunter. 'Get this entrance concealed and then we can get down to Cornwall and end this thing.'

45

The four men wore black suits and black rollnecks. Black leather gloves gripped matte black automatic pistols. The most horrific detail was the demon masks that covered their faces. Hideous, monstrous faces, twisted like gargoyles. In the middle of the group of men was his wife. The men stood behind his old, patched-up couch. His wife sat terrified in front of them, hands clasped together and shaking in her lap. The man on her right was casually pushing the muzzle of a SIG Sauer into the top of her head. Tears rolled down her cheeks.

Gates knew there would be no fight. A simple carving knife wasn't coming out on top of four SIGs.

Worse, they had a hostage. Susanna. He dropped the knife and raised his hands.

The man holding the gun spoke first. 'There's a good boy. Now turn around and put your hands behind your back.'

'Release my wife first,' Gates said. 'You can see I'm not armed. I'm no threat to you. Let her go and I'll come without a fight.'

'You're dictating terms, James,' the man said. 'Don't dictate terms.'

'Who are you?'

'You may call me Oriax.'

'Then please listen to me, Oriax.' Gates paused to lick dry lips. He kept his eyes away from his sobbing wife with all his willpower. 'You're here for me, not my wife. You don't need her. Take me and we can talk this through. We can come to an arrangement. Maybe I can get you whatever it is that you want. Please, be reasonable.'

Oriax heard the words. The demon's face nodded up and down in understanding. 'I already shot both of your dogs tonight, James. Your wife is alive because I want her to come with us. You think if I didn't want her to come with us, she would still be alive?'

The man's thin voice crawled into Gates's brain like

some kind of virus. These monsters had already killed Lucy and Zack? He felt his flesh crawl. He loved those dogs like they were his children. Rage began to grow inside him. He felt their deaths like a hot iron pressing into his back. Worse, he knew Oriax wasn't bluffing about his wife. If they didn't want her, she would already be dead. It was obvious what must happen next.

'Where are we going, Oriax?'

'An intelligent and pertinent question at last. It shows me you are just as bright as I was told in my briefing. You have already assessed the situation and decided you cannot win here tonight. There can be no running, no escape. There can be no bargaining. No cutting deals to save the life of the one you love. There is only surrender, blissful and complete.'

Oriax was right. Gates's only chance had been the gun safe, which was a couple of yards behind the men holding his wife hostage. It was also locked and the guns inside were unloaded. No way was he getting to it, opening it and loading a weapon before these demonic bastards could open fire and kill him and his wife. Any attempt at breaking free would have to wait for another opportunity. If there was one.

'You said you were briefed,' Gates said. 'That means you're working with other people. Who is your boss?'

'Not your concern. Yet.'

'This is about HARPA?'

'Not your business. Yet.'

Gates checked his frustration, parking it somewhere next to his fear. 'Okay, then how do we do this?' Gates asked, finally seeing his wife and registering the fear and disappointment in her eyes. Yes, he felt with a sickening realisation, Susanna had expected him to intervene somehow, to step in and rescue her from this nightmare. Instead, he was just giving up. He hoped she understood.

'You do what I just told you to do,' Oriax said through the mask. 'You turn around and put your hands behind your back.'

Gates broke eye contact with Susanna and obeyed Oriax's directive. When he was in position, he heard footsteps approaching him from behind. One of the men was directly behind him and forcing his hands into cuffs.

'Good work, Vepar,' Oriax said. 'Put him to sleep.'

Gates moved to turn, but before he'd moved an inch, he felt something heavy and fat crunching down on his head. He tumbled forwards, unable to reach out to stop himself from hitting the floor because of his cuffed wrists. Hands grabbed him to arrest his fall. Then he was struck again and it was all over.

46

As Blanco raced the SUV down the final stretch of the A395, Hunter opened his eyes and was met with the sight of wipers furiously trying to clear away rain lashing against the windscreen. 'I see normal British weather has returned.'

'It's been getting heavier since we drove past Exeter,' Blanco said.

'About par for the course.'

'Except Lauren, you were all asleep by then. You're the first to wake up.'

Hunter turned in the front passenger seat to see everyone else slowly coming back to life. 'Wakey, wakey, eggs and bakey.'

Jodie finished a big yawn. 'Piss off, Hunter.'

Blanco followed the satnav and pulled up on the coast, a few minutes away from Tintagel Castle. 'We're here. Everyone, get suited and booted.'

They climbed out of the SUV and went around to the back where Blanco dished out weatherproof coats and shovels.

Jodie took one of the shovels and just stared at it. 'If we get attacked by Lundquist's men, I'm sure gonna be glad I packed this foldaway shovel.'

'We're not in HARPA any more,' Amy said. 'We can't bring a load of guns we stole from mercenaries onto a commercial aircraft in our carry-on luggage, and besides, even if we could, we ran out of rounds for those guns in the last firefight.'

'If only you had some friends, Hunter,' Jodie said. 'You could have got some old army buddy to furnish us with something a little handier than these shovels.'

'Hey,' Lauren said with a smile. 'We're at the seaside. You have buckets and spades at the seaside. At least I did when I was five.'

Jodie turned away from her and lowered her voice as she walked past Hunter. 'She's really starting to annoy me, Hunter. Make it stop.'

Hunter smiled and checked his watch. 'All right. It's nearly dark and we have a lot of ground to cover.

What do you suggest we start with, Lauren? Xavier's clue was kind of vague.'

'I don't think Xavier hid the sword in Merlin's cave. Too many people have explored the cave over hundreds of years. I think Xavier buried it somewhere on the grounds of Tintagel Castle because that is where he was conceived. We start there, but we're stuck with preliminary exploration until Max's army friend arrives with the proper equipment.'

They began to descend a long set of steps leading down to the castle.

Amy stopped to take in the breathtaking view. 'This place is beautiful. How long has it been connected with Arthurian legend, Lauren?'

'The association starts when Geoffrey of Monmouth wrote about it in his famous history of Britain, *Historia Regum Britanniae*, in the 1130s. He described how Arthur's parents, Uther Pendragon and Igraine, fell in love and conceived Arthur here. His birthplace is less clear, with many locations vying for the honour.'

'But Xavier meant conception, right?' Jodie said.

'So I believe,' Lewis said.

'Then it's got to be here.'

They walked down a cliff path leading them around Tintagel Haven as the soft, creamy twilight over the Cornish coast slowly yielded to dusk. A cool breeze gushed over them, fresh from the sea. Hunter pulled up his collar and picked up the pace, acutely aware of the time and how much better things would be if they could get in and out without having to fight Lundquist and his men, whom he thought were still conspicuously absent. As was any sign of Sam Bodie and the men and equipment he had promised Hunter in their phone conversation.

They approached the castle as the last light faded. Hunter pulled a small torch from his pack, as did Amy and Blanco. Shining the beams over the ancient stone walls, Hunter felt a shiver go up his spine. 'This place gives me the creeps.'

'You can say that again,' Amy said.

'Which is why I'm so excited that we're here to dig a grave!' Jodie said. 'Yay, we're ghost hunters!'

'We're not gravedigging.' Hunter stepped ahead of the team, torch lighting the wet grass at his feet. 'Xavier hid the sword here because it was the site of Arthur's conception, not his grave.'

'I get that, Hunter,' Jodie said with a sigh. 'I literally just walked out of that tomb. I was making a joke.'

'Oh, sorry. Do let me know in advance next time so I can prepare myself for the aching ribs.'

'Down!'

The voice came out of nowhere. Hoarse, raspy and full of focused rage. It filled the night again.

'Down! Down!'

The team scrambled into a circle, watching each other's backs.

Amy spoke first. 'Lundquist!'

Men rushed at them from different angles. One vaulted over a crumbling waist-high stone wall, and another burst into view from behind some trees. They carried automatic weapons, machine pistols and handguns. Blanco reached for a knife in a sheath on his belt. Lewis was a step ahead of him, his blade glinting in the dying sunlight.

'Max!' Amy yelled.

Hunter blew out a sigh of relief. As one of the men approached him, his face obscured in camo grease and a Glock in his hand, Hunter laughed. 'Sam, you old bastard. Thanks for coming.'

Hunter turned and saw his team, dumbstruck.

'Max?' Lauren asked, her chest heaving up and down with fear.

A broad smile lit up Hunter's face. The other man smiled too, his teeth bright white in contrast to the black camo face paint.

'Relax, everyone,' Hunter said. 'And let me introduce you to Colonel Sam Bodie. Sam, let me introduce you to everyone.'

The man gave a mock salute. 'Good to meet you all. Sorry about the unusual welcome, but we got some intel that Lundquist and the Swedish team are inbound. When we saw figures approaching in the dark, we couldn't take any chances. Should've seen your faces, though!'

'It's all good,' Hunter said, shaking hands with Bodie. 'Just glad you could get here. Did you bring the gear?'

Bodie nodded. 'Miller, bring it over.'

A young soldier in combat fatigues, his face also disguised behind the camo grease, ran over to them in the darkness. He wore a heavy pack on his back but carried it with ease. When he drew up parallel to Bodie, he removed the pack and set it on the grass. Then he stood to attention. 'It's here, sir.'

'Good work.' Bodie turned to Hunter. 'Your very own ground-penetrating radar, as requested. My QM is a hell of a guy. Only took him two hours to rustle it up but it's all you'll need. As used in all professional geophysical surveys. On the rock underneath our feet, you're looking at a range of around fifteen metres. I'm sure your medieval wanderer went no deeper than that.'

'Thanks, Sam,' Hunter said. 'I owe you one.'

'You said you have intel about Lundquist?' Amy asked.

'That's right, but not much more than what I have already told you. I have a former navy friend with contacts in the world of foreign intelligence. I gave him Lundquist's name and asked him to look into the whole nasty business. He called me back less than twenty minutes ago to say they're on their way here from London City Airport.'

'But how?' Amy asked. 'It just doesn't make any sense. We just found the final clue about this location in Arthur's tomb in Glastonbury, not even four hours ago.'

'Maybe you have a spy on your team?' Bodie asked seriously.

'Never.'

Hunter saw Jodie glance at Lauren. 'Don't even say it,' he said.

Jodie looked at him sharply. 'Say what?'

'What you were thinking when you looked at Lauren. Don't go there.'

'She's only been with us for a couple of days, Hunter,' Jodie replied coolly. 'She's a specialist on the subject and now we find out Lundquist is somehow mysteriously winging his way to the Cornish coast without any possible way of knowing where we are.'

'I think we need to get off this,' Amy said. 'Max trusts Lauren, so we should all trust her. That's what being in a team is all about.'

'She's not in the team,' Jodie said.

Amy glared at her young protégé. 'You know what I mean. Now, shall we get the treasure before those crazy bastards turn up?'

'It's too late for that,' Lewis said, pointing into the eastern sky. 'Helicopter inbound. I estimate its arrival in less than five minutes.'

'Will they land here?' a concerned Lauren asked.

'Not unless they're insane,' Bodie said. 'We have anti-aircraft RPGs. If they come over here, they're going down in a fireball.'

'Which is why they'll land a way off,' Hunter said. 'Where they can see we don't control the landing area.'

'Then they'll make their way across the cliffs and onto the peninsula on foot,' Bodie added.

Hunter felt a surge of adrenaline, then the dampening effect of fear. 'We need to break into teams, fast. Lauren, Lewis and Jodie, start work with the GPR, and the rest of us fan out and set up in solid defensive positions around the east coast of the peninsula. The place is a natural fortress.'

'Agreed,' Amy said. 'Let's move.'

47

When Hunter got into position behind one of the castle's original crenelated walls, full night had wrapped its cloak around the windblown peninsula. Armed only with the spare Glock Bodie had handed him, he felt the gravity of the moment bearing down on him. If they had done their work right, somewhere behind him, Xavier had hidden Excalibur, once King Arthur's legendary sword, and before even those ancient days, if Lundquist had been truthful, the weapon wielded by the Archangel Michael to drive Lucifer from Heaven.

On the mainland, east of the peninsula, he watched a glossy black helicopter swoop down and land somewhere behind the Camelot Castle Hotel.

The howling wind scoured the rocks far below and drowned out the sound of the helicopter's rotors. The aircraft looked like it was maybe a Sikorsky Sea Stallion, which he knew could carry nearly forty troops. He doubted they were facing that much trouble. Lundquist seemed to prefer a smaller unit of special forces rather than the mob-handed approach. Still, the Swedes were going to put up one hell of a fight. He could count on that.

When he heard Bodie's comms crackling to life in his ear, he knew something was up.

'They're on their way, Max.'

'What do you see, Sam?'

'If I close my eyes, I see a beach in the south sea islands somewhere. It's 1974 and I'm on that beach sharing a cocktail with Britt Eklund.'

The colonel's reply made Hunter smile. 'And if you open your eyes?'

'Eight men, black combat fatigues and most in balaclavas. They're led by Lundquist, and I also see Kjell and Eklund. I can see their faces because they're going al fresco this evening. That means they're very confident of winning this thing and getting clean away with no witnesses.'

'Little wonder you were on that beach for a second

there,' Blanco said over the comms. 'Is there room for another, Colonel?'

'Sure is.'

'Great stuff. I wonder if Britt remembers the time I met her.'

Hunter frowned. 'Sal, you are a man full of surprises. You'll have to tell me that story.'

'Anytime, bud.'

'Where are they now, Colonel?' Amy asked.

Bodie's reply was cut off by the sound of gunfire. Hunter looked over the wall and watched the Swedish team fanning out just as his team had done. They left the approach road and began to stream down over the slope leading towards the castle. 'Lundquist is making his way to the bridge. He's going for the peninsula right away... straight for the jugular.'

'I see them,' Blanco said.

'And me.' Bodie's voice was thin, masked in crackle. 'I'm going in with Miller.'

Hunter watched Bodie and Miller break cover from their position behind the Beach Café and open fire on Lundquist and Kjell. The two Swedes were startled by the attack and spun around, returning fire on them as they changed direction away from the bridge and ran towards the cover of the castle's ruins. Having driven the two enemy mercs off course from the bridge and given the radar team some respite, Bodie and Miller broke off and ducked down behind some loose scree on the cliffs, held in place by rockfall netting.

'What's going on now?' Amy said.

'We're on it,' Hunter replied. 'You?'

'No luck yet. We've done about a quarter of the area inside the ruins up here.'

'Stay on it, Amy,' Hunter said. 'We're doing everything we can to stop them.'

He heard a wild volley of gunfire and saw one of the soldiers Bodie had stationed on the mainland, to the castle's west, drop his weapon and tumble off the cliff. 'Shit. We're a man down, Sam.'

'I see it,' Bodie said coolly. 'That was Ashworth. Good man.'

More gunfire. From his bird's eye view, Hunter watched Lundquist and Kjell attempting to break free from where they were pinned down. There was no sign of Eklund. 'They're making another break for the bridge.'

'I see them,' Bodie said. 'Looks like Enfield and Bow are giving them a hard time. They're good men too.'

'I can take a shot at Lundquist,' Blanco said. 'I need to break cover.'

'Hang on, Sal,' Hunter said. 'I've lost sight of Kjell.'

'I see him. I'm going in.'

Hunter saw Blanco climb out from behind his cover position on the other side of the Great Hall's ruins. He was gripping the MP7 Bodie had given him and crouch-walking behind a long wall directly above Merlin's cave. When he broke into the open, Kjell was already on the bridge with Lundquist a few paces behind him. Blanco raised his weapon and loosed a savage volley of fire, perforating Kjell and driving him over the side of the bridge. Seconds later, his dead body smashed into the rocks below, yards from the cold sea. Hunter's satisfaction with the mission's progress took a wild turn when he saw Eklund pop up from behind some rocks on the cliff near the Beach Café and fire on Blanco.

'No!' Hunter yelled.

Blanco was hit. Hunter watched his body convulse as he dropped the MP7 and then fall out of sight off the cliff. It was silent, almost peaceful. Hunter thought of Blanco's family in Brooklyn and felt sick.

'Max?' Amy's voice. She had heard him screaming.

'It's Sal. I think he's gone.'

The radios crackled, but the moment was broken by the Swedish team. Lundquist was halfway across the bridge, Eklund and another masked man right behind him, providing hellish cover and keeping Hunter from opening fire on them.

'It's going shit-shaped, Sam!' Hunter said.

'I concur, Max. Not least because one of Lundquist's men just shot me.'

Hunter was shocked. 'What? Are you okay?'

'It's a flesh wound. I'm still in the fight, but Lundquist is nearly at your position. There's only me and Miller left now, Max. We'll go around in an arc and approach the Swedes from the rear. Give them a two-front war.'

'Got it,' Hunter said, still thinking of Blanco's brutal death.

After this, things moved fast. Lundquist's team, diminished in number but still formidable, streamed over the peninsula like ants. With Blanco dead, and Amy, Lauren and Lewis up at the main site with the GPR device, the defence of the area was left to him and Jodie. When he heard Jodie cry out over her radio, he feared the game would soon be up. When his position was swarmed with men in black fatigues and balaclavas, his fears were confirmed.

'Drop the gun, Major!'

When he first heard the angry command, Hunter was confused. The Swedish mercenary was referring to him and his old army rank, but these days he had grown used to the term Doctor. No matter. He dropped the gun and raised his hands. Taking one look at the man's outfit, Hunter smiled and said, 'Have you brought any Milk Tray?'

The Swede screamed at him to shut up and pushed him down the path towards where Amy and the others were scanning the ground for Excalibur. On his way, he was joined by Jodie. She had also been captured and like him, she was being force-marched with her hands above her head. Her face was a frozen rictus of misery, and Hunter knew why.

Sal Blanco.

Hunter had no words, but the moment soon passed. When they reached the main site, they saw Eklund and two more men holding Amy and Lauren captive. They were standing beside the GPR unit with their hands raised. Lewis was being forced to lie on the ground with his hands behind his head. They weren't taking any chances with the former US Marine.

'Max!' Amy said. 'Are you okay?'

'I'm fine. Maybe a bruised ego.'

Amy turned to Jodie. 'Jodie, I'm so sorry about Sal. We're all devastated.'

Jodie looked not at her boss, but Lundquist. 'I'll even things up. Believe that.'

With everyone safely secured, Lundquist now strutted over to Amy. 'Thank you so very much for leading us here, Agent Fox.'

'What do you mean?' Amy said in disgust. 'I never led you here.'

'She wasn't bugged,' Jodie said. 'I checked her up and down when we got her out of the castle in Slovenia. Remember?'

Hunter nodded. 'I remember. She wasn't bugged.'

'Oh, yes she was,' Lundquist said. 'With GPS-trackable smart dust.'

Amy's face hardened. 'Tell me where Quinn Mosley is. Now.'

Lundquist looked confused. 'What are you talking about?'

'Quinn Mosley,' Amy repeated. 'She's one of my agents. You had your men kidnap her outside the castle in Slovenia.'

'I most certainly did not,' he said coldly. 'You seem to be labouring under a wild misapprehension.'

Hunter didn't know why, but he believed Lundquist. The man had no reason to lie, and it fit with their theory about the Illuminati snatching Quinn. It wasn't a big leap of the imagination to conclude that the same people had also taken Juliette and maybe even Jim Gates. If this were true, things were looking worse than ever.

In response to Lundquist's words, Amy furrowed her brow. 'Then where is she?'

'Your problem,' Lundquist said, peering at the GPR unit. 'My problem is finding Excalibur. Where is it?'

'We can't find it,' Amy said. 'Too bad for you, right?'

'She's lying!' Eklund snapped. 'She has to be. It's right here, beneath our feet. I know it!'

Lundquist raised his machine pistol and pointed it at Lauren. 'Agent Fox, you will proceed with the exploration of this peninsula or I will kill this young woman. And work fast, please. Our little disagreement a few moments ago will have certainly caught the attention of the local law enforcement authorities and they can be so very boring at times like this. Work. Now.'

Amy continued Lauren's work, pushing the GPR unit up and down in parallel strips as they had done before. It wasn't long before an alarm on the unit began to bleep, not unlike a metal detector. Amy peered down at the screen and gasped. 'Lauren, get a load of this!'

Lauren inched forward, but Lundquist stopped

her, swinging his gun in her face. '*Nej, nej, nej!* Get back where you were. And you too, Agent Fox. This is my treasure, not yours.'

Amy stepped back as Lundquist moved over to the GPR and stared down at the screen. 'Eklund, get over here. Now!'

When Eklund joined him, he nodded his head and smiled. 'This is what we have been seeking for so many years. This must be it.'

Lundquist looked up at Hunter. When he spoke, his voice was loud and arrogant. 'And what do you make of this, Dr Hunter? It looks like I won our little fight. It seems Excalibur will be mine after all. Mine, all mine! The sword of St Michael that drove Lucifer from Heaven will now be wielded by me and give me the power to—'

The bullet tore through the back of Lundquist's skull and blasted out of his forehead, a terrible gaping exit wound of blood, brain matter and skull fragments. Everyone jumped, horrified by the brutal gunshot wound as Lundquist's dead body collapsed to the ground. Eklund moved first, darting away from the group and heading for the western edge of the peninsula. He didn't get very far. Hunter watched as Bodie and Miller sprinted up the path from the bridge and located the fleeing Swedish professor. They both opened fire on him, perforating him like a sieve and sending his corpse cartwheeling out of sight, down the slope to the west.

Everyone was silent. Everyone was still. The wind gently howled off the sea and across their shocked faces. The next sound was Bodie's and Miller's boots as they crunched up the path and pulled up to a stop beside the team. Bodie looked at Lundquist's body and winced.

'Looks like I got the blighter.'

After a pause, Hunter spoke. 'That you did, Sam. That you did.'

'And Eklund, sir,' Miller said.

'And Eklund. Good work, Miller.'

'Thank you, sir.'

Amy stared at the GPR unit screen. 'Looks like a box, around a metre long, I guess.'

Hunter stared at the team. Jodie had been sobbing but was trying to hide it.

Then a heavy Brooklyn accent broke the silence. When Hunter turned, it was to see his old friend Sal Blanco staggering towards them, clutching his blood-soaked arm against his body.

'Sal!' Jodie cried out and ran towards him. 'You're alive!'

'So they say,' Blanco said. 'But it doesn't always feel like it. Not right now, and never on Monday mornings.'

Jodie hugged him.

'Bloody hell. I am glad you're okay, Sal! You're a top bloke,' Hunter said. 'I hope you decide to stick around instead of buggering off to make pizzas. How boring would that be?'

After the entire team had expressed their happiness and relief at his return, Amy checked her watch and resumed command. 'Lundquist was right. The police will be on their way. We don't have long. Get digging. This thing says it's one metre down.'

Half an hour later, they were staring down into the hole they had dug, exhausted, hungry and in desperate need of sleep.

Hunter stood over the pit and stared into it, wiping sweat from his eyes. It contained a rotten, crumbling oak box about the size of a large sword. After a short struggle, he managed to free the box from its muddy surroundings and pull it up to ground level.

'You do it,' Hunter said, handing it to Lauren.

The young archaeologist, now exonerated from any charges of betraying the team, carefully unwrapped the old, crumbling linen to reveal a shining silver sword, whose blade was covered in mysterious symbols. 'My God, Max. We found it. We found Excalibur – King Arthur's sword!'

Lewis whistled. 'And the sword of the Archangel Michael. Look at the inscription – *Gladius Sancti Michaelis*! The Sword of Michael. To me, that's even more impressive.'

'What do the symbols mean?' Bodie asked.

'I don't recognise them, sorry,' Hunter said. 'Lauren?'

She shook her head. 'Nor me, but I can't wait to start trying to decipher them. Imagine what they might mean!'

Hunter recognised the look of wonder and anticipation in Lauren's young eyes. "I know you'll do a great job deciphering them."

Lauren didn't need the compliment, but gave him a polite smile, one that soon faded. 'But what do we do now?' she said. 'Try and cover all this up? I don't know how any of this works.'

'Ordinarily, I'd argue against a cover-up,' Amy said. 'But we can't trust anyone right now. Because of what has happened here tonight, the local authorities will be involved and this place is going to become a major crime scene. We can't stop that, but we need to keep the sword safe until we know who we can trust.'

'Amy's right,' Hunter said. 'We can keep the sword

secret – we can hide it somewhere and let the police do their work. We'll be involved with the authorities anyway because Sal and the colonel are both wounded and need medical treatment.'

'And some food,' Blanco said. 'This is just a flesh wound, but man, I could murder a steak.'

With gentle laughter rippling over them then, they turned and limped back down to the bridge and the mainland. In the distance, they all heard the sirens of the emergency services and the flashing blue and red of their lights as they raced towards the coast.

48

Special Agent Amy Fox swung her legs out of bed and felt the thick, plush rug beneath her feet. She yawned and stretched her arms and gave quiet thanks that the day had dawned bright and warm. Sunlight streamed in through the curtains. She walked to them and drew them open, letting the bright morning sunshine flood into the room. Then she gave thanks that the UNESCO budget had stretched to the Camelot Castle Hotel. Somehow, she doubted Jim Gates would have had much success getting the US government to be so generous, even if she could get him to answer his phone.

Below her window, the cliffs dropped away to a dark blue sea. The strange promontory which hosted Merlin's Cave was much less foreboding in the fresh morning light, but looking at the place still gave her a shudder. She looked over at the ruins of Tintagel Castle and felt the same sense of awe and fear. Looking out across the scene, now crawling with British law enforcement after the events of the previous evening, she could hardly believe any of it had happened. It also meant the team would be staying put for a few days to answer their questions. There was no way out of that. There was also the urgent and unfinished business of tracking Quinn down, and by the looks of it, Juliette Bonnaire, too.

She picked up the breakfast menu, turning it over in her hands and giving it a quick once-over. It all looked great but she had no appetite. She knew it would be like this until she had her friends safely back and liberated from whoever had taken them. Despite the dark feelings of dread, she realised she was feeling more at home with herself than in a long time. She guessed that had less to do with Lundquist's untimely demise and the successful ending of the mission and more to do with what Max Hunter had told her before she'd gone to sleep. That he loved her and was sorry for his erratic behaviour. She would see about that. Maybe it also had something to do with Brent Reed texting her and telling her that HARPA's suspension had just been made permanent.

The team was over and she was homeless, at least in a professional capacity. It didn't frighten her, but it made her feel alone because it seemed to her everyone else had some other place they could go. Jim Gates was inches from retirement anyway and Quinn would vanish like her namesake 'ghost' and return to a life of hacking just for the hell of it. That was if she could be found. She shook the dark thought from her mind. Quinn was gone, but it was still possible that the problem with Jim was just a simple communications issue. Either way, she wouldn't stop until they were both safe.

As for the rest of the team, Jodie could return to the underworld and earn much more in the process. Lewis most likely would go to a theology department at a good college somewhere in the northeast. Hunter had UNESCO and, of course, they would all get together and talk about their new lives in Sal's pizza place in Manhattan.

That just left her, out in the cold. Heading back into the FBI was not something that was floating her boat right now, nor was a move into the even darker heart of the CIA. But these were a natural next step for her following the end of her career at HARPA. She'd a few days to think it over and had already tried to make plans if things didn't work out, but early signs weren't encouraging. She would need more time to make a good next move, she knew that. Take some time out. Talk to some trusted friends. She pushed it away and decided to take a shower. After the police's questions, she had a long flight back to DC later in the day and would try to eat something at breakfast so she could sleep on the plane.

In the shower, a few moments turned into nearly twenty minutes of relaxation and contemplation. The warm soapy water felt great on her naked body, and for the first time, she started seeing HARPA's downfall potentially as a positive development in her life, as a brand new start rather than something to be lamented and mourned. No one knew what was around the corner, and maybe that uncertainty was what made everything worth living. She was bright, capable, fit and young enough to start over. Screw whoever had shut HARPA down. She would find a better life.

She turned off the tap, stepped out into the bathroom and reached out for one of the fat, plush towels draped over the rail beside the sink. She dried herself and slipped into one of the complimentary dressing gowns hanging off the back of the bathroom door, then she wrapped her hair up into a towel turban and went back into the bedroom, feeling refreshed and energised. She knew she had a mountain to climb now she was out of work, but there was hope, and right now she had Quinn's rescue to focus on.

She got dressed and stepped out of her room, clicking the door gently shut behind her and making her way down the narrow wooden corridor. She walked down the stairs to the ground floor and wasn't surprised to hear Sal Blanco's big, booming laugh coming from the dining room off to her right. She joined them and poured herself a cup of coffee. After a brief breakfast, the talk returned to business.

'What's next?' Lauren said.

Amy looked at the young woman as only a mother could look at a naughty child. 'Next is, you go back to school and finish your education while the rest of us track down our missing teammate Quinn.'

Jodie laughed, then grew more serious. 'I can't believe we found the sword last night. Thank God we decided to hide it from the police, too.'

'It was quite a moment, I agree,' Hunter said. 'Now it's over to UNESCO to decide exactly where it ends up. But people must be able to study it. After all, it's one of the most important archaeological finds of all time, especially if it really does have any kind of heavenly provenance.'

'You can't believe that,' Jodie said.

'I don't know what to believe any more,' he said.

'Well, I believe it,' Lewis said. 'Last night, I touched the sword that the Archangel Michael used to drive Lucifer from Heaven during the war. I'll never be able to fully understand the significance of that moment. I feel blessed.'

'And I feel knackered but ready to find Quinn and Juliette,' Hunter said. 'They're both missing and they're going to need our help.'

'That's presuming Lundquist told us the truth,' Lauren said.

'Told *us* the truth,' Jodie said. 'You're not us.'

'No, I don't suppose I am. Unless you let me join.'

Amy gave her a look. 'There's nothing to join. We're not a team any more. We're officially homeless.'

'But you're still going after your friends,' Lauren said. 'I could help.'

'I vote for "no",' Jodie said tartly.

'We're not talking about this right now,' Amy said. 'It's not a club anyone can just join and leave whenever they want. And you have your education to pursue.'

'Amy's right,' Hunter said. 'It's important you finish your doctorate. You're very smart and you have a great future ahead of you. Don't throw all that away to join a team that doesn't even exist. It's not worth it.'

Lauren accepted the consensus but looked deflated. 'All right. Have it your way, but you can call me if you need me.'

'That's a deal,' Amy said. 'And thanks for all your help, Lauren. We appreciate it.'

'No problem, it was a privilege. Like Max says, now I can put finding the tomb of King Arthur and Excalibur on my CV. This may have implications for future career prospects!'

Hunter laughed, and then Amy frowned at him. 'And don't think I've forgotten about how you found that inscription on the plinth in Gargano after I already looked there. How did you find it?' she asked.

'I saw some scratches that looked a little too uniform, so I dabbed some spit on it with my thumb and it revealed the inscription. It needed the water to become visible, then when it dried, it disappeared again, at least back to the scratches. Not the first time I've done it, either. You'd be amazed what eight centuries of dust can do to a shallow carving.'

She looked at him and smiled. 'Good work, Max. Maybe if we get HARPA back up and running, we can...'

She stopped talking when her phone buzzed. 'It's from Jim!' Amy's voice was bubbling with excitement. She answered the call and flicked it to the speaker. 'Jim, hey! Why haven't you been answering my calls?'

'Listen very carefully, Agent Fox.'

Hunter felt his skin grow cold. The voice on the other end of Gates's phone was not their boss, but someone else, someone cold and distant. He had been expecting this, and it felt just as bleak as he had imagined it would. He saw from Amy's face that she was feeling the same as he was, that everyone else in the team was.

'Who is this?' she asked.

'You may call me Oriax.'

'Damn it,' Jodie muttered. 'Why do these guys always sound like a brand of detergent?'

'It's a variation of the name Orias,' Lewis said grimly. 'In demonology, it's the name of the Grand Marquis of Hell.'

'So, not a detergent?' Jodie was trying to look unfazed, but everyone could see her fear growing.

'What do you want, Oriax?' Amy said firmly. 'And why have you got Jim Gates's cell phone?'

'Because I am holding Jim Gates and his wife Susanna. I am looking at them right now. They are sitting beside Quinn Mosley. I have her in my possession, too. And Professor Bonnaire.'

Hunter felt a rush of relief and revulsion wash over him. Relief that they were alive and their abductors were now making contact, but revulsion at the use of the word possession, like they were some kind of asset to be bartered and not people at all. He leaned into Amy's phone and raised his voice to a snarl. 'What do you want, Oriax?'

'Could this be the infamous Dr Hunter?'

'You bet it is. What do you want?'

'A little patience would work wonders for you, Dr Hunter. As would some respect. Remember, the lives of four of your friends are in my hands. It's not wise to irritate a man with this power.'

'A man? I thought you were some kind of demon?' Hunter said.

Amy pushed Hunter away and resumed control. 'This is Agent Fox, Oriax. You called me today and I want to know why.'

'This is too complex to discuss over the telephone. Cell phones are so modern and impersonal and vulgar. I prefer to converse face to face. If you and your team want Jim and Susanna Gates and Quinn Mosley and Juliette Bonnaire to live to see another sunrise, you will do exactly as you are told. Is that clear?'

'Totally clear,' Amy said through clenched teeth. 'Go ahead.'

'I desire a simple trade. You will give me the Flaming Sword of St Michael, and I will give you your friends.'

'We can't let him have the sword!' Lewis said. 'This guy calls himself a demon! Remember, the sword was used by Archangel Michael to fight Lucifer out of Heaven! Who knows what he wants to do with it!'

Amy raised her hand in a gesture to make Lewis stop talking. 'I'm listening. Oriax.'

'You will be sent further instructions in good time. Don't do anything stupid in the meantime.'

He cut the line.

The team gawped at each other, stunned and speechless.

'We cannot give a man called Oriax the sword of St Michael!' Lewis repeated. 'We just don't understand enough about its power yet to make this kind of a decision.'

Jodie lit a cigarette. 'We know that loon is going to kill Quinn, Juliette, Jim and his wife unless we do what he says. We know that.'

'Max?' Amy asked. 'What do you think?'

Hunter stared out across the Atlantic Ocean, the fresh morning light almost mocking the horror that was about to unfold all around them. They had completed their mission for UNESCO. It had been successful. They had recovered not only the missing crown jewels as per Juliette Bonnaire's original brief but also discovered two of the greatest archaeological finds of all time, the tomb of King Arthur and Excalibur. It was over. Mission complete.

But now this. Quinn, Juliette, Director Gates and Susanna snatched and torn from their lives by this demon Oriax and his Illuminati mercenaries. His mind raced. One glance at the rest of the team and the anguish on their tortured faces reflected the turmoil inside himself. Outside, a storm was blowing in across the sea, heading towards the Cornish coast with foreboding menace. It matched the gathering sense of rage and dread he felt in his heart. Whatever he and his team had to do to rescue their friends would be dangerous and lethal.

* * *

MORE FROM ROB JONES

Another book from Rob Jones, *The Angel Prophecy*, is available to order now here:

https://mybook.to/AngelProphecyBackAd

ABOUT THE AUTHOR

Rob Jones has published over forty books in the genres of action-adventure, action-thriller and crime. Many of his chart-topping titles have enjoyed number-one rankings and his Joe Hawke and Jed Mason series have been international bestsellers. Originally from England, today he lives in Australia with his wife and children.

Sign up to Rob's mailing list for news, competitions and updates on future books.

Follow Rob on social media here:

facebook.com/RobJonesNovels

x.com/AuthorRobJones

ALSO BY ROB JONES

The Hunter Files

The Atlantis Covenant

The Revelation Relic

The Titanic Legacy

The Excalibur Code

The Angel Prophecy

THE *Hit* LIST

Every crime has a story...

THE HIT LIST IS A NEWSLETTER DEDICATED TO PULSE-POUNDING, HIGH-OCTANE ACTION THRILLERS!

SIGN UP TO MAKE SURE YOU'RE ON OUR HIT LIST FOR EXCLUSIVE DEALS, AUTHOR CONTENT, AND COMPETITIONS.

SIGN UP TO OUR NEWSLETTER

BIT.LY/THEHITLISTNEWS

Boldwood

Boldwood Books is an award-winning fiction publishing company seeking out the best stories from around the world.

Find out more at www.boldwoodbooks.com

Join our reader community for brilliant books, competitions and offers!

Follow us
@BoldwoodBooks
@TheBoldBookClub

Sign up to our weekly deals newsletter

https://bit.ly/BoldwoodBNewsletter

www.ingramcontent.com/pod-product-compliance
Lightning Source LLC
Chambersburg PA
CBHW010657100726
47900CB00010B/2699